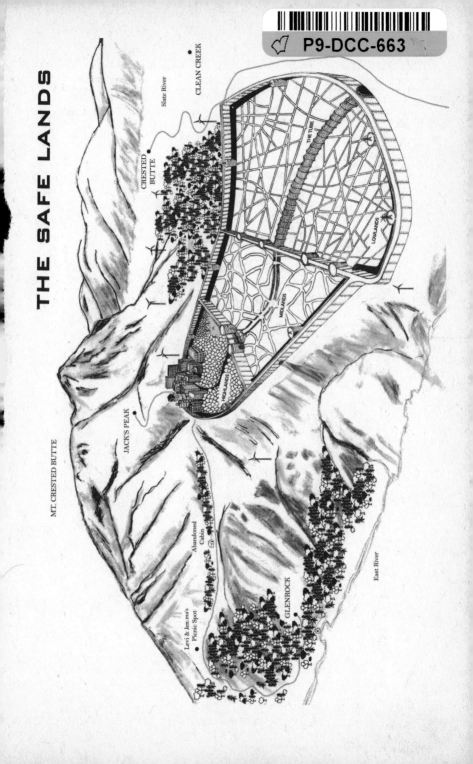

Books by Jill Williamson

Replication

The Safe Lands series

Captives

The Blood of Kings series

By Darkness Hid

To Darkness Fled

From Darkness Won

The Mission League series

The New Recruit

Chokepoint

Project Gemini

Nonfiction

*Go Teen Writers: How to Turn Your First Draft
into a Published Book*

OUTCASTS

BOOK TWO OF THE
SAFE LANDS SERIES

JILL WILLIAMSON

BLINK

BLINK

Outcasts
Copyright © 2013 by Jill Williamson

This title is also available as a Blink ebook. Visit www.zondervan.com/ebooks.

Requests for information should be addressed to:

Blink, 3900 *Sparks Drive, Grand Rapids, Michigan 49546*

Library of Congress Cataloging-in-Publication Data

Williamson, Jill.
      Outcasts / Jill Williamson.
        pages cm. — (Safe Lands ; book 2)
      Summary: "The remnant from Glenrock is now living as rebels within the Safe
Lands, looking for a way to find purpose in their lives. When a young rebel is
murdered and his death points to a rebel leader, it's hard to know who to trust"—
Provided by publisher.
      ISBN 978-0-310-72424-7
      [1. Government, Resistance to—Fiction. 2. Science fiction.] I. Title.
PZ7.W67195Ou 2013
[Fic]—dc23   2013033153

The author is represented by MacGregor Literary, Inc. of Manzanita, OR.

Cover designer: Brand Navigation
Cover photo credits: iStockphoto/Shutterstock/Steve Gardner, PixelWorks Studios
Interior design: Ben Fetterley and Greg Johnson/Textbook Perfect

Printed in the United States of America

13 14 15 16 17 18 19 20 /DCI/ 20 19 18 17 16 15 14 13 12 11 10 9 8 7 6 5 4 3 2

"Very truly I tell you, no servant is greater than his master, nor is a messenger greater than the one who sent him."
—John 13:16, NIV

To my sister Beth Britton, for wanting
to read book two so desperately.
Thanks for your enthusiasm and support.

PROLOGUE

JULY 2088

Almost there.

Kendall strode around the curve of Belleview Drive and fixed her gaze on the messenger sign at the end of the block. The flying white envelope on a red circle flickered in the night.

She wanted to run — to at least jog — but held back, forcing her legs into long strides. Kendall swung her arms and breathed in the scents of dryer sheets and waffle cones from the Belleview Laundry and Cinnamonster ice cream shop.

Barely four weeks had passed since she'd given birth in the Surgery Center, and only two since she'd moved out of the harem and back to the Midlands. Kendall's medic had told her to wait at least six weeks before doing serious exercise. So Kendall walked everywhere, determined to firm up her abdomen, look normal again. Determined to forget.

She wasn't supposed to work for six weeks, either. But staying home with no baby to hold ... Add to that her depressing thoughts, worry over the girls from Glenrock, and the task director general's summons — it had been too much. She'd begged Tayo to let her come back to the messenger office early.

Kendall picked up her pace. What could the task director want now? He'd taken everything from her. She'd served her term in the harem, had given the ultimate sacrifice. This couldn't be a surrogacy request. Safe Lands customs said she deserved a two-year reprieve for her service to the nation.

This summons had to be personal.

A taxi turned down Belleview and sped toward Kendall, its headlights blinding. She lowered her gaze. The vehicle passed — and the product expo on its side caught her eye.

The face of her son. "Welcome, Baby Promise" scrolled underneath.

Kendall stopped. She watched her son's face shrink away until the taxi vanished. Fortune was mocking her pain.

What kind of a name was Promise, especially for a boy? More Safe Lands strangeness. Her baby would always be Elyot to her.

Kendall choked back her sorrow and trudged the rest of the way to the messenger office. She used her SimTag to let herself inside and set her messenger bag on the front counter.

A single bulb cast yellow light and hard shadows over the messenger workstations and rows of nearly empty package shelves. Kendall crossed the lobby and slipped behind the counter, her running shoes scuffing over the concrete floor. She walked down the first aisle of shelves, her shadow creeping along beside her.

This place had always been ghoulie at night.

The task clock hung outside Tayo's office door, located at the back. Kendall tapped her fist on it, officially tasking out for the night, and started back toward the lobby.

A low moan rose from the dark. She jerked her head around, spine tingling. Cocked her ears.

No more sound.

Kendall peered through the shelves on her right. "Hay-o? Who's here?"

A gargled breath. "Help me."

The words squeezed her throat. For a moment Kendall couldn't move. Pushing down her fear, she forced herself around the end of the shelves. Peeked down the next row.

Empty.

She inched toward the third one.

Nothing.

Kendall glanced at her messenger bag. Her portable Wyndo was inside. She could tap Enforcer 10 for help.

She bit her lip, then eased around the fourth row. Halfway down, a man in a messenger uniform lay on the floor, one hand on his stomach, the other under his back. White-blond hair. Big feet.

"Chord?" Kendall ran to him.

Red everywhere, like a bottle of spilled Shower Paint. It had soaked Chord's white T-shirt and the top of his green shorts, puddling under him. Still spreading.

She swallowed the bitter burning of nausea. "What happened?"

Chord lifted his hand. Kendall reached for his bloody fingers, but he pointed upward, to a large box high on the shelves.

"You want the box?" she asked.

He nodded and choked out the word, "Hurry."

Kendall had to climb on the lowest shelf to reach the box. She held the shelf with her left hand and slapped the box with her right until it slid over the edge, careful to use her arms and not put strain on her stomach. She stepped down with the box, keeping her hand underneath to catch it as it fell. It was light and open at the top. She set it on the floor and pulled out a messenger bag. Chord's? She met his gaze.

"Deliver," he rasped.

"You want me to deliver your messages?"

"To the ... addressees. No one else. Secret."

She found four messages in his bag. Messages with no codes. In the Safe Lands, it was illegal to deliver mail off the grid. Enforcers monitored everything. She read the addresses. Chord worked the Sopris route, but these addresses were mostly in Old Town, which was her route.

"Chord, why do you ...?" She looked up to find him staring past her knees. Unblinking. Unseeing. His eyes dull, mouth half open, face slack.

A breath rattled past her lips. She spun around, slipping in the blood. Kendall ran to the counter, withdrew her Wyndo from her own messenger bag, and tapped one zero. Her thumb — shaking over the glass screen — produced a one-eight-eight. She deleted the numbers and carefully tapped one zero again.

One ring and a female face showed on the glass. She had silver hair, mimicking Luella Flynn, no doubt. "Enforcer 10. Where are you located?"

"Midlands-east-messenger-office," Kendall said, breathless. "A man's been hurt. He's bleeding. I think he's … dead. Oh, walls! Don't let him be dead!"

"Try to stay calm," the woman said. "Can you tell me what happened?"

Kendall gasped in a breath, panic clouding her thoughts, tears and hysteria lacing every word. "I don't know. I didn't see. I came in and found him here."

"You found him dead?"

She stared at the woman on her Wyndo screen and set her messenger bag back on the counter. "No. He was just talking to me, but now he's only staring." She looked back down the aisle to where Chord lay. No change.

"Okay, I'm dispatching Enforcer 10," the woman said. "I see two SimTags at the address you gave me. ID#5 – 71 – 36, Chord Prezden and ID#1-W1, Kendall Collin. Is this Kendall?"

"Yes. And Chord is hurt."

"Kendall, do you see any weapons?"

A new wave of horror seized her. "I didn't." Had Chord been shot or stabbed? "Should I go back and look?"

"No, stay where you are," the woman said. "I need you to preserve the scene until Enforcer 10 arrives. Do you know the victim?"

"Yes! Chord tasks here." Tears were flowing down Kendall's cheeks now. She paced the length of the counter. How could this be happening? Who would kill Chord?

The front door whooshed open, bringing the smell of dryer sheets and waffle cones inside the lobby. Kendall spun around. A man stood on the other side of the counter. She screamed and dropped her Wyndo, which snapped into three pieces on the concrete floor.

"Hey, sorry," he said. "Didn't mean to scare you."

The man looked familiar. He was wearing a messenger uniform, but he wasn't a regular here. Where had she seen him before? He had a 9X on his face. Was this Chord's murderer?

Trapped, Kendall crouched behind the counter to pick up her Wyndo. She was still holding Chord's messages in her hand and shoved them into the waistband of her shorts. She pulled the hem of her T-shirt over the messages and collected her Wyndo and the solar pack. Where was the back? She never understood how these things looked like transparent glass until they came apart. Technological magic was the worst kind. It made her feel ignorant for not comprehending how it worked.

Calm down! Look for it. She scanned the floor for any reflection.

The man stepped around the end of the counter, his messenger sneakers, bare legs, and green shorts a blur outside her focus. There! She spotted a rectangle of clear plastic across the floor, by the man's foot. She blinked and looked up to his face.

Alone with a strange Xed man who was blocking her way to the exit and might be a murderer. No Wyndo. Not good. If she survived this night, she vowed to reconsider a SimTalk implant.

The man's dark eyebrows rose, causing his forehead to wrinkle. "You okay?"

He was young, his voice soft and a little hoarse, like he had a cold. Cute. Boyish, though his jaw and upper lip were shaded in the soft scruff of a first attempt at a beard. He was likely harmless. Not every man was like Lawten. But this one looked *so* familiar.

The answer came a second later. Omar. The new rover. Tayo had introduced him at Monday's staff meeting. See? It was okay. He had a right to be here. So ... probably not a murderer, then. Right?

"Hey." Omar crouched and picked up the back of her Wyndo from the floor beside his foot. He held it out, baring thick black SimArt lines that swirled and knotted their way up his left arm. A chain. "Don't worry. It's probably not broken. For bits of plastic and glass, they're pretty sturdy."

She snatched the back from him and fumbled with the pieces, trying to put the contraption back together. She had the solar pack upside down, so she flipped it over and clicked it into place.

Enforcer 10 was coming. She'd be okay.

"Aren't you that Kendall girl from the ColorCast?" Omar asked. "The queen? The one who just had the, uh ... ?" His gaze flicked down to her belly.

"No," Kendall said, hating that she'd lied. Lawten had made her afraid of everyone. Her legs shook from squatting so long, yet she felt safer crouched against the counter.

She snapped on the back of the Wyndo, but when she tried to power it up, the glass remained dark. *No!*

"So, what's your name, femme?" Omar asked.

She met his gaze then. A risk. But perhaps conversation would distract him until Enforcer 10 arrived. His eyes were slate blue, rimmed in thick, dark lashes. Natural eyes that made her think he might have once been an outsider too. His skin looked healthy — she could see actual pores. No Roller Paint. But he was marked 9X. Weird. Outsiders weren't usually nines, but they did tend to get an X or two before they figured out how to live here. Especially the men. Maybe he hadn't been in the Safe Lands long. Maybe he wasn't like the others.

But maybe he was.

"Why do you want to know my name?" she asked, tempted to look at Chord's body, wanting to help him in case it wasn't too late, but wanting to get away even more.

Omar's lips spread into a slow grin that completely lit up his face. "Okay, never mind. Um ..." He ran his fingers through his hair, creating three thick waves that swooped back over his head. "Have you seen Chord? I was supposed to meet him."

His words threw the fear back in her face. "You were supposed to meet him?"

"That's what I said." His eyes narrowed. "Are you sure you're okay?"

Shards of ice slid down her back. If Omar had hurt Chord, would he hurt her too? Kendall couldn't help it. Her body betrayed her, and she glanced down the aisle to where Chord lay.

Omar followed her gaze and gasped. "Wait, what?" His voice rose in pitch, panicked. "Is that Chord?" He ran down the aisle. "No! Why?" He picked up Chord's messenger bag, reached inside it. "His messages are gone." He turned back to Kendall. "What happened? What'd you do?"

He wanted Chord's messages. The ones Chord said were secret. "*Me?*" Kendall stood, fumbled for her bag, and backed toward the end of the counter. "I didn't do anything. I just came in to task out for the night and found him there. He said — "

"He spoke?" Omar walked toward her, his eyes bearing down, intense.

Kendall turned and ran around the end of the counter.

"Whoa! Hold on!" Chord's bag clutched in hand, Omar jumped against the counter and slid his legs over the top, landing on the other side and cutting off Kendall's exit. He was standing so close she could smell the hint of metallic mint on his breath. He was a user.

She wanted to scream but had no lungs or legs or breath at all.

"What did he say?" Omar asked. "Did he say anything about his messages?"

Kendall shook her head, almost a tremble, back and forth, back and forth. Chord had said to tell no one about the messages. And if Omar had killed Chord, he would kill her too. She tried to walk around him, but he stepped to the side, blocking her way.

Where was Enforcer 10? *Hurry!*

"Please." Omar dropped Chord's bag on the floor and grabbed her shoulders. "It's important."

Beastly hands squeezing ... Kendall screamed.

Omar quickly let go, swallowed, and held up his hands, palms facing her. "I'm not going to hurt you. I just need to know what he said."

Lies. Lies. Her voice came in a rush, sounding like someone else. "All he said was, 'Help me,' so I tapped Enforcer 10." *Can I go now? Please let me go. Need to walk. Need to run.*

Omar closed his eyes and exhaled a breath that took four inches off his height. That stopped Kendall, confused her. He wasn't exactly acting like a killer. And the mention of Enforcer 10 being on the way didn't seem to alarm him. But why had he been going to meet Chord here? And why did he seem to be looking for the messages?

The sound of a siren grew in the distance — finally! — giving strength to her legs. Kendall darted past Omar, but he caught hold of her messenger bag and looked inside it, deflating again when he found it empty.

Kendall snatched it back and walked toward the door, holding her wrist against her hip to keep Chord's messages from sliding past her waistband. She stepped outside just as Enforcer 10 arrived.

The enforcers questioned Kendall and Omar, scanned their bodies for blood residue — finding it only on their shoes — then released them. The process took so long that Kendall had mostly calmed down by the end, though she kept Omar in sight. He hadn't hurt her, but he still could.

She tried to slip away, but a familiar voice called her name. "Kendall! Come say hay-o, you sweet femmy."

It was Luella Flynn, the ColorCast co-host and most famous face in the Safe Lands, waving her signature handheld microphone like a flag, her silver hair shining brightly under the streetlamps. Kendall groaned but knew if she ignored Luella now, the woman would simply invite herself to Kendall's apartment later. Might as well get it over with.

Kendall walked up to Luella and Alb, the cameraman who was Luella's shadow. Luella looked stellar, as always. Tonight she wore a purple-and-yellow houndstooth jumper over a silver bodysuit. She'd been wearing the tinsel weave in her hair for a few weeks now. Silver: a trend that had lingered longer than the celebrity usually allowed. Half the Safe Lands had been dressed in silver since Lonn's liberation four weeks ago. Maybe the purple and yellow was a sign that the fashions were about to get brighter.

Luella kissed both Kendall's cheeks and then spoke into her microphone. "Kendall Collin, our former queen, can you tell us what's happened here tonight?"

"I don't know if I'm allowed. The enforcers didn't say."

"You can tell me, femmy. Lawten okays everything I record before it's broadcasted, so no need to worry."

Lawten. The man was on a first-name basis with far too many women.

"I understand a man was murdered tonight?" Luella said, eyes shining as if death was thrilling. "Chord Prezden? And you called Enforcer 10."

"Well, I don't know if he was murdered. But he is dead." Though if Luella knew that Chord was dead, she knew all that Kendall knew — except for the messages tucked into the waistband of Kendall's shorts.

"Did you witness the murder?" Luella asked.

"No," Kendall said. "I had just finished my shift and found him when I went to task out. There was no sign of any attacker."

"Can you describe how he looked for the Safe Lands viewers? How was he killed? Did he suffer?"

"I …" Chord's dying body flashed back to her mind, helpless, bleeding.

"We really didn't see much of anything, Miss Flynn," a soft voice said.

Kendall looked just behind her. Omar stood there, his attention focused wholly on Luella Flynn. Where had he come from? And what did he want? Did he suspect she had the messages?

Luella's eyes narrowed. "And you are …?"

"Omar Strong. I'm the new rover. I came by just after Kendall

15

called Enforcer 10. Chord and I had plans for tonight. We were supposed to meet here and then go to Dreamland. Have you ever been?"

Luella pressed her hand over her chest, displaying her purple-and-silver-striped fingernails. "I adore Dreamland Disco. Most turbulent music in the Midlands." Then she smiled and set her hand on her hip. "And you're a clever raven to change the subject. How'd you get your X, Mr. Strong? Don't bother lying, either. I can look it up."

"Look it up then," Omar said. "Pleasure meeting you, Miss Flynn. Sorry we couldn't be more helpful. Kendall? Are you ready to go?"

His question took Kendall off guard, as did the way he held out his hand like they were a pair. Pairing up was all Safe Lands men ever wanted. "Um …" She *did* want to get away from the microphone and the woman holding it, but she didn't want to give Omar the wrong idea. She stepped beside him and glanced at Luella, who watched them with raised brows.

Omar took hold of her hand anyway. His palm was rough, like he tasked outdoors. She wanted to let go, embarrassed to touch a stranger in such a familiar way, but she didn't want Luella to ask any more questions.

"Good night," Omar said, pulling Kendall away from the camera.

"Maybe I'll see the two of you at Dreamland," Luella called after them.

"Maybe," Omar said, without looking back.

But Kendall looked back at Luella three times as they walked away, worried that the woman would follow them, see they weren't really together, ask more questions. Then she changed fears and hoped Luella would come so Kendall wouldn't be alone with Omar. But finally Luella waved her microphone at one of the enforcers and stepped into the crowd, Alb on her heels. Gone.

Kendall pulled her hand from Omar's grip, and they continued walking side by side, though Kendall's senses were on alert. It was only another few yards to the corner where she could wave a cab and get away from Omar. "You're asking for trouble, playing games with Luella Flynn."

Omar shrugged one shoulder. "You looked like you wanted to escape. I was trying to help."

She *had* wanted to get away from Luella. "But the way you cut her off and didn't answer her question about your X . . . You don't want her as an enemy."

He shoved his hands into his front shorts pockets. "Aw, she doesn't scare me."

Fool of a man. "She should. Luella Flynn is the most powerful woman in the Safe Lands."

Those bright eyes of his met hers again. "Why'd you say you weren't Kendall Collin?"

She didn't owe him any explanations. "How *did* you get your X?" Murdering someone, perhaps?

His smile lit up his face and eyes, making him look even younger. She wanted to ask how old he was but doubted she'd get the truth.

Omar stopped walking and turned to face her, hands still stuffed into his pockets. "Can I walk you home, Kendall?"

It could have been a line from one of the Old movies Kendall had seen as a child. Men didn't say such things in the Safe Lands. "No, thank you."

Omar pulled his hands from his pockets and stepped toward the curb. "Let me wave you a cab, then. I don't like the idea of you walking alone with a murderer on the loose."

Again with the chivalry. How could she know whether or not it was an act? He had a macho way about him, though he wasn't much taller than she was. He had some muscle on his arms as well, but if she wasn't recovering from childbirth, she'd bet she could run faster than he could. "I like walking. It's why I task for the messenger office."

"Okay." He pocketed his hands again. "Well, good night, Kendall. Be careful." He flashed one last wide smile and walked off down the sidewalk.

What a weird man. Boy. Guy. She forced herself to stop watching him and waved a cab. Sure, she preferred to walk, but Omar had made a good point. No need to tempt a murderer.

Not until she was safe in her apartment with the door locked did she remove the messages from the waistband of her shorts. She carried them to her kitchen table and spread them on the glass surface.

There were four white envelopes addressed to Dane Skott, Ruston Neil, Domini Bentz, and Charlz Sims. None had a grid code or return address. Three were private residences, and the fourth was an MO Box from her own branch.

She didn't recognize any of the names. But Kendall had lived in the Safe Lands only a few months before she'd gotten pregnant and been sent to the harem, so she'd never met many people outside the messenger office. Chord had always been kind, had never tried to pair up with her. He'd been a real friend. Kind and authentic. And if delivering these messages was his dying wish, Kendall would make it happen, murderer or not.

CHAPTER
1

Defying any government was a dangerous game. And while Safe Lands enforcers considered rebellion an X-able offense, the acts that inspired rebellion were far greater crimes, in Mason's opinion. Crimes against humanity and liberty. Crimes of manipulation and terror.

Ciddah would likely disagree.

Mason pushed the beautiful woman from his thoughts and entered the train station. Zane had told him to find locker 127. The lockers were located outside the gate, and he found number 127 easily and tapped onto the pad the code Zane had given him.

The locker clicked open. Inside, Mason found a small metal box. He opened the lid and removed a pair of black gloves that supposedly held a generic SimTag in the right hand. The metal box had somehow concealed the SimTag's location, which would now appear on the grid.

Ever since rebels had cut the official SimTag from Mason's hand, he had to choose whether or not to carry it with him. Today he'd left it in his apartment, hoping those monitoring him might think he was watching the ColorCast or sleeping. But he couldn't pass through the gate from the Highlands to the Midlands without a SimTag of some kind, hence these gloves.

He pulled them on and shut the locker, then walked to the Midlands turnstile and tapped his right fist — his right *glove* — on the SimPad. The turnstile light turned green, and Mason walked through.

Of all the remnant of Glenrock, only he, Mia, and Mia's mother, Jennifer, still resided in the Highlands. The others were now in hiding in the Midlands under the protection of the Black Army rebels. Except Omar, who had a Midlands apartment.

Mason took the train to the Belleview station and got off. He found locker 127 in that train station and deposited the gloves into the metal box inside. Now, without a SimTag on his person, he should be invisible to enforcers monitoring the grid. But that didn't mean he wasn't being followed.

He thought back to his trial before the Safe Lands Guild, and their accusations. Though they hadn't been able to prove he'd been involved in the harem escape, Lawten Renzor, the task director general of the Safe Lands, had warned him they were watching him.

So as Mason made his way down Belleview Drive, he scanned the street and sidewalks for suspicious persons. This was his first time in the Midlands, and its dullness surprised him. The structures and fake vegetation were the same strange colors — he passed a building of turquoise bricks with pale pink shrubs out front — but the place lacked the cleanliness and polished luxuriousness of the Highlands.

There were plenty of Wyndo screens flashing the latest mimic styles and product expositions to the public, but they were caked with dust and grime and the occasional cobweb. The streets were cracked and dirty. The buildings were flaking and had patches of paint that covered graffiti. Some had graffiti still, doubtlessly put there by rebels. Mason passed by some that said, "The Black Army wants you" and "Enforcers are evil."

And it wasn't only the scenery that was more rundown than the Highlands: Even the Midlands people didn't seem as extravagant. Sure, silver was everywhere as people mimicked Finley Gray and

Luella Flynn, but there was less Roller Paint here. And he couldn't be certain, but it seemed like less cosmetic surgery as well.

A plane flew overhead and Mason stopped to watch it. All his life he'd seen them and wondered. Now he knew the Safe Lands sent planes to Wyoming to trade and to other places to scavenge. Since there were people here in Colorado and in Wyoming as well, there were likely other civilizations in the world too. Perhaps the Safe Lands Guild knew of more.

Mason took a deep breath and continued on, recalling Levi's directions to the rebel meeting place. His older brother had never been great with details, but so far Mason had encountered no obstacles or confusion. He walked past the Get It Now store, past the charge station, and stopped in front of the Sim Slingers SimArt shop where Omar officially tasked, though his little brother also did various jobs for Bender that the Safe Lands Registration Department didn't know about. Besides Mason, Mia, and Jennifer, Omar was the only other outsider who was still officially registered as a Safe Lands national.

A steady beat throbbed from within the shop. The windows were Wyndo viewing glass, and Mason found himself watching the image of a technician altering SimArt on a computer while a SimArt flower on her client's shoulder changed colors. Such technology seemed similar to painting. No wonder Omar liked it.

Sim Slingers stood beside the Cinetopia Theater on Whetstone Road, separated by an alley. That was where Mason needed to go. He slipped down the alley, then poured on the speed, hoping to reach the corridor before anyone passed by on the street behind. He scanned the alley for the break in the wall that supposedly led to the back of theater nine, which was where Bender's rebels met.

Mason looked over his shoulder more often than he should, which caused him to almost miss the narrow opening in the cement wall of the theater. He darted into the corridor. Ahead, two men stood beside a door, looking like pillars.

Mason walked up to them and stopped, unsure what to say.

"Name?" Pillar One asked.

"Eagle," Mason said, which was short for his radio call sign, Eagle Eyes, and the code name Levi had told him to use for meetings.

Pillar Two pulled out a SimScanner and ran it over Mason's body, the dull buzz seeming to prolong the awkwardness of the moment. "He's clean."

Pillar One stepped aside. "Go on in."

"Thanks." Mason entered the building and passed down a dark hallway that let out in the left front corner of a small movie theater. The low rumble of Bender's voice signaled that the meeting had already begun.

The theater held maybe a hundred seats, all covered in thick red fabric. According to Levi, Jakk, the man who operated the theater, was one of Bender's rebels. Years ago, he'd built a wall over the interior entrance to theater nine to offer a secure meeting location for Safe Lands rebels. The only entrances now were through the back alley or a chute in the floor that led to an underground storm drain. The rest of the theater was open for business and showed the latest Safe Lands feature films to the public.

There were maybe two dozen people scattered in the seats in the front three rows of the theater, all eyes on the rebel called Bender, who stood in front of the darkened movie screen.

Bender looked to be in his fifties — too old to exist legally in the Safe Lands. His forehead was a mass of soft wrinkles, and a short gray beard covered his cheeks and chin. A scar had melted the skin over his left eye so that he always appeared to be squinting. He wore all black. Fitting for a man of the shadows.

Mason spotted Levi in the second row and made his way toward him as Bender continued his speech. Levi still had a small scab on the bridge of his nose, which was now slightly crooked since he'd never gotten it fixed after Omar had broken it.

" … learned a valuable lesson in all this. Liberations are a sham. They're not filmed live. We should've known, really. It's always been obvious that they edited things out. Just never suspected … I take full responsibility for failing Lonn."

Mason slid past the knees of those sitting in the second row: Shaylinn, Jordan, Levi. Jemma, Levi's wife, scooted down, leaving the seat between her and Levi open for Mason.

He sat down, thankful to have finally arrived. "Thanks, Jemma."

"You're late," Levi whispered.

"Sorry. My rebel skills are not as proficient as yours, brother." He truly didn't want to be here. The news he was carrying would only depress everyone further.

Zane sat in the row ahead of Mason. The rebel teen had been shot in the leg trying to help them free the women from the harem and still walked with a limp. He had short, spiky brown hair, was missing one ear, and had three spirals of gold metal looped through one nostril. He raised his hand and leaned back in his seat, which cracked under his weight. "You think Lonn is dead, then?" he asked Bender. "You think that's what liberation truly is?"

"Don't know what to think," Bender said. "I don't feel like he's dead. Either way, his liberation has people scared, and rightly so. We've lost eleven that I know of in the past year. We need to assure our followers that the Black Army is strong. That we have purpose and safety. And we need more members."

"Maybe you should stop using the messenger offices." Omar's soft voice came from the back of the room.

Mason looked over his shoulder and saw that his little brother was sitting alone in the very top row of the theater. The light on the end of the personal vaporizer he was holding to his lips glowed blue, which meant he was inhaling.

"Someone knew Chord was up to something," Omar said, his voice hoarse from the vapor.

"You were on watch, Omar," Bender said. "Why didn't you see anything?"

Omar didn't answer. He simply blew out a plume of black vapor.

Mason winced at his little brother's attitude. He understood it, but Omar was in a dangerous place right now, and picking fights with the head of the rebels was ignorant.

23

"We can't stop using the messenger office," Bender said. "It's vital to communication between rebels and potential recruits. Levi, since Chord was killed when one of yours was on watch, you provide a replacement."

"I don't think so," Levi said, and his tone made Mason flinch. "It's one thing to ask us to man your lookout posts, but it's another to ask us to make your deliveries. We don't want to get involved in your little war."

"I'm not asking," Bender said. "Find me a replacement for Chord, and I want your people helping us scout for new members."

Levi made to stand, but his best friend, Jordan, held him back. "Why should we help the Black Army?" Jordan asked. "We just want to get to our kids and get out of this dung pile."

"Levi and I made a deal." Bender scowled, which made his scarred eye close as if he were winking angrily. "I let you and your people stay in my bunker and keep you fed. In exchange, you do what I say. Once you're gone, you're gone. Until then, you work for me."

"You want my pregnant wife to walk up to people and say, 'Hey, you want to help take over the government?'" Jordan asked. "Are you nuts?"

"None of you will recruit," Bender said. "Just be on the lookout. I want the names of people who've been Xed, complainers, people who've lost a lifer. Ask questions. Listen. You get the feeling someone might join, tell me and we'll make contact. But be careful. Some of these people might be spies. Otley's not a shell. He didn't like that you outsiders got your women out of the harem and made him look incompetent."

"I'd like to volunteer," Shaylinn said. "To work in Chord's position."

"Um, no she wouldn't," Jordan said, glaring at his baby sister.

"*Yes*, I would," Shaylinn said. "I'm tired of staying indoors."

Jemma leaned past Mason's knees to look down to where Shaylinn sat at the end of the row. "It's not safe, Shay. Your face is plastered all over the Safe Lands."

"Then we can dye my hair or something." Shaylinn was tall for

24

fourteen, but it would be foolish for her to go outdoors with Safe Lands enforcers looking for her, since they'd made her pregnant in the Surrogacy Center just before the women had escaped the harem.

"We could certainly create a convincing disguise," Bender said. "Did you make a connection to Kendall Collin when you were in the harem, Miss Shaylinn?"

"Yes." Shaylinn leaned forward on her chair and bounced, as if Bender's attention were a special gift. "She was my mentor."

"Stop talking, Shay," Jordan said.

"She'll be perfect, then," Bender said. "I'll have Red come by this evening to work on a dis — "

"No." Jordan stood up and strangled the back of the chair in front of his. "She's not doing this."

Levi stood as well. "Omar will take Chord's place."

"But *Levi*." Shaylinn leaned past Jordan and fixed her gaze on Levi, big brown eyes blinking, lips turned in a frown. "I want to help. Please?"

"Omar already knows the messenger office, Shay, so he's the logical choice."

How very diplomatic of Levi to make it sound like Omar was merely the best candidate for the job when Mason knew his brother would never send a fourteen-year-old girl to be a spy. Omar was only sixteen, but Levi didn't have a lot of options.

"I'm just a part-time rover," Omar whined from the back. "I can't guarantee I'll get the right shifts."

"The shifts don't matter," Bender said. "New messages will show up in your sorter."

"Then that's settled," Levi said, sitting back down.

"Good." Jordan fell back to his seat as well.

Shaylinn slouched, scowling at her lap. She might not look pregnant, but that didn't change the fact that there was a child growing inside her. Perhaps once she began to show she would stop volunteering for risky positions.

"That's all I have for today," Bender said. "Levi, feel free to use the theater as long as you need to." Bender turned and walked toward the exit.

Over half the people stood to leave. Levi climbed over the front row seats and chased Bender. He caught up with him just before the exit. Jordan got up and squeezed past Shaylinn, then met Levi down front.

With the movement of so many people leaving, Mason couldn't hear what Levi and Bender were talking about. Shaylinn got up from her seat at the end of the row and scooted down until she sat beside Mason.

Jemma, still sitting on Mason's left, leaned over his lap. "Shay, why do you insist on antagonizing him?"

"I just want to do something important," Shaylinn said. "Soon I'll have a kid and my adventuring days will be over."

"I'm no expert on the subject," Mason said, "but my mother always claimed that raising her boys was her greatest adventure."

"Well said, Mason." Jemma patted his arm. "See, Shay? Adventure is coming! Oh, Levi is waving me over. Excuse me."

Mason twisted his knees to the side to let Jemma pass. Once she was down the stairs, Shaylinn lowered her voice to a whisper. "Were you able to find an answer to my question?" She winced, like she wasn't quite sure she wanted to know.

Mason could relate. "I'm sorry, Shay. I've been distracted lately with the trial." And there was the fact that Mason wasn't eager to learn the answer. This mystery donor from Wyoming, who was supposedly the genetic father of the baby Shaylinn was carrying, troubled him. But the alternative was to hope she was carrying Omar's child, which was an equally disturbing idea. "I should be able to find out this week." A promise he would have to keep this time.

"Thank you," Shaylinn said. "I mostly just want to make sure I wasn't infected during the procedure. I heard Levi and Jem talking, and, well ... Levi thinks I am."

Mason's older brother was paranoid. "The goal of the Surrogacy Center is to produce healthy children, Shay, don't forget."

"But Kendall got infected."

"Yes, but my understanding is that Kendall's donor was infected."

Shaylinn wrinkled her nose. "And you think mine wasn't?"

Oh, he hoped not. "That's my theory."

She smiled the same smile her siblings, Jemma and Jordan, had. One that bared full lips and perfect teeth. "Is it frightening living up there all alone?"

"The trial was a difficult time," Mason said. "But since they acquitted me, I've been treated like any other Safe Lands national. And when I'm working, I'm too busy to worry." Worrying wasn't logical, anyway.

"If you'll all quiet down, we need to discuss some things," Levi said, facing those who remained: the remnant from Glenrock and Levi's Safe Lander friend Zane. Levi stood in front of the movie screen, in the same place Bender had spoken from. Jemma and Jordan now sat in the front row. "First, I want to hear from Mason."

Wonderful. May as well get the worst over with. Mason scooted to the edge of his seat. "I'll start with some news from the harem. Jennifer and Mia are both pregnant."

The other women gasped and murmured around him. He wondered how their reactions might differ if they knew Mia had gotten pregnant on her own just days before she was scheduled for her ETP procedure. It was a fact he'd decided to keep to himself. But that now made two people from Glenrock who had contracted the thin plague. Omar and Mia.

Mason needed to find a cure.

"That's regrettable," Levi said. "But remember, we've already voted that we're not going after Mia and her mother. It's too risky to try to rescue those who will likely refuse to come. So this is no surprise. They made their choice."

"Thank you for telling us, though," Aunt Chipeta said to Mason.

Indeed. Better to find out from him than from Luella Flynn on the Safe Lands ColorCast. A sob from Mary spurred Mason to change the subject. "How am I to communicate with you without the radios?" Mason asked. Omar had destroyed that communication line before his change of heart. "Are we strictly sending paper messages now?"

"I'm getting you an untraceable Wyndo," Zane said. "I'll have it soon. Levi, Jordan, and Omar already have them. You'll be able to tap them on that. Just know that everything deletes after it's sent or read. That way, if you lose it or someone tries to take a look, everyone is safe."

"What did you find out about the kids?" Levi asked.

Mason took a deep breath. "The nursery is on the sixth floor of the Medical Center. I haven't been able to get over there yet. The older kids are in the boarding school. I've studied the school from the outside, but it's as much of a fortress as the Safe Lands itself. Penelope's class seems to walk to the park every Tuesday. I'm going to attempt to make contact with her next time."

"Tell her I love her," Aunt Chipeta — Penelope's mother — said.

"What's taking you so long?" Jordan asked. "It's been a month since we got the women out of the harem. You should have talked to Penny by now."

"I'm being cautious," Mason said. "My concern is that one of the teachers will see us speaking and perhaps not allow her to leave the school anymore."

"Still, you could have tried," Jordan said.

"With tasking in the SC and the trial, I haven't had time," Mason said. "And even though they acquitted me, I'm afraid I'm being watched."

"Of course you're being watched," Jordan said. "Figure out who it is and ditch them."

"It's not as easy as someone following me everywhere," Mason said. "I'm not even sure what to look for. I mean, I found a MiniComm in my apartment."

"What's a MiniComm?" Jemma asked.

"Exactly," Mason said. "I've since learned that it's some sort of recording device."

"They transmit," Zane said. "I'll come sweep your apartment."

"Thank you," Mason said, thankful that Zane was their friend. "But don't disturb anything you find. I don't want them to know I know they're listening. If something disappears, I'll look suspicious. Like I have something to hide."

"You do," Jordan said.

"No, he's right," Zane said. "Leaving things be will keep them off his back."

"Another thing," Mason said. "When I first spoke to the task director general, he mentioned that I could task in Research. I might ask him for a reassignment."

"Why?" Jemma asked. "You're in a good place in the Surrogacy Center."

Mason looked at his hands clasped together between his knees. "Ciddah put the MiniComm in my apartment."

"You're sure?" Jemma asked. "Why would your boss do that?"

"And what was she doing in your apartment?" Jordan asked.

Mason didn't want to lift that boulder, so he kept talking. "I think she's assisting Lawten — the task director general. So I can't imagine I'll be able to learn much under her ... observation."

"But you need to be at the Surrogacy Center for Mia and Jennifer," Aunt Chipeta said.

"It's too late to help Mia and Jennifer," Mason said. "But if I left the SC and tasked in Research, I'd have better access to learning about the disease. A better chance at finding a cure."

"Hang finding a cure, Mason," Levi said. "A cure is not our goal. Stop wasting your time and get to the kids."

"The Tasker G is not going to let you learn anything, anyway, you know," Omar said from the back of the theater. "All the man does is lie."

"And if you go to a new task, you'll have to start over," Jemma said, her soft voice a soothing change from Levi and Omar's criticism. "You need Ciddah."

He *wanted* to spend time with Ciddah, but he didn't need anyone. Mason had always been fine on his own. "I don't trust her."

"Mason," Jemma said, "you can't trust the task director general either."

Point taken. "I simply think it would be good to put distance between myself and Ciddah." Why couldn't he be stronger? Tell Levi no. Or be strong enough to smash his feelings for that infernal woman.

"It doesn't matter if you trust her," Levi said. "You can't trust anyone in the Safe Lands. Stop thinking of her as a person. She's the enemy, Mase. Use her to get what you need so we can all get out of here."

Use her. Mason had already abused his relationship with Ciddah a great deal, and he didn't like the heaviness his actions had brought to his heart. Ciddah had abused their relationship too, planting that MiniComm. But somehow Levi's suggestion seemed worse. More cutthroat. Sinister. Evil for evil.

Though why should Mason care? Ciddah had been toying with him from the start. None of her words could be trusted. Levi was right. Mason needed to forget his feelings for Ciddah and do his job, find out how to free the children so they could get their people out of the Safe Lands before any more became infected.

But he couldn't give up his search for a cure, either. Especially not now that both Omar and Mia were infected.

Yes, the children needed to come first. But Mason would continue his search for a cure, no matter what Levi said. There was simply too much at stake.

CHAPTER 2

Y ou. Have a. SimTalk tap. From … Red."
    The electronic voice of Omar's SimTalk implant roused him from his stim nap. The remnant from Glenrock was still here, so he hadn't been nodding long. "Answer," he said.

"Hey, trigger, where are you?" Red's voice came tinny in his ear.

"Theater."

"Be there in five. Wait for me?"

"Sure." Omar sucked in a long breath on his personal vaporizer. He watched his brother Levi ascend the theater steps to where Omar had claimed a seat in the back. His PV was filled with a combination of meds, grass, and brown sugar — low doses of the stims to keep Levi from strangling him. Though that looked like it might be about to happen anyway.

Omar closed his eyes and held the vapor in his lungs, savoring the way the stims eased the ache in his soul.

Levi's footsteps scuffed in the row in front of Omar. "How could you mess this up?"

Omar blew out a stream of vapor and opened his eyes. He still hadn't gotten used to the way Levi's nose looked. His brother hadn't gotten it fixed — on purpose, as a reminder to Omar of his betrayal. "Don't yell at me."

"You were late, weren't you? You were late meeting Chord."

Omar paused to think how to answer, hesitating enough that Levi kept talking.

"Why were you late, Omar?"

"Between Sim Slingers and the messenger office, I'm tasking two locations. Give me a break." But he didn't deserve one. Chord was dead. It should have been him.

"You told me you were done at Sim Slingers at five. You were supposed to meet Chord at eight. Was three hours not enough time for you to get from Sim Slingers to the messenger office? What is it ... three blocks?"

Levi's interrogations only made Omar feel worse. "I went to dinner."

"Where?"

"Does it matter?" What was done was done. The dead didn't come back.

Levi's expression actually softened a bit. "Look, Bender put me in charge of certain things. I don't like it any more than you, but I'm in his debt right now. So where were you?"

"Just because you're elder — "

"*Where*, Omar?"

"At the Paradise, okay? Eating dinner — "

"With Red."

It wasn't a question. Levi had been on Omar's case for spending time with Bender's errand girl — a crazy, wild, and physically friendly femme. Omar narrowed his eyes. "What makes you think I was with Red?"

Levi barked out his disgust. "Omar, I'm not stupid. I know she lives in the Paradise."

"I'm not stupid, either." *I'm not.*

"Could have fooled me, brother. All you had to do was show up at eight at the messenger office and bring the messages back to Bender.

Simple. Now Chord is dead. The messages are missing, and Bender is all worked up over it."

"See, I don't get that," Omar said. "They've never been *Bender's* messages before. And if Bender wanted them, why not ask Chord for them himself?"

"Zane thinks Chord was murdered because he discovered something important. My guess is that Bender knew Chord had information to bring him and wanted your help throwing Otley off track. But Otley's men got to Chord before he delivered his messages. So thanks to you, we'll never know what they said."

Great. Just what Omar needed: more guilt. "I didn't kill him, Levi."

"No, but you're so consumed with this place, with that ... vapo stick, that you can't even think straight."

"Do you hear me sniffing, brother? No, because I'm vaping my allergy meds. And the ACT treatment." And a little added sweetness to take the edge off Levi's lectures.

Levi paled a bit at Omar's mention of the ACT treatment. *Elder Levi* hated that Omar was infected with the thin plague. So Omar did his best to bring it up as often as he could.

"I wish you'd get your act together," Levi said.

That was all the lecture Omar could take for today. "No one respects me. I'm sick of it." At sixteen, Omar was too young to rally older men to the rebels' cause, and those who knew him knew he'd betrayed their village to Safe Lands enforcers. And even after he'd helped Levi, Jemma, and Zane escape the prison and apologized to everyone, people still treated him badly.

"It's going to take time, Omar. It hasn't even been two months since Glenrock was destroyed."

"But working two jobs isn't fair. And now I've got to worry about Otley's men watching me too."

"Contrary to what these flakers in the Safe Lands believe, life is not fair, Omar. Sometimes you get dealt a bad hand. Sometimes you earn it. But you can deal with it or drown. I'm not going to coddle you. I need you to do your share."

"I'm fine doing my share. But why should I do more than everyone else?"

"You have a lot to make up for. You want people to respect you? Show them you've changed. Stop whining. Stop sucking on those poison sticks. Start acting like you want out of here someday."

Did Omar want out of here? "I don't know what I want."

"Figure it out, Omar. Or it's going to be more of the same. And stop hanging around with those flakers. Red, especially."

"They're people, Levi. Like you and me."

"They're the enemy. Stop pretending they're not."

"I'm a flaker too. It won't be long until my skin looks like theirs. So does that mean I'm the enemy?"

"This is about us and them. Catching their sickness doesn't make you one of them. Don't be stupid. And stop treating your body like a canvas."

"Stop telling me what to do."

"I'm elder, Omar. Telling you what to do is my job. And for now, I want you following that Kendall woman. Bender thinks she might have the messages."

"You just said Bender thought Otley had the messages."

"No, I said Otley got to Chord before he delivered the messages. But Otley didn't get them. If he had, Bender said this place and our bunker would be compromised and they would've already raided us. Either Chord hid them or he gave them to someone. Bender thinks it's Kendall Collin. Find out." Levi walked away, not giving Omar a chance to argue.

Not that he wanted to.

Now, Kendall Collin, the girl with the sweet face and the silky brown hair ... that wasn't a bad assignment. Omar would very much like to get to know her better. He sucked in another hit from his vaporizer, closed his eyes, and enjoyed the thrill, letting the fog seep from his lips. He could never tell how much time passed when he vaped the hard stuff. He nodded off again, thinking of Kendall Collin.

"Hey, trigger."

Omar opened his eyes. Red stood before him, looking glossy in a short silver dress with black boots that went up over her knees. She sometimes mimicked the clothing, but never messed with her hair, which was vermillion red, not carrot orange like Belbeline's had been.

Walls, he missed Bel.

Omar looked past Red to the bottom of the theater. Levi, Jordan, and Zane were still there, standing in a huddle by the entrance, but everyone else had gone.

"I thought you were sleeping," Red said.

"Not sleeping." He held up his PV.

"Ooh, gimme." She snatched his PV and took a long drag.

Red reminded him of a warrior. There was a hardness to her. An inner metal. He'd met her three weeks ago when he'd started up with Bender and the rebels. Omar and Red were both angry deep down, their souls ravaged by this city. They seemed to understand each other's pain.

She sat on his lap crosswise and put her arms around his neck. She smelled nice, softer than the spicy smells Belbeline wore.

"Want to go dancing tonight?" she asked him.

"Can't."

She ran her fingers through his hair at the nape of his neck. "Why not?"

"Levi's mad at me for missing my meeting with Chord."

"Yeah, that's a bummer about Chord. He was a valentine."

Her words pricked Omar's nerves. He hated how Safe Landers shared each other. He wanted a girl who wanted him and no one else. He wanted what Jordan and Naomi had. What Levi and Jemma had.

But Red thought like Belbeline. The word *commitment* didn't exist in their vocabulary. They just wanted to play.

Red seemed to sense she'd upset him, because she fisted the front of his shirt and tugged. "Hey, he's not as valentine as you, though."

"Really." He didn't believe her. Not even a little. But he liked her aggressive ways.

She set her forehead against his and stared into his eyes. "You have gorgeous eyes."

When she set her mind to it, Red had a way of saying just the right thing. *Her* eyes were pink today. It was weird, how she changed her eye color each day like Omar changed his shirt. She kissed him then. She was a good kisser. Almost as good as Belbeline.

"Get a room, Omar!" Jordan's voice carried from below.

Omar ignored him.

But Red pulled away and grinned. "That's a good idea." She hopped off Omar's lap and stood. "Let's go, trig." She pulled him out of the seat and down the steps toward the exit. They passed Levi, Jordan, and Zane at the door.

"You dirt bunnies make me sick," Jordan said.

"We try, shell," Red said, blowing Jordan an air kiss.

A few more steps through the darkness of the corridor, and he and Red left the theater. Red stopped to give one of the guards at the door a lingering kiss. On the lips. One of her old conquests, Omar assumed. Mad annoying. But if he said anything, they'd fight. Omar just needed to get used to how things worked here.

Or maybe find a girl who wasn't from here. A girl like Kendall. She was an outsider too. Maybe they'd make a better match.

Finally they reached the sidewalk, passed Sim Slingers, and headed toward his apartment. Red walked with her arms around him, one hand fisting the front of his shirt, the other tucked into his back pants pocket. It made him uncomfortable, like he didn't know her well enough for such a public display of affection despite the intimate things they'd done in private. The thought gave him pause, didn't make sense.

Omar took another drag of his PV, and the stims relaxed him. Red's hands did too. Kissing while walking wasn't the easiest of tasks, so they made several stops on their walk to his place to enjoy each other. Red made him feel alive, like the brown sugar. He wanted to feel alive. He needed to.

Find pleasure in life, right? That's what they always said in the Safe Lands.

It was during one such stop in the park that the sound of an owl drew Omar's attention.

"What's wrong?" Red asked.

Omar stepped back from Red, his gaze flitting over the branches above. "I heard an owl."

"So?"

He kept looking, every rustling leaf a potential perch. "I didn't know they came into the Safe Lands."

"Who cares?"

Omar did. And when the curved shadow of the bird panned across the lamp-lit street that edged the park, Omar chased it.

"Where are you going?" Red called.

Omar sprinted down the sidewalk after the receding shadow. He ran for three blocks and lost the bird somewhere over the Outrunner building. He stopped to catch his breath, consumed with the image of the wingspan stretched across the center of the street. He needed to draw.

"You. Have a. SimTalk tap. From ... Red."

"SimTalk off," Omar said.

He ran all the way to his apartment in the Alexandria. He walked inside and tripped over the dumbbells he'd left on the floor by the door before he remembered to turn on the lights. Once he could see, he grabbed a fresh sheet of paper and nub of charcoal and fell onto the tile floor in the middle of his kitchen, which was really more of an art studio now. His hands quickly drew the shape of the owl's wings. He blended the shadow with the side of his fist, caressing the paper, creating the look of freedom. Wings that could carry him away from this place. Away from the chains that bound him so tightly.

Oh, how he wanted to be free.

Five sheets of paper later, Omar sat back on his heels and studied his work. He'd drawn the face of an owl on the body of a man. A flowing cape framed the figure.

It was the Owl — Omar's favorite superhero from the comic books of Old that his Grandpa Seth had given him years before he died.

Levi was right; life wasn't fair. But that was okay. Because if everything was fair in the world, nobody would win. And Omar was sick of losing.

He was also sick of numbing his pain with temporary pleasures. There had to be another way to deal with his grief and guilt. A way that would prove to Levi that Omar wasn't a worthless flaker. That he could be a hero too.

He could become the Owl, a superhero for the Safe Lands.

He grabbed a fresh canvas and propped it on the easel, then began to paint the Owl.

"Omar?"

He jumped at the sound of Red's voice in his apartment. *Maggots.* He didn't want her here, but he'd added her ID to his door lock a week ago, and now she could come and go as she pleased.

He kept his back to her, hoping if he ignored her, she'd leave. But her footsteps crossed the room. She crouched just behind him, blocking some of his light, and reached up the back of his shirt. Her long fingernails scratched lightly up his spine and caused goose bumps to stand out along his arms.

He didn't want to want this girl. He wanted to paint. He wished she would go away. Why couldn't he just tell her that? *Go away, Red. Leave me alone.*

Instead he allowed her to take the paintbrush and palette from his hands. She set them on the paint-splattered floor, then turned him to face her, slid her fingernails up the backs of his hands and over his wrists and forearms, slowly sliding her hands up his arms, up, up, until her fingers locked behind his neck.

He let out a happy moan and thought, *Go away, Red.*

But she kissed him. And he kissed her back, weakling that he was. How could someone so weak become any kind of superhero?

He couldn't.

Women were nothing but trouble for superheroes. As soon as she left, he'd reprogram his door lock so she couldn't get inside next time.

Next time. It would be easier to resist her next time.

CHAPTER
3

Mason paced along the sidewalk in front of the G.I.N. vending machine that sat across the street from the Safe Lands Boarding School. It was Tuesday morning, and the older students should be walking to the park soon. The boarding school housed kids from age three to thirteen. He'd seen Penelope and Nell, who were both thirteen, in the group before, and he was determined to speak with one of them today.

The clamor of children's voices that came from behind the red brick wall surrounding the school antagonized him. Somewhere inside, children from Glenrock were playing. Were they afraid and lonely? Or were they enjoying themselves? Mason had found much of the Safe Lands fascinating, and he could only imagine what Safe Lands novelties might distract children. For a brief moment he imagined that the children would refuse to leave when he and others from Glenrock finally arrived to rescue them, preferring this eternal playground to home.

Surely a longing for their mothers would trump such innovation.

An iron gate yawned open to his left, and a line of students departed the school, single file, down the sidewalk toward where he was standing. Excellent. He turned to face the vending machine, but instead of examining the contents for purchase, he used the glass's reflection to monitor the passing students.

"Get the flakes," a boy told him.

Mason turned and met the boy's cheeky grin as he walked by.

"Flakes are the best," the boy called after him.

A dark-haired girl grabbed Mason's arm. "Buy me a fizzy?" She had long fake eyelashes and a familiar face. Penelope. "Pen — Please?" Mason said, looking for the teacher and hoping he hadn't been overheard. "Um … Don't forget your manners."

"Please!" a dozen children seemed to yell at once.

"Leave the gentleman to his shopping," the teacher said from the end of the line, her tone stern yet bored. "Keep the line moving."

Penelope slipped something into Mason's hand and stepped back into line.

Mason watched her go, then thought better of it, and turned back to the vending machine. He had planned to simply follow the class today, but perhaps Penelope's idea was the better one. He purchased a package of chocolate chews from the vending machine and followed the students, keeping a dozen yards behind. Up ahead, the street ended, forcing traffic to the left or right along the road that bordered the park. The line of students trailed across the street, blocking traffic. Mason went into a Lift on the corner, which was an establishment that sold hot and cold beverages with the option of added "lifts" or supplements, be they vitamin, adaptogen, or stimulant.

He sat at a table at the window and watched the students enter the park. He unfolded the paper Penelope had given him.

There are two ways kids sneak out of the school. A storm drain leads off the southeast corner of the basement in the boys' dorm. Kids have been using it for years and getting caught, so right now it's boarded up. I'm trying to talk this girl into taking me, because she's always bragging about all the places she's been. But she could be lying.

The girls' dorm roof is five stories high and the same level as the roof of the Nordic Apartments. Kids sometimes go up on the roof to vape and drink alcohol. There's a wooden plank up there that is long enough to stretch from the dorm roof to the Nordic roof. I went out with a few kids last week. We didn't leave the Nordic. But we were able to get over there and back without getting caught. So that might be our best plan. It will be hard to get all the kids together at once without being seen. But if you tell me the date and time, I think we'll be able to do it.

Love you!
Penny

Mason's nerves, heart rate, and muscles relaxed. There was hope here. And Penelope still wanted out, which probably meant most of the others did too. Good.

He left the Lift and walked back past the school. He scanned the skyline, considering the placement of the Nordic Apartments, the roads, and the yellow cameras that were everywhere in the Safe Lands. Zane had promised he could take care of the cameras. The Nordic was located on the three-way corner of where Emmons Road crossed one end of Treasury Road. To the east, Treasury dead-ended at the Midlands wall. He likely wouldn't be able to get the kids through the Midlands gate. Perhaps there was a way to take the storm drains, which would make the basement exit ideal ... But if they couldn't get to the drains through the boys' dorm and had to use the roof of the girls' dorm, they'd still need to come out of the Nordic and get underground.

Levi would need to explore the drains underneath the school.

If they were going to have to get out through the roof, it would be nice to speak with someone who'd attended the school, especially a female. But the only female in the rebel group was Red, and Levi had forbidden Mason from involving her in their plans.

There was Ciddah, of course. But ever since Mason had found the MiniComm in his apartment he'd been avoiding Ciddah, working beside her in near silence.

Levi's words came to mind: *"Stop thinking of her as a person. She's the enemy, Mase. Use her to get what you need so we can all get out of here.*"

Was Ciddah Rourke his enemy? Despite the MiniComm, he simply couldn't accept that — at least not as harshly as Levi had put it. No one who treated patients with such gentle care could be all bad.

Ciddah had been his friend. And she had gone to the boarding school and had the information he needed. Though she'd never help him. Not with this. He couldn't even risk asking her about the school because she might report his suspicious questions to enforcers. But he had to risk it, didn't he?

He didn't know what to do. He liked Ciddah too much to play the games Levi had asked of him. But she was his only option. That woman made him an irrational mess.

Enough of his pathetic emotions. Getting out of the Safe Lands and finding a cure for Omar and Mia was all that mattered. Mason could lament his poor choice in women once all of Glenrock was safely outside this diseased fortress.

He took a deep breath and walked away from the boarding school, headed back to his apartment. Tomorrow he would engage Ciddah in a conversation that would, hopefully, lead to some answers. Time to "use her," as Levi had said, the way she'd been using him from the start.

CHAPTER
4

Twenty-six days had passed since the women had escaped the Highland Harem. And that was how long Shaylinn and Naomi had been banished to the underground bunker in the Midlands. In that time, Shaylinn had been allowed to leave only twice, both times to attend Bender's rebel meetings with her brother.

Naomi hadn't been allowed to leave at all. She was far too pregnant now. And she took more naps than a cat.

When Shaylinn wasn't in the bathroom on her knees dealing with tedious amounts of morning sickness, she entertained herself by cleaning the bunker. It was hard work, but the place was gross, and she didn't like the idea of her new nephew crawling around in such filth — though hopefully they'd all be long gone before the child learned to crawl.

Shaylinn filled a bucket with soapy water. Jemma wanted her to use bleach, but Shaylinn couldn't tolerate the smell. She carried the bucket out of the main living area and into the corridor. The space was concrete and cold and stretched out like a very long and wide hallway. It smelled of moss and metal. Burnt sienna stains painted stripes down the walls where rusty water had run and dried. Omar had taught

Shaylinn the color burnt sienna, and the rusty stains reminded her of the boy she loved.

Maybe she was too young to love a boy. She hadn't meant to. If she had, she would have had the sense to love someone who might love her back, someone who wasn't so ... lost. And stupid.

Tears flooded her eyes, thinking about Omar being infected with the thin plague. Why had he done everything Elder Eli had warned them not to do?

She wished her mother were here so she could talk to her about all this. Mother had always been a good listener. Jemma was too intent on fixing everything, but some things just couldn't be fixed.

Shaylinn reached into the warm water, squeezed out her sponge, and scrubbed at the stain on the wall. The bright color smeared, coming off easily. Drops of burnt sienna water rolled down the wall, leaving clean stripes of gray behind.

A while back she'd had a dream that had showed a happy future. Shaylinn and a man in a home with several children. The dream had helped her when she'd needed confidence to get through the procedure in the Surrogacy Center. But that had been almost a month ago, and her confidence had waned since then.

It wasn't fair. Pregnant without ever having kissed a boy. Unless she was to count kisses from her father or the time Ewan, one of the harem enforcers, had kissed her without asking. But Shaylinn didn't count those kisses.

She thought of Omar and that day at the kissing trees when he'd —

The seal on the iron door that separated the bunker from the underground storm drains cranked open, echoing slightly in the concrete corridor. Shaylinn took a step back to stay in the shadows. She wasn't expecting anyone for another hour.

Two men and a woman stepped through the door. One of the men had wide shoulders and was as tall as Jordan. The other was shorter. They were not from Glenrock. Shaylinn's stomach turned, and she pressed against the wall, straining to get a good look at their faces.

She recognized the shorter man first. It was Rewl, who reminded

Shaylinn of a grown toddler … until he smiled. He'd gotten SimArt implants in his teeth, which gave them diagonal black pinstripes. So gross.

Next came Red, the woman who was always with Omar. Red hadn't been the one to infect Omar, but Shaylinn hated her anyway, even if it was wrong to hate. Red looked like a skeleton wearing a flesh jumpsuit, but her chest was so large Shaylinn wondered how she could walk and not fall over. She had electric pink eyes and wispy, chin-length, maroon-colored hair that looked fake. That's what she was: 100 percent fake.

Red stepped deep into the corridor, holding a fat bag. Rewl and the other man pulled the door closed until the clamp clicked into place, sealing off the bunker again, which would keep the water out if it rained. The men turned toward the entrance to the main room, and Shaylinn recognized the second man.

"Mr. Bender," she said, relaxing and stepping into the light.

The leader of the Black Army reminded Shaylinn of Grandpa James. He had wrinkled skin and short gray hair. A strange scar over his left eye made him squint, like he was always thinking about winking but never made up his mind.

All three wore black gloves. Shaylinn had never seen a Black Army member without gloves.

"Miss Shaylinn," Bender said, his voice low and kind. "Exactly the femme I'm looking for."

Shaylinn squeezed the sponge. A trickle of water splashed on the floor, which made her step back and lighten her grip. "You want to talk to *me*?"

"Why don't we go in and sit?" Bender said. "It'll be more comfortable."

"Okay." Shaylinn dropped her sponge into the water and picked up the bucket. She went to open the door to the main room, but her hand slipped on the knob, still wet from the wash water.

Rewl darted forward. "Let me help, Miss Shaylinn." He opened the door and held it there, baring his striped teeth in a smile.

Shaylinn walked past him and into the main room. It was warmer than the corridor. It had a one-wall kitchen on the front end, a TV and sofas on the other end, and three round tables in the middle. Shaylinn set her bucket in the kitchen sink and dried her hands on a towel, turning it slightly orange from the rusty water on her hands.

Bender made his way to the sofas and sat on the brown one, which was the one with the least holes. Red stayed with him, sitting beside him on the sofa. Rewl closed the front door and stood in front of it like he was guarding the place. Something about his posture made Shaylinn's neck tickle. She decided then that she didn't like Rewl either. She wondered if he were carrying a gun.

"Yesterday at the meeting, you volunteered to work in Chord's position," Bender said.

Shaylinn walked to the other end of the room and stood beside the Old TV set. "Omar is going to do it," she said with a glance at Red. But Bender knew that already.

"I have a proposition for you, Miss Shaylinn," Bender said. "I need to find out if Kendall Collin has the messages Chord was supposed to bring to me. You think you could find out?"

"Oh." Why was he asking her? "I'd like to help, but it would be wrong to go behind Levi's back. Or my brother's." Plus Jordan would yell and scream.

"I understand. And I admire your loyalty to your brother." Bender sighed and stretched his arms up on the back of the sofa, one behind Red. "It's a shame about Kendall, though. She seems like an honest femme."

Red gasped and pressed her hand against her gigantic chest. "You're not going to kill her, are you, Bender?"

"Not me," Bender said. "I'll have Rewl do it."

"What?" Shaylinn couldn't have heard that right. "Kill Kendall?"

"I wish I didn't have to," Bender said, "but without knowing for certain if she's got those messages and what she's going to do with them, I don't have a choice."

Of course he had a choice. No one was putting a gun in his hands.

"You can't take the risk," Red said, patting Bender's knee. She looked at Shaylinn, and those pink eyes seemed electrified, like Red was a robot. "It puts the entire Black Army in jeopardy. And the outsider shells too."

Did it? But Shaylinn couldn't allow them to kill Kendall. "I guess I can try to find out if she has them, but you're wrong to mistrust her. She hates the Safe Lands government. They took her baby."

"You get burned enough, femme, you don't trust anyone anymore," Bender said.

"And why would she care about them taking the kid?" Red said. "It's what they do. He's not *her* baby."

Shaylinn folded her arms. "Of course he's her b — Wait, aren't you a rebel? Don't you think the Safe Lands is wrong to take babies?"

Red snorted and flicked her hair over her shoulder. "I don't like the government telling me what to do. But babies aren't my interest."

Shaylinn pursed her lips. "Men are your interest, right?"

"That's right." Red giggled, low and secretive as if she knew something Shaylinn didn't. "You'd better not hurt Omar," Shaylinn said.

This comment seemed to make Red's pink eyes even more electric as she glared at Shaylinn. "Omar knows what he wants. And he wants me."

A rush of anger welled up in Shaylinn. "No, he doesn't. He's sad and confused because of everything that's happened. And you're taking advantage of him."

Red cackled like an evil witch in an Old movie. "Omar can wipe his own nose, femme. He doesn't need you sticking your — "

"Focus," Bender said. "Kendall Collin?"

Shaylinn scowled at Red once more before giving Bender her full attention. "Can you bring her here?"

"Nooo. She can't know about this place," Bender said. "You're going to be a spy, Miss Shaylinn. Spend time with her. Get her to tell you about the messages without mentioning me *or* the Black Army."

"But how can I go outside when I'm supposed to be hiding?" Shaylinn asked.

"I've got a couple ideas," Bender said. "I can get you hired at the messenger office as a janitor during Kendall's shifts. Or Rewl can drive you around, follow Kendall, and you can bump into her when she goes to the G.I.N. or wherever. Or we can get you moved into the apartment beside hers."

The idea of having her own place thrilled her. "I'd like the apartment, please. But ... Jordan. When he finds me gone, he'll come and get me and lock me up." And yell and scream. But if he didn't know about the apartment, she could always sneak out again.

"Then you'd better act fast, femme," Red said.

Shaylinn didn't like the way Red looked at her and bossed her, so she kept her side of the conversation between her and Bender. "My picture is on the ColorCast all the time. And Jordan said he saw it on the train too. What if someone recognizes me?"

"Red is going to give you a little makeover," Bender said. "No one will recognize you when she's done."

As a last-ditch effort to get them to leave her alone, she said, "But I'm pregnant!"

"You're not even showing yet," Bender said. "You'll be fine."

Shaylinn looked back at Red then, and met those electric-pink eyes. "As long as she doesn't make me look like her."

Red smiled, and it was an ugly, fake smile. "Why would I do that? One of me is all the Safe Lands can handle."

Shaylinn hummed as if considering her comment. "It's all I can handle too."

A few hours later, Shaylinn was standing alone in her new apartment that was located next door to Kendall's in the Belleview Building. The kitchen, sofa, and bed filled one small room. And then there was a tiny bathroom. The whole place was decorated pink and green and reminded Shaylinn of the polka dot chair in Tyra Grant's office.

Thoughts of the harem's beauty care specialist sent Shaylinn walking toward the mirror for the fifth time since Bender, Red, and Rewl had dropped her off downstairs. She'd been worried that being underground with no access to InstaWraps and SkinnySticks would have made her get fat again, but it hadn't. Silver was still the hot trend, set by Finley Gray and Luella Flynn, the hosts of the Safe Lands ColorCast. Shaylinn had refused to allow Red to cut her hair, so the woman had straightened it and given her a tinsel weave, which mixed in strands of metallic silver hair with her natural brown hue. Shaylinn's hair now reached her elbows in a flat, shaggy mop. Red had also given Shaylinn a pair of contact lenses that made her eyes look a natural green, and black lace gloves with no fingers that held a SimTag so she could enter buildings and pay for taxis or whatever she might need.

That had been more than enough to transform Shaylinn into a completely different person from the picture of the frightened girl that had been plastered all over the Safe Lands. Red had also given her several sets of clothes, enough to last the week. They were sexy clothes that clung to Shaylinn's body and showed off her growing chest.

She hadn't needed breast implants after all. The pregnancy had taken care of that.

Shaylinn had always wanted to be beautiful, but she wasn't certain she liked what Red had done. She looked like someone from *C Factor*. And even though Red had promised this new look would help her blend in with the other Safe Lands women, Shaylinn was sure it would only call attention to herself.

A bell chimed. Rewl had rigged up the bell to signal whenever Kendall's apartment door opened. Shaylinn ran over to the peephole on the wall and looked in.

Kendall was home. She walked to the kitchen table and set her messenger bag on one of the chairs and a box of chicken from Leghorns on the table.

Shaylinn drew back. Bender wanted her to wait until she and Kendall bumped into each other on the stairs or outside. To create a coincidental meeting. But Shaylinn had no intention of doing things

Bender's way. The moment Jordan realized she was gone, he would come looking. If Shaylinn was going to help Kendall, she needed to do it now.

She left her apartment and knocked on Kendall's front door. She heard footsteps, then saw movement in the peephole. The door opened, the chain keeping it from going farther than a few inches.

"Yes?" Kendall said.

"Hi, Kendall." Shaylinn leaned close and whispered, "It's Shaylinn. From the harem."

Kendall's eyes narrowed and studied Shaylinn from head to toe. The door pushed closed, the chain rattled, and the door opened again. "Come in."

Shaylinn slipped inside, awkward in the high-heeled shoes Red had given her. The smell of fried chicken made her stomach flutter. *Oh no.*

Kendall closed the door behind her and came to stand by the kitchen table, arms folded. "You escaped the harem. I've seen your picture on the ColorCast. What do you want?"

Shaylinn pressed up against the front door and fought to hold back the sickness, but the smell of the chicken ... She looked around the apartment and spotted the bathroom door in the same place it was located in her new apartment. She ran for it. "Need to use your bathroom."

Shaylinn fell to her knees at the toilet and wanted to cry. She had no control over how smells affected her anymore. How was she supposed to keep from throwing up all the time? When she finished, she washed her hands and rinsed out her mouth, then tottered back into Kendall's kitchen/living room/bedroom.

"I put the chicken in the oven and opened the windows," Kendall said. "My morning sickness only ever came in the mornings. But they say if you get it really bad, it means you're having a girl."

"Maybe," Shaylinn said, tickled at the idea of a daughter to take care of.

"What about Jemma and Mia and the others?" Kendall asked.

"We got out in time. I'm the only one who was made pregnant."

"And Naomi?"

"She's safe too. And she's huge! That baby is coming any day, Jemma says. What about you? Have you seen your baby?"

"Once." Kendall's jaw hardened. "They don't allow that, really, but Lawten had promised I'd be able to hold Elyot whenever I wanted. But after the first time I went to the nursery, they wouldn't let me back in." Tears pooled at the corners of her eyes. She blinked rapidly. "So, who glossed you up? You look like a dancer."

"You're a shell!" a strange voice said. "Tch tch tch."

Shaylinn jumped and looked toward the window where a rounded cage sat on a narrow table. Something moved inside the cage, flying from corner to corner. A little bird. It was yellow and blue with black-and-white wings. "What's that?"

Kendall waved her hand as if the topic bored her. "Oh, that's my bird, Basil."

"He talks?"

"Give me a kiss," the bird said in a dull, almost electronic voice. "What time is it?"

"I'm sorry, but ... why are you here, Shaylinn?"

"I have something important to tell you, but I need you to let me finish before you interrupt me or get angry. Do you promise to listen until I'm done?"

"Okay."

Shaylinn took a deep breath. "Well, since we escaped the harem — "

"Budgie. Basil's a budgie. Tch tch tch. Give us a kiss."

Shaylinn grinned at the bird.

"Just a minute." Kendall walked to the cage and pulled a drape over it. "Good night, Basil."

"Good night, Basil. Tch tch tch."

"Will he go to sleep?" Shaylinn asked.

"Yeah. He's funny that way. You were saying?"

"Right. Um, the Black Army has been hiding my people. Levi befriended their leader, Bender. Well, Bender is their new leader now that Lonn has been liberated."

"Go on."

Shaylinn hoped she was explaining things correctly. "Bender thinks you have messages Chord Prezden was meant to deliver. He said if he couldn't figure out whether or not you were trustworthy, he was going to have you killed. So I volunteered to spy on you so I could warn you."

Kendall paled. "Kill me?"

"I know you're not a murderer, Kendall. So if you have Chord's messages, I figure you have a good reason."

"I have them," Kendall said, her eyes glossy with tears.

Shaylinn breathed out a sigh, hoping Bender would leave Kendall alone once he had the messages in his possession. "Can I have them? To give to Bender?"

Kendall's bottom lip trembled. "When I found Chord, he'd been attacked. With his dying words he asked me to deliver the messages to the addressees and no one else. I think Chord knew someone else would come looking."

"Maybe Bender is worried the addressees will be exposed to enforcers," Shaylinn said. "Maybe he's just trying to protect his rebels."

"Maybe Bender killed Chord."

What a terrible thought. "Why would he do that? He's a good guy."

"Anyone who threatens to kill someone is not a good guy."

Yeah. Good point.

"I've had the messages for three days," Kendall said, "trying to decide if I should deliver them or destroy them. Let's read them."

"That seems a little nosy," Shaylinn said.

"It's the only way we'll find out the truth." Kendall walked to her refrigerator and opened the freezer. She removed the ice bin and dumped its contents into the sink. Then she peeled a plastic bag off the bottom of the bin and left the bin in the sink.

She carried the bag to the kitchen table and sat down. Shaylinn pulled out the chair beside hers and sat too. It felt good to get off her feet. The high-heeled shoes were painful after wearing them too long.

Kendall opened the plastic bag and set four messages on the glass tabletop. "Three are private residences. But this one"—she tapped the message addressed to a Ruston Neil—"is an MO Box from my branch."

"What's the difference?" Shaylinn asked.

"This Ruston doesn't get mail at a residence. He picks it up at the messenger office."

Shaylinn read the names on the envelopes: Ruston Neil, Dane Skott, Domini Bentz, and Charlz Sims. "I know Charlz's name. He helped Omar get Levi and Jemma out of the RC." And it had earned him an X after his number, same as Omar.

"Let's open that one first, then." Kendall ripped open the envelope and removed a single white card. There were only three lines of text.

> Want freedom?
> We have answers.
> Cinetopia, Theater 9.

"Sounds subversive," Kendall said. "If Chord was involved in some rebel cause ... that might explain his death. People who rebel in the Safe Lands don't rebel for long. As Luella Flynn would say, 'Rebels are a blemish that must be painted over.'"

"Chord was a rebel," Shaylinn said, feeling as though that supported Kendall's theory. "And theater nine is where we meet—the rebels, I mean. To talk about our plans. I bet this is an invitation for Charlz to join the rebels."

"So this Bender man wants to kill me in case I might expose his potential recruits?" Kendall asked. "That doesn't seem like adequate motive."

"Let's open the others," Shaylinn said, curious if they were all the same.

The messages to Dane Skott and Domini Bentz were identical to the one addressed to Charlz Sims, but the message to Ruston Neil was totally different.

Mr. Neil,

Zane told me to contact you if I ever needed someone to trust and he wasn't around. Since Zane didn't answer my tap today, and I didn't think it was safe to leave a voicemail, I'm writing to you.

I left my messenger bag at the warehouse yesterday, and when I went back to retrieve it, I overheard Bender take a tap from General Otley. I couldn't hear what Otley said, but Bender asked how Otley's plans were coming along. He also said that once Otley was the task director general, Bender would be the enforcer general.

Nothing else notable was said, but before Bender ended the call, he said he'd take care of it, whatever that means.

While I can't imagine that I misheard, I felt the best plan was to bring this to your attention. Bender summoned me to the warehouse today. I'm afraid he somehow found out I'd overheard his tap, so I decided to write this letter in case something happened to me.

Thanks for your time,
Chord Prezden

"Bender must have killed Chord," Kendall said. "What are we going to do?"

Shaylinn's head tingled. So did her arms. Hot and cold all at once. Bender kill Chord? She jumped up and trotted toward the door. "I have to go! I have to tell Jordan and Levi."

"Wait!"

Shaylinn reached the door and slammed her glove to the SimPad. It swung inward, but Kendall arrived and pushed it shut.

"What are you doing?" Shaylinn pounded her fist against the SimPad again, tears blurring her vision. "Let me out! If Bender killed Chord, he could kill any of us. Whenever he wants! I have to warn them!"

But Kendall closed the door again and this time took hold of Shaylinn's shoulders. "Just think for a minute, Shaylinn. Please. We have to be very careful and very smart. If Bender sent you here, he could be outside, watching. If you go running out of here, upset like you are ... It will look bad, okay?"

"Okay." Shaylinn scanned the room, wishing there were another exit, but Kendall's words slowly sank in. She took a deep breath. "Okay."

"Come back and sit at the table so we can decide what to do."

Shaylinn obeyed, rubbing her eyes as she clomped across the kitchen. She fell onto the chair and took another huge breath. "What if we delivered them but kept copies of the messages. We'd need new envelopes, and we'd have to make them look as dirty and rumpled as these. But I could take the copies to Bender, and you could mail the real ones."

"I don't know." Kendall paced to the fridge and back to the table. "What if we get caught? If Bender never delivers any of the messages, then these people show up at your theater meeting with the original letters ..."

Good point. "Then we'll make new envelopes and give these originals to Bender." Shay gathered the recruitment cards. "But we need to deliver the original letter to Mr. Neil and give Bender a copy. That's the only way to make Bender leave you alone and still honor what Chord risked his life for."

Kendall stared at the letter to Ruston. "I suppose. But won't Ruston's letter expose Bender? If Bender gets proof that Chord saw him and wrote a letter telling someone, he might assume that Chord told others as well. And if he thinks any rebels know about his deal with Otley, he might—"

"Tell Otley where my people are hiding!" Or worse, kill them. That left only one option that Shaylinn could see. "So we give Bender the three recruitment letters and that's it. But we also have to go to Levi right away and hope he can come up with a plan before Bender betrays us all."

CHAPTER 5

"You sent her where?" Levi fought to bottle his anger — *Refrain from anger, and turn from wrath* — but the careless look on Bender's face almost put him over the edge. They were in the main room in the underground bunker. Levi had brought Bender and Rewl in for a quick discussion about recruiting Omar's friends Charlz Sims and Dane Skott, but instead had found Jemma in hysterics over her missing sister.

Bender had confessed straight away, as if his forcing Shaylinn to work for him was no big deal. "You worry too much." Bender leaned back on the sofa and set his arms along the top. "The girl is stronger than you think."

"That's not the point." Levi tapped his chest. "Where my people are concerned, *I say*, not you."

"Where did you send her?" Jemma asked, her voice quavering.

"We set her up in her own apartment next door to Kendall Collin's place," Bender said. "I need someone Kendall trusts to be the one spying on her."

Levi motioned to his brother, who sat at the table, vapo stick hanging from his lips. "I sent Omar to spy on her."

"She's got a bird," Omar said. "It sits in her window and sings."

"Omar won't get the answers we need," Rewl said. "My sources tell me Kendall doesn't trust men."

"Go to Kendall's place and bring back Shay," Levi said to Omar.

Omar nodded and stood, exhaling a cloud of black vapor. "On my way."

"There's no need." The soft voice drew Levi's gaze to the door. A woman stood there, wearing a glimmering silver tank top, black half-gloves, tight black pants, and silver shoes with spiky heels. Her hair hung to her waist, long and straight like a horse's mane and streaked with strands of silver.

Who in all the lands was this? And how had she gotten in?

"Shay!" Jemma set her hand over her heart.

"Walls," Omar said, his eyes round.

Shaylinn? *Really?* Levi squinted at her as she thumped across the room, unsteady on those ridiculous shoes. Her eyes were green and she'd changed her hair. And he could hardly even look at what she was wearing, but, yes, her face was there. Little Shaylinn, looking far too grown up.

"Red cleaned her up nicely, don't you think?" Rewl smirked, his eyes locked onto Shaylinn's body in a way that made Levi want to throw him out into the storm drain.

"Red did this?" Omar said, still staring at Shaylinn.

Shaylinn stopped before Bender and tossed three messages onto his lap. "Kendall didn't deliver them. Chord asked her to, but she was too scared. She was keeping them in her freezer. When I asked about Chord, she gave me the letters. Will you leave her alone now?"

"Of course." Bender shuffled through the stack. "This was it?"

"Yes. I hope they were worth it. You scared me and Kendall practically to death."

"Oh, they were worth it, femme." Bender smiled up at Levi. "I told you this one has talent. We could use her to — "

Levi grabbed the front of Bender's shirt and pulled him to the edge of the sofa. "You talk to my people again behind my back and … we're done. You get me?"

The click of a gun cocking stiffened Levi's spine.

"No!" Jemma yelled.

Rewl had pulled a handgun — what looked like a real one, not a stunner — and had aimed it at Levi. "Let him go."

Levi shoved Bender back against the sofa cushions and glared at Rewl, wondering if the kid could shoot. "Omar, show Bender and Rewl to the door, will you? It's time for dinner."

"You know what? I'm ready to go, anyway." Bender stood and walked toward the door. "Thanks, Miss Shaylinn."

Shaylinn glared at Bender, and Jemma wrapped her in a hug.

Omar got up and followed Bender, staring at Shaylinn until he nearly walked into one of the tables. Rewl kept his gun pointed at Levi as he waited for his boss.

Levi pretended he wasn't looking and sat on the couch, but he watched out of the corner of his eye until they were gone. Then he tore into Shaylinn. "What were you thinking?"

Shaylinn folded her arms. "He threatened to kill Kendall if I didn't help him."

"I don't care who he threatened or —"

"She's my friend, Levi," Shaylinn said. "I knew he was tricking me." She glanced at the door as Omar returned and locked it. "Bender and Red both tricked me. But I didn't see any other way. And you should know something about Bender. He — "

Levi jumped up from the couch and clapped his hand over Shaylinn's mouth. "Not here," he whispered. Their gazes locked, and Levi raised his eyebrows until Shaylinn nodded. He released her and turned to face the table. "Omar, we're going out. Shaylinn, go change. You're coming with us but not dressed like that. Is there a SimTag in those gloves?"

Her face paled. "Yes. But Bender said it wouldn't show up underground."

"Probably a ghoulie tag," Omar said.

Levi sighed. Bender said a lot of things. "Give me the gloves." He walked over to Shaylinn and waited for her to take them off. "Naomi? Tap Jordan, please. Tell him we've got Shaylinn and to meet us at Café Eat."

"What about dinner?" Jemma asked.

"Eat without us, Buttercup. We'll be awhile."

Levi, Omar, and Shaylinn all put on pairs of gloves that held ghoulie tags, which were SimTags Zane made that reflected numbers on their cheeks and hands but were off-grid. And just in case, Levi tossed the lace gloves Bender had given Shay into a dumpster.

When they arrived at the café, Jordan and Zane were already eating at a table in the back corner. Levi, Omar, and Shaylinn joined them, and within seconds, the waitress appeared.

"Where were you?" Jordan asked Shaylinn. "And what happened to your hair?"

"In a minute," Levi said, nodding at the waitress. "First, let us order."

Jordan fell back in his chair and shoved a handful of fries into his mouth, while Levi and Omar ordered burgers and fries and Shaylinn ordered a salad.

"Back in three or it's free," the waitress said, walking away.

"Jordan, you can talk with Shaylinn later about what she did," Levi said, knowing Jordan would want to discipline his sister. "Right now, we need to address how it happened and what she found out. Bender came into the bunker when he knew Shaylinn was alone, and he tricked her into helping him spy on Kendall Collin."

"That cud-chewing maggot." Jordan glared at Shaylinn. "How'd he trick you?"

Shaylinn cowered a little under her brother's glare. "He said he thought Kendall had Chord's messages and that he was going to have Rewl kill her in case she was working with Otley. I knew he was talking down to me, but I didn't see any other way to save her. So I volunteered to see what she knew."

"He tried to scare you," Zane said. "Fear is one of Bender's favorite methods."

"And the rest of the story?" Levi said, eager to know himself. "Tell us what you found."

Shaylinn glanced at Zane. "Are you sure?"

"I trust Zane." There was really around 1 percent doubt in Levi's mind as to Zane's loyalties, but he had to trust someone in this place, and Zane had yet to let him down. "We're here to ask his advice on all this. Tell us what happened."

"Kendall and I couldn't figure out why Bender wanted the messages. So we decided to open them." Shaylinn reached into her back pocket and pulled out a folded piece of paper. "There were actually four messages. Three of them were rebel recruitment cards. But the other one was a letter from Chord. We put the recruitment messages into new envelopes, and I gave them to Bender. But not this one." She held up the paper.

Zane frowned at Shaylinn. "He didn't suspect?"

"He didn't seem to," Levi said. "But he did act like there was something missing."

"And what does the message say?" Zane asked. "The fourth one."

Shaylinn unfolded the piece of paper, but the waitress arrived then with their food.

She set it all on the table and asked, "Can I get you anything else?"

"Just some privacy, please," Levi said. "Thanks."

"Right, well, thanks for visiting Café Eat. Find pleasure tonight."

Levi watched her walk away, and only when he was sure she was out of earshot did he say, "Go ahead, Shaylinn."

Shaylinn handed the message to Levi. "It basically says Bender is working with Otley."

"What!" Jordan slapped his hands on the table and stood. Levi and Omar's sodas sloshed over the side of their cups.

"*Jordan.*" Shaylinn grabbed a napkin and mopped up the spilled soda.

"I'm not surprised," Omar said. "Bender is a maggot."

The mere idea sent fire through Levi's chest. But people were staring. Levi raised his eyebrows at Jordan. "Have a seat, Jordan."

Jordan plopped back to his chair and folded his arms.

Shocked and confused, Levi read the message, then passed it to Zane.

"Is it bad, brother?" Omar asked.

"Yeah." But why would Bender partner with Otley? A month ago he'd wanted Levi to shoot Otley. Was this a recent move? Or had Bender been talking with Otley even back during Lonn's days? Maybe that was how Lonn had gotten caught, which painted a terrible theory of the botched Lonn rescue in his mind. Well, if Bender had killed Chord and turned on Lonn, he wouldn't hesitate to betray Levi's people. They had to move. Now.

Zane sighed and passed the letter to Omar, but Jordan snatched it away before Omar managed to touch it.

"Hey!" Omar said.

This conversation might be too scary for Shaylinn. "Omar, you and Shaylinn go sit at the counter, will you?"

"You don't want me to hear something?" Omar scowled and gestured at the letter in Jordan's hands. "I don't even get to read it?"

"Not you, brother." Levi nodded to Shaylinn, who was picking at her salad.

"Fine," Omar said. "Let's go, Shay." He whisked her plate out from under her hands and carried it to the counter.

"Hey!" Shaylinn said, getting up to follow him.

Once they were both seated at the counter, Levi asked Zane, "Is Shaylinn safe? What she did with Kendall ... defying Bender like that. What if he knows? What if he put one of those MiniComms in Kendall's apartment or put one on Shaylinn somehow? I mean, look at that hair. There could be anything in that mess."

"I don't think he'd put an ear on her," Zane said. "But he's been watching Kendall since Chord was killed. Rewl and I followed her a few times."

"You think Bender had Chord killed?" Levi asked.

"He must have. My guess is Rewl did it."

Rewl. Maybe that kid *could* shoot. "Who's Ruston Neil?"

"How much rebel history do you know?" Zane asked. "Have you heard of the FFF?"

"I've seen graffiti in the storm drains," Levi said.

"The FFF was the first resistance movement in the Safe Lands. Where the Black Army is mostly made up of disgruntled Safe Landers, the FFF is the real underground made up of Naturals. Been around almost since the beginning. Stands for Freedom for Families."

"Wait. Families? Here?" Levi asked.

"This place didn't just start out the way it is now, peer," Zane said. "Things happened. Over time. And in the beginning, there were people who didn't like what was happening. Anyway . . . Ruston Neil is the current leader of the FFF. Ruston and Lonn were friends, worked together on a lot of things."

"So Chord figured Ruston needed to know about Bender and Otley," Levi said.

"We all needed to know," Jordan said. "We need to take down that maggot."

Zane shook his head. "Don't do anything yet — at least not to Bender."

Levi couldn't just sit around and wait to be arrested or killed by Otley. "What if I went to Dayle up in the Department of Public Tasks?"

"Dayle would just go to Ruston too," Zane said.

"Does Bender know Ruston?" It seemed like all these rebels knew each other.

"Yes, but he doesn't know where he lives. Ruston keeps off the grid as much as possible. He's only got a few guys who run for him. Bender can't find him. No one can."

"Can you?" Levi asked.

Zane smiled and ate one of Levi's fries. "I can find anyone."

"That's what we want," Levi said. "We have to leave the bunker. I can't keep my people vulnerable to Bender. Plus I'm sick of him telling me what to do."

"I've got a place," Zane said. "No one knows about it. Not even Rewl or Bender knows. It will be a tight squeeze. But you could bring your women there. At least until I can talk to Ruston about someplace bigger."

"Oh, no," Jordan said. "I'm not getting separated from my wife again."

Levi didn't like the idea of dividing their flock either. "Can we all go there?"

"Yeah, sorry," Zane said. "I meant all of you. You'll fit." But he didn't look so sure. "We'd have to move you at night or really early in the morning, go through the storm drains, at least until we're on the outskirts of the city."

"Our leaving would tip off Bender that we don't trust him, though," Levi said.

"It won't be a problem if he can't find us," Jordan said.

"What about Omar?" Zane asked. "You want him to stay on grid and task?"

"No," Levi said at the same time as Jordan said, "Yes."

"It's too dangerous," Levi said.

"If Omar goes into hiding, Otley will know," Jordan said. "Bender said the enforcers were still watching him."

Right. "But *Bender* said, Jordan. He could have been lying."

"What if he wasn't?"

"What if Omar runs into Bender?" Levi said. "What if he asks Omar about me or where all our people went to?"

"Omar tells him you got the women out one night, and that they're back in Glenrock," Jordan said.

Levi didn't like that plan. "It puts Omar in a vulnerable place."

"Look, I'm going to take this letter to Ruston and get the new place ready," Zane said. "I'll tap you with the plan. Until then, play like you know nothing about Bender and Otley."

"Who?" Levi said.

Zane smirked and stood. "I'll tap you. Oh, here." He removed a Wyndo from his pocket. "This is for Mason. Remind him that messages automatically delete once they're read. I'll start on the ones for the femmes when I can get the parts."

"Thanks, Zane," Levi said.

"Part of my pleasure." Zane limped out of the café.

"I don't like this, Levi," Jordan said. "I want out of here yesterday."

"Me too. Hopefully Mason will have a plan come Saturday. Once I get him this Wyndo and we can talk without having to send paper messages, things will move faster." At least he hoped it would. He had no idea what was taking Mason so long up there.

"Mad good." Jordan slapped the table. "Then talk to Omar about staying away from Shaylinn, will you?"

"Since when?" Levi turned on his chair. Omar and Shay were sitting at the counter. They were both laughing, using plastic forks to smash Omar's french fries into mush. It was the first time in a long time that he'd seen his little brother acting his age. "What's he doing wrong?"

"Nothing yet," Jordan mumbled. "But he will."

Levi wished Jordan would let up on Omar a bit. But saying so would only start a fight. "Shaylinn isn't stupid. You're going to have to trust her at some point."

"Like you trusted Omar? Look where that got all of us."

Levi gritted his teeth through that insult. "Omar and Shaylinn are different people."

"Not as different as you'd like to think. They're both youngest kids, family misfits, insecure, and looking for meaning in the world. Omar thinks he's found it. And I don't want him showing his version of 'meaning' to my sister."

"He knows right from wrong," Levi said. "He might be trying to justify his actions now, but he'll grow out of it."

"Until he does, keep him away from her."

Levi didn't think Omar would dare touch Shaylinn, but he didn't really know Omar that well. Probably never would. "He's going to die slowly before our eyes."

"It's what he deserves," Jordan said, as if Omar's impending death was no big deal.

Levi couldn't let that comment slide. "You forgave him. Don't act like you didn't."

"I know. But ... I loved my father. I loved yours. And every time I look at his face, I ..."

"They would have forgiven him," Levi said.

Jordan stared at Levi, his eyebrows high. "Elder Eli would have. Our fathers? I don't think so."

Levi checked himself. He had the tendency to glorify his father's memory, but Jordan was right: Levi's father would never have let Omar live this down. "But you agree forgiveness is right?"

"Not when I see him living like an animal and loving every minute of it. He was repentant before. And I could tell he was sorry then. But lately ... he's been acting like a maggot again."

"I don't think he's loving it," Levi said. "I think he's miserable."

Levi climbed into bed and snuggled against Jemma's back, pulling her close. It was selfish to wake her, but he wanted to talk. The elder of Glenrock was responsible for much. No one helped him with the pressure like Jemma. He played with her hair and tickled the back of her neck until she stirred.

She moaned in a deep breath and turned in his arms. Her eyes fluttered open and met his. "Hello, my Westley," she mumbled.

He smiled. "Did you sleep well?"

She blinked sleepy eyes. "Until you woke me up."

He pulled her on top of him for a long kiss. When he released her, he combed his fingers into her hair. "Bender is working with Otley. We're all moving in a few days."

Her eyes widened, and she pushed off him and sat up. "You're certain?"

He nodded, feeling slightly guilty for ruining her night. "You know, I never really trusted Bender. There had always been something off about the man."

"What are you going to do?" Jemma asked. "When are we moving? And where?"

"Zane has a place. We'll probably go tomorrow night or the next."

"And you're sure you can trust Zane?"

"Yes, Buttercup. I'm sure." He was 99 percent sure, anyway.

Tears flooded her eyes. "I want to go home."

"I know. Me too. I need to talk to Mason. We need to get the children out before more get hurt." Or infected or impregnated or brainwashed.

Jemma ran her finger over the wrinkles on his forehead, then down to the scab on his nose. "I hope nothing bad has happened to any of the kids."

He caught her hand and pulled her down beside him, cradling her in one arm. "They're tough kids, Jem. They're smart."

"Did Jordan behave with Shaylinn? Did he make her cry?"

"He reined his temper enough. But he hates Omar, and I can't change his mind."

"Jordan has always held grudges too long. Omar *is* trying. I see it."

"But he's so caught up in the ways of this place ... I feel responsible. Yelling at him has done no good. I've thought about beating him up or letting Jordan —"

Jemma smacked his arm. "What good will that do? You can't force his mind. God has given us all freedom to choose our own path. Violence will only push Omar away."

"I don't like him spending time with Red. Can I forbid him that?"

"I wish you could, but she treats him like a man. And that is why he likes her. Omar has only ever wanted to be one of the men. To be a part of *your* life. So, set an example: Respect his freedom. Praise his good work, and he'll find his way back."

"But I'm afraid for him. That Red will break him when she decides she's bored. That the plague will make him waste away in front of me. That he'll suck down so much vapor it will kill him. The way these flakers live, indulging every craving of the flesh with no regard for the consequences? It's madness."

"They're bored," Jemma said. "And spoiled and lazy. They have no serious responsibilities to give them purpose in life. It leaves them aching for meaning. So they fill themselves with pleasure. It won't ever satisfy in the long run. They need the Lord."

The Lord. Levi had always assumed he'd have time to read the Bible when he was older. And as village elder, it was his responsibility to train the next generation in their faith. But how was he supposed to do that when he barely understood it himself?

"I'm worried about Naomi's baby," Jemma said. "I can handle helping her through a regular birth, but what if something goes wrong? I'll need Mason's help."

Not this again. "Jordan won't allow it. End of discussion."

Jemma sat up and shot him that look, like he was wrong, wrong, wrong. "And if Naomi's life is at stake?"

"Are you certain Mason truly knows more than you?" Because Levi didn't think so. Mason had witnessed one human birth before their village was attacked. Jemma had helped in at least a half dozen.

"I don't know. But I'd feel better if I wasn't alone during the delivery. Ciddah's help would be ideal."

"Well, you can't have Ciddah's help. Mason's either. Start training Eliza and Aunt Chipeta to help you. They've had plenty of babies. They must know something." Suddenly Levi was tired. He'd woken Jemma for sympathy and support, and she'd stolen the conversation.

"I'm worried about Mason too," Jemma said. "The look on his face when you told him to use Ciddah ... I think he loves her."

"Mason in love with the medic?" Levi couldn't imagine Mason in love with anything but a book. "I'll believe it when I see it with my own eyes."

"He blushes when she's near," Jemma said. "She's a nice person, you know."

"She's a Safe Lander. They're all adulteresses."

"Levi!" Jemma folded her arms. "What a horrible thing to say."

He rolled onto his side and propped his head on his hand. "It's true. You've seen how they live. The men too."

"They're people, Levi. People who don't know any other way."

"I can't spare sympathy for these people, Jem. As elder of Glenrock, it's my duty to get our people out of here before they're destroyed like Omar."

"Omar is not destroyed," Jemma said. "He's mending."

"Not if he keeps sleeping at the Paradise with Red."

"I know." She sighed as if Omar were her responsibility and she were failing. "Levi, I'm tired. Will we ever get our 'happily ever after'?"

"Of course, Buttercup."

"But there is so much pain around us. And we're all still grieving the loss of our elders. I miss my parents so much. How can I help Shaylinn? She's going to be a mother with no husband and no prospect of one. Mother would know what to do, but I don't."

"I'll tell you what to do: Sleep. There will be plenty of time to worry about Shaylinn once we are free from this place."

She hummed and smiled. "I'm proud of you, Elder Levi."

"What for?"

"You take on so many burdens. You're a good man."

"If I'm good, it's only because I married a good woman."

CHAPTER
6

When Mason arrived in the SC Wednesday morning, Rimola said, "Ciddah wants to see you in her office."

Mason circled Rimola's desk and started down the hall. "Good morning to you too."

"Sorry," Rimola called after him. "Just ... be nice to her."

Mason stopped and turned around, taken aback by such a plea. "When have I ever been otherwise?"

Rimola rolled her eyes and turned back to her desk.

Odd.

At the door to Ciddah's office, Mason knocked, still puzzled over Rimola's words. Had he said something to offend Ciddah? He had in the past, but he'd barely spoken to her since he'd discovered the MiniComm. Perhaps his silence had been offensive. Who could understand women, anyway?

"Come in," Ciddah said.

Mason set his fist on the SimPad beside the door, and the entry swung open. Ciddah was sitting behind her desk, her posture rigid but beautiful as always, with golden hair, a perfect body, and electric-blue eyes. He entered, and the door closed behind him.

"Have a seat," she said.

As usual, Ciddah's office was messy. He gathered a stack of files off the chair in front of her desk.

"You're been avoiding me," Ciddah said before he'd even managed to sit. "Have I done something to offend you?"

Wait. She thought *he* was offended? Mason set the files on the end of Ciddah's desk, waiting to make sure they were balanced before letting go. Then he sat down and met her icy gaze. "Silence from a man is not evidence of vexation." Though in this case...

"Were the beets *that* awful?" she asked.

Mason thought back to the night he'd gone to Ciddah's apartment and she'd cooked dinner. That had been a good night, despite the tension of his role in breaking the women out from the harem and the horror of seeing his mother's face on the liberation broadcast. "On the contrary, the beets were quite good."

"It's because I asked you to stay, then, isn't it? I scared you away."

She hadn't scared him. She simply hadn't been able to wrap her mind around his morality. What Ciddah and Mason deemed moral were polar opposites. He didn't like this conversation. It felt like an attack, like she wanted to fight. He was not suited for romantic missions. Levi or Omar had no difficulty speaking with females, but Mason never knew what to say.

"The beets were quite good," he said softly, hoping she would think him funny.

But Ciddah sighed and looked away.

See? He'd already said the wrong thing. How could he fix it? Was she seeking some kind of reassurance? "I do not disdain you for your advances, nor do I fear them."

Her head turned slowly, and the cold look on her face made Mason shiver. "You're being temporarily reassigned to the pharmacy in the lobby," Ciddah said, her voice aloof and businesslike. "One of the pharmacy techs is taking two weeks off, and you're going to fill in."

The pharmacy? "Why me?"

"Because there's no one else who's trained, and I think you can handle it."

But ... "This is not a punishment for my poor communication skills?"

Ciddah began to sort through the mess on her desk, as if suddenly too busy to give him her full attention. "No. Though I would dock your credits if I could."

He blinked, trying to ascertain which words he'd said that had been bad enough to penalize his earnings. "By how much?"

"It was a joke, Mason." But Ciddah wouldn't meet his eyes. "The head pharmacist downstairs is named Philo Brock. He's expecting you."

"I'm to go right now?"

She picked up a stack of papers and scanned the top page. "Yes."

How was he to get Ciddah's help if they were apart? And how was he to find a cure for the thin plague? "Will I be back?"

She flipped to the second page. "In about two weeks — on the thirteenth of August, actually."

Well, this would never do. "Can I ... um — ?"

The speaker on Ciddah's desk beeped. "I just put a patient in exam two for you," Rimola said.

Ciddah pushed a button on the speaker. "I'm on my way." She set down the papers and stood. "See you in two weeks, Mr. Elias."

The pharmacy in the lobby was a Pharmco, which was the only type of pharmacy Mason had seen in the Safe Lands besides those located inside G.I.N. stores. This one was a single black counter in the corner of the City Hall lobby. Mason announced himself to the girl behind the counter, whose name badge read Saska, and she called Philo Brock out to the front.

Where Saska was dark and round, with black hair and bronze skin, Philo was light and thin with skin the color of milk and hair like a baby chick. The Old rhyme *Jack Sprat* came to mind as Saska and Mr. Brock spoke to each other just out of Mason's hearing, though it wasn't likely these two were a couple.

"Mr. Elias. Excellent!" Mr. Brock opened a half-door on the end of the counter. "Come on back."

Mr. Elias. Mason expected such formality from strangers like Mr. Brock, but not from Ciddah. Her coldness upstairs had shaken him. It had been a grave error to ignore her for so long. Had he lost everything he'd worked so hard to build? There must be some way to salvage it.

Mason followed Mr. Brock behind the counter, where rows of shelves were stocked with bottles of medications. Mr. Brock passed them all and turned down the last row, where a long desk was covered in equipment.

"First of all, you touch none of this. I work back here. You assist. Got it?" Mr. Brock looked at Mason, his eyebrows raised over a pair of bulging eyes in a gaunt face. He must have been nearing the liberation age of forty.

"Yes, sir," Mason said.

"You'll start each task shift by checking in with me. This branch is only open during business hours, so I'm always here. I eat my lunch here. I take my breaks here. Ciddah told me you're bright, but I'll judge that for myself. This is *not* a task that tolerates errors. With every prescription passed over that counter, someone's life is at stake. Got it?"

An extreme view of pharmaceutics, but technically accurate. "Yes, sir."

"You deal with the customers. You answer the phones. You check the order report. You process prescriptions. Can't read the prescription? Don't ask me. Call the medic and find out. *My* time is valuable. *Your* job is to let me do mine. Got it?"

So ... never speak to Mr. Brock again? "Yes, sir."

"Well, at least you're polite," Mr. Brock mumbled.

Saska showed Mason how to check the order report and process prescriptions. Then she showed him how to work the credit register.

"If you think you've got it, I can get caught up, and then have more time to show you things."

"I believe I can handle the register." But a line soon formed, made up of people with crossed arms, tapping feet, or glaring eyes.

Saska came back to help Mason, and together they worked faster. She handed Mason a prescription for the next man at the counter, then left to find it.

Mason scanned the prescription over the register and read from the screen. "Ten credits."

"It's always been five," the man said.

Mason met the man's narrowed eyes, then turned to look for Saska, who had gone halfway down the first row of medications. He went over to her. "The customer says his prescription always costs five credits."

She rummaged through a bin of prescriptions. "Tell him to take it up with his medic."

Mason repeated Saska's words to the customer, who said, "My medic told me five."

"I'm sorry, sir," Mason said. "You'll have to check with your medic again."

The man stormed off, mumbling something about incompetence.

A short woman stepped forward. "Could I have more of the blue juice I take every morning?"

"Do you have a prescription?" Mason asked her.

"Of course I do." She waved her hand at the register. "Look it up."

"Um ..." Mason glanced over his shoulder for Saska, but she was busy. He squinted at the register and saw an icon that said SimTag. "SimTag, please?"

The woman set her fist against the glass, and the register beeped. A list of prescriptions came up. There were eight, all current. Much to Mason's disdain, he had to call Saska for help, and Saska had to open boxes for each prescription on the list until she found the juice that was blue, which of course, she didn't open until her seventh try.

By then, people in line had begun to grumble, and the woman at the counter said, "They're always so slow here."

Inconceivable nonsense, in Mason's opinion. "Perhaps if you were to bring the empty vial with you next time or recall the name of the medication, we could assist you more quickly."

The woman snatched the med box from Saska and stomped away.

The frenzied rush continued for the next forty-five minutes. When the line finally vanished, Mason's frustration level hovered near the breaking point. "How can you stand to task here?" he asked Saska. "It's maddening."

"It pays well. And it's days. The customers *are* hard sometimes, though. If they don't get their way, everything is your fault."

"Yes, I gathered that." Mason didn't think he could tolerate tasking here for two weeks. Even if there was some clue that might aid his search for a cure, when would he ever have the time to discover it?

"Line," Saska said.

Mason returned to the counter where Rimola stood waiting. "Oh, hello."

Rimola winked and tapped her fingernails on the counter. "Hay-o, raven. How you doing down here?"

Mason set his hands on the counter. "The pharmacy is not my favorite place to task."

Rimola chuckled and set her hand on his, rubbing her thumb over the back of his hand. "That doesn't surprise me, trig."

This woman was incapable of understanding personal boundaries. Mason pulled his hand away. "Do you have a prescription I could help you with?"

"Not me. I always pick up for the SC after my lunch break."

"Oh." Mason went to find Saska again. "Rimola is here to pick up prescriptions for the SC."

"I'll get them," Saska said.

A moment later Saska set a plastic tub on the counter that had three little red boxes inside. "The SC's ID is SC000," she told Mason. "Pull them up, then check out each one."

Mason recognized the little boxes as what Ciddah gave to women to help them conceive. They were fertility stims. He ran the first one over the glass. The register beeped and displayed *Tsana Beshup JP28*.

A chill ran across Mason's back. He knew that name. He scanned the second box: *Alawa Kitchi JP14*. And the third: *Sunki Hinto JP16*.

The enforcers must have seized the people of Jack's Peak, the settlement up the mountain from Glenrock. Could this be the real reason Ciddah had wanted him out of the SC? So he would not be present to cause her trouble as she processed these women he knew?

He fought to maintain his composure as he completed the transaction and handed the plastic tub to Rimola.

"Thanks, trig," she said. "You know, she's not as grouchy when you're gone."

"It's nice to know I have such a pleasing effect on people," Mason said.

She batted her impossibly long eyelashes. "You do on me, raven. You let me know if you change your mind about pairing up."

He looked away and caught Saska's wink, which, combined with Rimola's advances, released more blood flow into his cheeks. Infernal place, anyway. Was there no dignity here? "Your offer is flattering, Rimola, but I will not change my mind."

"Yeah, I'm not surprised." She patted the counter and smiled at Saska. "Watch out for this one, femme. He's no fun at all."

"Good," Saska said. "Maybe we'll actually get some tasking done around here."

The rest of Mason's shift dragged by. When three o'clock arrived, Saska told him he must take a fifteen minute break, so Mason took the elevator to the fifth floor.

He arrived in the SC and walked through the reception area and around Rimola's desk as if he were just arriving to task. Rimola was speaking to someone through her ear implant. She turned to watch Mason as he moved past her desk and down the hall, but she did not try to stop him. He lifted the CompuChart from the slot by the wall of exam room one and read the patient's name.

Kosowe Elsu.

Mason had met Beshup, his wife, Tsana, and her friend Kosowe at a celebration in Jack's Peak when he was eleven or twelve. He remembered Kosowe as being quite lovely, with dark skin, hair, and eyes. The chart said she was here for an embryonic transfer.

So soon? How could Mason have missed that the Jack's Peak women had been in the Safe Lands? There had been no mention of it on the ColorCast.

He knocked and slipped inside the exam room before Ciddah could catch him. Kosowe was alone in the room, strapped to the exam table, a number four bright against her dark skin. Her eyes met his and widened. "Mason of Elias? You reside in this place?"

The medic screen in the corner showed three circles: embryos that sat under the microscope.

Why three?

He needed to speak quickly before Ciddah arrived to see her patient. "How long have you been here, Kosowe?"

"Two weeks."

Mason reeled. Ciddah had to have been keeping this from him. Scheduling appointments with the Jack's Peak women on his off days. And now moving him to the pharmacy. "Did they attack Jack's Peak? Did they kill your men?"

"They attacked at dawn. Our men *and* women killed many enforcers before we were paralyzed with their lightning guns. Chief Kimama and my father were taken alive. I know not what other men live." She lifted her head from the exam table. "What of Levi?"

"He's alive," Mason said.

"And his woman?"

Mason fought a smile. What was it about his bossy brother that the ladies liked so much? "Levi and Jemma are married now."

Kosowe let her head fall back to the table. "Explain our purpose here. What do they want with my people?"

"They're dying, and they want you to bear them children."

Her eyes seemed to darken, or maybe she was simply glaring at him. "And if we refuse? They will violate us?"

"Not like you think," Mason said, glad to have a shred of positive news to convey. "They use technology to make you pregnant."

Her face paled. "Their medicine woman?"

"Sort of."

"This is unnatural. Chief Kimama would not allow it. *I* will not allow it."

The door swung in, and Ciddah entered the room. "Let's see, did I leave my chart — *Mason.*" She pursed her lips and snatched the chart from his hands. "What are you doing here?"

"You've been keeping this from me," Mason said.

She shook out her hair and looked at the chart. "I don't report to you."

He shouldn't be surprised by her dispassion. "You can't have this both ways, Ciddah. Either we're friends or we're not."

"Why should my task have anything to do with — "

"I will not have a technology baby," Kosowe said, her voice cutting through the tension.

Ciddah stared at Kosowe, her eyes moist, then grabbed Mason's arm and pulled him toward the door. "Join me outside. Now." Ciddah dragged him into the hall.

"This is why you changed my schedule," Mason said. "You didn't want me to see them here."

Ciddah pursed her lips and waited for Kosowe's door to close behind them. "Mason — "

"The chart says she's here for ETP. And it says three embryos. *Three?*"

Ciddah sighed and rubbed her temple as if Mason were a small child with so little understanding of the world. "We always use three if we can get three. The more embryos transferred, the higher the likelihood of multiples."

Another blow that threatened to knock Mason over. "You always try to create multiple babies?"

"Of course. Now, what did you say to my patient?"

Could this mean Shaylinn was carrying more than one child? And if the donor had been infected, that would mean multiple babies who were doomed to a life of —

"Mason! What did you tell her?"

Mason snapped his attention to Ciddah, whose expression looked fiery enough to melt the Safe Lands walls. "I ... told her the Safe Lands would force her to bear a child."

"Mason!" She shoved him. She actually shoved him. So hard he stumbled. "That's not your place."

He got his feet back under him and straightened his spine, trying to salvage a scratch of dignity. "I'm a medic, Ciddah. My patient asked a question. And why wouldn't you tell her?"

Again she moved toward him, but this time she merely shook her finger. "She's *not* your patient. You do not task here at the moment. I could have you arrested for trespassing."

"That would most certainly mend the rift between us."

She closed her eyes, pressed her fingers to her temples, sighed, and then fixed her gaze on him again. "Mason, this is an honor for Kosowe. But you make it sound like some kind of nightmare."

"It's only an honor to people who want it. To outsiders, a nightmare describes it perfectly, especially when you do so without their consent or knowledge. Kosowe is a human being, not an animal in a laboratory."

Ciddah inhaled a deep breath, as if to hold herself together. "Being a surrogate is a thing of beauty, Mason. I would be thrilled to be in Kosowe's place."

"Kosowe is not you. Have you asked her if she wants to be pregnant? Or have you already denied her the choice?"

"If you can't assist me without poisoning the patients against me or the Safe Lands, I won't be able to use you in the SC anymore."

He was already tasked to the pharmacy. "Fine by me."

Tears welled in Ciddah's eyes. "Perhaps they'll keep you permanently in the pharmacy, then."

"That is also acceptable." Which it wasn't. At all. Why was he saying such things?

"Yes, well … Bye-o then." Ciddah nodded and went back inside the exam room.

Mason stood alone in the hallway a moment, morose at yet another failure on his part to befriend Ciddah, not that that was why he'd come here on his break. What good was he to his people if he'd lost his only Safe Lands source? But Shaylinn came to mind then. He owed her some answers. That much he could do.

He walked to exam room two, lifted the blank CompuChart off the wall by the door, and went inside. The room was empty. His hands were shaking as he pulled up Shaylinn's file, and Ciddah's last words haunted him. This was for the best, really. He had grown far too attached to that infuriating woman.

It took him a moment to find the date of Shaylinn's ETP and to read through Ciddah's notes. He found what he was looking for at the bottom.

Two embryos transferred.

He clenched his teeth a moment, trying to keep his head. It would not do if Ciddah tapped enforcers to remove him from the SC.

But why two embryos for Shaylinn, three for Kosowe, and only one for Kendall Collin? Perhaps they had failed to remove three embryos from Kendall, or the others fetuses may have died during the course of her pregnancy.

Mason took a moment to look up Kendall's history, but he could find no results for an ETP at all. Her first appointment in the SC had been on November 18, 2087. Reason: pregnancy test.

Kendall had gotten pregnant by natural means. Interesting.

Mason backed the CompuChart to Shaylinn's appointment history. The day Ciddah had confirmed Shaylinn's pregnancy had been a Monday. Ciddah hadn't announced it over the ColorCast because she liked to wait at least four weeks before making a pregnancy public, and the Glenrock women had escaped before then.

Mason clicked the calendar icon and paged back to Monday, June 28. He found Shaylinn's name, clicked on it, and located Ciddah's notes.

Pregnant with twins! Fortune be praised!!!!!!!!!!!!!!!!!!!!!!!!!!!

Ciddah's use of multiple exclamation points was further proof of the wall between them. She was set on repopulating the Safe Lands, no matter the method, and Mason was set on getting his women out of the Safe Lands. How could he have ever entertained thoughts of a life with a woman with such different views of love and family? He had not been thinking clearly in her presence. She had a way of intoxicating him.

Little Shaylinn, the mother of two?

And now Kosowe in the next room undergoing a similar procedure?

Lord in heaven, help us fix this.

But there was still one question left unanswered. Mason paged back to Shaylinn's ETP appointment and looked in the little slot titled "Donor."

9-G1.

G stood for Glenrock, which meant the donor was one of their own. So that Wyoming man's sample had not been used to impregnate Shaylinn. Good. Mason's Safe Lands ID number was 9-G25. Jordan and Levi, who'd gone to the Registration Department together, had been given the numbers 9-G26 and 9-G27.

Mason could only guess who had been the first member from Glenrock to become a Safe Lands national. But he knew the identity of the only Glenrock man to comply with demands to be a donor.

Omar.

Mason sat in the air-conditioned lobby of the Westwall apartment building where he and Ciddah both lived, watching the parking lot, waiting for her to arrive. He had to make peace. For no other reason than to use her, of course — like Levi had said.

Three shiny black cars pulled into the drop-off zone out front. The front seat passenger in the second car got out and opened the back door. Mason watched Ciddah climb out and turn to speak to someone in the back seat. She smiled as she spoke, then stepped back, revealing the task director general, Lawten Renzor, still in the car. Ciddah waved good-bye to him.

Mason closed his eyes, bracing himself against the fracture that seemed to be cracking him in two. This was nothing new. He'd known she was friends with Lawten. She was likely working for him. Maybe more. It didn't matter.

As the procession pulled away, Mason got up and walked toward the elevator, then turned back, uncertain if he should abandon his plans to speak with Ciddah or not.

What did she see in Lawten, anyway? Mason had found the man to be an ailing bully. True, Mason knew little about women, but he was fairly certain such traits were not highly prized in a man. Perhaps it was merely Lawten's power, then, that Ciddah found so alluring.

Before he managed to make up his mind, she entered the lobby. Her smile grew cold when she saw him. Not good.

"Waiting for the elevator?" she said.

"Yes." Technically.

She leaned forward and pressed the elevator button. "It might help to call it."

"Right. Um ... Just finish your task shift?"

"Yes, and I'm hungry." She pushed the elevator button again.

Mason forced the words from his mouth before he lost the chance. "I owe you an apology."

She looked at him then, the crystal blue of her eyes sending a chill over his body. How could one woman invoke in him such visceral emotions? Was that normal?

"I was wrong to come to the SC today," he said, determined to regain her good favor. "And what you do ... your task in the SC ... It's not my place to intervene."

"Thank you." She pushed the elevator button again.

"Pushing the call button repeatedly will not make the elevator come faster," Mason said. "Once the button is pressed, the call is sent to the computer that controls the elevator. Pressing the call button again does nothing."

She shot him a dirty look.

Perhaps he shouldn't have said that. "I understand if you don't want to be friends. I simply ..." He paused, searching for the right words.

"Simply what?" Ciddah said.

He tapped his hands against the sides of his legs. "Well, since I've come here, I ..." He had planned to tell her she was his only friend, but such a confession seemed terribly pathetic, despite how true it might be. "I want to ask you on a date."

What? Where had *that* archaic idea come from?

She seemed genuinely surprised by this. "Now?"

"Friday," Mason said quickly. "We both have the day off, and I need time to make plans." Though he doubted a year's worth of planning would prepare him for such an event.

"Oh-kay ..." A small smile. "What time on Friday?"

"All day." All day? Really? Why had he said that? "I'll, uh, come to your apartment at eleven. Don't eat lunch. Or dinner." Don't eat dinner? This was a nightmare.

His comment induced a frown. "What should I wear?"

What did that matter? "Whatever you like. Something ... comfortable."

"Comfortable. Friday. Eleven in the morning?"

"Precisely." Then, desperate to end this infernal conversation, he added, "See you then?"

"Okay." She smiled a little again, looking at him strangely, as if he had food on his face. He wiped his hand over his mouth, just to check.

The elevator opened and Ciddah stepped inside. "Are you coming in?"

"Not now, no. I've got an errand to run." A suicide to commit...

"Bye-o, then."

Mason held up his hand. The elevator doors slid shut, and he let his arm fall.

A date? What had he been thinking? He hadn't. And there lay the problem. He only ever maintained decent conversation with Ciddah Rourke when disagreement was involved. How would they ever manage an entire day of polite conversation? Plus, he knew nothing about dating rituals. He took the stairs to his apartment to leave his SimTag behind, then went to the train station, used the spare SimTag from locker 127 to cross to the Midlands, then took the train to the Belleview exit. He didn't stop moving until he'd reached the underground bunker.

The door clanked and echoed in the corridor when he closed it. "Hello? Anyone here?"

No answer came, but he heard footsteps in the main room. He found Jemma there, standing around the side of the refrigerator, pressed up against the wall as if she were hiding from him. A pot bubbled on the stove. Peculiar.

"Mason!" She relaxed and came to give him a hug. "Is something wrong?"

"I would ask you the same thing. Why were you hiding?"

She rubbed her hand over her face. "Oh, Mason. We're not supposed to talk about it in case ..." She tapped her ear and mouthed, *Someone is listening.* Then, "Why are you here? Are you looking for Levi?"

"I have a date. Like in Old movies. With Ciddah."

Jemma's lips curved in a slow smile.

Must she? "Don't tease me, Jemma, please. Just ... help?"

"Is your date tonight?" she asked.

"No, Friday." He'd done that much to help himself, at least.

"That was smart thinking, to ask in advance."

"I didn't do it to be smart," Mason said. "I simply knew we both had the day off."

Jemma took his arm and led him toward the sofas. "Mason, you can do this. If you let me tell you what to do, it won't be authentic. Ciddah likes you and wants to spend time with you. Not me."

Mason pondered her words. "I wasn't asking you to take my place."

Though she did raise an interesting point. Why *had* Ciddah accepted his offer? Did she truly like him? Even after all his animosity toward her profession?

Jemma giggled and sank onto the couch with its back to the kitchen. "Sit. Let's talk this out. You want to know how to behave, right?"

The three couches were arranged in a C. Mason sat on the edge of the couch opposite Jemma's, which seemed to be the only one without holes. "Mostly I don't want to end the experience with her liking me less she does now."

"Oh, Mason. That's not possible. She can't help but like you."

Her words were kind, as always, but Jemma was not familiar with Ciddah's ever-changing moods.

"You should take care, though," Jemma said, lips pursed in a sudden frown. "I can see how much you like her. Is it wise to spend time with her like this? She doesn't think like you do or believe the same things. I don't want you to get hurt."

Yes, these were all valid points Mason had considered time and again. "I'm well aware of our different philosophies, Jemma. Frankly, I like that she and I have much to debate. But if you're concerned that I will become brokenhearted over this woman, don't be. I cannot trust her, and trust matters more to me than how many lives she believes in or that she thinks copulation is equal to a game of checkers."

Jemma burst into laughter then, going on for so long that she clutched her sides and lay down on the sofa.

Frustration simmered within Mason. "I wasn't trying to be funny."

The door opened then, and Levi and Zane entered. Zane's hair was flat today — no spikes — but he still wore his gold spiral nose rings.

"Mason," Levi said. "Jemma, what's wrong?"

Jemma grabbed the top of the sofa and pulled herself to a sitting position, looking over the back at Levi and wiping her tears. "He has a date."

Zane limped toward the couches, but Levi slowed to a stop by the tables and crossed his arms. "They do that here? I thought that was ancient stuff."

"Of course," Zane said, sitting on the couch between Jemma and Mason's. "Why wouldn't we date?"

"I mean date like they did in Old movies," Levi said, making his way to the back of Jemma's couch. "I'm well aware of how people … trade paint, as you say."

"What if that's what she's expecting?" Mason asked, suddenly twice as apprehensive as he had been. "Is that what 'date' means in the Safe Lands?"

Zane rolled his eyes. "Despite what you people think of us *flakers*, not every Safe Lander looks to pair up on the first date. Who is she?"

"Ciddah Rourke," Mason said, intrigued by Zane's missing ear. The entire pinna was gone, leaving only the tragus and the dark hole of the ear canal.

"Okay, I know her." Zane shifted on the couch so that the spot where an ear should be was out of Mason's view. "She's a quiet one. Smart. A bit pretentious. Used to see her with Renzor a lot before he became the TDG."

Lawten again. Mason didn't want to hear about him. "She told me once that the men here don't listen. That she wanted someone to care and not leave." It seemed important, somehow.

"Might be looking for a lifer, then, which means she's a softie." Zane combed his fingers through his stringy brown hair. "Okay, if it were me, I'd take her dancing."

A terrifying proposition. "I don't know how to dance," Mason said.

"Does she?" Zane asked. "If not, you could take a dance lesson together."

"Oh, yes!" Jemma clapped her hands together. "That sounds perfect."

"No," Mason said. "I don't want to dance. I don't want to make myself more nervous than I already am. I need something I can't mess up."

"Why?" Levi said. "You should be focused on getting the kids out of the boarding school, not trying to make some flaker like you."

Unbelievable. "You told me to make her like me, *Elder Levi*. You said to use her to get the information I need. She's not apt to give me information if she dislikes me."

Levi came around the end of the couch and sat beside Jemma. "Fine. Sorry. I forgot." He took hold of Jemma's hand and she leaned against him.

"Go on a picnic — that's what Levi always did." Jemma kissed Levi's cheek. "I love your picnics." Levi turned his head and kissed her lips. Mason looked back to Zane.

"Go on grid and look until you find something fun," Zane said. "There's tons to do here."

"Mason," Jemma said, "you're going to have to talk to her and look at her."

Mason nodded his understanding. "I can do that."

"Talk about things she's interested in, though," Jemma said. "Not just things you know about. And eye contact, Mason. Look at her a lot. Count to five before you look away. And let her touch you. At least three seconds before you move."

"Three seconds." Wait. Three seconds or five? Better go with five on everything, just to be sure.

"Brush up against her arm as you walk," Zane said. "Make it look accidental. That's what I do. And if you run out of things to say, compliment her."

"Say she looks pretty," Jemma said.

"Again and again or just once?" Mason asked.

"Send her a pre-date text tap," Zane said. "Say you're looking forward to the date. And text her right after the date to say you had a nice time. Then wait, like, four days and make another date. Don't wait longer than a week or she'll think you don't like her. And not sooner than three days, or she'll think you're gummy."

Perhaps Mason should have brought along a notebook and pen.

"Where are you getting all this?" Levi asked Zane.

"I took a class," Zane said. "They've got classes for everything."

Mason doubted he had time to take the class.

"That reminds me," Levi said to Mason. "Zane got you a private Wyndo. Tap me when you're in a secure location because I need to tell you about some developments we've had since I saw you last."

Tonight, Jemma mouthed. *We're leaving the bunker.* She pointed at the door, making her fingers move like a walking person.

Leaving? That must be why Jemma had been hiding behind the refrigerator.

"Communicate with Ciddah on your regular Wyndo, though, since hers is monitored," Zane said. "The one I made you is only for talking with us."

"I understand," Mason said, though Zane didn't seem to be worried about anyone monitoring their conversation. Who but General Otley and Lawten Renzor were they afraid of?

"So you think the medic knows something?" Levi asked. "About the boarding school?"

"Um …" Mason didn't understand. Was it safe to talk about this? It must be or Levi wouldn't have asked, right? "She knows everything about it. But I made her angry today when I … Oh! I forgot." Thoughts of the date with Ciddah had turned his brain to mush. "Enforcers attacked Jack's Peak a few weeks ago. I saw Kosowe today in the SC. She'll have had her ETP by now. Three embryos. And I also discovered Shaylinn is carrying twins and they're Omar's. Twin pregnancies have a higher incidence of nausea, so that's likely — "

Jemma gasped and clapped both hands over her mouth.

Levi groaned and set his face in his hands.

" — why Shaylinn has been so sick." Clearly Mason had gone about sharing that news in the wrong way as well. Could he do nothing right today?

Yet Zane chuckled as if this were great entertainment. "You people are better than watching *C Factor.* I see why you're worried about your date, though, peer. Tact is *not* your strength."

CHAPTER 7

Red tugged on Omar's hand, trying to pull him off the sofa. "Come and dance, valentine."

Omar pretended not to hear her and took another puff from his PV. If she thought he was completely juiced, she'd leave him be. And that's what he wanted. To be alone.

She eventually got the hint and sauntered off to the dance floor on her own. The disco lights made reflections float around the room and over the dancers. Omar watched Red from the sofa, not ever looking directly at her. She approached a couple and started dancing with the man, whose partner didn't look pleased about the intrusion.

Typical Red. She could turn on the charm for anyone. Omar really didn't like her very much. Or did he? He couldn't decide. She was just so … pushy.

Relationships in the Safe Lands weren't exclusive. If a guy saw a femme he liked, he went after her. By that logic, Omar could have gone after three girls today.

And Shay yesterday.

The thought brought on the familiar aching guilt that haunted him. Levi was right: Omar made all the wrong decisions. He was using

Red ... and abusing his body with the stims. He'd already contracted the thin plague. It was his fault so many of the Glenrock elders had died. And then to have such thoughts about Shay?

Truly, if he was looking for fairness in life, death was the place to start. He deserved to die for the things he'd done. No question.

He took a long drag from his vaporizer but knew this concoction wouldn't kill him. Why couldn't he be consistent with his doses? When he wanted more, he cut back. And when he thought he was getting too crazy with the juice, he pushed it further.

Who was Omar Strong, anyhow? What was his life worth? The people of Glenrock saw him as a traitor. Could he ever change that perception?

He took another drag and closed his eyes, wanting the buzz to be more than it was, wanting it to pull him under, to escape to that euphoric place where nothing mattered.

"Hay-o, Strong."

Omar opened his eyes in time to see Zane fall into the chair across from him. He'd slicked back his hair tonight — no spikes. The disco lights sparkled on his nose rings. Omar focused on the place where Zane's ear should be. Creepy. "What happened to your ear, anyway?"

Zane rubbed the side of his head. "You here with Red again?"

"Fine, don't tell me." Omar shrugged one shoulder. "Came with Red. Hoping not to leave with her."

Zane chuckled. "I hear you, peer. I lived that nightmare myself. Can't believe you've lasted this long." Zane stared at Omar, squinting his eyes a little. "You talk to Levi today?"

"About the move? Yeah." He had to be over at the bunker at three in the morning. He should probably be home sleeping right now. Zane hadn't responded and was still staring. "What?"

"So you roughed up a few times. Move on. Don't cower at your brother's feet like he's some kind of enforcer rank."

"I never cower at anyone's feet." Except maybe Belbeline's. Maybe Zane could help him get into the Highlands where he could try to find

Bel. Like it would matter. "I have to do what Levi says. He's the village elder."

"What village? You people are in the Safe Lands now. Look, this place will destroy you. I know it's hard to resist. That stuff..." He nodded to Omar's vaporizer. "And that..." He nodded to the dance floor where Red was dancing with a girl with FloArt lightning bolts up her arms, which glowed neon blue and pink under the black lights. *Wow* ... Zane kicked Omar's foot, ripping his gaze away from the girls and back to him. "You've got to fight it, peer. If you let yourself get lost in it, you lose who you are."

"What's it matter?" Omar asked. "I never knew who I was, anyway."

"Who you are and what you're about are the only things that do matter. Don't let this place turn you into a mimic."

"I'm not a mimic." Omar might wear some of the popular colors, but he'd never color his hair or skin. He preferred SimArt to Roller Paint.

"There's more to mimic than fashions. This place kills the soul. Most people are walking around half dead. And from the look of you, you're well on your way. Fight it, peer."

Omar still didn't know why it mattered. "What about you? You're infected, right?"

"Yeah ... and I still have moments of weakness. It burns to live your whole life separated from reality, to be trained to resist only to find out training isn't enough. The temptation is too strong. And it feels good to give in. Real good. And suddenly you wonder about everything you were ever taught. Who was right? Does any of it even matter?"

That sounded about right to Omar. "Does it?"

Zane stood up and limped over to stand in front of Omar, looking down. "What you do doesn't matter as much as who you are. But you have to decide who you are. Who you *want* to be. And no one can decide that for you. Not your donors, not your brother, not some flame, and not that juice. You decide. Then you stick to it with everything you've got. Once you know who you are and what you stand for, you'll know what matters and what to do about it." He slapped Omar's shoulder twice as he moved around the sofa. "Figure it out before you die, okay, peer?"

"Yeah, sure." Easier said than done, though.

Zane left, and Omar watched Red and the FloArt femme dance, thinking over what Zane had said.

Who was he? Back in Glenrock, he'd always wanted to be a hunter, but that was over now. Then he'd wanted to be strong. He supposed he still wanted that, but lifting weights wasn't enough. He wanted to matter to people, to be a hero. And he wanted a nice girl like Kendall Collin or Shay.

Omar left Red on the dance floor and exited the club. Outside, the temperature was cool. He paused to watch a helicopter sail overhead and wondered what the enforcers were doing. Enforcers were the only ones who used helicopters in the Safe Lands, and only a select few had access.

A yell pulled Omar's gaze down the street where some guy was kicking an electric sign that had once hung on the marquee of the Night Owl dance club. The electric orange pipes that outlined the owl sparked each time the guy kicked it.

Omar had always liked that sign. Someone had painted intricate feathers on the owl, but in the dark, he could see only the orange outline of the bird and the yellow circles that were its eyes.

Owls were solitary, watchful, intelligent, nocturnal — different from most birds. Misunderstood, like Omar. He sometimes thought he even looked like an owl with his round face and large eyes.

A sudden rage took over — likely stim-induced. "Hey!" Omar ran toward the guy, ready to defend the sign if need be. But the guy took off down the street, abandoning his prey.

Omar stopped and stared at those yellow circles. "You and me," he told the sign. "We need to make some changes." He picked up the dented metal, careful not to cut himself on the broken glass piping, and carried it back to his apartment.

When he walked through his apartment door, the sign whacked against the dumbbells he'd left on the floor. He really needed to put them somewhere else. It was 11:57 p.m. He had to be at the bunker in three hours. Might as well pull an all-nighter.

He set the sign on the floor in the middle of his kitchen and marveled at the workmanship that had gone into its creation. It wasn't glitzy like most of the Safe Lands signage. Someone had painted each feather with black, brown, yellow, and white paint — they were all unique. Omar grabbed a screwdriver from his art box and set to work removing the brace bands that held the glass piping in place.

The people of Jack's Peak saw owls as an omen of death and destruction. And while Omar found such superstitions foolish, he liked the idea of an owl as a messenger, the way Bender used the messenger office to communicate with other rebels.

Owls were also hunters. Omar had never been skilled at hunting deer, elk, or bear. But owls hunted smaller game. They were cunning. And they had the ability to notice things, to see and hear better than most. Omar had those strengths too.

He needed to prove himself — redefine who he was and who he wanted to be. He didn't want to be "traitor" anymore. He didn't want to be "juicehead" or "flaker," either. Or any of the names his father had called him: crybaby, wimp, girl, sissy.

Omar wanted to be a hero.

He took a draw from his PV, and the burning taste told him it was empty. He pocketed it and grabbed a beer from his fridge, drank half of it, and set the can on the floor under his easel.

He removed the thin sheet of painted aluminum from the sign's frame and carried it to his bedroom. He stood before the mirror, holding the sign in front of his chest. Squinting one eye, he imagined himself with wings. He carried the sign back to the kitchen where his easels were set up and dug out his canvas of the Owl superhero he'd started a few nights back.

Omar had been branded a traitor. It would not be an easy image to change in people's mind. But if he could hide his face behind a mask … create a hero people loved … maybe then, when he finally revealed himself, he would have a chance at redefining his image.

He needed a costume. Perhaps the sign could be formed into a breastplate of owl armor, but reshaping the aluminum would cause the paint to flake. He could get fresh metal and paint it after it was shaped, but aluminum or steel wouldn't stop an enforcer's SimScanner or stunner — or bullet, if someone were to use a real gun. If he couldn't protect himself, why not be comfortable? Maybe he should just design SimArt that would display feathers all over his body. He'd been getting tired of the chain design on his arm, which had been the first SimArt he'd done himself.

Omar stared at the sketch of the Owl, his thoughts sloshing in his mind like colors in an ink tumbler. He recalled Levi telling Jordan about how the stunners hadn't worked on the chest waders he'd worn into the Safe Lands. If Omar could find a suit of rubber, perhaps he could craft himself a different kind of armor.

The enforcers had taken Levi's chest waders, but Shay had found an old black-and-white wetsuit when she and Aunt Chipeta had cleaned the bunker. She'd put it on and flapped around the bunker like a penguin until everyone was laughing.

What had she done with it? He'd have to ask her the next time he saw her.

But he didn't want to wait. He wanted to make his suit now. He glanced at the clock on his Wyndo wall screen. 12:26 a.m. He had time. He finished his beer then headed out into the night. He stopped at a stim store to fill his PV. They had a special on something called a stim cocktail. It was half the credits of what Omar usually vaped, so he decided to try it.

He entered the storm drains and headed toward the bunker, using his off-grid Wyndo to light his way. The water wasn't terribly deep, so he waded through it even though he was unable to keep his feet where he wanted them. Too much beer, perhaps.

He sloshed down the tunnel, vaping and dreaming about his costume. Oils would take too long to dry. He did have some tubes of fabric paint that he'd used to paint wings on his curtains. He'd likely need to buy more, though.

By the time he reached the bunker, he was shivering and his pulse was racing. He was glad they were moving above ground. The door seemed extra loud, especially when he closed it. His steps too. The air around him felt electric, like time was going faster than it was, yet he could see it moving ... so did that mean it was really moving slower?

He stood in the corridor outside the main room for a moment, holding his Wyndo above his head, trying to remember which room Shay slept in.

The one on the end. With Mary.

Omar walked that way, mumbling to himself. "Where's the penguin suit, Shay-Shay? I'm going to turn the penguin into an owl so it can fly." He giggled and cracked open her bedroom door, then shifted and held his Wyndo inside first. He squinted to make out the forms on the beds inside. One was much larger than the other.

That would be Mary.

He crept inside, trying not to laugh. He held his Wyndo close to Shay's head to make sure it was her. The tinsel in her hair shone in the white light. He tap-tap-tapped the Wyndo glass against her forehead.

"Shaaay," he whispered. "Oh, Shay-Shay. Wake up, Shaylinnnnn."

Her eyelids fluttered, then opened. She'd taken out the green contacts and her eyes were brown again. Burnt umber, actually, like the tube of the color he bought from the Task of Art store the last time he'd been in the Highlands, thinking of Shay's eyes, quicksand eyes that made him sink into their depths, never to return.

Walls, his thoughts were coming super-duper fast from whatever was in that stim-cock-a-doodle-doo-tail.

"Omar?" Shay said. "What are you doing?"

"Shhhhh. Don't wake Big Mary." He threw back her covers. She was wearing a tank top and shorts. The top had twisted around her waist, making her body look ... well, perfect. He stared at her, mesmerized. Such a pretty girl, Shay was. When did it happen? How did he miss it? "Pretty, pretty, pretty, pretty—"

"What are you doing?" She tugged at the covers, trying to pull them back over her.

So Omar slipped into the bed and rolled onto his side, facing her. The bed was warm and smelled like honey, which made his stomach growl, and he wished he had something to eat. He shivered under the soft warmth of the blankets and snuggled into them. "You smell good."

"Well, you smell funny. And you're wet."

"I'm making something special and I need your help. Say you'll help me, Shay-Shay, please? I want to turn a penguin into an owl."

"Omar, it's one in the morning," Shay whispered.

"When did you get so beautifully pretty?"

Her eyes flashed wide, and she pulled the covers tight under her chin. "What are you doing here? And what's wrong with your eyes?"

"I want to paint you, your eyes and your hair, so I can hang you on my wall and see you all the time and stare." He snickered. "That rhymed, Shay-Shay. Did you hear it? Hair and stare. Paint your hair so I can stare, stare, stare at your hair."

"Why are you talking like that?"

Why was he? He blinked, trying to remember. And it came to him in a breath, like there was too much air to breathe and it gave him a pulsing rush of energy. "I need the wetsuit with the penguins. I mean the black-and-white one you put on that day to look like a penguin when you made everyone laugh so hard they cried and then you took it off. What did you do with it? Please say you kept it and didn't throw it away because I need it for my special project of making an owl into a pink . . . into a p-penguin." *Deep breath. Wow. Can't focus.*

"Uh . . . it's hanging in the closet."

His cheeks were tingling. "In this room?"

"Yes."

He threw back the covers and hopped out of bed, but he couldn't see the closet. He felt for his Wyndo, but it wasn't in his pockets. Where was it? Where? He spun around, looking at his feet, then back to Shay's bed. She was sitting up now, clutching the blankets to her chin. He wanted to pull them away and stare at her again, but he ran his hands through his hair, trying to remember why he was here.

To kiss Shay and paint her and smell her and drown in her eyes of burnt umber quicksand.

He pressed his hands over his face. They were trembling, and he stayed that way, standing in her room, covering his face, trying to remember, his cheeks and head tingling, his heart racing, his vision blurred.

Something tickled his arm. Bugs. Crawling on him. He swatted at his arms, trying to brush them off, but Shay was there and she grabbed him and held his arms down at his side and he could smell her honey sweetness and he wanted a sandwich or a beer or hair ... honey that smelled like hair. He tried to pull away, but she hugged him.

"Hey, it's okay," she said. "Calm down."

So he did. He closed his eyes and stood in her arms, his forehead resting on the top of her head where he could smell her honey hair. And he dreamed he was eating bread with honey and butter and it tasted good and he was rocking and then he lay down and was so very warm.

A moment later he opened his eyes, panicked. The enforcers. He was in the health clinic, tied to the bed. They were going to operate. He broke free from the restraints.

"You should rest, Omar." Shay was sitting on the foot of his bed.

"We have to get out of here." Omar's arms shook as he searched the room. Someone was in the bed beside his, under the blankets. Someone big. "He's there," Omar whispered, pointing to the lump on the bed. "Otley."

Shay frowned. "That's my aunt Mary, Omar." She picked up something from the bed and held it out to him. "Here's the wetsuit. You wanted it, right?"

The wetsuit. Yes. It would make the perfect disguise. He took it from Shay and shook it out so that it lay on top of him. He kicked off his shoes, leaned back on the bed, and pushed his feet through the legs. Then he slid out of the bed and jumped, pulling the suit up until he could put on the arms. It was tight over his clothes, and he wrestled with it until he got it on. He spotted his Wyndo tangled in the blankets and tucked it into the top of the suit, then zipped it up. "We have to go," he said, running out the door and into the corridor.

"Omar, your shoes."

He cranked the hatch wheel on the bunker door, and it squeaked. Otley would hear it. He had to hurry. The door banged when he broke the seal, then *squeeeeeeaked* open, and Omar stepped out into the tunnel. He turned back and waved Shay to follow. "Come on."

She shook her head. "Stay here, Omar. Please?"

"Otley is going to catch us," he hissed. "We have to go."

"I'm going to get Levi." She jogged down the hallway.

"Traitor!" Omar turned and ran. He should never have trusted Shay. She was on Otley's side now, and he'd have to forget about her quicksand eyes and honey hair.

His foot hit something sharp, and he cried out. Where were his shoes? Why couldn't he see? He fumbled to get his Wyndo out from the wetsuit and tapped the flashlight add. White light lit the storm drain around him. Better.

"Omar?" Levi's voice.

Omar spun around and saw lights in the tunnel behind him. Walls! Otley must have tricked Levi into helping him.

Omar turned and ran, splashing through the water and not slowing down until he got back to his street. He still felt like he was being followed, but when he noticed he wasn't wearing his shoes and that he was wearing the wetsuit, the thought occurred to him that he'd vaped some dirty juice.

The stim store was still open, so Omar went in and complained about the cocktail.

"Grass will help you come down," the barkeep said. "Want me to switch your juice to grass?"

"Yes, yes, yes." Anything to feel normal again. To stop shaking.

Omar vaped grass the rest of the way home, still wondering if someone were following him. No more cocktails for him. He got home at 1:57 a.m. and tripped again on the dumbbells he'd left by the door. Stupid chunks of metal. He turned on the lights, too excited to sleep.

He wanted to paint his costume. He took off the wetsuit and dug out all the fabric paint he could find. He started with the torso, since the wetsuit legs were soaked. Feathers of gray and black and brown — burnt umber quicksand eyes.

Shay. He'd left her to Otley. He put down his brush and palette and ran to his windows and pulled the curtains closed. Otley's enforcers could be watching. The curtains were too thin. He should paint the windows black so no one could see inside.

Wait. Otley wasn't here. The stim cocktail was still messing with him. He took another drag of grass and went to sit on his couch for a minute, but the knob on his front door rattled, and someone pounded on the door.

"Omar? Are you in there? I saw your lights go on from the street. Open up."

Red. He'd reprogrammed his door locks to keep her out — his chicken attempt at trying to wean himself of her company. The pounding continued. If she kept it up, Otley would hear. But he couldn't risk Red seeing his costume. She might be Otley's spy.

He took the costume off the easel and hung it in his closet, then went and opened the front door.

Red was a skeleton. Her cheeks and eye sockets were sunken in her pale face and her figure, except for her chest, was all sharp angles, the opposite of Shay's soft round warmth. "What do you want?"

"You ditched me at the club hours ago," she said. "And why can't I get in?"

Omar looked away. He should tell Red the truth. End this like a man. He stepped over the dumbbells this time and walked back to his easel, though nothing was on it now that he'd hidden the costume. The aluminum owl from the Night Owl marquee was clipped to his second easel. He'd been repainting the places the glass tube had chipped and scratched the paint.

He grabbed his oil paint palette, dipped a fresh brush into the burnt umber, and dabbed at one of the feathers, thinking of Shay and searching for the words to end this mess of a relationship with Red. *Go away? I don't like you? You're too gummy?*

Her footsteps crossed the hardwood floor behind him, drawing nearer until she appeared at his side. "Is that the sign from the Night Owl club?"

"Some juicehead trashed it," Omar said. "I brought it home."

"Walls. Why are you painting on trash?"

He studied the sign. "Why not?"

She crossed her arms, watching his brush strokes. "Why couldn't I get in?"

"I changed my code."

"Why would you do that?"

He released a trembling sigh. "I can't do this anymore, Red. It's not really working. I think we should stop."

"Stop what, Omar? Stop talking. Stop kissing? Stop trading paint?"

"Yeah. Stop everything."

She changed her posture, stretched her shoulders back, straightened her spine. She stared at Omar with her neon pink eyes. "Why would we do that?"

"Because it's … weird. It's no fun anymore."

She narrowed her eyes, as if getting angry might actually change his mind. "You're such a liar, Omar. You can't tell me you're not having fun when we're together."

"I'm not. Seriously. It's too … crazy."

Which instantly seemed the wrong choice of words.

"I'm *not* crazy!"

Omar inched to the side.

"What? You're afraid of me? Is that it?" She lunged toward him, and he flinched, which made her cackle. "I can't believe you're afraid of me." But then her bottom lip trembled and tears welled. She blinked, clearing two heavy streams of tears from her eyes. "You want someone else?"

"No. It's not that." Though he guessed it really was…

"Then what, Omar? What is it?"

"I just … I don't know." He again recalled the word Zane had taught him. "It's just too gummy. I want some space."

She stepped close to him. "You didn't want space when I first met you."

He stepped back. "Well, I want it now."

"You're dim!" Red pounded her fist against Omar's chest. Once. Twice. "You stupid shell!" Then both fists, alternating, nonstop. He stood still, taking her abuse, wishing she'd stop. Otley might hear.

Why did he keep thinking about Otley?

"I hate you!" Red went to the front door, picked up a dumbbell, and came back to the kitchen. She lunged past him and heaved the weight at his easel, knocking it over, sending the old Night Owl marquee and his tray of paints skidding across the hardwood floor. The dumbbell thudded against the floor. Bottles and tubes bounced and rolled. Red kicked over the stool, then spun around, glaring.

Omar's lips parted to speak, but he supposed she really wasn't hurting anything. Let her get her anger out and be done with it. But then she ran toward his stack of canvasses and grabbed his painting of the owl's shadow on the street.

"Red, don't. Calm down."

"*Calm down?*" She held the painting before her as if trying a new outfit. Then she slammed the canvas against her bent knee, ripping a hole through the center.

"Hey!" Omar grasped for her arm, but she slipped away and seized another canvas, this one of Jemma.

"No! Come on, stop."

"You like this one, don't you, you pathetic little boy?" Red held it up and punched her fist through Jemma's face.

Omar lunged toward her and grabbed her arms, squeezing hard.

She screamed. "Let go of me!"

"When you calm down."

"You going to beat me up, tough boy? That what you're going to do? You want to fight?"

Omar released her at once. "Of course not. Just stop wrecking my stuff."

"'Of course not. Just stop wrecking my stuff,'" she mimicked.

"Oh, very mature."

"So I'm crazy *and* immature?"

"I didn't say that."

She turned and ran into his living room, pulling over a floor lamp as she passed by. It crashed on the floor, and bits of glass shot across hard wood.

"Red! Come on, quit it."

Omar followed her through the living room. She shoved a chair over, knocked over an end table, and pulled the cushions off his couch and threw them at him. When she picked up the floor lamp and ran toward his Wyndo wall screen, he grabbed her around the waist and pulled her back.

She bucked against him, dropped the lamp, and dug her fingernails along his arms and his left cheek, then bashed the back of her head against his face. His lip split on his own teeth, and salty blood filled his mouth.

He pulled her to the floor. They lay on their left sides, Omar holding Red's back against his front. Her body trembled, her shallow gasps proof that she'd let her anger morph into tears.

Red's behavior made no sense. Why would she care if they broke up? She had lots of guys. Said she liked it that way. But he didn't know what question he might possibly ask to understand her, so he remained on the floor on his side, sucking on his bloody lip and holding this shattered human being.

Another life he'd help ruin.

CHAPTER
8

"A re you sure you're okay?" Jemma asked, sitting on the end of Shaylinn's bed. "He didn't hurt you?"

Shaylinn sat up and leaned against the wall. Her eyes stung from the early hour. If Levi and Aunt Mary and Jemma weren't awake now, she might have thought Omar's visit had been a dream. "No, I told you. He just wanted the wetsuit."

"He wanted to go swimming in the middle of the night?"

"I don't know," Shaylinn said. "It was scary. His eyes were all red. And he was saying such weird things."

"Levi thinks it was because of his vaporizer," Jemma said. "Like being drunk."

"I suppose." Why did Omar have to be so stupid? And if he'd been drunk, he likely hadn't meant it when he'd said she was beautifully pretty.

"Honey, I'm sorry." Jemma patted Shaylinn's leg through the blanket. "You know, I need to tell you something. Mason came to see us last night after you were in bed. Before Omar's ... visit. It's about Omar, though."

Shaylinn already knew he was dying. She'd heard Levi and Chipeta talking about it. "It takes a while to die from the thin plague, doesn't it?

"Oh, Shay, not that." Jemma wrung her hands.

"Stop it." Shaylinn leaned forward and grabbed her sister's arm, pulling her hands apart. "You're frightening me."

Jemma looked up, frowning. "It's just that ... you asked Mason to find out who the donor was, for your pregnancy. Well, he found out two things, Shay. You're carrying twins, and they're Omar's."

Shaylinn's body tingled all over. Omar's twins ... "You're sure?"

"Mason said so. I guess Omar was the only one from Glenrock who complied with the Safe Lands demands on the men. Plus his Safe Lands ID number was listed in your medical record for the ... whatever they call it. The procedure."

Tears blurred Shaylinn's vision. It was as if God had taken everything she'd ever wanted and twisted it into a knot. Could such a mess be untangled? But then she recalled her dream. The children blowing dandelion clocks. The faceless husband. Could he have been Omar?

Jemma hugged Shaylinn then, pulling her back to the present. She hadn't realized she was shaking until she felt her body trembling against her sister's. "Does he know?"

"Not yet."

Shaylinn pulled out of the hug. "Does Jordan know?"

Jemma winced, as if there was no right way to deal with this whole mess. "Levi wants to tell Omar first, then he'll tell the others. Right now, only you, me, Levi, and Mason know."

Shaylinn was thankful. She could only imagine what Jordan might do to Omar. "If Omar's drunk or whatever, what if he doesn't show up? It's only an hour until three now."

"Levi went to look for him. He'll bring him back."

But would he be in any state to help them move? And if Levi told him about the babies, would he even remember in the morning? And if he did, what would he say? What would he do? Nausea raged in Shaylinn's stomach, and she pressed her hand over it, hoping the pressure might calm it.

"Might as well pack now, since we're all up. Can I help you?" Jemma asked.

"No, I'll manage."

Shaylinn had few belongings anyway. As she folded the last of her clothes and tucked them inside her pillowcase, someone knocked on her door.

"Come in."

The door swung in, and Omar stood there holding a cardboard food box in one hand. His hair was flat, hanging down over his forehead like he'd showered recently but hadn't bothered to brush it. He was wearing a black hooded sweatshirt and jeans. He smelled like minty wood and fried eggs.

Shaylinn's eyes swelled so wide the air tickled them, and she blinked to stop the strange feeling. The smell of eggs turned her stomach. "Did you talk to Levi?" she asked.

"About what?" He gave her a small smile. A nervous smile. The whites of his eyes were red, but he looked calm, sober, and a little curious.

He didn't know. Should she tell him herself? But she couldn't! How could anyone deliver such news? She wanted to crawl into bed and sleep, maybe cry.

"I, uh … wanted to apologize for last night, um … I mean, a few hours ago," Omar said, scratching his finger over the top of the cardboard box. "I don't remember much, but I know I came here and woke you up."

Shaylinn hugged her pillowcase. "You scared me." And how was he even awake right now? Shouldn't he be passed out?

He hung his head. "I'm so sorry, Shay." He looked up, his eyes pleading. "I'd never hurt you. I swear."

"I wasn't afraid for me. I was afraid for you."

"Oh, well, I'm fine now." He smirked. "No more cocktails for me."

Whatever a cocktail was. "That's good."

"I brought you some breakfast." He handed her the cardboard box, and the eggy smell attacked and made her stomach churn.

She backed away, shaking her head. "The smell."

"You think it smells bad?" He lifted the box and sniffed it, and the movement sent another wave of odor to Shaylinn.

She pushed past him and ran to the bathroom, embarrassed that her stomach had ruined his thoughtful gift.

When she returned, she found Zane, Jordan, and Naomi waiting at the bunker door. Levi and Jemma were standing just inside the entrance to the main room, arguing in low voices. Aunt Mary, Chipeta, and Eliza were standing in front of Levi and Jemma's room.

Shaylinn went into her bedroom and grabbed her pillowcase. She stepped back into the corridor. "Where's Omar?"

"He took the eggs into the kitchen," Naomi said. "Levi's going to eat them."

"I'm here." Omar squeezed past Jemma and Levi at the door to the main room, which only increased the urgency of their whispers. When he reached Shaylinn, he rolled his eyes. "Married people, huh?" He darted a glance at Jordan and Naomi and waggled his eyebrows. "Hey, I'm sorry about the eggs, Shay. What *can* you eat?"

"Breads are the only thing I can keep down lately," she said. "Meats and eggs — I can't even stand the smell." But Omar's minty wood smell was nice now that he'd gotten rid of the eggs.

"Sounds mad annoying. Can I carry your, uh, pillowcase?" He smiled that smile that lit up his face, took the fat pillowcase from her hands, and swung it over his shoulder.

"Thank you." Her cheeks burned, and she hoped she wasn't blushing.

"You follow Shay, Omar," Jordan said. "Make sure she doesn't fall. I'll be right behind you, so don't mess up."

"I got it," Omar said.

Shaylinn grimaced and stared at the floor. Goodness. Why did her brother always make everything more awkward than it already was?

Finally, Levi and Jemma walked toward them.

Levi stared at Omar, then Shaylinn, and the intensity of his gaze tempted her to run to the bathroom again. "Tap me when you get there," Levi said to Jordan.

"You're not coming?" Shaylinn asked.

"I have a meeting with Bender," Levi said. "Zane says if I go with you right now, I won't be back in time."

"Why meet him at all?" Omar asked.

Levi glanced at Jemma. "That's what my wife said. I think it's best to maintain peace with Bender until I'm certain you all are safely moved. If I don't meet him this morning and he comes looking ... It's not worth the risk."

Which left no time for Levi to tell Omar he was going to be a father. How very awkward. Maybe Shaylinn should try to tell Omar, though she couldn't begin to think of what she might say.

Levi kissed Jemma good-bye, then Zane led the eight of them out of the bunker and into the dark storm drains. It was just after three in the morning, so the only light came from the Wyndos they carried, Zane and Jordan's flashlights, or distant lamplight shining through the occasional grid overhead.

They moved very slowly. Zane in the lead, followed by Eliza and Jemma, who kept turning around to check on Aunt Mary. Then Chipeta, who was carrying Aunt Mary's things. Then Shaylinn, followed by Omar, Naomi, and finally Jordan.

Shaylinn held her Wyndo in one hand and kept her feet on the sides of the pipe, one foot on each side of the water, which was only a few inches deep in the center. Thankfully it had been a while since it had rained. Aunt Mary kept one hand pressed against the tunnel wall and slogged through the water.

"How long will this take us?" Jemma asked.

"It's about an hour to Prospect Drive," Zane said. "There I've got a friend with a van, and I'll drive you the rest of the way."

"What friend?" Jordan asked.

"He's safe," Zane said. "His name is Nash. He and I go back about as far as two people can, okay?"

"Nash, who lives in the Mountaineer?" Omar asked.

"That's right," Zane said. "Why?"

"I met him once, that's all," Omar said.

"Fine. Remember that we need to be quiet," Zane said. "Enforcers have been exploring the storm drains, and we don't want to be overheard."

Zane led them through the storm drains all morning. Omar stayed behind Shaylinn the entire way, which made her neck prickle. They barely spoke, just walked. Shaylinn's racing thoughts made the silence worse. Plus it was stuffy, and she almost threw up twice when strange smells overwhelmed her.

They came out of the tunnel in the basement of a small house. Zane took them upstairs and let them rest and take turns in the bathroom, then they all went into the garage and got into the back of a white van. Jordan and Zane shut them in. They never met Nash.

The back of the van had no windows. It seemed almost darker than the storm drains had been. The engine started, and the vehicle rolled out onto the road. Shaylinn's emotions got the better of her, and she started to cry. Hormones, anyway...

"Hey, Shay." A gust of minty wood rolled over her, and she felt a body slide up against her side. Omar's fingertips grazed her leg, her elbow, and then trailed down her arm to her hand. He took hold of it and squeezed. "This is nice, huh? Who needs to see?"

The feel of his hand in hers rendered her speechless for a few seconds. "You do," she finally said. "To see colors."

"Aw, I've got them all in my mind. But you're right. Colors are good. Real good. You know what else is kind of good?"

"Smells? Not eggs, of course. But flowers. And mint." And wood.

"True." His head touched hers and he inhaled a deep breath. "You smell like honey."

Which made her think of his visit last night when he'd crawled into her bed with his wet pants and shoes.

His head was still beside hers when he whispered. "Jordan is riding shotgun."

Shaylinn smiled wide in the darkness and bet it could be heard in the tone of her voice. "That's the 'kind of good' thing?"

"He only told me to make sure you didn't fall. He didn't say I could hold your hand or smell you. I don't think he'd like that."

Boldness came over Shaylinn in the dark. "I do."

When the van stopped and the back doors were opened, Omar helped Shaylinn stand, and he passed her to Jordan, who helped her get out. It was still dark, but she could see that she was standing on a gravel drive in a forested area. She inched away from the van to leave room for the others to get out, and her eyes adjusted to the outdoors. She could see the bright light of the city in the distance, separated from where she stood by a sea of darkness. She turned around and found the tiny red lights that stretched along the outer wall of the Safe Lands. It was only about a hundred yards away, through the trees. Until now, she hadn't realized there were houses inside the Safe Lands that weren't in the city.

"So close to the wall," she said.

"You'll be perfectly safe as long as you don't come and go during the daytime," Zane said.

But what if someone came to them? Someone like Bender? Where would they go? She hoped Levi was right to trust Zane and his cabin in the woods.

Inside, Zane gave them a quick flashlights-and-Wyndos tour. "Leave the ceiling lights off until Omar gets a chance to paint the windows," Zane said. "Can you do that tomorrow?"

"Sure," Omar said.

And then Zane left them.

The cabin had four beds in the basement. On the main floor were three bedrooms and a separate kitchen, living room, and bathroom. There was also a tiny attic with two more beds. The living room had two shabby green couches with a matching chair that faced a small

Wyndo wall screen, which Omar had turned on now that dawn light had started to spill in through the windows.

Shaylinn walked to the long picture window opposite the TV. She could now see that the cabin sat on a hill on the edge of the Midlands in a grove of pine. In the distance, the top of City Hall poked above the treetops. It was a lovely view.

"It reminds me of home," she said to herself.

Naomi came to stand beside her. "Except for that looming wall in the distance."

"Naomi," Jordan called, "come tell me which room you want."

"I already told him. The one nearest the bathroom." Naomi rolled her eyes at Shaylinn, then waddled down the hallway, leaving Shaylinn alone with Omar in the living room. He was sitting on one of the couches, watching the wall screen, but when she glanced at him, she found that he was staring.

"What?" she said.

He grinned, which always seemed to make his eyes sparkle. "Nothing. You look so different, that's all."

She thought of his compliments last night. Beautifully pretty. "I'm not ugly anymore?"

He tilted his head a little. "Ugly?"

"You told me I was an ugly crybaby. That day at the kissing trees when I was eleven."

"I did? When you were *eleven*?" His eyebrows pinched together, and he looked at the floor, then suddenly jerked his gaze back to hers. "I remember. I was mad because — "

"Levi and Jemma had started holding hands."

He huffed a laugh. "At thirteen, I knew I was going to marry Jemma. And I thought Levi had stolen her from me. Joel had dragged me to the kissing trees to try to cheer me up."

Shaylinn would never forget. "But when he told you who was in the tree, you yelled, 'Shaylinn is ugly!' So I climbed down and I was crying, and you called me an ugly crybaby and I ran all the way home." She took a deep breath. She hadn't intended to say all that, but the confession had gushed out of her, leaving her embarrassed and jittery.

Omar stood and walked toward her. "I'm sorry, Shay. I was, uh, having a bad day."

"Yeah. Me too."

"I was dumb. I didn't mean it. I was mad at Levi. We were kids." These statements popped out one after the other, as if he was trying and failing to find the right thing to say.

But his saying sorry had been enough. "We're still kids, Omar."

He sighed and combed his fingers through his hair, making it stand up. "I don't feel like a kid."

"Me either." She folded her arms across her belly, wondering what Omar would do when he found out about the babies. Would he reject her? Them? And what did she want him to do? She didn't want him to feel like he had to be with her. If she was going to marry someone someday, she wanted that man to love her. Was that too much to ask?

But if Omar stayed in the Safe Lands forever, could Shaylinn raise *two* children on her own? Yes. She could. She was tough. But still, she wondered. "Will you stay in the Safe Lands when we leave? Or will you come home?"

"Home ...?" Omar said. "I'm not sure I know where home is, anymore."

She wanted to tell him that home was with her, but as much as she thought she loved him, things had changed. Before, her crush had been an obsession, but now she needed to be smart. She was going to be responsible for raising two children. And Omar's dependence on those vaping pipes made him crazy. She couldn't have a crazy person around her children. She needed to find out if he could stop. If he was capable of putting others before himself. If he even cared enough about her to try.

She would give him a mission, see if he was worthy of making sacrifices for her. "Would you do me a favor?"

"If I can."

"I need something to do. To keep me busy. I'd like some soft fabric. Then I could make something for the baby."

"*Your* baby?" Omar said, as if he'd forgotten she was pregnant at all.

Babies, now, Omar. If you only knew. "No. Naomi's." She forced a smile. "Mine don't ... It doesn't feel real yet."

He licked his lips and nodded. "Soft fabric, then? What color?"

"Whatever you find. I'd need some needles too, and thread. Or a sewing machine, but I won't press my luck."

"I'll try." He ran his fingers through his hair again, and it looked like a furrowed field. "Shay, I'm sorry this happened to you. It feels like my fault."

She fought her smile, knowing how true his statement was, though if Omar had not been the donor, the medic would have chosen another. Perhaps this was for the best in some strange, God kind of way. "Some days I'm angry or scared. But then I think that God chose me to bring life into this world. And that feels pretty special."

He heaved a deep sigh and looked out the window. "This world isn't the best place to bring life."

"This world is what we make it, Omar. And I'm keeping a positive outlook. If I don't, I'll go crazy."

Omar looked down on her and smirked. "Keep at it, then, Shay-Shay. There's enough craziness in this place as it is."

Sometime that morning, Omar left — without having painted the windows. And Jordan had a fit. There was no food in the cupboards, so for lunch Aunt Mary cooked up some noodles she'd brought from the bunker — plain noodles, which Shaylinn barely kept down.

Jordan made the sad lunch all the merrier with his lectures. "No one comes or goes during daylight. Do you all hear me?" He pointed at each face around the kitchen table. Shaylinn was secretly glad Jordan would never be village elder.

"Where would any of us go?" Naomi said.

"When I get my hands around Omar's neck, I'm going to —"

"Baby ..." Naomi nodded at Shaylinn, as if there were children present and Jordan should save his rantings for later. Like everyone wouldn't be able to hear right through the walls, anyway.

After lunch everyone vanished to their bedrooms, though Shaylinn didn't see what anyone could be setting up. They owned so little. Perhaps they all just wanted to be away from each other again. Staying cooped up together got old fast. At least in the city, Levi had kept Jordan busy.

Of the three bedrooms on the main floor, Levi and Jemma would have one, Jordan and Naomi another, and Shaylinn would share the third with her aunt Mary, who didn't do well with stairs on account of her knees. Chipeta and Eliza had first claimed the attic, but quickly declared it hot and stuffy and moved down to the cooler basement.

Maybe when Omar came back — if he came back — he could have the attic.

Dinner was more plain noodles, after which Shaylinn sat in the living room with Eliza and Chipeta, tapping through the ColorCast channels until Jordan told them it was getting dark and they should shut it off. So they sat talking instead. She wished they had some games, at least a deck of cards.

Levi arrived an hour later, carrying two bags of groceries. Jordan must have tapped him that there was no food. Or maybe Omar had told him. Shaylinn couldn't see where he and Jordan were standing in the kitchen, but she heard Jordan rant about Omar leaving during daylight that morning and that he had neglected the windows.

"Yes, he came back to the bunker to wait for me," Levi said. "He knows not to do it again."

"And the meeting with Bender?"

"He still wants Shaylinn to spy for him. I told him no. He wasn't happy. I'm glad none of us have to see him again."

Bender still wanted her? Why? And who did he want her to spy on now?

Levi went looking for Jemma. Eliza and Chipeta went to bed, leaving Shaylinn alone.

Jordan came out of the kitchen and stood in the span of the arch that led from the living room to the hallway and kitchen. He leaned against the impost. "You okay?"

"A lot bored. But I'm fine."

"I'm going to bed, so why don't you get some sleep too?"

It was only just after ten o'clock, but she'd been up so long that she was pretty tired. "Yes, oh, brotherly warden."

"Hey, how about a little less bark with that bite? I don't think I can handle sarcasm from *two* women."

Shaylinn laughed, knowing he deserved every bit of sarcasm Naomi gave him. "Tell Naomi good night from me?"

"Will do, kid." Jordan crossed the living room and kissed the top of her head, then retreated to his room.

Shaylinn got up and looked out the picture window. The lights of the city sparkled in the distance. She couldn't live like this for long. Sitting here, day after day. Even if Omar found her fabric, she needed more from life. To be a part of things. To help. To make a difference in this place.

Maybe she could go on a little walk. It was dark, so that was allowed, right? She knew what Jordan would say, but he was with Naomi now. And Shaylinn could use the exercise.

Shaylinn went to her room and found her hooded sweatshirt. She put it on and left the cabin, walking down the dark, gravel road. It was probably stupid, but there wasn't another house in sight and she wanted to explore a little. She followed the winding road until she met another — Kokanee Lane. According to the sign, their cabin was at the end of Redrock Road. She could see the lights of a few large homes to her right, but the land around her was so dark that she couldn't tell if there were trees or grass or water around her. She went left on Kokanee, toward the city lights. She quickly reached Prospect Drive, a road she found familiar.

The road was dead now, but once she got closer to Gothic Road, there would be lots of traffic. Shaylinn didn't want to meet any traffic on this road, alone and in the dark. So she walked in the ditch, keeping away from the road. It wasn't until she'd passed the sign for a place called Wildhorse Village that she saw her first car. She crouched in the ditch until it passed, watching the swell of yellow light grow and fade around her.

The rest of her walk went the same until she reached Gothic Road. She hadn't intended to come this far, but now that she had, she wasn't going to stop. She walked all the way to the Belleview Building where Kendall lived. If she knew where Omar lived, she would have gone there instead.

Without the lace gloves Bender had given her, she had no way to enter the apartment next door to Kendall's place. If Kendall wasn't home, she'd have to walk all the way back without a rest. But when she knocked on Kendall's door, Kendall opened it right away.

"I thought you said your brother wouldn't let you out again."

"I snuck out," Shaylinn said. "I want to be a messenger."

Kendall's eyes widened and she opened the door fully. "Come in."

Shaylinn entered, and the two girls sat on Kendall's blue-and-red-plaid sofa. The drape was over the birdcage. Not a peep from Basil.

"I don't really have much sway over who Tayo hires to task in the MO," Kendall said. "But you're off-grid anyway, right?"

"Not that kind of messenger," Shaylinn said. "I want to deliver my own messages. To give people hope. And I thought you could give me an idea of who I could deliver to. People interested in becoming rebels, maybe?"

"Besides those four names from Chord's message bag, I don't know who the rebels are. Didn't you say Omar took over Chord's route? You should ask him."

She'd like to. "I'm afraid he'll tell Levi or Jordan." Especially once he learned what she was going to do.

"He's cute. Omar, I mean," Kendall said.

The comment sent shards of ice through Shaylinn's heart. Kendall was gorgeous. If she liked Omar, of course Omar would like her back.

And Kendall was so much nicer than Red, which somehow made the thought even worse.

But was it fair for Shaylinn to be possessive of Omar? He hadn't asked to be the father of her children. And he'd never given her the impression that he liked her more than a friend. Not when he wasn't drunk on a "cocktail," anyway, though he had held her hand in the dark. And smelled her. The memory made her smile.

Worry would not do. Shaylinn should just be honest and leave the details of her life in God's hands. "I've loved Omar since I was eight and he was ten."

"How cute!" The declaration made Kendall laugh. "Does he know?"

"No, of course not." And Shaylinn wasn't about to tell him, certainly not now.

"But how will you know if he likes you if don't ask him?" Kendall said.

"It's not really the best time to be thinking about romance," Shaylinn said. "We're trying to free the kids from the school and get out of this place. And now I'm going to have twins. I don't want to create any more problems."

"Twins! Oh, Shaylinn, I didn't know there were two."

"I just found out today. Jordan wants to hide me away and keep me safe. But I can't sit around and wait eight more months for my life to begin. I need to do something."

"Then let's deliver a message, you and me. Off the grid. To one of those addresses — the one you said was Omar's friend. Then you'll know how to deliver a message. You'll have to figure out who else to send them to on your own, though."

"Okay. Thank you, Kendall." Perhaps Shaylinn would think of another way to get names without having to ask Omar.

Shaylinn asked for a sheet of paper and wrote a message she felt would be encouraging to a young man who was thinking of joining the rebellion.

I believe in the sun, even when it is not shining. And I believe in love, even when there's no one there. I believe in God, even when he's silent. I believe through any trial there is always a way. "We are hard pressed on every side, but not crushed; perplexed, but not in despair; persecuted, but not abandoned; struck down, but not destroyed." *Do not lose hope. You are not alone.*

A messenger

"That's beautiful," Kendall said.

Shaylinn beamed at the praise. "Jemma says I'm a good encourager." She put the message in an envelope and addressed it, using Chord's original message envelope. Then she and Kendall took a cab to make the delivery. It was a little after 10:30 p.m. when they set out.

Charlz Sims lived in the Twister in part of what Kendall said was her Old Town messenger route. The taxi made quick work of the journey, and Kendall paid the tab.

When Kendall knocked on door 322, a young man answered, wearing a gray jumpsuit that had Midlands Public Tasks embroidered on the front pocket. He was built like Jordan but had crusty skin, buck teeth, and the number 6X on his face and right hand. "Isn't it a little late for messengers?" He looked down at the message, then at the girls. "Off-grid, huh?" He stepped back and held open the door. "Come on in."

Shaylinn and Kendall glanced at one another, then slipped inside.

"Go ahead and sit." He motioned to a table cluttered in several types of stunners. "Sorry about the mess. I'm cleaning my guns."

"You sure have a lot of them," Shaylinn said. Maybe one of them shot more than electricity. Maybe one of them had killed Chord.

No, she was pretty sure Rewl had killed Chord.

"I collect them," Charlz said, digging through a pile of papers on a shelf. "Here we go." He carried a box of envelopes to the table and sat down. He pushed back the guns to make a clear spot and set the box there. He ripped open the card and read it. "What's this supposed to be?"

Kendall shrugged as if she had no idea. "We just make the deliveries."

"Right, sorry." Charlz flipped over Shaylinn's message and scratched a marker over the back. He wrote, "Enforcers asking questions. Tap me." He refolded the message and put it in the envelope. He wrote "Dane Skott, 607 Outrunner" on the outside and tossed it on top of the pile of guns.

"They following you too?" Charlz asked.

Shaylinn's eyes widened and met his. "Who?"

"Enforcers. They keep passing by my place."

Clearly Charlz thought they were rebels. "I don't think so," Shaylinn said, suddenly concerned that enforcers might swoop in and catch her.

"Chord thought he was being followed too," Charlz said. "Where is he, anyway? I haven't seen him in a week."

He didn't know about Chord? "He — "

"We don't know," Kendall said, shooting Shaylinn a warning glance.

Charlz chuckled, and it was a dopey, snorting sound. "You femmes don't know much, do you? Aw, it's probably better that way. Then if they catch you, you can't give up any secrets, right?"

"Right," Kendall said.

Now Shaylinn wanted to leave. Too much talk of enforcers catching her.

"Why did you join?" Charlz asked Kendall. "Because they took your baby?"

The blood drained out of Shaylinn's cheeks. He recognized Kendall. As much as her face had been displayed everywhere this past year, it shouldn't have come as a surprise. At least he didn't seem to recognize Shaylinn.

"It's okay. You don't have to say." Charlz handed Shaylinn the envelope. "You femmes be careful out there."

"Thanks," Shaylinn said.

They left the apartment. The cab had gone, so they made their way to Gothic to hail another. Shaylinn's eyes were peeled for enforcer vehicles.

"What do we do now?" She was ready to go back to the cabin.

"We deliver this." Kendall held up the message Charlz had given her. "Normally, when someone gives me a message, I use my scanner to print a code on the envelope, imputing each message into the grid. Off-grid messages are against Safe Lands law."

"So if a neighbor leaves a note on your door, that's breaking the law?" Shaylinn asked.

"I doubt the Guild would prosecute for that, but they could if they wanted to."

Kendall waved a cab, and they rode to Dane Skott's Outrunner apartment. The girls went up to the sixth floor, found apartment 607, and knocked on the door.

A short young man with long, frizzy hair opened the door and looked them up and down, a wide smile claiming his face. He had the number seven on his face. "Well, hay-o, femmes."

"Dane Skott?" Kendall said.

"Oh, you've heard of me. I'm not surprised the femmes are talking."

Oh, dear. Shaylinn never knew what to say to such bold and confident males.

"Messenger office." Kendall handed him the message.

"Oh, right." Mr. Skott held out his fist.

"That's not necessary, Mr. Skott," Kendall said. "This message wasn't coded."

"Off-grid. How ghoulie." He waggled his eyebrows and opened the message. After he read it, he slid the paper back into the envelope and looked at Kendall. "Walls, femme. You look familiar. Have we paired up?"

"Of course not!" Kendall said. "Would you like to send a reply?"

"Yeah, you would have remembered it, I'm sure. You femmes want to come in? Or how about the three of us meet up later? Drinks at Nob Hill, then dancing at —"

"We don't dance," Shaylinn said.

"Okay, just drinks then. We could come back here after, or there's this place in the park where couples can —"

"Tap the MO if you decide to send a reply, okay?" Kendall said, walking away.

Mr. Skott stepped out into the hall. "Hold on! Is there a reason why you femmes won't come out with me?"

"Do we need one?" Shaylinn asked, running after Kendall.

Mr. Skott pushed out his bottom lip in a pout. "It's a little prude not to give one."

"Call us prudes, then," Kendall called from the elevators.

"But I'm a lot of fun," Mr. Skott said. "Some women say I'm gratifiable."

"I'm sure you are." Kendall stepped into the elevator, Shaylinn alongside. "Thanks for using the messenger office!"

"Maybe this was a bad idea," Shaylinn said once the elevator doors had closed.

"No, you did fine," Kendall said. "But if I were you, stay outside, even if they invite you in. I only went in Charlz's place because you said he was Omar's friend. Normally, I'd never go inside anyone's residence."

"I didn't like Mr. Skott," Shaylinn said. "He reminded me of Ewan the harem guard." She didn't want to bring him another message. At least not when he was home.

"Eww. Ewan gave me the ghoulies," Kendall said. "Always staring. Safe Lands men can be like that. Kind one minute, beastly the next. That's why Omar intrigued me so much when I met him. He was such a gentleman. I kept waiting for him to make a move, but he didn't."

Everyone gave Omar a hard time, but Shaylinn had always known he was kindhearted. "I think Omar is adorable."

Kendall waved another cab. Shaylinn asked to be dropped off outside a house on Kokanee Lane and said good-bye to Kendall. Once the cab's taillights vanished in the darkness, Shaylinn made the trek back to the cabin. She half expected to find Jordan prowling out front, but the cabin was dark. No one had missed her.

It didn't seem like Charlz had even read her message. Maybe it was because they'd been watching him. But then he'd used the paper to write to Mr. Skott. Her plan seemed pointless if people weren't going to actually read her words. But she wasn't ready to give up yet. Who else could she send messages to? She knew the names of the rebels who attended Bender's meetings. And she'd met some people who tasked at G.I.N. and Café Eat in the Midlands. Energy coursed through her at the idea, and she wanted to write down the names before she forgot.

Levi and Mason had their plans to free the children, and now Shaylinn had a plan for herself that just might make the next few months bearable.

CHAPTER 9

A t exactly 11:00 a.m. on Friday, Mason rang Ciddah's doorbell and waited, moving his hands behind his back to hide the red rose he'd bought her.

Jemma had insisted he bring Ciddah a single red rose.

The backpack he wore felt heavy on his shoulders. He'd spent all week planning this day, and, though he didn't want to admit it, he was terribly nervous.

The door swung in, and Ciddah stepped out. She was wearing a bright blue shirt with long, poufy sleeves; a pair of black crinkly pants; and knee-high boots with flat soles. She'd painted blue on her eyelids and outlined her thick eyelashes in black. "Hay-o, Mason."

Mason held out his flower. "This is for you."

Her eyes widened and she grinned. "Oh, it's lovely." She took it from him and smelled it. The red petals were bright against her pale skin. "Let me put it in some water." She went back inside, leaving the door open.

Mason stepped into the doorway and drummed his hand against the side of his leg. He could hear water running. She hadn't asked him in, so he didn't dare cross the threshold, but a quick glance showed a heap of clothing falling from the couch to the floor, dirty dishes cluttering the surface of the coffee table, a stack of file folders on the end of the counter, and two G.I.N bags filled with cans sitting on the floor just inside the door, a lone shoe beside them. He'd been to Ciddah's apartment only once before. It had been spotless then.

She came to the door and shut it quickly. "Did you see my mess?" she said, closing the door behind her and smiling sheepishly.

"Did something happen?" He imagined enforcers tearing apart her home in search for some prohibited object.

"Oh, no. I'm just messy. You've seen my office."

Which was always a disaster. "But the night of Lonn's liberation …?"

"I hired a cleaning service." She slapped her hands against her sides. "So now you know my secret. Do you still want to go out?"

Uncertain whether or not that had been a rhetorical statement, Mason said, "Why should your lack of organization affect our plans?"

Ciddah bit back a smile and looked away. "So where are we going? To a play?"

He hadn't thought to take her to a play. "No. You'll see."

They walked to the elevator and rode to the lobby. For some reason, neither spoke. The awkward silence finally prompted Mason to say something. "Did you know elevators are twenty times safer than escalators? They're also safer than vehicles."

"You sure do know a lot about elevators," Ciddah mumbled.

"I read about them in the History Center one night." But her dry response made him realize he'd done exactly what Jemma had warned him against: spouting useless trivia. He needed to ask questions of Ciddah and then be a good listener.

They left the Westwall and started across the parking lot. The day was clear and already quite warm. He hoped they wouldn't get too hot out in the sun. He had taped his official SimTag to his hand with an adhesive bandage today so that he could pay for things and be seen, if anyone was watching.

"We're walking?" Ciddah asked.

"To the train station, yes."

"Tell me where we're going. To the Noble Gardens?"

"Stop being impatient," Mason said. "You'll know when we arrive." The train station was only a short walk from their apartment building, but Mason's conversation attempts made every moment grueling. Zane had given him several safe topics. He could ask about her task aspirations, classes she'd taken at the Highland Civic Center, or foods. "Have you eaten an orange?" Mason asked as they got on the train.

"Um, yes." Ciddah walked to a pair of seats and took the one against the window.

Mason sat beside her. "Do you like them?"

"Oranges? Sure, they're okay."

"I'd never eaten one until I came here. I'd read about citrus fruits, but I understood that they only thrived in tropical locations. I was surprised to find one in the G.I.N. Are oranges imported?"

"I don't know."

"Oranges cannot be grown outdoors in this climate, but with Safe Lands technology, a regulated greenhouse might create the perfect environment for such tropical — "

Ciddah grabbed his hand, which had been absently tapping his leg. "Mason, stop."

He looked at her, wondering what he'd done to offend her. Zane had said food was a safe topic.

"Relax," she said. "I know you're clever. There's no need to continually try to prove it."

Mason slouched and stared at the back of the seat in front of him. "I wasn't trying to be clever. Only to start a conversation. Food seemed like a safe topic we might not argue about." He glanced at her. "You said I always argue."

She fought back a smile. "So you wanted to know my favorite food?"

He shrugged, discouraged. "I don't know."

"My favorite food is steak. That's why I made it for you."

"Oh." That made sense. "My favorite food was raspberries, but now it's oranges."

She laughed and said, "How surprising." Then her expression sobered. "So, what other safe topics do you want to talk about?"

Mason took a deep breath. He could do this. "Classes you've taken at the Highland Civic Center?"

"Only cooking classes. One on how to bake bread and one on how to bake cakes."

"Before or after you burned the spice cake?" he asked, recalling the charred cake in Ciddah's kitchen sink.

"Before." She elbowed him. "I also took a dancercise class."

"What's that?"

"Exercise by dancing."

"You like to dance or exercise?"

"Dance." She wrinkled her nose. "But only when no one's watching. Have you taken any classes there?"

He shook his head. He didn't even know the location of the Highland Civic Center. "Any suggestions?"

"Classes for Mason Elias, who already knows everything . . . hmm."

"Ciddah, I don't know every—"

"Shh, I'm thinking." She tugged on her bottom lip. "There are science classes . . . speed math. You might also like the wonders of nature course, though knowing where you grew up, you could probably teach it. I had a friend take a robotic craft course that sounded fun for . . . smart men. But I think your favorite class might be brain fitness."

"What does it mean, 'brain fitness'?"

"It's a class that teaches techniques on focus, memory skills, concentration, reaction time, and reshaping your brain through plasticity—things like that."

"Fascinating. And what's plasticity?"

"Neuroplasticity, actually. It's the brain's ability to be changed, modified, and in some cases, repaired."

Retraining the brain was certainly plausible, but modifying? "Are you certain it's not a brainwashing class?"

She chuckled. "If you ever go, I suggest you avoid the classes on seeing into your past lives. I don't think you'd like that very much."

"That much is certain," Mason said.

The train stopped at Champion Park South Station, and Mason stood. "This is our stop."

"We're going to the lake?" Ciddah asked.

"Stop guessing. You'll know soon enough."

They exited the train and walked across the platform toward the stairs. Mason flew down the steps to street level.

"*Mason*, wait up!" Ciddah called from behind.

He stopped and turned to wait, realizing he'd already forgotten most of the tips Jemma and Zane had given him. When Ciddah reached his side, though it went against every instinct in him, he reached out and took hold of her hand. "Sorry," he said.

She beamed at him, then bumped her cheek against his shoulder. Mason marveled at the power human touch had over this girl. She'd touched him often when they'd first met, but after Lonn's liberation, she'd kept her distance. Who could comprehend females?

They walked into Champion Park, which was a half mile of forest, lake, and concrete walking trails. There were quite a few people out, many walking dogs. In the distance, the north side of the park ran along the Highlands-Midlands wall. If not for that eyesore, Mason might have felt like he was back in Glenrock.

They walked to the docks and a rowboat rental shop. Mason paid for the rental with his SimTag.

"We're going in a boat?" Ciddah asked.

"Yes, is that acceptable?"

"Sure. I've never been in one."

"Me either."

They both put on life jackets. Mason helped Ciddah into the boat first, then he stepped in. The craft rocked under his feet. Ciddah grabbed his arm to steady him, and he managed to sit on the bench seat, facing her, without capsizing the small craft.

Mason had used the grid to research how to row a boat, and he did his best to do so confidently. He rowed toward the island in the center of Lake Joie, enjoying the breeze and the view.

He asked Ciddah her task aspirations next, and while she told him about wanting to rank a level twenty medic, he practiced stints of five seconds of eye contact, marveling at her beauty. He knew eyes did not glimmer, that such an effect was produced when light reflected off the cornea, but Ciddah's eyes seemed to be proving otherwise. And her skin ... Some Safe Lands women looked painted, but not Ciddah. She had a little makeup on her eyes and lips, but besides the slight fade to the number seven on her cheek, he couldn't tell she was wearing Roller Paint at all. If he hadn't seen her tears wash it away the day of Lonn's liberation, he wouldn't know now. She was perfection.

Hunger panged in his stomach. He checked his Wyndo and saw it was 12:36. Time for lunch. He'd forgotten how stimulating conversation with Ciddah could be. He'd also gotten off course with his rowing and had to steer them back toward the island.

Mason got out first, secured the craft, then helped Ciddah out. They left their life jackets in the boat. He took hold of her hand and led her down a winding path that entered a forested area. Ahead, on the side of the path, a small crowd of people was clustered around a bronze statue of a man and a woman wrapped in a loving embrace. The man was kissing the woman's neck, and the woman's head was thrown back, her face frozen in laughter.

"What does this sculpture represent?" Mason asked Ciddah.

"It's the Champion Memorial." And at his blank stare, Ciddah continued. "Loca and Liberté Champion founded the Safe Lands in the aftermath of the Great Pandemic."

Ah, yes. Papa Eli had spoken of this pair. They were not heroes in Glenrock history, but hedonistic megalomaniacs. Strange that the Safe Lands and Glenrock cultures each deemed the other in such negative light.

The crowd moved on, and Mason stepped closer so he could read the words inscribed under the couple's feet. "'Find pleasure in life.' The task director said that to me."

"It's the motto of the Safe Lands," Ciddah said. "Loca and Liberté wanted to create a place where people were free to enjoy themselves, where cost wasn't a factor."

"Yet the pursuit of such pleasure cost the people everything," Mason said, "the thin plague being a blood-borne virus."

Ciddah's posture stiffened. "Mason, you don't understand. Everyone was already infected. Because of the Great Pandemic."

"Is that what they teach in your boarding school? Ciddah, my great-grandfather met Loca and Liberté Champion. And when he saw how carelessly they treated the virus, he and his friends fled this place. That's why my people aren't infected and yours are. The blood-borne strain came after the 'Safe Lands' were founded, not before."

Ciddah didn't answer, so Mason looked at her. She was staring at him, tears in her eyes.

"I'm sorry," he said. "I broke my rule and argued."

She sniffled and brushed a lock of hair from her eyes. "You like to be right."

He looked back to the statue. "I'm always happy to be proven wrong."

But Ciddah made no comment.

They left the statue and continued through the forest until Mason found a flat, grassy spot under a tree. "This will do." He removed his backpack and unzipped it.

"Will do for what?"

"For lunch." Mason removed a blanket and spread it over the grass, then set out the meal he'd packed, which consisted of a chicken salad sandwich for Ciddah, a peanut butter and jelly one for him, potato flakes, apple wedges, and cupcakes from BabyKakes. "One spice cake and one chocolate."

Ciddah groaned but smiled. "Did you make these sandwiches?"

"I bought them at the G.I.N. store."

They enjoyed their meal, and Mason was careful to keep the topics away from anything controversial. He asked her what it was like to be raised in the boarding school, but she had little to say on that subject. Did she suspect him of trying to gather information to free the children?

After lunch, they rowed back to the boat rental return, then got on the train headed west.

"You realize we live the other way?" Ciddah said. "Don't tell me. It's another surprise."

"The day is not over yet."

It was only one stop to the second location on Mason's agenda. They got off the train and walked two blocks until they stood outside what looked like a huge warehouse.

"Virtual Floors?" Ciddah said. "Is it a home décor store?"

"It's a museum," Mason said, pleased that she'd never been there. He held the door open for her, then took hold of her hand again when he joined her inside a small room.

A man stood at a counter, and Mason paid the entry fees.

"Welcome to Virtual Floors," the man said after they both tapped in their SimTags, "a journey into your imagination. Each chamber will transport you to a different place in time, from the heights of City Hall, to the depths of Calamity Cliffs. Stepping on and touching the floors is encouraged. You cannot ruin the art. Press your SimTag to each door and it will open only when the next chamber is empty, allowing you a private experience for each room. Your tour begins through those doors, but beware of the beasts that lurk in the waters. They aren't often fed, and may find you quite appetizing."

Ciddah's eyes lit up, and she smiled at Mason.

"Let's go in," he said, pressing his fist to the pad beside the door to the first chamber. It opened right away. Ciddah took hold of his hand again and they walked through the door.

Inside, the room felt damp and smelled of hay and mildew. It looked like the outside of one of Jemma's fairy tale castles. Walls of stone and ivy were in fact only painted to look that way. A three-dimensional image of a drawbridge was down and passed over a moat that was filled with crocodiles with teeth as long as Mason's hand. The reptiles seemed to be snapping at their heels. It looked so realistic that Mason jumped.

"It's wonderful!" Ciddah said.

Mason slid his shoe back and forth over the edge of the drawbridge and the crocodile's teeth. It was completely flat. He bumped Ciddah's side, knocking her onto the painted water. "Look out!"

She laughed and pulled him with her. Mason jumped onto a crocodile's head and pretended he was trying to keep his balance. Ciddah pulled his hand again and stepped onto the blue water.

"You got eaten," she said.

"Well, you're drowning." He motioned to her feet. "Omar would love this place."

"Your brother?"

"The younger. Omar's an artist. He paints and draws everything."

"Do you miss him?"

The question gave him pause, and he realized that from Ciddah's view, Omar had gone into hiding last month as a rebel. "I miss the way things were when we were younger. Levi's relationship with Jemma turned everything into a competition with Omar. Ever since, things have been difficult."

The second chamber was a forest. It smelled of pine and wildflowers. A raging, three-dimensional river rapids stretched diagonally across the floor. An inflated yellow raft had been painted just above a waterfall, and Mason and Ciddah sat cross-legged on the painting of the boat.

Ciddah giggled and lifted her hands. "We're going to go over the edge!" She pretended to slip out of the boat, but Mason grabbed her waist, and she fell across his lap on her back.

"You saved my life," she said, staring up at him.

"You're welcome," he said, making sure to count to five before looking away.

The next room was an aerial view of the buildings in the Highlands with the walls painted to match the surrounding view — even the ceiling was blue and filled with clouds. A soft breeze wafted through the room, and Mason could smell metal and tires and a hint of popcorn.

He stood on top of City Hall and looked toward the forest that once had been Glenrock. It was nothing but trees. The experience chilled him. "How do they make the smells?"

"I don't know," Ciddah said," but I think it's wonderful."

Some of the other chambers they passed through were a cathedral, a cavern with a rope bridge, a room where the floor was crumbling underfoot, one where monsters were crawling up from a fiery lava pit and trying to grab their ankles, a nightclub, and a burning building. Each one seemed tangible and incorporated smells and appropriate temperatures, which Mason found absolutely brilliant.

By the time they finished the museum, it was 5:26 p.m.

"Are you hungry?" Mason asked, taking her hand as they left Virtual Floors.

"Yes."

"Good."

They took the train back to the heart of the Highlands. According to the grid, Below Zero was a restaurant bar made of ice. Mason had thought it would be a nice touch after Virtual Floors, but now he wondered if it would only be more of the same.

But when Ciddah saw the sign, she squealed. "I've always wanted to come here!"

"Why haven't you?" Mason asked.

"They don't allow minors, and once I started working, I never had time."

They stepped inside the restaurant, and an instant chill clapped onto Mason's arms. The place was small, no bigger than the front half of his apartment. The blue and white walls glowed brightly, coated in real ice and frost. A bar chiseled from ice stretched down one side of the room and maybe a dozen people on barstools sat there, draped in animal pelts. Mason quickly counted eight booths made of ice on the opposite wall.

A woman approached them. She wore a bright blue fur coat that made her look huge, though her face was slender. "Name?" she asked them.

"Mason Elias," Mason said, glad he'd made a reservation.

The woman left and returned with two fur coats. Mason was given a black one, Ciddah a white one. The woman in blue also gave them matching fur caps. They helped each other put them on, laughing at how silly it all seemed.

The hostess seated them in a small booth with a view of a man chiseling a statue from a block of ice in the middle of the room. Mason ran his finger over the table, then the bench. Both were made of real ice. Fascinating.

Mason ordered a zucchini grinder sandwich. Ciddah ordered a polar bear burger, which the waitress said was beef, not bear. When the food came, Mason's sandwich was a long white bread roll, sliced horizontally and stuffed with chunks of baked zucchini, red and yellow peppers, marinara sauce, and melted white cheese. Ciddah's was a stack of three chubby, square patties topped with a square bun. It reminded Mason of City Hall.

"How am I supposed to eat this?" Ciddah asked.

Mason fought back a laugh. "One bite at a time?"

They ate and watched the sculptor chisel away at the ice, which slowly took the shape of a woman riding a bird.

"That's from a movie," Ciddah said. "*Gogo Magie*. It's the story of a girl who finds magic in everything she touches and uses it for all kinds of frivolous reasons, yet when a boy she loves is injured, and she tries to use the magic to heal him, she discovers that the magic had been flowing out of her all along, not in. And now she's empty. She wasted her magic in pursuit of her own pleasure, and the boy suffered a premature liberation."

"*That's* a Safe Lands story?" It seemed to speak to discipline, rather than the pursuit of pleasure.

"It's a cautionary tale to remind us that each individual is sacred, as is each life," Ciddah said. "It reminds us that we come into this earth with great potential, and we should give pleasure to each other in each life, not simply live to please ourselves."

Intriguing. But Mason wanted to point out that had the girl used her magic on others, she still might not have had any left to heal the boy. The only way for her to have had magic available for the boy was if she had hoarded it all her life, which was also selfish. But he'd agreed not to argue, so he remained silent.

When they finished their meal, they returned the fur coats and hats and walked outside. A gust of warmth surprised Mason. The sun had not set fully yet. "It was quite cold in there," he said, taking Ciddah's hand.

She smiled at him, so he held her gaze and counted to five. Six ... seven ... eight ... nine ... lost again in her eyes.

"What?" she asked, her lips curving into a smile.

He shook his head and led her down the sidewalk. Below Zero was close enough to their apartment building that they were able to walk home. Mason told Ciddah one of his favorite childhood stories on the walk. It was the story of how the tortoise beat the hare in a race.

"I'm a lot like the tortoise," he said. "I might not be the fastest or strongest, but I'm persistent and smart. It helps me remember that size or speed isn't everything and that defeating the stronger adversary is possible." Like Otley or Lawten or the thin plague or, when he was younger, Levi.

"I like that story," Ciddah said. "I think I'm a tortoise too."

They reached the Westwall and rode the elevator to the third floor.

At the door to Ciddah's apartment, she turned to face him and bounced on her tiptoes. "I had a great time today, Mason."

So had he. And he'd learned nothing about the boarding school. Figured.

"Do you want to come in?" She looked hopeful, waiting for his response.

Did he? Mason stared at her. He did. But also ... he didn't.

Ciddah leaned against the wall beside her door. "*Mason*, you've been sending me signals all day."

"Have I?" Of course he had. He'd done everything Jemma and Zane had suggested. He might not have understood why those things had pleased her, but he could see that they had.

Ciddah eyelashes fluttered. "I like you very much, Mason. And I think you like me too. I know you're uncomfortable with the way things are done here, but I imagine that even in Glenrock it would have been unfair to flirt with someone if you didn't intend to see that person again."

He'd *flirted*? To be honest, he hadn't expected any of it to work. And Zane had said to wait until Tuesday to arrange a second outing. Since Zane's advice had worked so far, it seemed wise to stick with it. "But I'll see you in the lobby. And when I return to the SC to task, I'll see you —"

"I want you to kiss me," she said.

Oh. He started tapping his leg as his mind raced, looking for escape. "Some scientists of Old hypothesized that the practice of kissing originated from animal feeding rituals when a mother masticated food, then passed it to her offspring by mouth."

Ciddah blinked and tilted her head to the side. "Mason, I want a kiss, not your regurgitated sandwich."

"Sorry." His stomach clenched, and he looked at the floor. Nothing to do now but kiss the girl and hope she found it satisfactory. Or he could just run for it.

He didn't want to run, though. He liked Ciddah very much. She was perfect — except for being the enemy, of course, and for her views on procreation, and the fact that she had the plague. And he should likely weigh her dishonesty more heavily against her as well. And her friendship with *Lawten*.

Why did she have to be the enemy?

He looked up and found her staring, and in her gaze, he lost his train of thought. Such a lovely girl. Smart too. It would hurt when she betrayed him again. It seemed almost as if she'd taken his heart from him already. Put it in a box. He felt fragile and empty at the very idea of walking away and never seeing her again.

He couldn't.

For Levi, right? For Glenrock? A little pain was worth the cause of freedom for his people. Even if it bound him to this woman.

He inched forward, and the soles of his shoes scratched over the carpeted floor. Should he do something with his arms? In Old movies men were always grabbing a woman's face or waist or pushing them up against a wall.

Mason reached out and took hold of her hands, threaded his fingers with hers. He dove toward her lips, but their noses struck. Ciddah turned her head, but Mason pulled back. "Sorry."

Ciddah tugged on his hands. "You've never kissed anyone, have you?"

Mason's cheeks burned. "I have." Though Eliza had instigated the act. Apparently there was more to instigation than he had surmised. Flustered, his hands began to tremble. He tried to pull them free.

But Ciddah held tight. "Why don't you try again?"

Try again? When he'd rather go home and avoid Ciddah for the rest of his life?

But he couldn't very well do that, not after all the work he'd put into today. And he couldn't stand outside her door any longer, either.

Twelve. He'd been twelve the last time Eliza had kissed him, and he felt twelve all over again. He hadn't anticipated kissing Ciddah, or he would have researched the topic on the grid.

Mason leaned toward her, slowly, hands still trembling. She turned her head a little and closed her eyes. Mason waited until he was certain of his aim before closing his eyes.

Their lips met. His were stiff and puckered, hers soft. She released his hands, and hers slid around his neck, pulling him closer. The space between them seemed to disintegrate. While Mason was awkward, Ciddah was confident. And just as hormones flooded his bloodstream, creating a sense of euphoria, Ciddah pulled away, leaving Mason winded and wanting.

She smiled, resplendent, and set her fist against the door pad, never breaking eye contact. "Good night, Mason."

He released a quivering breath. "Good night."

She went inside and closed the door, abandoning Mason to the hallway. He stood there, still stunned by the effect she'd had on him. He'd thought he was going to lure Ciddah into his trap, but somehow things had gotten completely turned around.

CHAPTER
10

Levi rode with Zane in a black bullet truck through the Midlands. It was Saturday, after lunchtime. Levi had been up since 4:30 a.m., which was the only way to get a ride from the cabin if he needed to visit the city in the daytime.

The electrified gauges on the windshield and the silence of the engine still amazed him, but his thoughts dwelled on Beshup from Jack's Peak. Zane had confirmed that Beshup was in the Safe Lands and tasking in the Midlands. If Chief Kimama had heeded Levi's warning and helped him back when he'd asked, things might be different now. But there was no point in saying "I told you so" since they were all in this prison now. They may as well work together — if Beshup would agree.

Zane took Gothic Road to Outrun. Once they passed 4th, warehouses ran all along both sides of Outrun. Zane pulled into a parking lot outside a long building labeled Leather Works Design.

"Will anyone care if I just walk in?" Levi asked Zane.

"Doubt it. Manufacturing isn't the loftiest of tasks. That's why it's in the Midlands. Here." Zane reached across Levi's lap and opened the glove compartment. He pulled out a large padded envelope. "Say you have a message for your peer, and someone will call him to the front. Don't take too long. Make plans to meet later."

"What's in this?"

"A clean Wyndo. I was going to give it to you for Shaylinn, but I figured she could wait."

"She can. Thank you, Zane." Levi took the envelope, got out of the truck, and entered the building. He stopped inside a small reception area. The air smelled of oil and leather.

A woman looked up from a desk. "May I help you?"

"Message for Beshup."

"Beshup Chua?"

Beshup must have taken his son's name as a surname. The five-year-old had likely been taken to the boarding school, away from both his parents and his little brother Matsiku, who'd be in the nursery. What a mess.

"Yes," Levi said. "Beshup Chua."

"One moment." The woman tapped her GlassTop screen, and when she spoke again, her voice came out through speakers in the ceiling. "Beshup Chua, you have a message in reception. Beshup Chua to reception, please." Another tap and she looked at Levi. "Go ahead and take a seat, if you like." This time her voice didn't amplify.

Levi perched on the end of a chair, anxious to see Beshup.

"What salon you go to, valentine?"

Levi turned his attention back to the receptionist. "I'm sorry? We're you talking to me?"

"Are those plugs?" She touched her hair.

"I'm not infected." Maybe he should quit bathing. Then these people would stop staring at him everywhere he went.

"Walls! How'd you manage that?" she asked.

"I'm an outsider. Was."

"You need someone to show you around, outsider, you give me a tap. I'm here Wednesday to Saturday, eight to four."

She could dream. "I'm married."

She leaned forward, as if she'd misheard him. "You're what?"

"Levi of Elias," a deep voice said.

Levi looked toward the doorway behind the reception desk and saw his friend standing there. Beshup was a few inches taller than Levi and had long blond hair, which he wore in two braids. He was wearing a thin, gray jumpsuit like the one the medics had given Levi after they'd captured him and taken his clothes. The number four glowed white on his cheek.

Levi got up, trying not to grin. "I have a message for you." He held up the envelope, then glanced at the receptionist, whose gaze bounced back and forth between Beshup and Levi. "Why don't we step outside for a moment?"

"If you insist," Beshup said.

Levi pushed open the door and held it wide for Beshup. When they were both standing outside, Beshup clapped his hands onto Levi's shoulders.

"It is good to see you alive, my friend. You always were a wild rabbit. I'm surprised you haven't waged war on this place."

"And what about you?" Levi asked. "Didn't you say Jack's Peak would kill all who stood in your way?"

"I'm still determining whether I can do so and see my family and tribe live."

"I may have a way," Levi said. "I heard through Mason that Tsana is well."

Beshup's eyes widened. "How? Did he see my wife?"

Levi explained how Mason tasked in the Surrogacy Center, how the Safe Lands had the Jack's Peak women in the harem, and how Levi was trying to find a way to free the Glenrock children.

"Are your women in this harem as well?" Beshup asked.

"Not anymore." Thankfully. "We got them out."

"Then you can help me free the women of Jack's Peak."

If only it were that easy. "We can't talk here." Levi handed Beshup the padded envelope. "Inside is a Wyndo that can't be traced. It works like a CB, but more high-tech. My number is programmed into the memory. We have a meeting tonight. Do you have transportation?"

"I have two feet. But my tasking shift ends in a half hour. Can you wait?"

Would Zane want to wait? Doubtful. "See that black truck that looks like a bullet?" Levi nodded to Zane's vehicle. "That's our ride. I'll see you soon."

Zane didn't want to wait, so they ran some errands and came back. Then Zane drove Beshup to his apartment and explained how the SimTags worked to track them. Beshup had no desire to wait until they met up with Mason. He cut out his own SimTag and wrapped toilet paper around his hand.

Once that was done, Zane drove them to the small house where they'd left Jordan that morning. Apparently, it was the same house the people of Glenrock had come in through the basement after deserting Bender's bunker on their way to the cabin. Here they would have the men's meeting while they waited for it to get dark enough to return to the cabin and meet with everyone. Getting the men together in advance allowed for more purposeful talk, as some of the women tended to get emotional.

Zane parked out front and they went inside. The place reminded Levi of the Old houses in Crested Butte. It had a small living room that opened into a kitchen in the back of the house. A cluster of mismatched recliners and kitchen chairs were circled up in the center of the living room. Mason and Omar had joined Jordan, and all three greeted Beshup and expressed concern for the people of Jack's Peak.

"What happened that day?" Jordan asked. "Did someone in your village betray you?" He shot Omar a dark glance.

"No. Their warriors came before dawn. They came in the copters. The noise woke us, but their lightning guns quickly put our men to sleep. Once we knew what was happening, our men and women fought bravely and killed many enforcers. But our ammo ran out and theirs did not. By dawn, it had ended. The children were loaded into a copter. Then it returned for the women, then the men. My father was taken and Chief Kimama as well."

"Elsu lives? And Chief Kimama?" Levi couldn't believe it. The woman was almost ninety.

"They took them alive," Beshup said, "but I have not seen them since we left the City Hall."

"Liberated, like my mother," Levi said.

"What does this mean, liberated?" Beshup asked.

"We don't exactly know, but we're trying to find out." Too many things to worry about and too little time.

Beshup asked more questions about the harem, so Mason did his best to explain what he knew, how he'd helped free the women, and how Mia and Jennifer had chosen to stay behind.

"They are fools," Beshup said. "Dancing with the coyote is a dangerous game."

"I think everyone who lives here is dancing with the coyote," Levi said, which made Jordan laugh.

But Beshup nodded solemnly. "The coyote is always making mischief, but time is evolving again. We saw America come and go. And now we will see the Safe Lands come and go. Mother Earth must purify the land before it can be renewed."

"I don't know what that means," Jordan said, "but I'm all for it."

Levi knew. Beshup was speaking of the typical Jack's Peak superstitions. "He means that even though the Safe Lands has a lot of power right now, and they were able to destroy our villages, they can't continue with their way of life forever. What they've done here is not natural. They're already failing. And they can kidnap and pillage all they want, but over time, they'll still fail. Life will find a way to return — whether by Beshup's Mother Earth or Papa Eli's Creator Father."

"There are only six Jack's Peak men that I know to be registered here," Beshup said. "Tomorrow I will gather them and cut out their tags so they can attend the next meeting."

Mason passed around the letter he'd gotten from Penelope, which gave Levi hope they would be able to get the kids out of the school.

"I was thinking we could schedule a rescue for the fourteenth of

August," Mason said. "That would give us two weeks to plan and two more Tuesdays for me to speak to Penelope."

"What about the women in the harem?" Beshup asked.

Levi knew Beshup would keep bringing this up, and he could hardly blame him. "We'll help you free your women, but not until after we get the children out."

"I cannot leave my wife to become pregnant while I wait for two weeks to pass," Beshup said.

"I understand, Beshup, I really do." The mere idea of Jemma being captured, especially now that she was Levi's wife … maddening. "But we've been working on our plan to free the children for a while now. And if you and your men will help us, we'll free the Jack's Peak children as well. Are you with us?"

"I cannot see any reason to stand against you," Beshup said, though he did not look at all pleased.

"I brought supplies for Jemma to use when Naomi goes into labor." Mason patted a fabric sack on the chair beside him. "And has Shaylinn reduced physical activity? Omar, how are you two holding up?"

Nuts. Levi looked at his baby brother, who straightened in his chair.

"Me?" Omar said. "What about me?"

"I haven't told him," Levi said. "It's been a little crazy with the move and Bender's demands and everything." But he felt like a coward. He'd talked to Omar at the bunker on Thursday. He should have told him then. And he hadn't exactly tried to track him down yesterday. He should have.

"Told him what?" Jordan asked.

Maybe the news would be best received in a group. More bodies to hold Jordan back when he tried to kill Omar. "Why don't you tell us now, Mase?" *Coward. Elder Coward.*

Mason stared at Levi a moment. "Gee, thanks, brother." He shifted in his chair. "Um … well, first of all, Shaylinn is carrying twins."

"*Two* kids?" Jordan asked. "Hogs teeth! How can you possibly know that?"

"I looked up her file in the CompuChart," Mason said. "And

140

Ciddah told me that when they do embryo transfers, they always try for multiples. Beshup, you should know that they're trying for three with your friend Kosowe."

"My cousin is no man's wife," Beshup said. "And now she never will be."

Levi rubbed his hands over his face. The nightmares never ended in the Safe Lands.

"Speak English, Mason," Jordan said. "I can't understand doctor talk."

"They put multiple babies in every woman in hopes that she'll birth more than one," Mason said.

"They're trying to repopulate the Safe Lands," Zane said. "That's just the way things work in the harem."

"Poor Shay," Omar said, rolling his vapo stick along his thigh. "It's not right."

Levi could only stare at Omar. How was he going to respond when Mason told him the rest?

"What else?" Jordan said, practically yelling. "You're all acting like maggots. Is Shaylinn infected? Is that what you're hiding?"

"No. Her donor wasn't infected at the — uh …" Mason took a quick breath. "He was from, uh … Glenrock."

"What!" Jordan stood, and the rocking chair he'd been sitting on bounced back and forth behind him. "I never donated a thing." His eyes were wild and desperate as he looked to each of them as if to prove his point. "Levi?"

Here we go. "Neither did I."

Mason sighed. "Nor I."

"If none of us made donations, who's the father of Shaylinn's babies?" Jordan asked.

Mason looked at Omar.

Jordan's head turned slowly, and his desperate expression morphed into an angry one. "You dung-licking maggot!"

Omar's eyes bulged, and he looked from Jordan to Levi to Mason. "You can't know it was me."

"I can, actually," Mason said. "The donor's ID number for both fertilizations was 9-G1. What was your Safe Lands ID number, Omar?"

Omar's face went very pale, and a soft moan seeped from his lips. "I – I … didn't know that, that it would …"

Levi couldn't help but feel sorry for his brother, but he needed to say something elder-like. "What did you think would happen?"

"You didn't think, as usual." Jordan growled, and it grew into a scream as he pulled at his hair. "*My* sister. Hogs teeth, my *sister!*"

"I must point out that Shaylinn would be pregnant whether or not Omar donated," Mason said. "She was ranked first. If they hadn't used Omar's sample, they would have used another."

"That's true," Zane said.

Omar cowered in his seat, his hands on the sides of his face. "I'm sorry."

"You'll have to stop seeing Red," Levi said, glad for any reason to get his brother away from that conniving woman. "If you're going to be Shay's husband."

Omar's eyes met Levi's. "Husband?"

"Oh, no," Jordan said, pacing inside the circle of chairs like a bull in a pen. "Don't any of you think I'm going to let this pathetic excuse of a man-child anywhere near my sister."

Levi folded his arms. "But he's the father, Jordan."

"I'd rather Shaylinn's children think their father died beside mine in the raid than have this maggot in their lives."

Omar lifted his vapo stick to his lips and inhaled, his eyes closed.

"Now, wait just a minute, Jordan," Levi said. "That's not really how things work. Plus, Shaylinn should have some say in this, don't you think?"

"She's too young to have a say," Jordan said. "I'm her guardian." He poked his chest. "I say."

"Shaylinn is smarter than you think." Omar, still hunched like a scared dog, blew out a quick breath of black vapor and glanced at Jordan. "And she's —"

Jordan lunged across the open floor, grabbed Omar's shirt, and lifted him out of the chair. "Don't you dare speak her name, you—"

Levi jumped up and wedged himself between Jordan and Omar. "Come on, that's enough. We've got important things to discuss here." He elbowed Jordan in the ribs. "I said, back off, Jordan. Let go."

Jordan snarled and pushed Omar back into his seat, then thundered out of the living room and into the kitchen. Levi followed him.

"I don't want to talk about it," Jordan said when Levi reached him. "I mean, why'd she have to be first? She's only fourteen. Why not Aunt Mary or Eliza or one of the others? Why Shaylinn? And why *him*?"

"I don't know," Levi said. "But, Jordan, Omar and Shaylinn might have gotten married any—"

"No. It wouldn't have happened. Your father was going to send Omar to Jack's Peak. And then Shaylinn could have married Trevon," Jordan said. "I like that kid."

Levi had to bite back a laugh. "Trevon is ten!"

"So? Four years matters little to adults. When Trevon is twenty, Shay will be twenty-four. Not a big deal."

"You want her to be alone for ten years? Raising two kids?" Levi said. "Jemma thinks this is God's way of making a match."

Judging from the snarl on Jordan's lips, he did not agree with that theory. "How long have you known it was Omar, Levi?"

"I found out Wednesday night. I wanted to tell Shaylinn and Omar first thing Thursday before we moved, but then Bender wanted that meeting and there was no time to talk to Omar before you all left for the cabin."

"Jemma told Shaylinn?"

"Yes."

"So she didn't tell me, either?" The anger faded from Jordan's face, and he just looked tired. He slapped Levi's chest. "Finish your meeting, Levi," he spat, then walked back to the living room.

The men didn't get much done after that. Jordan and Mason both sank into moody silence, and Zane, Levi, and Mason spent the next few hours answering Beshup's questions about the Safe Lands.

When darkness finally settled over the city, they all piled into Zane's fancy truck and drove back to the cabin. The women had dinner ready, so they gathered around the kitchen table to eat while Beshup shared his story about the attack on Jack's Peak again for those who hadn't heard it.

Levi couldn't help but notice that Omar continually stayed on the opposite side of the room from Shaylinn and took three trips to the bathroom during dinner.

While Omar was still in the bathroom on his third trip, Mason leaned over to Levi and whispered, "He needs to run away and paint. It's how he deals with things."

But there was no painting left here. Omar had already done all the windows. "It won't be much longer." Levi picked up his butter knife and tapped it against his water glass. "If everyone will quiet down, we'll get started."

All heads turned toward him. He stood at the head of the table, nervous for some reason. Because of Beshup and Zane? Maybe. He met Jemma's adoring smile and the fear melted away.

"I'd like to open this meeting with a prayer." Levi had never prayed publicly before, and he wasn't thrilled to start doing so now. But he agreed with Jemma's concerns that their people needed consistency during this traumatic time, so in an attempt to be more like Papa Eli he recited the prayer Jemma had helped him write based on Psalm 13. "Father in heaven, you didn't promise us peace. Look on us and answer, Lord. How long will you forget us? We wrestle with sorrow. Day after day we weep as our enemy triumphs over us. But we trust in your unfailing love. In the hope of your salvation. Bring us victory, Lord. Set the captives free. Amen."

"That was lovely, Levi," Aunt Chipeta said.

"Lovely words don't bring my husband, Mark, back," Eliza said. "They don't bring my children back to me. Why did this happen? We follow God. Yet it seems like he's punishing us."

"Where in the Bible does it say God's people will be safe from violence?" Mason asked Eliza. "Where does it say his people will always be rescued here on earth?"

"It's unfair," Eliza said, tears filling her eyes. "And what if this is just the beginning? What if we're stuck here forever? What will become of my babies? Will they remember me? What I taught them? Or will they become like him?" She gestured to Zane.

"What did I do?" Zane said.

"Train a child in the way he should go and when he is old he won't turn from it, Eliza," Aunt Chipeta said, handing Eliza a napkin. "Trust that to be true."

"I know it's taking us longer to get to the children than we hoped," Levi said, eager to change the subject. "Mason, how about you give the ladies your update?"

"I saw Penelope when the students walked to the park. She passed me a note, which told of two ways she thought the kids could sneak out of the school."

"How was she?" Aunt Chipeta asked of her daughter.

Levi removed Penelope's letter from his pocket and handed it to his aunt.

"Bright and smiling. Tenacious as ever," Mason said. "I also hope to get some information about the boarding school from Ciddah."

Aunt Chipeta narrowed her eyes. "I thought you didn't trust her."

"I ... don't." Mason stretched the neckline of his shirt as if it were too tight. "But I'm trying to know her better, and questions about one's childhood are relevant in courtship, are they not?"

Eliza snickered, her cheeks still wet with tears.

Aunt Chipeta gave her a one-armed hug. "See, Eliza, you can trust God to always use Mason to provide comic relief."

Mason's eyebrows sank as he looked at the women. "I don't see what made my question humorous."

"Once we determine which route is safest," Levi said, "we'll plan the escape and get word to Penny. We're hoping to do it two weeks from today."

"Two more weeks," Mary murmured.

"What about the nursery?" Eliza asked.

"The nursery is another matter," Mason said. "We need to enter at night as well, and we need to knock out the cameras."

"I can do the cameras," Zane said. "But I've never been in there, so I don't know where to send you."

"It would be best to do both escapes on the same night," Levi said. "Otherwise we tip off enforcers that we're after the children, and they'll tighten security more than ever on the other location."

Someone knocked on the front door.

All eyes focused on the entrance, Levi's included. Heat flashed over him. Who else knew they were here? He glanced at Zane, who shrugged one shoulder.

Levi pushed back his chair as silently as he could, but Shaylinn hopped up from her seat and jogged to the door.

"I'll get it," she sang. "It's probably Kendall."

Levi and Jordan exchanged shocked glances. Both jumped to follow her.

"Shaylinn, stop," Jordan growled.

But Shaylinn glanced through the peephole and pulled open the door. "Yep, it's her."

Indeed, Kendall Collin stood alone on the porch, gaze bouncing from one person to the next in the crowd of people staring at her.

Shaylinn had invited someone here? When? And what had she been thinking?

Kendall stepped inside and Shay shut the door behind her. "I've recruited my first rebel," she said, smiling.

"Can I talk to you, please?" Levi grabbed Shay's arm, towed her into the living room, and pulled her to sit beside him on the sofa. Jordan and Jemma followed.

Before putting his attention on Shaylinn, Levi watched Omar in the kitchen. He pulled out a chair for Kendall, who was smiling at his little brother like they were about to climb the kissing trees.

Wonderful. Just what Omar needed after news of Shaylinn: another female distraction.

"Why, Shay?" Jemma said, pulling Levi's attention back to the problem.

"We weren't supposed to tell anyone about this place," he said.

Shaylinn looked from Jemma to Levi. "No one said that."

Seriously? Levi sputtered to find a response that didn't involve shaking some sense into the girl.

"No one should have to say that," Jordan said. "It's completely obvious."

Shay's eyes misted. "She tapped me that she wanted to join the rebels. I told her Bender's group wasn't safe. She's one of us, though. She's an outsider too." Shay's gaze slipped away from Levi's to the kitchen table where Omar and Kendall were chatting it up, and her eyebrows sank. See? Even she could see this was a bad plan. But maybe that was the best angle.

"Omar and Kendall seem to be hitting it off," Levi said.

Jordan glanced over his shoulder. "That dung-eating maggot. I told you."

"She's not right for him," Shaylinn said. "But only God can show him that."

Oh-kay. Time to backtrack. "How is someone not from Glenrock one of us? And why didn't you consult me first?"

Shay focused on Levi again. "I'm sorry. But she was taken from her home too, and her child is also in the nursery. She's been there, Levi. The task director general let her hold her baby once. She can help us get inside. And Zane is here, and Beshup. They're not from Glenrock."

He hated that she was challenging him this way, that she'd put him on the spot. "It's not that I disagree entirely, Shay. But the Elder Council approved Zane and Beshup in advance. We did not approve Kendall. If we're going to build a new village and keep everyone safe, we all need to follow the same rules. Tell Kendall that we'll discuss this and let her know what we decide. Fair enough?"

Shay blinked at him, eyes wide and disbelieving. "You mean she has to leave?"

"I'm sorry. But yes."

"I'll get rid of her," Jordan said.

Shay jumped up and grabbed Jordan's arm. "No, I will." She pushed past him and walked back to the kitchen table.

Levi couldn't hear what was being said, but both Kendall and Omar's gazes shot to him as Shay explained. He walked slowly back to the table.

Everyone stared as Kendall stood, cheeks flushed, and walked toward the door, keeping her gaze on her feet.

"I'm really sorry, Kendall," Shay said as Kendall opened the cabin door and left without uttering a word.

"Wait!" Omar ran after her, jerking the door open. "I think someone should walk her home," he said to Levi. "After all, she did risk everything to come. Plus, what if she was being followed and led someone else here? I'll look around, make sure no one else is out there."

"Fine," Levi said. "Make it quick." Which he knew was impossible as far as they were from Kendall's apartment in the city.

"I'll try," Omar said, "but don't wait for me to continue the meeting." And Omar left.

Great. Levi hoped his baby brother wouldn't do anything stupid.

CHAPTER
11

Omar raced after Kendall. Any excuse to get out of that cabin and away from the never-ending guilt. "Hay-o!"

Kendall turned. She was really cute. Maybe that was the cue for him to turn back. After what Mason had just told him about Shay, he'd be wise to stay away from all girls until he figured out what to do.

He just wanted to be the Owl. That was all. He'd barely finished his costume this morning before Levi had tapped him and told him to go meet Mason and Jordan at Zane's house. Maybe he could try it out tonight.

"I did *not* lead anyone else here," Kendall said, her peachy face flushed. "And if someone was following me, you should know since you've been following me all week."

She'd seen him? The Owl wouldn't be very effective if he couldn't even follow a girl without being seen. "Bender had to make sure he could trust you."

"Chord asked me to deliver the messages and keep them a secret. If you wanted to know that, you could have asked me yourself, like Shaylinn did."

His stomach tightened at Shaylinn's name. "You're mad at me?"

She shoved him. "Yes, I'm mad at you! I've been terrified ever since I read that message." She folded her arms and stalked ahead, her shoes crunching over the gravel road.

Omar ran to catch up, and they walked in silence until they reached Kokanee Lane.

"Did I get Shaylinn in trouble with Jemma's lifer?" Kendall asked.

Omar chuckled at the very idea. "I don't think that's possible. Levi gets mad fast, but he worships his wife. And Shaylinn is his wife's little sister, so …"

"It was my fault," Kendall said.

"It was Shay's fault. She should have asked Levi before inviting you. Then everyone would have voted you in already and we'd be in the meeting instead of out here in the dark." Though Omar was glad to be out of that cabin.

"You're so sure? I don't think that Jordan fellow likes me."

"Join the club," Omar said.

"The Jordan Hater Club?"

"No, the Hated by Jordan Club."

"Why does he hate you?"

Why didn't he hate Omar? But right now, it was because of Shaylinn.

Omar was going to be a father. A dad. So weird.

They reached Prospect Drive and turned right onto it. Kendall stayed beside him. So far they'd seen no cars, but it wasn't that late. Only nine thirty or so.

"Well, anyway," Kendall said, "I don't understand how Jemma and Levi can be married if marriage doesn't exist here."

"Jordan married them," Omar said, glad to change the subject. "In our village you need an elder to marry you."

"And Jordan is an elder?"

"Enforcers killed all our elders, so Levi and Jordan and Mason are the last of the men."

"And you," Kendall said.

"But I'm not an elder." And never would be, with his mistake record.

"Why not?"

He opened his mouth, but no sound came out. No point in bragging about his stupidity.

"You have ranks. Is that what you mean?"

"Sort of. Levi's the boss. The rest of us do what he says. And Jordan makes sure we do. And Mason's smart. But I'm not an elder because it's my fault we're all here."

"Shaylinn told me. Omar, I don't think you should blame yourself. The task director general, he ... he's a bad man. He would have come for you all eventually."

Maybe. No one could ever prove that, though. They walked in silence until they passed Wildhorse Village.

"So you and Shaylinn, huh?" Kendall said, smirking at him.

Twins. His stomach churned. He took out his PV and inhaled a long drag. "Did she tell you that too?" he asked, his voice a croak from holding his breath. Couldn't girls keep their mouths shut about anything?

"That's bad for you, you know." She gestured at his PV.

He blew out the fog. "Yeah, I've heard that."

Again they walked in silence. Omar wasn't sure what he was doing with Kendall. This walk was way too long. But the train station was just up ahead at the corner of Prospect and Gothic. He'd have to get the gloves from the locker if he was going to go home and try owling tonight.

"You like SimArt?" This time Kendall pointed at his arm. "Wait. Where is it?"

Omar winked, liking her confused expression. His SimArt didn't work when he wasn't wearing the gloves that held his official SimTag. "I like real art more." He stopped at the crosswalk to Gothic and watched the cars pass. "You want to see some of my work?"

"Where?"

"My apartment. I live in the Alexandria."

Kendall chuckled low. "I don't think so."

She thought he was trying to pair up. "I'm not trying to get you to come to my apartment for — I mean, you'd be coming only to see my paintings." Why was he even asking her over? He should go home and get to the business of owling.

The light changed, and they crossed the street. "Paintings?"

"Yeah, I have a couple dozen." He'd have to hide the ones of Belbeline, though.

Three yards from the entrance to the train station, someone stepped in front of them and cut them off. It was Red. Her eyes were bloodshot, the centers were green tonight, and she wasn't wearing any Roller Paint. She looked awful, her skin like crackle paint.

"Hay-o, trigger." Red leaned in to kiss him, but he stepped back. "Oh, so it's like that, is it?" She jerked her head at Kendall. "You upgrading to a queen?"

Kendall looked from Red to Omar, her eyes large and sad. Puppy dog eyes.

"Shimmer, you don't want to get involved with this one," Red told Kendall. "It's all a game to him and his peers. They dare each other — "

"What are you talking about?" Omar couldn't believe this was happening. "She's lying."

"Men." Red rolled her eyes. "They always deny everything."

"I'm going to go," Kendall said, stepping around Red toward the train.

"Wait!" Omar yelled after her, then to Red, "What is wrong with you?"

"Nice meeting you, Kendall Collin!" Red waved, as if they were old friends. "See you around, Omar." And Red strode away.

"Why did you say that?" he yelled after her, but she pretended not to hear. Or she outright ignored him. Either way, Omar stood alone on the platform, gritting his teeth. He decided to try to catch up to Kendall, but by the time he reached the right platform, the train was rolling away. Stupid Red. It was probably for the best.

Omar used the gloves in locker 127 to ride downtown. Rather than putting them back in that station's locker, he kept them on, hoping to make use of the ghoulie SimTag for his owling quest.

He went to check in at the messenger office but found nothing in Chord's former sorter, so he went home and donned his Owl costume. It had turned out great. It wasn't quite as tight as the costumes worn by the superheroes in his Old comic books, but he liked that better. Though he'd been lifting weights and could tell it was making a difference, skin-tight clothing would only call attention to how tiny his muscles still were.

Owls had two features that aided their hunting skills: they were silent flyers and their feathers camouflaged them in the forest, making them difficult to spot. Both features allowed them to sneak up on their prey.

Omar's goal was simply to not get caught.

He'd painted the wetsuit in shades of brown with white accents and made a mask to match. He'd also made a brown cape from fabric he'd bought when he'd gone shopping for Shay's fabrics, which he still had sitting beside his door. He wanted her to have them; he simply didn't know what to say to her now.

He looked at himself in the mirror, flexed his arms, and tossed his cape over one shoulder. Not too bad, actually.

What should be his first heroic act? Was he just supposed to lurk in dark alleys until he witnessed a crime? It might be best to start small. Do a good deed. Something safe. Something people would see and talk about. Something to build respect for his new persona.

Bender ran a safe house in the warehouse district. People who were looking for a place to hide or get clean could crash there. Once a week someone brought food, but the people were mostly on their own, many of them hungry.

Omar used his off-grid Wyndo to tap Café Eat and order fifty cheeseburger meals to be delivered to the safe house in a half hour. Then he tapped a cab. If the cab driver found Omar's costume strange, he didn't comment. Omar supposed with all the pierced and painted people in this city, his Owl costume wasn't that odd. But when he tapped to pay the fare and a woman's face appeared on the windshield, Omar realized he shouldn't use ghoulie SimTags for anything but riding trains. Good thing he was wearing the mask.

He'd have to find a way to be the Owl without credits.

The cab dropped him off at the warehouse. Omar waited outside until the Café Eat truck arrived with the huge box of cheeseburger meals. The Owl went inside and started handing out food. Everyone looked at him strangely. He scared one woman half to death. Whenever someone asked, "Who are you?" Omar simply replied, "The Owl."

By the time all the meals had been handed out, a crowd had formed in the doorway.

"That's all the meals I have for today," Omar said, then raised his voice to the whole room. "The Owl is wise. The Owl sees all. Trust the Owl for answers." He ran out the door, across the street, and around the next corner. He didn't stop until he was certain no one had followed him. He felt awkward and embarrassed, like he'd just made a fool of himself.

Maybe he had.

What now? It had probably been dumb to leave his apartment in the costume. He couldn't keep coming and going from there dressed like a superhero. He slipped into an alley and removed his costume, which left him in his boxers.

He was an idiot.

He rolled the costume around his arm until it was a small bundle, then he started back, trying to keep to the darker streets so no one would see him in his underwear.

As he made his way home, he critiqued himself. His slogan was too wordy. Plus he had no real powers to impress anyone. He wished he knew how to build a hang glider, but he'd likely get himself killed trying to fly between the buildings.

He needed to think this through. What was his goal? It wasn't about playing superhero like a child or even a vigilante. This was about revenge against the Safe Lands government for how they'd used him. It was about justice for himself, for Glenrock, and for all Safe Lands nationals. Renzor and Otley had everyone trapped, but most nationals didn't have a clue. Omar wanted the people to see the truth. Then, if they still didn't care, fine. But if he could expose the lies of the Safe Lands for all to see, then people could make an educated decision about who they were going to serve.

But how? Where did superheroes find trouble? Clark Kent had been a reporter. Peter Parker a photographer. And the commissioner had used the Bat Signal to call Batman.

Omar needed a mark. A symbol of his identity. A way of being recognized. He could use that mark to build up intrigue, leave it all around the Midlands.

When he got back to his apartment, he got out a pencil and paper, ready to create a symbol for the Owl. But what should it be?

The Black Army used a bird's wings to symbolize flying to freedom. Omar liked that. For his mark, he drew fat owl's wings, arching up in a V for victory, with talons at the bottom, clutching the Safe Lands bell logo. When he was happy with how it looked, he created a stencil that would make spray painting his mark a quick and simple act.

He used some scraps of fabric from his cape and made a belt bag to hold his cans of paint. Then he put his costume back on and went out again. He crept along Cinnamon Mountain Road until he reached Belleview Drive, turned down Belleview, passed the messenger office, the Cinnamonster ice cream shop, and the laundry. He left his mark along the way, adding words like, "Trust the Owl," "The Owl sees all," and "Hoo is the Owl?"

That last one made him smile. If he did this every night for a few weeks, he could mark the entire Midlands. Once he'd done that, he could do the same in the Highlands.

But graffiti alone didn't make a superhero. He needed a master plan.

He returned home and had barely changed out of his costume when the doorbell rang. His fear was that Red had returned, but a look through the peephole showed it was Zane.

Omar opened the door. "You're out late. How was the meeting?"

"It was a meeting." Zane limped in, punching Omar's arm as he did. "This place is a pit. What goes on here?"

Omar looked around his apartment. It was still a mess from Red's hissy fit. He'd really only cleaned up his studio — kitchen — so he could finish his costume. "Levi keeps me too busy to clean, and Red wasn't much help."

"I'll bet." Zane sat on the back of the couch, his feet dangling. "So, where'd you stash your owl suit?"

Omar shut the door and turned to look at his guest. "What?"

"The ghoulie tag you stole from the train station made a purchase outside Bender's warehouse. So I went to check it out. I saw Owl Man handing out burgers. Recognized your voice."

Great. "Please don't tell anyone. It's just ... You were right. I wanted to do something that made a difference. I'm a loser and a traitor to my people, plus now that I'm going to be a father, I — "

"Calm down, peer, I get it. I do. But if you're going to do this thing — which I think is stimming awesome, by the way — you need a voice modifier. And I'm going to build you one."

Omar relaxed. "You're not going to tell anyone?"

"Walls, no. Clearly you don't think the rebels' plans are enough. And I agree with you. The Safe Lands people need something like this. Someone who'll voice their darkest fears. The things everyone wonders but is afraid to ask. People are talking about what you did tonight, *Owl Man.* If you keep it up, it won't be long before you have more press than a harem queen. But you're going to need help to keep from getting caught. Let's work together to make you someone the public can trust. The Owl Man sees. Trust the Owl Man. It's good."

"It's just the Owl, not the Owl Man."

"Fine."

It *would* be nice to have a partner. "But Levi can't know."

"No problem," Zane said. "Let's keep this between you and me."

"Deal," Omar said. And they shook on it.

For the next hour, they talked about their plans, and only after

Zane had left and Omar cleaned up the floor of his place did he find the message that had been slipped under his door. It was unmarked, off-grid. The mere sight of it filled his stomach with dread. He opened the envelope and read:

Omar,

Blessed is a man who perseveres under trial. But remember: God tempts no one. A man is tempted when he's dragged away by his evil desire and enticed. Once desire is conceived, it gives birth to sin, which when fully grown, gives birth to death.

God did not create you and cause you to live with the purpose of wishing to die. I believe, in my heart, you were intended to value life and enjoy it. So falls the rain after the fire, and this too shall pass. Remain steadfast.

Love from

a messenger

This wasn't from Bender. Omar's first thought was Jemma, for only she could quote words that touched the aching soul. But he knew Jemma's handwriting — still had a birthday note from her in his desk back in Glenrock. This wasn't from her.

The dread had not wholly vanished from his heart. But it was no longer dread for himself. It was dread for this messenger, who was attempting something very brave yet very foolish.

Just like him.

CHAPTER
12

Shaylinn's days in the cabin were far too quiet. There was nothing to do but cook, clean, or watch the ColorCast, all of which Shaylinn was sick of. Clearly Omar had forgotten to get her some fabric.

Or maybe he'd found out the truth and was avoiding her.

It had been only two days since he'd chased Kendall out the door. Perhaps no one had told him still.

After dark, Jordan returned to the cabin and set several grocery bags on the kitchen table. "I got you some fabric." He pulled out a wad of blue denim. "It should make a nice pair of pants."

Shaylinn took the fabric and stroked it. Denim was exactly the type of fabric her brother would have picked out for his son. Thick and sturdy and tough. What kind of fabric would Omar have chosen?

Before they'd escaped the harem, Luella Flynn had said on her show that Naomi's baby was a boy. Naomi said Ciddah had confirmed it. Shaylinn wondered about her own babies. Kendall had predicted girls. She strained to remember her dream, to recall if the children had been boys or girls. But she couldn't remember.

She'd just have to be surprised.

A door down the hall opened and Naomi jogged into the kitchen, holding her belly with one hand as she moved faster than must be comfortable. "Hey, baby!" She crushed herself to Jordan. "What did you bring me?"

"Cookies, cookies, and more cookies."

"Good man." She dug a package of cookies out from one of the bags and tore into them. "You having any cravings yet, Shay?"

"No. Everything's revolting."

"I still can't believe you're going to have two babies."

Shaylinn forced a laugh. "I'll be huge."

"Surely Omar will take some responsibility in this," Naomi said. "You can't raise two kids on your own."

"She won't be on her own," Jordan said. "She can stay with us."

Shaylinn glared at her brother and Naomi. "I know what you're thinking. You're thinking I'm your responsibility now, like I can't take care of myself."

"Can you?" Jordan asked.

"I've always been a decent hunter. And I fish better than you. I respect you, Jordan, and I love you both dearly, but my babies are not yours. You and Naomi are not my parents. And I won't let you take over my life."

"I don't want him in this house," Jordan said.

"This is not *your* house, brother. And stop acting like Omar took advantage of me. No one is to blame for this but our captors. I don't need your pity."

She grabbed the fold of fabric, stomped to her bedroom, and slammed the door. She fell onto her bed and let the tears come. She had never been a crier until she'd become pregnant. Now the tears came whether she wanted them to or not. It was so unfair. Her pity party was short-lived, though, as nausea sent her running to the bathroom.

After yet another bout of sickness, she washed her hands at the sink and tried to decide if it was safe to return to her room.

Someone knocked on the bathroom door, and Jemma cracked it open. "Can I come in?"

"Why does Jordan hate Omar and Mason so much?"

Jemma came inside and closed the door. "He doesn't hate them, honey. He's still angry at Omar for betraying our village. He may be angry about that for the rest of his life. And Mason ... it's only because he doesn't understand Mason."

"I'm not afraid of these babies." The dream she'd had showed a peaceful, happy future. "Don't you see? This is God's will."

"How come I never knew that you liked Omar?"

Shaylinn lowered the lid on the toilet and sat down. "I hid it from everyone. Even Penny and Nell. I miss them, Jemma."

"You have me."

"It's not the same. I know you love me, but we've never spent much time together. You're always with Naomi or Levi."

"Well, that can change, can't it?"

"I suppose." But Shaylinn didn't think it ever would.

"And change, it shall. It might take Omar a while, but I'm sure he'll come around. Honey, try to remember: he's only sixteen, and you're only fourteen. That's very young to be dealing with these things. I'm so proud of how brave you're being."

Yes, Shaylinn could be brave, but that didn't make her any less lonely. She convinced Jemma that she needed a nap, then returned to her bedroom to work on her messages. She'd used Jordan's Wyndo to find out where the people on her list lived and was almost ready to make another delivery trip. If she couldn't give hope to herself, at least she could give it to others.

When everyone was sleeping, Shaylinn went out into the night. Mapping out her route on the Wyndo in advance would have been wise. She'd backtracked three times already and still had two messages left.

She left the Twister apartment building and crossed the parking lot, heading back toward the Paradise.

"Hay-o, Shaylinn."

She jumped and scanned the dark lot. Rewl was leaning against a black car beside an opened back door. Shaylinn wanted to run, but Rewl's friendly smile compelled her feet to keep a steady pace. *Just act calm*, she told herself. But all she could think of was Bender's threat that Rewl would kill Kendall.

"You've been delivering messages." Rewl's eyes seemed to devour her. He held out an envelope. "I have one for you."

Someone had written back? Shaylinn walked up to the car and reached for the envelope. Rewl pulled his arm back a little and grinned. The SimArt on his teeth made them look rotten in the darkness. Shaylinn reached farther. Rewl held the message above his head. Shaylinn sighed and reached up, knowing he'd only move it again. But this time he grabbed her around the waist and pulled her into the back of the car.

Hot fear seized Shaylinn, and she screamed. "Let go!" She kicked and clawed at Rewl, but he held on. The door rolled closed and the car pulled away from the hotel. Someone else was driving? She strained to look, but the car had a divider that hid the driver from view.

Rewl lay on top of her, chuckling, like this was fun and games. He squeezed her waist tighter. "Simmer, shimmer. I just want to ask you some questions."

Shaylinn stopped struggling, and Rewl released her. She slid over against the opposite door and tried to open it, but she didn't have a SimTag anymore.

"Jumping out of a moving car ... much more dangerous than some quick words with me. I'm just pointing that out."

Shaylinn's body trembled all over. "Let me out."

"First tell me where you're staying now. Levi just up and moved away without telling Bender a thing."

Oh no. What if he followed her? What if he already knew where the cabin was? "He doesn't owe Bender any explanation. Bender doesn't own us."

"No, but he invested in you people. Levi owes him."

She wished Jordan were here. "You'll have to take that up with Levi. I don't know anything about it."

Rewl stared at her, ran his tongue over his creepy teeth. "Then why don't you explain why you've been delivering messages that are off-grid. Where did you get them?"

Her heart thudded inside her. "I wrote them myself."

"This isn't Levi's way of recruiting his own people?"

This question brought a different kind of fear over Shaylinn. "No! Levi knows nothing about this. I just wanted to write to people. To encourage them."

Rewl chuckled and slid his fingers over her knee. "Convince me."

She pulled her knees closer to the door. Maybe if she let him read one of the messages she'd yet to deliver, he'd let her go. But he had no right to boss her. "You don't scare me." Such a lie.

"Which is why your voice trembles every time you speak. Are you pairing up with Omar?"

His question made Shaylinn gasp. "You're rude."

"And you're prude. Ba-boom. Poetry, shimmer. It's a gift." He slid closer to her on the seat. He smelled spicy and sweaty, and Shaylinn wanted to get away. "Look, Shaylinn — that's such a pearly name, you know it? I don't want to hurt you. But you've been poking around, stepping into parties you haven't been invited to. I need to know why. If you don't tell me ..." He shook his head and grabbed her knee again.

Shaylinn couldn't get any closer to the door, so she pushed his hand off her knee. "I'm trying to help people, that's all. Stop touching me."

He chuckled and moved back a little. "I've seen you and Kendall Collin make deliveries together."

"Once," Shaylinn said, "just so I would know how to do it."

"I don't trust Kendall Collin. I've seen her talking to enforcers. Getting picked up in fancy cars from City Hall. Plus, she was helping Chord."

The name sent another jolt of fear through Shaylinn. "What's so bad about that?"

"Chord was a traitor. Making things up about Bender. Spreading lies to everyone. Trying to help Otley."

Could that be true? Was Chord's message to Ruston a lie?

Rewl chuckled and stretched his arm over the back of the seat. "Not so sure anymore, are you? You thought you could trust Kendall. You know she's after Omar, don't you? I've seen her coming and going from his place."

Tears flooded Shaylinn's eyes. *Don't believe him!* "You're a liar. I want to get out now. Please stop the car." Shaylinn examined the car door again, looking for some kind of emergency latch.

"In a minute, shimmer. Look, you need to stop with the messages. Even if they're harmless, they're confusing people, and Bender doesn't like it. So why don't you move into that glossy apartment we got you, relax, play, and come dancing with me tonight."

She watched him warily. If he tried to touch her again, she'd punch him. "I don't think I'm a very good dancer."

"I know Levi told you to stay away from us Safe Landers, but Levi doesn't know something about me. See, I'm not infected."

More lies. Shaylinn pursed her lips.

"Have you heard of Naturals?" Rewl asked. "Some people call them ghosts."

Ghosts? Shaylinn frowned, trying to remember where she'd heard that term. It seemed like something Jordan and Levi had been talking about.

"It means I'm not a regular Safe Lander. I wasn't born in the MC. I wasn't raised in the boarding school. I grew up with the rebels in the basements. I have parents, like you."

A chill ran over Shaylinn. "There are people here who have parents?"

"Everyone has parents, shimmer, whether they admit it or not. I just happen to have been raised by mine. Bender is my dad."

Dad. A term she'd never heard a Safe Lander use. But if Rewl was Bender's son, of course he'd claim his father's innocence. But what if he *was* innocent? Maybe Chord had been working for Otley. Maybe Rewl and Bender were the good people.

She needed to speak to Kendall.

"I like you, Shaylinn," Rewl said, his voice low. He scooted close, right up next to her, leaving only an inch of air between them. "You're kind and beautiful."

Why did she only ever hear she was beautiful from drunk men or men she didn't like? "I'm pregnant," she said, hoping that would make Rewl stop saying such things.

His breathy laugh warmed her ear. "Yeah, I don't mind."

This confused her. What did he want? Only to dance? "I want to get out now."

Rewl sighed and leaned back against the seat. "Okay, femme." He rapped his knuckles against the dark glass separating the front seat from the back. The car slowed to a stop. "Thanks for the talk, shimmer. Think about dancing sometime. I'll find you."

Shaylinn's door slid open, and she jumped out without a backward glance. The car sped away. Tears flooded her eyes, relief that she was free.

She was standing in the parking lot of the Paradise, almost exactly where Rewl had grabbed her. Should she tell anyone what had happened?

What if Rewl had been telling the truth? Maybe he was a good guy. And if she stopped delivering the messages, maybe Rewl would leave her alone.

She started to cry. She'd been so stupid to think she could make a difference, do something good. All she'd done was put herself in danger. And now she had to be careful getting home because Rewl could be watching. If she was going to keep this up, she needed to find a new way to and from the cabin. A way that Rewl couldn't follow.

CHAPTER
13

"Try it," Zane said.

Omar tapped "voice" on his flexible Wyndo wristband, then said, "The Owl sees. Trust the Owl." His voice came out magnified, deep and distorted, from speakers Zane had installed in his new helmet and gloves. Perfect! He grinned at Zane. "It works!"

"Of course it works," Zane said. "Now toggle back to me."

Omar tapped "nest" and said, "Owl to the nest. Do you hear me?"

"Excellent." Zane's voice came through the SimTalk implant in Omar's ear as simply as if he had used it to tap anyone.

They were in a secret room in the basement of Zane's house in the Midlands, a room filled with computers and guns — both killers and stunners. Omar was sitting on a chair before a green wall, which Zane said would enable him to project any image behind Omar. Across the tiny room, Zane sat before a GlassTop desk. A Wyndo wall screen covered the length of the wall above him. Zane had assured Omar that this was the ideal location for their base of operations — or "the nest," as he'd been calling it. The Owl was about to make his first broadcast to the Safe Lands.

"We ready, then?" Omar asked.

"I think so. I can only hack the ColorCast for thirty seconds at a time before they can track me. We can't let them find us, so if I have to, I'll pull the feed early. Read your lines from the Wyndo wall screen, and I'll do the rest. Now put your voice back on."

Omar tapped "voice" again, and when he said, "Ready," it came out amplified and deep. His heart was racing, but it was pure adrenaline. When Renzor and Otley saw this broadcast, they would be furious.

"Okay, Owl," Zane said. "You're live in three, two, one." He pointed at Omar and nodded.

Omar took a deep breath and read from the wall screen. "This is not an error. The Messenger Owl has truth to deliver to the people of the Safe Lands. Truth brings freedom. Listen well. Liberations are not filmed live. They are prerecorded and edited so you hear only what the Guild wants you to hear. This ColorCast is a tool for the Safe Lands Guild to tell lies. The Owl speaks the truth. There are not nine lives, but one. Make yours count."

"Done." Zane jumped up, fists raised in the air. "That was perfect!"

Omar relaxed and pulled off his mask, unable to stop smiling. The Owl was real now — to the people of the Safe Lands, at least. A real vigilante. A messenger of truth.

"We'll do that every day at different times so they won't know when to expect it," Zane said. "Messenger Owl. Stimming brilliant."

Omar felt free and worthy, like he was making a contribution for the first time in his life, like he mattered. Only one thing nagged him. "If this mysterious messenger person has been sending notes to people beside me, the enforcers might go after him, thinking he's the Owl."

"Then we'd better find out who he is and warn him," Zane said. "Rewl's in charge of sending Bender's messages. He's probably already looking into this mysterious messenger's business."

"But we're not telling Rewl about the Owl."

"No way. Rewl and Bender can't know. I can't trust them anymore."

"Agreed." Omar still wasn't sure what to say about Levi if he ran into Rewl or Bender. He was supposed to say that Levi made other arrangements, but that just seemed like fighting words. At least now

Omar had his own way of fighting. He could do so much as the Owl that Omar Strong could never do. "That was fun — the broadcast. But is it enough?"

"It's a good start. People are going to see it on their Wyndos and wonder what just happened. Plus you're going to do a graffiti patrol each day to keep the marks fresh, and one sighting, right?"

Zane wanted Omar to be seen in person somewhere every day. "I'm doing Midlands West today," Omar said.

"Good. But it will get old fast. Safe Landers are all about the next big thing. We have to keep this, you know, new and different. So let's talk about where we're taking this thing. Creating doubt and unrest in the people is great, but I know what it's like to live here. People might doubt the Guild, but besides the rebel groups, no one does anything about it. The Owl speaks to everyone, and that will unify doubts. But we need to build on it each week. Toward something huge."

"An assassination? Renzor or Otley?" Omar would love to see either go down.

"That would certainly get people's attention," Zane said. "You going to do it? Because as much as I hate them both, I could never go out and kill someone — unless they were shooting at me first. I'm just being honest here."

Omar wanted to say that he could, but it would be a lie. His one act of aggression against Levi still haunted him. And Levi hadn't bothered to have anyone fix his nose, so his face constantly reminded Omar of how he'd betrayed everyone.

"Lonn was always saying the rebels need to unite," Zane said. "He used to say the different groups were like flocks of birds. We were all pecking, but if we pecked at the same time, we might actually make a difference."

Made sense. "That kind of talk is great for rallying people, but someone needs to be in charge for that to work, and Bender can't be the guy in charge." Even if Bender believed that as enforcer general he could do some good, Otley would betray him. Bender was a fool to think he could trust that animal. "We need to use our heads. We need a lynchpin."

"What's that?" Zane asked.

"It's a fastener that keeps a wheel from falling off the axle — on a vehicle. The point is, a lynchpin is tiny compared to a vehicle. But without it, the vehicle is useless. We need to find something small that, when taken out, the lack of it will cause the Safe Lands to fall."

"Like taking a can from the bottom of a stack of cans?"

"Exactly." The mere idea of finding the right thing thrilled Omar. "So what can't people live without?"

"Same as everywhere. Water. Food."

"And where does all that come from?"

"Water from the dam. Food ... from the Lowlands, I guess."

The Lowlands. Omar had never been there. "Sounds like we've got some investigating to do. If we can figure out how to stop the water or the food, people will get desperate — the government included."

"It's worth a try," Zane said, spinning on his chair to face his GlassTop. "I'll ask around."

That night Omar went out and painted more graffiti. When he returned to the nest, Zane was limping from green screen to GlassTop.

"We've got a problem," Zane said. "I tapped Rewl and asked about this mystery messenger. It's Shaylinn."

Hearing her name made Omar tremble. "That's mad. How can it be Shaylinn?"

"She delivered about twenty messages this week. Started at the Larkspur and worked her way across downtown. Spends a lot of time at Kendall Collin's apartment. Rewl said he picked her up a few days ago and tried to scare her into stopping, but she's still at it."

"He 'picked her up'?" What did *that* mean? "How did he scare her?"

"Didn't say. But he did say she makes her deliveries at night."

Omar couldn't believe it. Shay wandering the Safe Lands in the middle of the night? How could Jordan not know? "I shouldn't have used her name. 'Messenger,' I mean. I put her in danger." Rewl must think that Shay was the Owl.

"Nah. She did that to herself before you came along. Why don't you drop by the Belleview tomorrow night? Rewl said she gets there about one a.m., though he can't figure out where she's coming from. Wants to know where Levi's got everybody stashed. Rewl says she goes into theater nine when she's done, so she must be coming into the city through the storm drains. You should warn her that Rewl is trying to track her. I'd hate for her to run into him underground."

"If she didn't listen to Rewl, why would she listen to me?"

"You're the guy from home. The daddy of her babies. And, if she still won't listen, you could always tell Jordan."

"Yeah, she'd love that," Omar said. "But you're right. That would end it."

The next night, Omar waited in an alley across the street from the Belleview. Sure enough, at 1:06 a.m. Shay came walking down the street. Alone. She'd changed so much since they'd come here. She was no longer the chubby shadow of his cousin Penelope. She might only be fourteen, but she didn't look it. That hair alone would turn any man's head. And if she were out walking alone every night, any creep could grab her. Rewl already had.

He didn't like the idea of Rewl watching her, much less "picking her up" and trying to scare her. She should at least put her hair up under a hat or something.

He still couldn't believe he was going to be a father. What was he going to say to her about that? Did he have to say anything? Couldn't he wait until the kids got here?

Why was he such a coward?

The moment she entered the building, Omar crossed the street. Apartments in the Midlands weren't like those in the Highlands. No doormen. Some had SimLocks on the entry door, but most were broken and never got repaired. He shuddered to think what things might be like in the Lowlands.

Omar slipped inside the Belleview in time to see Shay's boots turn on the landing halfway up the first flight of stairs. He crept behind her, not eager to see Kendall again after what Red had told her at the train station. Every time he turned around he seemed to face a new humiliation.

This too shall pass.

He smiled at the words from Shay's note. Her words had done him good, yet here he came to put an end to her good deeds. It didn't seem right.

He peeked around the landing and saw Shay standing outside Kendall's door. He couldn't blame her for wanting to do something good in this place. In fact, he admired her for trying.

When the door swung open, Omar ran for it, not bothering to be quiet. Halfway through the doorway, Shay turned, eyes wide. Kendall stood behind her, staring at him too.

"Omar?" Shay's eyebrows sank low over her eyes. They were sculpted now where they used to be thick.

"Let's get inside, shall we?" He put his hand on her waist and walked into Kendall's apartment, pulling Shay along. She felt odd in his arms. Thicker where Red had been all bones. Healthy. Nice.

"What are you doing here?" Shay asked, looking from him to Kendall and back. "Do you come here a lot?"

Oh. She thought something was going on between him and Kendall. Maybe that was good. Then if something did happen...

Curse his foul mind. Why couldn't he stay focused? He was here to help Shay, not himself.

A low squawk made him jump. He'd forgotten that Kendall had a bird. He walked straight for the window where a black, art deco wire cage with a scalloped top sat on a narrow table. The bird was small and bright like the colors of his paints. He had a tantalizing turquoise belly, a custard-cream head, a purple moon beak, and black-and-white-striped wings. "Hello, angel," Omar said in a soft voice. "Aren't you beautiful?"

"He's a boy," Kendall said. "His name is Basil."

"You've never been here before?" Shaylinn asked, her words tinged with hope.

Omar kept his eyes on the bird. "No." He wanted to look at her, but he was thankful this fluttery little distraction gave him an excuse to gather his courage first. "He's a parrot?"

"A parakeet, actually," Kendall said. "I was told he was a *budgie*, but … I don't really know what that means."

"Budgie. Budgie. Basil's a budgie," the bird said, his voice soft and raspy.

A thrill ran through Omar. "He talks!"

"What time is it? Give me a kiss. Tch tch tch." The bird's beak barely moved, but he jerked his head from side to side in quick movements.

Omar laughed, which only egged Basil on.

"Budgie. Basil's a budgie. Give us a kiss. Tch tch tch. Juice off, Lawten. Juice off! You're a shell! Tch tch tch."

That got Omar's attention. He straightened and focused his wide-eyed surprise on Kendall. "*Lawten*? As in Task Director General Lawten Renzor?"

Kendall shrugged like it didn't matter that the bird had insulted the ruler of the Safe Lands. "He picks up most anything he hears. It doesn't have to be from me."

"Sure." Omar grinned and tapped the cage with his fingers. The bird's glassy eyes twitched at the sound. "Where'd you get him?"

"He was a gift from … um, I mean, the Safe Lands Guild gave him to me to make up for taking Elyot."

"Who's Elyot?" Omar asked.

Shaylinn stepped beside Omar. "He's her — "

"It's doesn't matter," Kendall said, shooting Shaylinn a look that seemed to say, "Shut up." Then she turned her bossy expression his way. "What are you doing here, Omar?"

"Yeah." Shay crossed her arms and mirrored Kendall's angst.

"I need to talk to you about the messages," he said.

Shay stared at him as if she might deny knowing what he was talking about. Omar stared back — at burnt umber eyes with specks of cinnamon — and Shay was the first to look away. She sighed and sat down on a kitchen chair. "Rewl talked to you, didn't he?"

"Yeah," Omar lied. "He's worried about you. And so am I. You're supposed to stay in the cabin. Enforcers are looking for you."

"I look different since Red did my hair. They don't recognize me."

"You don't look *that* different."

She flinched, as if his comment had been a slap.

"Budgie. Basil's a budgie. You're a shell!"

"Hey, I'm sorry." Omar pulled out a chair and sat beside her. Kendall walked around the table, watching them. "I didn't mean that as an insult. Shay, look at me."

She did, but there was fire in her eyes. "I'm going crazy locked up in that cabin, Omar. I want to do something that helps people. My messages — "

"Are wonderful," he said. "I got one."

She blinked long and dark lashes, and, when she opened her eyes, she was looking at her lap.

"Shay, you have to be more careful. Rewl has been following you, trying to figure out where Levi moved everyone. Plus, Rewl ... he's different. I don't trust him and I think — "

"I'll be more careful. I'll wear a hood or something."

"I'll help her find a better disguise," Kendall said.

Omar wanted to tell Kendall to stay out of this, but before he got his chance, Shay said, "Please don't tell anyone."

Her plea melted him. "I'm just worried about you. I don't think it's safe for you to — "

"Don't take this away from me, Omar. I haven't told anyone about you."

Me? He frowned and searched her eyes. "What about me?"

"The *Messenger Owl* speaks the truth?" She pursed her lips and cocked one eyebrow.

Omar's lips parted in a gaping stare. How did she know? He'd only done one broadcast.

"You're the Owl?" Kendall sat down in the chair on Omar's right. "But you're so young!"

"Uh …" Omar ran his hand through his hair. "How did you know, Shay?"

She grinned, and her whole face shone like a ColorCast model. "You love owls. And you got the wetsuit from me, silly. It turned out gorgeous. But how did you change your voice?"

"And how did you hack the ColorCast like that?" Kendall asked.

"Budgie. Budgie. Basil's a budgie," the bird rasped.

Omar rubbed the scar on the bridge of his nose. This was terrible! If Shaylinn knew, who else? Kendall now. And Basil the budgie.

"Hey." Shay pulled his hand away from his face and continued to hold it. "You always rub your scar when you're upset. Someday you'll have to tell me why."

Omar pulled his hand from hers. He'd never told anyone what his father had said that day. He certainly wasn't going to tell a girl.

"I didn't mean to upset you," Shay said. "I didn't tell anyone about you being the Owl, and I won't. I promise. Who would I tell?"

He looked pointedly at Kendall, who grinned like this was all a big joke, so he looked back to Shay. "Naomi, Jordan, Jemma, Levi. Levi can't know, Shay. Please."

"I think he'd be proud of you," Shay said. "You're helping."

"Oh, no. You don't know Levi. He wouldn't see it that way. He's pretty straight-lined."

Shaylinn's lips curved into a small smile. "And you're a curvy line?"

Yeah, right. "I'm a knot."

She giggled, which made everything about her shine. "I like knots."

"What time is it? Give me a kiss. Tch tch tch."

"Oh, be quiet, you!" Kendall walked to the cage and pulled a blanket over it.

Shay kept her gaze on Kendall. "I need to write those messages, Omar. It's important to me. I need something to do."

The fabric! This was his fault. "I'm sorry I haven't brought you your fabric. I got some. I just never brought it to you."

The confession brought her focus back to him. "I'd like to have it."

He needed to say more. To make everything right, somehow, even though it was impossible. "Look, Shay ... I'm sorry. About ..." He reached for her, toward her stomach, then pulled his hand back. "What I'm trying to say is ... I've really messed up my life. And everybody else's. I've been thinking that those ... kids. They're probably the only kids I'm ever going to have. So, uh ... Please, protect them. Stay in the cabin? I'll bring you anything you want, I swear."

Her brows sank as if she were considering his offer.

Please say yes, Shay.

"Will you deliver my messages? As the Owl?"

"Sure," he said before thinking it through. What would Zane have to say about that? Likely something about fingerprints. "You'll have to wear gloves when you write them. There can't be any fingerprints."

"I have been wearing gloves." She sat up straight and bounced in her chair, proud of herself. "I'm smarter than you think, Omar. But if you'll bring me fabric and deliver my messages, I'll stay in the cabin. For you."

For him. He sighed and smiled, relieved that he'd convinced her to listen. "Thank you."

She leaned over and kissed his cheek. "No, thank *you*."

Emotions raced through him. Not a desire for her body, but something else. Something foreign. He wanted to please her. To impress her. To bring her joy. To make her proud of him. None of it seemed at all likely to happen, but with an icy certainty that surprised him, he knew he would die trying.

He was going to die anyway. He may as well make the time he had left worthwhile.

CHAPTER
14

As Zane had suggested, Mason text tapped Ciddah on Sunday to thank her for coming with him Friday. Then he waited until Monday to ask her to dinner the following Saturday. She said yes and challenged him to come up with at least four non-argumentative conversation topics.

So Mason spent the rest of the week brainstorming topics and planning a way to trump last week's outing. Would she expect something similar? He specified dinner this time, not an entire day of entertainment. Might that disappoint her? And what might it take to get her to open up about her time in the boarding school?

Mason had settled on ordering a meal to be delivered from Le Nuit, a fancy Highlands restaurant. The chef owed Zane a favor, and for whatever reason, Zane was willing to donate his favor to Mason's cause. Once the meal was taken care of, Mason went out and rented a fancy black suit. It looked similar to the suits men had worn before the Great Pandemic, except that the jacket only reached his waist and the shirt had a ruffly red fringe than ran down the front. He also bought some ornate dishes, a vase, and a tablecloth so that he could take their meal to the roof for an evening picnic.

He figured red roses and picnics was a safe theme to repeat, and the roof would offer the opportunity for private conversation away from the MiniComm she'd left in his apartment.

Friday morning before his task shift at Pharmco, he was sitting on the couch in his apartment eating a plate of scrambled eggs for breakfast and wondering whether or not Ciddah's friends would be a safe conversation topic if she mentioned *Lawten,* when there was a knock at his door.

"S.L.E., open up."

Mason stared at the door for a moment, then got up and looked out the peephole. Enforcers. At least three of them standing in the hall outside his apartment.

What did they want? Should he answer the door? Pretend not to be home?

An enforcer pounded on the door again, which made Mason jump. "Mr. Elias, we tracked your SimTag and know you're home. Open the door."

SimTag, right. Since he'd been about to leave to task his shift at Pharmco, he'd already showered this morning and used the small round adhesive bandage to attach his SimTag.

Mason opened the door. "Yes?"

"Safe Lands Enforcers, sir," an enforcer said. Bron, according to the name on his patch. He looked the definition of "brawn" as well with a muscular build and a short beard. "We have a warrant to search your apartment and your person."

A warrant. Mason stepped back from the door, and the men filed inside. There were five enforcers and a plain-clothed bald man with brown SimArt "hair" that looked more like some kind of helmet.

General Otley was the last to enter, making Bron look like a child. The man had to be six and a half feet tall with shoulders that rivaled the old bull Mason used to feed each day back in Glenrock. He wore yellow contacts and had several lip and eyebrow piercings, including a golden tusk through his nasal septum. Mason could barely see the number eight that glowed on his cheek beneath his bushy moustache and beard.

A surge of anger and fear twisted Mason's stomach. He gritted his teeth in the presence of the man who'd killed his father, his uncle, and Papa Eli. Yet he didn't dare speak, knowing he had no power in this moment. Otley always had the power.

Four of the enforcers instantly began their search: two went to his bedroom on the other side of his apartment; one rushed to the living room, which was on the opposite side of the wall that divided the living space from the kitchen; and the last remained in the kitchen, not far from the apartment entry. This left Bron, the man with the SimArt hair, and Otley standing inside the open entry door.

Otley jerked his head toward Mason's kitchen table. "Sit, little rat."

Mason walked to the chair and sat. Kitchen cupboards slammed as the enforcer opened one after another, rummaging through Mason's meager possessions.

"Mr. Elias, sir, my name is Webb Bron. I'm an investigator with the Safe Lands Enforcers. We're looking into the theft of pharmaceutical products that disappeared from the City Hall Pharmco last Wednesday. We have reason to suspect your involvement."

"Seriously?" Mason said. "Why me?"

"The meds were stolen the day you started at the City Hall Pharmco," Bron said.

"And that makes me guilty?"

Bron pulled out a chair and sat beside Mason. "That makes you a suspect."

"Well, I didn't take anything."

Another kitchen cupboard slammed and dishes clanked together.

"We'll see, Mr. Elias." Bron waved the bald man over. "This is Reed Yarel. He's an enforcer field medic. He's authorized to test your blood."

"For what?" The bald man set his case on the table and opened it. "What was stolen from Pharmco, anyway?" And was it really worth a search of his apartment?

"ACT treatments."

177

That was all? "I don't have the thin plague," Mason said. "Why would I steal treatment?"

This gave Bron pause. He looked to Otley.

"He's an outsider," Otley said, looming over them like a monster about to pounce. "Outsiders are usually clean."

"I see," Bron said. "Well, a blood test will confirm that."

How could Mason get out of this? "I don't consent."

Bron's eyes narrowed. "You have something to hide?"

"The thin plague is blood-borne," Mason said, watching the enforcer in the living room pull cushions off the couch. "How can I be certain you haven't come to infect me with the virus?"

"Mr. Elias," Yarel, the enforcer medic, said. "I am a professional and quite capable of taking a blood sample without contaminating my patient. If you're concerned, inspect my equipment yourself." Yarel handed Mason a standard blood test kit, still in its sanitized packaging. Mason supposed there was no way for that to be contaminated.

"I still don't understand why you need to test my blood."

"It's standard procedure in a theft of this type," Bron said. "To verify that you haven't used the stolen goods."

Then there was no option but to let his blood prove his innocence. Mason nodded, and Yarel proceeded to take a sample of Mason's blood and test it with a blood meter. Mason perceived nothing subversive in the medic's actions. He used the same tools when he worked in the Surrogacy Center, so he was able to understand the readings when the machine finally stopped whirring.

The test was negative.

Though he knew this already, relief filled him to see Yarel corroborate his word.

"No sign of ACT, General Otley," Yarel said. "He's stim free as well. And there is no indication of the thin plague."

Otley growled and paced to the table. "My turn, little rat. Hook him up."

Medic Yarel removed another device and held it out to Mason. "SimTag, please?"

Mason froze, terrified that things were about to go badly. The bandage holding his SimTag in place was small, but if Yarel saw it...

Mason twisted his hand so the bandage faced him, then reached out and set his fist against the screen, trying to look calm, praying Yarel had no reason to inspect his implant location. Might a question be distraction enough? "What does this do?"

"It's a lie detector, Mr. Elias," Yarel said, eyes blessedly focused on the machine and not Mason's hand. "So be sure to tell the truth."

Mason pulled back his hand and clasped it with his other, then put them on his lap under the table. *Thanks, God.* He eyed the little black box, curious how it worked. It consisted of the SimPad and three tiny bulbs that were dark.

Otley stepped up to the table on Mason's left. "When did you leave the Pharmco last night?"

"A little after six o'clock, just after we closed." Mason looked at the lie detector. A green light flashed in the bulb on the far right.

"And you went where?" Otley asked.

"Here. To my apartment. And I haven't left." The green light flashed again. Green must mean truth. Mason stopped looking at the lie detector. He knew he was telling the truth, after all. Instead he glanced at the enforcer who was rummaging through his refrigerator, saw him put something in his mouth. He was eating Mason's food?

Otley slapped his hand on the tabletop. "Pay attention, rat. You've been here since returning from task yesterday?"

"I have."

Otley's yellow eyes pinned Mason. "Can anyone verify that?"

"The doorman."

"The doorman can verify that you were in your apartment all night?" Otley raised one eyebrow. "Was the doorman with you?"

"Of course not. I spoke with him when I passed through the lobby. Probably around six fifteen."

"You know Ciddah Rourke?" Otley asked.

Her name made him flush with the memory of their kiss. "Yes, she's my — was my task director in the SC."

"Have you ever paired up with Miss Rourke?" The question was intrusive, but with Otley's growling voice, it seemed downright mean.

"No." For some reason Mason looked at the lie detector. Green.

"Miss Rourke claims otherwise."

What? "She does?" Why would Ciddah say such a thing?

"She said that you and she are almost lifers."

She did? "After one date?" Mason doubted any man was *that* good at wooing a woman. "Did you use the lie detector on her?"

Bron chuckled and covered his mouth with his hand.

"Let me ask you this, Mr. Elias," Otley said. "Do you know a Droe Rivan or Losira Kent?"

"Never heard of them."

"They're Ciddah Rourke's donors," Otley said. "You would call them parents."

A chill gripped Mason's arms. What was Ciddah up to?

"Did you know that the ACT treatment differs per patient?" Otley said. "What I take and what Medic Yarel takes are different."

Mason considered this. "Because of your different body weights?"

"Partly," Yarel said. "And also because each person has an infinitely different strain. The virus mutates within us, and depending on our DNA, it affects us differently."

"The materials stolen from the Pharmco are a match for Losira Kent and Droe Rivan," Otley said.

Ciddah's parents were sick? Possibly sicker than most Safe Landers? Emotions fought for precedence in Mason's heart. He felt bad that her parents were suffering. But she had reassigned Mason to the pharmacy the day the vials went missing. It was too convenient to be mere coincidence. Every time he got close to that woman, she did something to push him away. This was his own fault. He'd never been a regular man getting to know a regular woman. He'd been trying to get information from Ciddah, so how did she keep managing to use him first? "It sounds like you should be questioning Ciddah."

"We have. She claims to know nothing about any of this. And she has an alibi for last night." Otley smiled, and his teeth were surprisingly white. "For the *entire* night."

That didn't mean she'd been with a man. It didn't. And ... "Did you use this thing on Ciddah and her alibi? Maybe they're the ones lying."

"Oh, I don't think so, little rat. I think *you're* lying. I think Ciddah told you her donors weren't doing well, that they were too sick to task and planned to go into hiding, and that they needed to take treatment with them. I think you wanted to help them — to help her. Why not admit it?"

"I admit nothing." Mason was angry now but reminded himself of his company. General Otley was not an honest man. This could be some sort of trap. But that theory didn't ease his fury.

Otley circled around half of the kitchen table until he was standing directly across from Mason. "Do you care for Ciddah?"

"Of course. She's a nice ... person." When she wasn't yelling at him for defending his people. Or framing him for theft.

Otley leaned on the table with both hands, which made it creak and tip toward him. "Do you *love her*?"

Seriously? "How is such a question relevant to stolen pharmaceuticals?"

"It goes to motive, little rat. A man will do anything for the woman he loves."

Even in the Safe Lands? "Well, I *like* Ciddah very much. But I wouldn't steal — "

"Do you love her — yes or no?"

Love. How could he love a woman he couldn't trust? "No," Mason said, determined that it was the truth.

But the bulb on the far left flashed red.

Mason's eyes bulged, staring at the tiny pinprick of crimson. How could a machine know something he didn't even know himself?

Otley laughed and straightened, and the table creaked back to a level state. "Surprised? Femmes will mess with your head if you're not careful. Now, tell me you stole those missing vials, and we'll be done here."

"I didn't."

Green light.

"Did you give them to Ciddah when you were tasking there?"

"No."

"Did she ask you to leave them somewhere?"

"No."

"Did she tell you she planned to steal them herself?"

"No."

Otley walked back to Mason's side. "If she came to you tomorrow and asked you to steal them, would you?"

"No, I wouldn't." Green. Good. Mason stared up at Otley.

"All right, rat. All right."

An enforcer walked up and handed Otley the MiniComm Ciddah had placed in Mason's apartment. Otley held it up for Mason to see. "Do you know what this is?"

"It's a MiniComm." Green light.

"And what does a MiniComm do?"

"Records?" The center bulb flashed orange. "What's that mean, an orange light?"

"It means you're guessing," Otley said. "That you don't know either way."

"That's incredible! How does this device work?"

"Focus, little rat," Otley said. "How did the MiniComm get here?"

"I don't know." Red light.

Otley raised his eyebrows and waited.

Mason released a long sigh. "Ciddah put it there. At least I think she did. I didn't see her do it."

"So she was here? When?"

"The morning after Kendall Collin gave birth."

"This has been here for over a month and you knew it and you left it be? Why?"

Mason leaned his elbows on the table. "I didn't want Ciddah to get in trouble." Red light.

"Try again."

"I don't know." Red light.

"Third time rings bells, rat."

"Because I didn't want whoever was listening to know I'd found it." Green.

"Why not?"

"Because it would make me look … subversive. Like I had something to hide." Green.

"Do you?"

Mason thought about how to answer that. "Don't we all?"

That was the end of the lie detector questioning. The search went on for another half hour. Mason sat at the table watching. He had so few things, he didn't know what was taking them so long. Otley asked him about the gloves Levi had given him to hold his SimTag when he wasn't at work and why he had two handheld Wyndos, to which Mason answered, "Winter is coming and I wanted an upgrade."

Otley merely grunted.

When they finally left, carting out bags of "evidence," Mason went to look for his things and found that his portable Wyndos and the gloves were gone. If anything else was missing, he couldn't remember.

He put the couch back together and sat down, staring at the dark Wyndo wall screen. "Wyndo: power. Grid: locate: Ciddah Rourke: ID#7 – 69 – 23."

The Safe Lands logo rotated while the Wyndo worked, then Ciddah's face filled the left side of the screen. It was a nice picture. She'd been smiling and looking at the camera, which made it feel like she was smiling at him. He glanced at the map to the right of her picture. It showed downtown Highlands. The pulsing orange dot showed Ciddah's location was in City Hall. Text to the side said: "Surrogacy Center."

He looked to her face again and fell back against the couch cushions. He should have known better. It seemed as though she had betrayed him yet again.

CHAPTER
15

From the moment Otley left his apartment until the time of Saturday night's date, Mason agonized over how to handle the situation with Ciddah. If it was true, and the enforcers really had questioned Ciddah first, she must know that they would have come after him. Should he tap her and cancel? Confront her over the Wyndo? Or continue with the date as planned, pretend to know nothing? Did she even expect him to show up? Maybe she thought he'd be in prison. What if he went down to her apartment to meet her and she was off with her *alibi*, celebrating Mason's demise?

Her alibi had better not be Lawten.

One consolation in all this was that Zane's off-grid Wyndo couldn't be tracked. The auto-delete feature cleared the memory instantly after every use. Mason had taken a trip to the Midlands last night to warn everyone not to tap him at that number anymore, and Zane had given him a new off-grid Wyndo and an emergency ghoulie tag in a tiny metal box. Then he'd come back with Mason to check his place for any new MiniComms that might have been left by Otley's people. Zane had found two, so that, at least, was something Mason needn't worry about now.

Ciddah was still a problem.

Since he'd already arranged most of the evening, he decided to pretend nothing was amiss — at first. Rather than going to the roof, now that the MiniComms were gone, Mason set his kitchen table — moved to the living room — for dinner, and put on the suit he'd rented. His only post-interrogation purchase was a dozen red roses, one of which he would give to her. If he could get her into his apartment thinking all was well, he'd have a better chance of conducting his own interrogation.

Tonight Mason would finally get some answers from Ciddah Rourke.

When the time came, he went down to her apartment and rang her bell. The door opened, and Ciddah smiled at him and stepped out, resplendent in a short, fitted red dress and matching high-heeled shoes. Even her lips had been painted to match.

Red, he decided at that very moment, was Ciddah's color.

Her gaze took him in as well. "Walls, you look good! Oh, thank you." She took his proffered rose into her apartment, and again Mason heard water running as Ciddah most likely put the flower in a vase.

He reminded himself that her beauty was irrelevant. He must maintain control of the evening's events and discover once and for all if Ciddah Rourke could be trusted.

She returned and closed the door. "Are you going to tell me where we're going yet? Or is it a surprise like last time?"

"We're going to my apartment." Mason offered her his hand, and she took hold of it, her nearness shrouding him in the scent of vanilla and cinnamon. That and her touch made him want to pretend that Otley's visit had never happened. As they made their way to the elevator, Mason considered that this evening would be harder than he had originally anticipated.

She tugged on his hand. "And what are we going to do at your apartment?"

Her suggestive tone strengthened Mason's resolve and reminded him that this woman was very likely his enemy. "Eat and talk."

"About safe topics?"

He thought about how to answer that without scaring her away. "Perhaps."

They got on the elevator and Mason pressed the button for five. It was difficult, trying to remain calm in light of Otley's interrogation. He wanted to confront her now, yet her touch — merely being in her presence — completely flustered him. So he reminded himself that he did not yet have proof that she was guilty of any wrongdoing. At this point, everything was circumstantial.

Yet the window of doubt for her innocence was microscopic.

"I've missed you in the SC," she said as they got off on the fifth floor. "Zolan is capable, but I have to tell him everything twice. Plus he's older than me, and I don't think he likes working under a female."

"Is he noncompliant?" Mason asked.

"No, it's just his attitude, I guess. He's not friendly, like you."

Friendly. Little did she know he was leading her into his cage. He opened the door to his apartment and held it for her. She walked inside and oohed at the sight of his preparations. It had taken him all afternoon, but he'd turned his living room into a private restaurant. The table was covered in the white tablecloth he'd planned to use as a blanket on the roof. He'd set out the special dishes and filled the vase with the remaining eleven red roses for the table, found orchestra music to play on his Wyndo wall screen, and programmed the picture Wyndos, which usually looked out onto the Safe Lands, to show a thick forest. That likely made him feel more at home than it did her, but she seemed pleased.

"Did you cook too?" she asked.

"I did not. I felt it unwise to risk my own cooking skills on such a special occasion. If you'd like me to cook for you some other time, I'm happy to oblige, though you might consider having something ready to eat in your apartment when you get home, just in case things were to go badly."

"I can't imagine they would. Mason, I don't think it's possible for you to fail at anything."

He tried not to let her words gratify him, but his pride absorbed her compliment like a sponge did water. He pulled out her chair and helped her sit.

Her gaze followed him as he walked to his seat. "So what are we eating tonight?"

"First we have an appetizer of roasted red beet hummus. Then a potato leek soup, followed by persimmon caprese salad. Then for our main course, I am serving butternut squash and pear ravioli with rosemary sauce. And then, if you are still hungry, a maple and cranberry crème brulée."

"That sounds amazing. Where did you get it?"

"Le Nuit."

She gasped and scooted to the edge of her chair, her electric-blue eyes practically glowing. "How? They only seat ten couples a night. I don't believe they let you order takeout."

Mason shrugged off her question. "Whether or not you believe does not alter the facts." A comment that Mason felt encapsulated most of their differences.

He served the dinner course by course. It was agonizing to wait so long to broach the topic of the ACT meds, but he had put a lot of effort into making this night perfect. He figured, the happier she was, the more apt she might be to answer truthfully.

When the dessert course came and Ciddah was humming delightedly over her crème brulée, Mason attacked.

"Ciddah, I have some questions to ask you, and I would be very thankful if you told me the entire truth."

"If I can," she said, taking another bite.

An interesting reply. Could there be some reason she'd lie? He hadn't considered that someone might be forcing her to act. "I find you to be an intriguing woman. You're intelligent, beautiful, and kind. Yet there have been moments of contradiction that tell me my initial observations of you were false and you're only pretending to be kind, or," he added in light of her comment, "that someone has asked you to do something contrary to your nature."

She was staring at him now, her spoon limp in her fingers. Mason inhaled deeply to compose himself. "General Otley and his men were here yesterday, in my apartment."

Her eyes widened. She blinked a few times, as if forcing away tears. "Whatever for?"

Indeed. "Since you said you would speak the truth only *if you can*, know that Otley's men took the MiniComm device you left here the morning after Kendall gave birth. I also had someone come here last night and search for more listening devices. He found two Otley's men must have left. All that to say, this apartment is clean. Only I can hear what you say here."

Tears welled in Ciddah's eyes. She took a drink of water, apparently willing to let Mason say what he must. He struggled over which question to ask first and chose to follow the historical time line of the evidence against her. "Who asked you to put the MiniComm in my apartment?" He held his breath as he waited for her answer, praying she would finally be honest.

"Lawten."

Though the name twisted his stomach, he thought to himself, *Good*. Perhaps he'd finally discover the whole truth. "What else did Lawten ask you to do in regard to me?"

She closed her eyes, and when they fluttered back open, she was staring at her dessert, unwilling or unable to meet his gaze. "I was supposed to seduce you, to pair up with you and try to get pregnant."

Mason slumped back in his chair. He had not expected such an answer, though it did confirm why Lawten had let him skip donations for so long. None of it had been real. She'd never been attracted to him. He was only her task assignment.

She set down her spoon. "I'm sorry." A single tear ran down her cheek.

"I see." And he did see now. Everything made sense. Lawten had tricked Mason from the start, sent him to Ciddah on purpose. All with the plan of getting what he wanted from Mason. How cruel. Forced donations would have been better than such emotional trickery.

There was nothing left to ask at this point. Even without an apartment filled with MiniComms, he could not trust Ciddah Rourke. She was Lawten's spy.

Her breath shuddered from those perfectly painted lips that matched her dress. "Mason, I know you're angry. And you have every right to hate me, but I ... I want you to know that when Lawten first asked me to do this, I was excited. You were intriguing and handsome and I so desperately wanted to carry a child for my nation that I — "

"I don't want to hear it." Mason pushed back his chair. "I appreciate your honesty, but perhaps you should leave."

"Please, let me say this." She got up from her chair and came around to where he sat. She knelt on the floor at his feet and reached for his hand.

He pulled it away before she could touch him. "Do not think you still have a chance of completing your mission."

She clenched her hands in her lap. "Mason, you don't know me. The real me. No one does. At first I was eager to do what Lawten asked of me, proud even, that I might get pregnant by natural means. But the more I got to know you and the more I thought about my donors and their relationship, I realized I wanted that for us. Because I fell in love with you."

Mason abandoned his chair and put a few steps between them, stopping when he reached the couch. "How stupid do you think I am? Our entire relationship has been built on lies." There was no point in dragging any of this out further.

Tears dropped from both eyes and ran down her cheeks and into her lap, pat, pat, pat against the silky fabric of her dress. She stood up and used his napkin to quickly dab her face. "You're the smartest man I've ever known."

He huffed a breath out his nose. "Then I may as well confess that I am 99 percent certain you *love* Lawten."

"No!" Another shuddered breath and she sat on his chair. "Okay, I'll tell you everything. I did love Lawten once. I told you that he was a medic in the SC when I did my first internship. I was still in boarding school and so naïve, and, believe it or not, five years ago, he was quite handsome. I quickly discovered that I had to share Lawten with many other women. But that was the way of things here. And while I didn't like it, I coped as best I could."

"Gee, Ciddah. You're really making me feel better about all this." As if he wanted to hear about how many women loved Lawten Renzor.

"I'm not done! Be patient for just a few more minutes and then you can throw me out, okay?" She wrung his napkin in her hands. "All my life I've wanted to give the Safe Lands a baby. Like most little girls, I was enthralled by the Safe Lands Queens, whose glamorous lives were broadcasted over the ColorCast. But I was interested in medicine too, so pregnancy enthralled me.

"I told you how I applied for revealing when I turned fourteen, that my donors were lifers. I was their second child of four. And when I told Losira how devastated I was that I had failed to bear a child for the Safe Lands, she said that Fortune had blessed me. And she told me the story of her labors and the horror she experienced when each child was taken. Her testimony was so backward from everything I'd been taught, I didn't want to believe her. But as I tasked in the SC, and even though I've only seen one child born, nearly all of my patients suffer from depression, and none more than those who have given birth."

Ciddah had never spoken of this. "You've always seemed so bent on defending every procedure in the SC no matter how the patients responded."

"I know. But my task long ago proved that pregnancy is not as glamorous as the ColorCast had made it out to be. There is a dark side to what we do. So when Lawten became the task director general, I broached this topic with him, thinking he would understand since he'd been a medic for so many years. I hoped he might change some things now that he was in a position to do so. Because Lawten has always wanted his own child too. But that's another story."

Lawten wanted a child? Mason sat on the arm of his sofa, curious what else she had to say.

"Anyway, Lawten said the procedures were too complicated to change all at once, at least in light of the infertility. That was our first concern, he said. Once our women were conceiving again, we could worry about the emotional side of pregnancy. So I set about researching ways to help. But my rank wasn't high enough to get the research I needed. And Lawten said he couldn't help me. That's when I first knew he was hiding something."

Which explained her frustrations when Lawten had granted Mason access to the History Center. "That still doesn't explain why you've lied to me."

"I'm getting there. Skip ahead to your arrival and Lawten's *mission* for me, as you put it. I'd met you that afternoon, and though I had my fears, my childhood dream of pregnancy tempted me more, and I accepted the challenge. I secretly hoped you'd fall in love with me and we'd be lifers. But you were always so calmly adamant. And even though I didn't understand your reasons, your logic matched my research. It made me angry. And scared. Because you were not only speaking to my suspicions and fears, you were tearing apart the fabric of my nation. I hated you for it, yet I knew I was falling in love with you."

Mason could only stare at her now. He didn't want to believe a word she said, yet this felt true. This matched up with everything they'd been through.

"When you asked me to come watch Lonn's liberation, I thought I'd have my chance to win you over. So when Lawten asked for an update, I told him things looked promising. Then he told me to use a MiniComm that night. I'd almost forgotten that your brother had turned rebel and that you were all trying to escape. So I had the MiniComm turned on when you arrived, but I turned it off when we started talking about my donors. I wanted to be honest with you and didn't want Lawten to hear. And he was furious with me the next time I saw him. But I told him that I loved you and wouldn't betray you. Then he betrayed me."

"How?"

"He threatened my donors. Told me he was going to change their prescriptions in the CompuCharts until I got my priorities straight, and if I continued to defy him, he'd liberate them. I thought he was bluffing until my donors started getting sicker. So I promised to try again. But I can't, Mason. I'd rather see you arrested for theft and forced to donate than be a fly in my web for one more day. I love you too much to destroy you. And I figured if I could steal what I needed to help my donors and save you at the same time ..."

Framing him for theft had been her way of saving him? He wanted to believe her. He did. "Every time I begin to think there might be something real between us, I meet an obstacle. Our different principles. The MiniComm. Now I've learned that you were assigned to seduce me, then set me up as a thief. How can I believe you? How could I ever trust you?"

She dabbed her eyes with the wrinkled napkin. "You don't have to spell it out, Mason. I know full well why you can't trust me. And I don't blame you."

A small consolation in all this. "Be that as it may, Ciddah, if how you feel about me is true — if everything you've said is true — I can't walk away. I want to, but I can't."

Her forehead wrinkled, brows scrunched together. "Why not? I'd think you'd run away as fast as you could."

"I don't deny the temptation." But he loved Ciddah. The lie detector had raised the subject in his mind, and he couldn't deny it. There would never have been anyone from Glenrock or Jack's Peak who was a better fit for Mason than Ciddah. Wasn't it worth the risk to see this though? "Lawten blackmailed you. If I had been in your situation, I may have done the same to save my parents."

"Donors," she said. "Parents are what you had, people who raised you. Mine didn't. I grew up in the boarding school."

Was she trying to change the subject or merely rambling? "Fine. Donors." He walked back to the table, moved her first chair next to his, and sat in front of her, their knees almost touching. "My concern is: Lifer or no, we still view courtship very differently. I see such shallowness in this place. But I want the promise of forever. I want someone willing to sacrifice to make forever work even when difficulties arise.

I want honesty and trust. But I suspect I'm wasting my time trying to explain, since there is nothing like that here in the Safe Lands."

"You haven't looked hard enough, Mason." Ciddah took hold of his hand and squeezed. "If you're willing, I'd like to take you to meet my donors."

CHAPTER
16

Shaylinn sat at the kitchen table. She had before her the Wyndo Zane had given her, a stack of paper, a stack of envelopes, several pens, and a long list of names with notes beside each. Half of the list consisted of names she'd added herself, but Omar had started giving her names and addresses for any letters he got in his messenger box, so she'd added them to her list as well. She investigated each person to try and figure out what he or she might be going through in order to do the best job possible penning each message.

The first name on the list was Dillard Betta. Shaylinn entered his name in her Wyndo and found his profile on the grid. He was twenty-seven, lived in the Midlands, and tasked as a chef. He had two Xs: both for assault. They were bar fights, according to the note on his profile page. How embarrassing that the Safe Lands posted a person's failures on the grid for all to see.

Shay prayed that God would give her the right words for Dillard, then she wrote the message, doing her best to write an encouraging statement about anger and pride.

Next was a woman. Elani Rood was only nineteen, but she had been Xed for trying to kill herself. She'd spent almost a year in the RC for counseling, but Shaylinn could tell from the things she wrote on her profile that Elani was still depressed. She'd had two miscarriages, and Shaylinn felt that they were the key to her sorrow.

She prayed for healing and closure for Elani. She prayed for purpose too, that Elani might find joy in a task that she was created for. Then Shaylinn wrote Elani's message, using as many loving and hopeful words as possible.

She wrote messages until Naomi, Eliza, and Chipeta came out and made dinner. Shaylinn's hand was cramped from holding the pen for so long. There were now thirty-six names on her list, and Shaylinn had written messages to each of them. She ate lunch with everyone, telling them all about the hurting people she'd written to.

"Did you check with Levi about this?" Jordan asked. "It seems like something the elder should approve, that's all. He should be back soon."

Levi had gone into the city today with Beshup to search the storm drains underneath the boarding school.

"They can't trace the messages to me, Jordan," Shaylinn said.

"I think it's a lovely gesture," Aunt Mary said.

"Thanks," Shaylinn said, smiling.

Jordan took a bite of his sandwich and asked with a full mouth, "How will you deliver them?"

"Omar said he would come and get them."

Jordan swallowed his bite. "When did you talk to Omar? Was he here last night?"

"Don't be a grouch, Jordan," Shaylinn said, and thankfully her brother said no more.

After dinner, Naomi, Shaylinn, and Jemma cleaned the table and spread out the blue denim Jordan had bought. Aunt Mary, Chipeta, and Eliza went out into the living room to watch the TV.

"I think it will make adorable pants," Naomi said.

"I was thinking overalls," Shaylinn said.

"That will make it hard to change the diaper," Jemma said.

Diapers. Shaylinn hadn't thought about that. She knew little about infants. As the baby of her own family, she had never had any younger siblings to help take care of. Would that make her a bad mother? Surely she could learn, right?

There was a small Wyndo on the microwave's door, so Jemma turned on the cooking show the ladies were watching in the living room as Shaylinn and Naomi started cutting out the pieces for a pair of pants and a little dress. The cooking channel was the only one Jordan didn't make a fuss over when they watched. Everything else made him terribly cross about the Safe Lands. Food, however, he liked — no matter who created it.

The woman on the Wyndo wall screen was explaining different ways to sauté onions when the screen blinked off and then showed the Owl's face in front of a busy city street.

Omar.

"This is not an error," the Owl said through the mask in his low, electric voice. "The Messenger Owl has truth to deliver to the people of the Safe Lands. Truth brings freedom. Listen well. Everything on the ColorCast is screened and approved by Lawten Renzor before you see it. Fortune's numbers are based on genetics, not divine knowledge. Life numbers identify people with similar DNA. What is liberation, really? Soon you will know. But there is only one life before Bliss, not nine. Make yours count."

The screen blinked, and the cooking show resumed.

"That guy's a freak." Jordan stood leaning against the impost between the living room and kitchen. Shaylinn had been so captivated by Omar that she hadn't seen him come in.

"Why?" she asked. "He's trying to tell the truth."

"Seems pretty brave to me," Naomi said.

"He's a freak because he's dressed like a bird," Jordan said.

"He can't very well show his face," Shaylinn said. "Enforcers would arrest him."

"I guess," Jordan said. "But why does he think he can figure out what liberation is when people like Zane don't even know?"

Shaylinn had no answer for that. She prayed Omar would be careful.

Shaylinn and Naomi finished cutting out the pieces for the two items of clothing. Naomi went to bed early, so Shaylinn bundled up the dress pieces to sew later and carried the pants pieces to the couch perpendicular to the one Chipeta and Eliza were sitting on. Once situated, she began to baste the pants together. Her stitches were never as nice and small as Jemma's, but babies grew so fast that it likely wouldn't matter if these pants were imperfect. She sewed for an hour, watching more of the cooking channel while Jemma and Aunt Mary baked in the kitchen, and Jordan sat in the armchair cleaning the pistol he'd gotten from Zane. When Shaylinn finished basting the pants, she decided to take a break from them and baste the dress too.

She had finished the skirt portion and was starting the top when someone knocked at the door. Shaylinn froze. She hated living like this: always wondering if they were caught again.

Jordan went and opened the door, his muscular body blocking the opening. "What do *you* want?"

"I've come to see Shay." Omar's voice.

Shaylinn's heart soared. He'd come! Her messages were going to get delivered.

"She's busy." Jordan started to shut the door.

"*Jordan.*" Shaylinn glared at her brother's back. "Let him in."

Jordan backed up a step, barely cracking the door. Omar turned sideways and squeezed through. He held shopping bags in both hands. He stumbled past Jordan, who was purposely making it difficult.

Omar carried his bags into the living room and set them on the floor in front of the couch Shaylinn was sitting on. He looked so handsome. He'd combed his hair back over his head, but the long ends fell off the sides of his head and curled around his ears. "I see you managed to get some fabric already," he said.

"I brought her some." Jordan was now leaning against the arch impost with his arms crossed, watching them.

"Eliza," Chipeta said, "let's go see if Mary needs help with those pies."

"Okay." As Eliza followed Chipeta into the kitchen, she elbowed Jordan as she walked past. But he didn't budge.

Omar's forehead wrinkled as he looked down on Shaylinn. "Sorry I was so slow."

"No matter." She gave him a big smile, hoping to make it clear that she wasn't upset. It had taken him a little longer than she'd hoped, but he'd passed her first test. "Forgive me for not getting up. I'm sort of trapped by these dress pieces until I get them basted together."

"You're fine." He sat on the edge of the other sofa and watched Jordan.

Her brother walked back to the armchair he'd been sitting in, picked up his handgun from the coffee table, and sat, keeping his gaze locked on Omar, whose couch sat opposite the chair. Jordan took apart the handgun again, one piece at a time, until the parts lay on the table. Then he grabbed a scrap of the denim that he'd taken from the trash and began polishing the pieces. Again.

Poor Omar. Her brother was trying to intimidate him, and from the look on Omar's face, it was working.

"Three babies," she said, hoping to distract Omar from her brother's gun. "Soon there will be three little ones around here. We'll need lots of clothes, so I'm glad you brought more fabric. Did you know they don't sell baby clothes in the Safe Lands? Since no one has children, there's no need to buy them things. Isn't that sad?"

Omar opened his mouth as if he were going to speak, but Jordan suddenly started piecing the gun back together, as if racing someone. The metal clicked and clacked until he finished. Then he aimed the gun at Omar, squinting one eye.

"*Jordan.*" Shaylinn scowled at her brother. "Could you go away, please?"

"I'm your chaperone," he said.

Shaylinn glared at him. "That's really not necessary."

"Of course it's necessary." He gestured to Omar. "I can't leave you alone with a ... boy."

She rolled her eyes. "What's he going to do? Get me pregnant?"

Omar snorted, fighting back a laugh, and the women giggled in the kitchen.

Jordan stared at her, then stood and stepped toward Omar, towering above the sofa. "It's not funny, maggot."

"Jordan!" Shaylinn said. "Please, go away. Please!"

Jordan set his jaw as if biting back a volley of curses, which likely involved at least two uses of the word *maggot*. He finally said, "You touch her, you die," and he tapped the barrel of the pistol against Omar's forehead.

"I won't touch her." Omar shrank down in his seat and lifted his hands out to the side.

"Good." Jordan turned and stalked from the room.

Shaylinn didn't hear his bedroom door close, which meant Jordan was likely in the kitchen, eavesdropping. Such a pain. "It's not loaded," she said to Omar. "Zane gave it to him, but he doesn't have any ammo for it yet."

Omar sighed and nodded.

"So?" Shaylinn gestured to the bags. "Are you going to show me what you brought?"

"Yeah." He stood and handed her one of the bags.

She reached in and pulled out a jar of pickles. She held it up and wrinkled her nose. "Pickles?"

He ran his hand through his hair, causing it to stand up in waves. "Levi said pregnant women crave weird things. I went on the grid to see, and it said pickles."

"Oh, well, maybe pickle cravings come later." She peeked inside the bag. He'd also brought her an assortment of breads and crunchies.

"You said you could only eat breads."

Aww. "Thank you, Omar. That was very thoughtful."

He lifted the bag of food off her lap and replaced it with two bags of fabric. Omar had chosen fabrics so soft they felt like fur. There was a blue-and-green print, a red-and-brown stripe with fat white dog bone shapes, a purple-and-yellow plaid with little smiling duckies, a fluffy pink fabric that looked like a blanket, and some of the same in light blue. There was also a pink-and-white plaid flannel, and a blue-and-white flannel with funny little cars.

"These are amazing!" she said. "Where did you get them?"

"Zane knew about a warehouse where they make fabric for the nursery."

"They're precious. Thank you so much."

He smiled — he was so cute when he smiled! "There's some needles and thread in that second bag. And some yarn too. I couldn't remember if you knew how to knit or crochet, so I bought both kinds of tools."

"I can do both." She peeked in the second bag and admired the different textures of yarn. "Omar, you're much better at choosing fabrics than my brother."

"What?" Jordan's voice. Then, "Let go of me, Aunt Mary."

"You stay right here and let them be," Aunt Mary whispered loudly.

Shaylinn and Omar laughed, but Omar quickly cut off his laughter, though he was still smiling. "Well, denim is good too," he said, loud enough for Jordan to hear.

"It's *sturdy*," Shaylinn said. "Jordan's child will be a hunter, boy or not."

"He's a boy!" Jordan yelled from the kitchen. "That doctor woman said so."

"Will you stop it or must I send you to bed?" Aunt Mary scolded.

When no other sound came from the kitchen, Omar said, "I have one more thing for you."

"You've given me so much!" Shaylinn said. "I'll be sewing the rest of my life."

"Well, this one is a present." He pulled a small canvas out from the last bag and handed it to her.

She flipped it over in her hands and looked into her own eyes. It was a painting of her, Penny, and Nell, the way they would have looked had Omar painted them when he'd promised to that day months ago. It was just their faces, with Shay in the center and a forest in the background. Tears sprang to her eyes. "Oh! Omar ..."

"I had to do it from memory, so it's not very accurate."

But it was. "It's perfect. I love it." She pushed aside the bags and the sewing and got up from the couch. She stepped to where Omar was standing and kissed his cheek.

He looked at the floor, and his cheeks flushed. Oh, he was so adorable. She didn't dare hope that he would be there for the babies, did she? Omar had never been the most reliable person, and he'd almost died once from smoking his weird pipe. She would just keep praying that he'd learn to fight the temptations in his life.

Because she wanted him to stick around.

CHAPTER 17

O mar is the Owl?" Levi asked.

"That's what Kendall told me," Jemma said.

Kendall? "When did you talk to her?"

"She tapped me on my Wyndo, looking for Omar."

Levi growled at this. That woman needed to stay away from Omar. Levi and Jemma were sitting in the dusty living room of Zane's abandoned house waiting for Omar to arrive before Zane took them to meet the mysterious Ruston Neil. Jemma had been begging to come out to the city with Levi, and he figured today was a safe day to placate his wife.

But he couldn't believe how continually stupid his brother was. "And Omar told her this?"

"No. Shaylinn figured it out," Jemma said. "We all should have. I mean, an owl? Omar? It should have been obvious."

Levi had never understood his brother's obsession with owls. "I guess."

"I think it's wonderful," Jemma said.

"It's a mess, Jem. Hijacking the ColorCast will only make Otley and his goons angry."

"And what's wrong with that?" Zane asked, walking into the living room from the kitchen. His hair was flat today, like he'd just rolled out of bed. At this hour, he likely had.

"Because Otley will tighten security and increase enforcer patrols until he catches the Owl." Which would also make it harder for Levi to free the kids.

Zane sat in the rocking chair across from the sofa Levi was sharing with Jemma. "Don't you think people deserve the truth?"

"Safe Landers aren't my business," Levi said. "And they're not Omar's business either."

"TeleFlash, peer," Zane said, "I think Omar feels more like a Safe Lander than an outsider. And I think he wants to help people."

Levi scooted to the edge of the couch. "He needs to help his *own* people. He doesn't know what he's doing, and he's liable to get himself killed."

"I see what this is really about," Zane said. "He went behind your back, and that burns you because you want to be the boss of him."

"I *am* the boss of him," Levi said. "I'm the village elder."

Jemma's hand touched his back and moved side to side, scratching lightly, comforting him.

"Look, I know what it's like to come into this place naïve and get taken in," Zane said. "To ruin your life because, even though you were warned, you didn't know any better. I didn't want that to happen to you, Levi. Which was why I helped you that day at Café Eat. But I didn't know you yet. And now I know that never would've happened to a rule monger like you. And that's fine. But Omar. That kid ..." Zane shook his head. "He got taken by this place, like I did. Now he's trying to turn it around. But you're standing in his way with your list of rules. Get out of the way, Levi. Let the kid do what he's got to do to make up for his pain."

A pang of remorse shot through Levi. He should be the one standing up for his brother, not Zane. "But nothing will ever make up for his pain. Sometimes consequences are just too great."

"Maybe. But Omar has to walk that road himself. You can't tell him how it's going to be. You can't wish him better. This Owl thing ... it's a good idea. It's making people ask questions and doubt the Guild."

Hang the Guild! Levi wanted to scream. "But what does that have to do with getting our kids out of the Highlands?"

"Your agenda is all that matters to you, isn't it?" Zane asked. "Why should I let this meeting happen? You want to meet Ruston so you can figure out how to get your kiddies, not so you can figure out what Bender is up to. Am I right?"

Levi glanced at Jemma, who was still scratching his back. "The kids are my top priority."

"Well, maybe I'm tired of doing cartwheels for your priorities, Levi. You expect a lot from everyone you meet. But I don't owe you anything. So, I'll do the meeting today, but for Omar, not for you. You want my help in the future? You're going to have to start caring about more than your own pet agenda."

Ouch. Levi glanced at Jemma again. Her eyes were wide and empathetic, supporting him even when he was being insolent. He'd never been good at thinking about other people's feelings. When he had a job to do, the job consumed his thoughts until it was done. "I feel a lot of pressure to take care of my people. I guess I get a little obsessed. I'm sorry."

"Just try to be flexible, okay?" Zane said. "And stop jumping to the worst-case scenarios all the time."

Was he pessimistic? "Troubleshooting the worst is an elder's job."

"Then do it in your head and wait for the facts before you start yelling. Do you even know how to — "

"He's here," Jemma said.

Omar shut the front door behind him. Zane limped over to greet him.

"Ask him about Red," Jemma whispered.

Talk about pet agendas. Not again with this. "Omar and Shaylinn's business is their own," Levi told his wife.

"But Kendall said Omar is still with Red. Shaylinn needs him now, Levi. And Omar needs your guidance."

"He's never listened to me before. Why would he now?" Besides, Omar was only sixteen. Shaylinn fourteen. They were too young to be worrying about getting married, though it might happen eventually. Levi was much more concerned about the whole Owl thing. Omar was a puppy picking a fight with a mountain lion.

Levi walked toward his brother in time to overhear Zane say, " ... skip patrols tonight. Oh, and Levi knows."

"What?" Omar's shocked expression shifted from Zane to Levi. His jaw tightened into a scowl. "I can't believe she told you."

As if Levi would be spending time with Kendall Collin. "She told Jemma."

"But she promised ... Whatever." Omar pushed past Levi, walking farther into the living room.

Levi grabbed his arm. "Hey, let's talk about it." He chose his next words carefully. "It seems pretty dangerous."

"Are you worried your little brother might get hurt?" Omar asked.

"I am, actually."

"Well, don't bother. I'm dying anyway. I may as well do something good with my life on my way out." Omar flopped down on the couch beside Jemma, and a cloud of dust puffed around him.

This was the kind of talk that really scared Levi. "That's what this is? Suicide?"

"I'm just not afraid anymore, okay?" Omar said. "Let them come and get me. I'm putting up my best fight."

"This isn't our war, brother," Levi said. "We need to get our people out and — "

"Maybe it's not your war, but maybe it is my war." Omar tapped his chest. "I made the deal that got us here, as you like to remind me. And they lied to me. I can't forget that. I need to do something. And since I've been the Owl, I've felt lighter than I have in weeks. I haven't had a puff from my PV all day. So, maybe I can get high off my new purpose instead of stims."

"That's great, Omar," Jemma said.

Levi didn't think any of this was great. "They're going to catch you."

"Nah," Zane said. "I've installed a SimTag detector in his Wyndo wristband. It alerts him when someone approaches, and he can identify who it is by looking on the grid."

"Wait. You're helping him?" Levi asked. "Why didn't you say so?"

Zane shrugged, the beginnings of a smile on his face. "You didn't ask, peer."

"Zane is my partner," Omar said.

"More like his sidekick tech wizard," Zane said. "I work from the nest."

"What's the nest?" Jemma asked.

"Our lair." Omar grinned and jumped up from the couch. "Want to see it?"

Zane and Omar led Levi and Jemma down to the basement of the house, which was nothing but a small room with cement walls. The air was colder down there. A ratty old couch sat across from a washer and dryer. And a long bookshelf filled with cardboard boxes stretched along the wall opposite the stairs.

"*This* is your lair?" Levi asked. Because it wasn't a bit impressive.

"Watch and see," Omar said. "It's mad wild."

His brother's enjoyment annoyed him. This was a game to Omar. He was playing superhero, like a character from the Old cartoon comic books he liked so much.

Zane grabbed hold of the shelf and pulled it back. Wheels clacked over the cement floor. Levi hadn't noticed that the shelf was on wheels. Behind the shelves, a black-and-green-checkered blanket hung on the wall. Omar drew it aside and held it, which revealed a door that Zane pushed open. Zane stepped up into the doorway and into who knew where.

"Ooh! A secret door?" Jemma ran forward to peek into the darkness.

"What every lair needs," Omar said, grinning.

Refrain from anger. Levi fought to keep his expression neutral and hurried to catch up to his wife, who thankfully had not jumped through the doorway until he could investigate. "Do we have time for this? We're supposed to meet Ruston any minute now."

"Trust, peer," Zane called from within the secret room. "You need to work on it."

Fine. Levi climbed inside what turned out to be a tunnel. Jemma followed and took hold of his hand. Behind them, Omar pulled the shelf back into place, straightened the blanket, then shut the door. Darkness engulfed them. Levi put his arm around Jemma, but before he could say anything, light spilled into the tunnel from the other end.

Zane stood there, a black silhouette rimmed in a rectangle of pale yellow light. "Welcome to the nest."

They made their way out of the tunnel and into the center of a small room. A Wyndo wall screen covered the entire wall on one end, hanging above a GlassTop desk. The opposite wall was painted bright green. Another entrance stood directly opposite the one they'd come through. Shelves lined the side walls and were filled with guns, all types of portable Wyndos, pre-packaged food, jugs of water, and enforcer uniforms. No ammo.

"Is that a green screen?" Jemma asked, pointing at the green wall. "I learned about those at the entertainment orientation in the harem."

"That's where we film Omar for his reports," Zane said, sitting on the chair in front of the GlassTop, but facing toward them. "I can change out the background to make it look like he's anywhere. Raises the intrigue."

Levi didn't like this whole Owl thing, but knowing that his little brother wasn't alone in it, seeing that Zane was keeping him safe … It made it easier to swallow. "Who's equipment is all this?"

"Ruston's," Zane said.

"So he's in on the Owl thing too?" Levi asked.

"He knows about it, but he's not helping us, other than letting us use this place," Zane said. "Still, this is a big risk, bringing you people here. Ruston hasn't taken a risk like this in … well, since I've known him."

"And how long have you known him?" Levi asked.

Zane waggled his eyebrows. "All my life."

A moment of silence passed, and Levi went to inspect the weapons on the shelves. Omar sat on the chair in front of the green wall.

"Omar, I haven't seen Red around in a while," Jemma said. She was standing in the middle of the room, arms crossed, ready to fight.

Levi groaned inside as he admired a shelf filled with stunners. This wasn't the time to fish for details about Omar's love life, but his wife was determined to get a happily-ever-after for her sister.

"We broke up," Omar said. "She's crazy."

Levi couldn't argue there. He'd been a victim of Red's lies too.

"She destroyed my apartment," Omar said. "Ruined a bunch of my paintings."

"I wish she'd get help," Zane said. "But she'd rather destroy apartments."

"Help for what?" Jemma asked.

"They've got classes at the Midlands Civic Center that teach women to disconnect when a guy moves on," Zane said. "Wash off the paint."

"You mean like counseling classes?" Jemma asked.

"I guess."

Jemma squealed like an angry child. "Where are the heroes in this place? Where are the men willing to die for true love? Where are the Westleys and Mr. Darcys?"

Zane looked at Levi. "I don't know what she's talking about."

Levi picked up one of the stunners and gripped it. Jemma's love of romance stories was fine between the two of them, but he never talked to other guys about it.

"So I'm a scoundrel in a fairy story, is that it, Jemma?" Omar asked.

"Yes," she said, her voice laced with tears. "You *are* the scoundrel. You're Mr. Wickham!"

"Jemma…" Levi said, putting the stunner back on the shelf. "Let's do this another time, okay? We're probably already late for our meeting with Ruston."

But Omar wasn't done. "Maybe I am, Jemma. But Red doesn't think like Eliza Bennett, Jem. She's more like the wild little sister. And the sister liked Mr. Wickham and was too stupid to know he was a maggot."

Levi fought back a laugh and inspected a pistol on the next shelf down. Not loaded. He wondered where they kept the ammo.

"Which is why Mr. Darcy swept in to set things right," Jemma said. "Mr. Wickham and Lydia got married."

"You want me to marry Red?" Omar said. "*That's* what you want?"

"No! I want you to …" She took a deep breath, and Levi knew she wanted to tell Omar to marry Shaylinn. "I want you to stop living like Mr. Wickham and start living like Mr. Darcy."

"What do you think I've been doing? Look around you! But you know we've already got us a Mr. Darcy, Jemma." He pointed at Levi.

"I hate this place," Jemma said. "How can a society exist without true love and commitment and sacrifice and families?"

"There are families here," someone said.

Levi spun around, pistol in hand, though he knew it wasn't loaded. A man stood in the second entrance to the nest. He had black buzzed hair, a bushy chin beard, and was wearing jeans and a black T-shirt. He looked like he could have been from Glenrock.

"Hey!" Zane jumped out of his chair and limped over to the man. "Meet Ruston, peers. Ruston, this is Omar the Owl, Levi the elder of the Glenrock remnant, and his wife, Jemma the softie." Zane winked at Jemma, who stuck out her tongue in return.

"Pleased to know you." Ruston focused his attention on Jemma. "To answer your question, there are families in the Safe Lands, like the ones from your softie stories. They're called Naturals. Some call them ghosts."

Levi put the pistol back on the shelf and gave Ruston his full attention.

"Rewl told Shaylinn he was a Natural," Omar said. "That he didn't have the thin plague."

"It's true," Zane said. "Rewl is *technically* clean, even if he's dimmer than a dead Wyndo."

"A Natural is a person who exists but has no record," Ruston said. "Someone born in secret. Off-grid. They were raised in the basements. And enforcers call them Naturals because they were conceived the natural way."

"How would they keep such little children hidden, though?" Jemma asked.

"We have our ways," Ruston said with a smile.

"You're a Natural, aren't you?" Omar asked Zane.

"Sure am." Zane lifted his gloved hands and wiggled his fingers. "That's why I always wear gloves. Fingerprints are the only way enforcers can register Naturals, since we aren't in the grid. And when enforcers register our prints, we become ghosts in their system. Faceless problems."

"Is Bender a Natural?" Levi asked.

"Yes," Ruston said. "As are my sons, Nash and Zane."

Jemma clapped her hands over her heart. "Zane! Why didn't you tell us?"

"That was Ruston's call, femme," Zane said.

"How many of you are there?" Levi asked.

"There are about sixty-two Naturals who live in the basements almost exclusively," Ruston said. "And we've got twenty-six men who work with Bender, though the FFF is their true loyalty."

"The family thing?" Levi asked, recalling the graffiti he'd seen.

"Freedom for Families," Ruston said. "It was started by my great-great-grandfather and his friends back in 2029 when the government required all minors to move into the boarding school. It didn't sit well with some people, so they moved into hiding, eventually into the basements and storm drains. Been there ever since."

"What about Bender and Rewl?" Levi asked.

"Lots of people leave the basements," Zane said. "I did. Ran off when I was fifteen. Thought I knew everything. But I came back. Some don't, though. Some think the Black Army's plans are better than the FFF's. Bender joined the Black Army a long time ago, so when Rewl got old enough, he followed."

"Mr. Neil," Levi said, "we're planning to rescue our children from the boarding school soon, but Zane tells me the storm drains are no longer safe. Do you agree?"

"Some of them are and some of them aren't," Ruston said. "Enforcers have been exploring storm drains in the Highlands and have closed all the drains on the perimeter wall, so if you're hoping to get out the way you came in, it's not going to work."

Which was just about the worst news Levi could have gotten. "I'm not sure we'll be able to keep the children inside that cabin once we get them out."

"They'd be welcome in the basements," Ruston said. "You all would be. But it's going to be tough to get the kids out of the school."

"Tough times never last," Jemma said, taking hold of Levi's hand, "but tough people do. Faith makes all things possible. And we have plenty of faith."

"Good," Ruston said. "You're going to need it."

CHAPTER
18

The next night Omar helped Zane haul a truckload of food and supplies to the cabin. Omar wore his Wyndo watch, and the SimTag detector made it easy to know that no officials were following them. He didn't want to go inside, though. He still couldn't believe Shay had told Jemma he was the Owl after she'd promised not to. He'd convinced himself Shay was different from other girls.

Wrong again.

Omar managed to stay outside the cabin, enjoying the soft breeze and leaving things on the porch for Jordan to take inside, but when his aunt Chipeta asked him to carry a box of clothing inside, he couldn't really say no.

He lugged the box after his aunt, who led him to Shay and Mary's room. Shay wasn't inside.

"Just put it on one of the beds," Aunt Chipeta said.

Omar dropped the box on Shay's bed and spotted the painting he'd given her hanging on the wall above the headboard. His heart seemed to bob, like it was trying to soar but had been anchored by Shay's big fat mouth. He fled the house, made it to the front porch, down the steps...

"Omar."

So close. He took a deep breath and turned around. Shay walked down the steps and across the gravel, clutching a stack of envelopes in her hands. Maybe he should just let it go, forgive her for telling. Levi had freaked out at first, but he was already accepting the Owl now that he'd seen the nest and knew Zane was helping. That wasn't the point, though. Shay had promised not to tell. She wasn't any different than Bel or Red or any other blabbermouth girl.

"What's wrong?" Shay asked, stopping very close to him.

He looked down on her face. The curl had come back into her hair, framing her face in tangles of brown and silver, the soft wind making it sway. Her burnt umber eyes stared into his, and he felt himself slip, the quicksand pulling him in. "You told Jemma I was the Owl," he said before falling completely under her influence.

She brushed a strand of hair out of her eyes. "No, I didn't."

"Now you're going to lie?"

Her eyebrows pinched together. "I'm not. I swear it on the Bible."

Omar frowned, unsure how much the Bible mattered to Shay. She'd memorized much of it. Could she be telling the truth? Was there some misunderstanding here?

An urge seized him. Kiss her, it said. She could be yours.

Kiss Shay? He inched back, afraid of himself, of how carnal he'd become. "I don't want to talk to you right now," he said. "And stop giving me those stupid messages to deliver. I'm done helping you."

Her eyes swelled with tears, but she said nothing. Just stared at him. Why wouldn't she fight back? Didn't she care that he'd insulted her messages?

His posture sagged at her silence. He wanted her to say something. Anything. But she just stood there, staring, fighting back tears, clutching her letters to her chest. He felt terrible and mean. His words had hurt her. He should apologize, say he'd keep delivering her messages anyway, tell her they were good messages. Wise. Hopeful.

Instead he turned and walked away.

Omar vaped his entire PV on the walk back to his apartment and looked forward to taking a short nap before a late night as the Owl. Sleep and a refill were the only things that would help him get his mind off Shay. But when he reached the lobby of the Alexandria, it was so packed with people that he couldn't even get in the front door.

"What's going on?" he asked a guy in the doorway.

"Art sale," the guy said, showing Omar the flyer in his hands.

Exclusive Art by Omar Strong
Make an Offer
Monday, August 9, 8:30 p.m.

The flyer had three images of Omar's paintings on the bottom. One he'd done of City Hall, one of a forest, and the one of Belbeline's face.

What in all the lands?

"Here he is!" a familiar female voice sang, and everyone applauded.

Red. She was standing on the stairs inside the lobby, pointing at him.

"I want the painting of the girl," the guy at the door said. "I'll pay fifty credits."

"*Fifty*?" Omar couldn't believe it. "Do you know how long it took me to paint that?" He wouldn't sell it, ever, but it was worth at least five hundred credits, in his opinion.

The crowd mobbed Omar, asking about the paintings on the flyer, if they could see his other work, if he did commissions.

"There's been a mistake!" he yelled. "I'm not having an art sale. You can all go home."

"I'll pay a hundred for the painting of the girl," the guy at the door said. "Final offer."

"Still no." Omar squeezed around people, fighting his way across the lobby. Red smiled as he passed her on the stairs, and all he could think to say was, "Real mature."

"He'll be opening the art exhibit momentarily," Red called to the crowd.

"No, he won't!" Omar yelled. "You can all leave. There's nothing for sale!"

The people grumbled and continued to ask him about the paintings. Stupid Red, anyway. It took Omar a half hour to get inside his apartment. He went straight to his bedroom and found a spare vial of grass. He crawled into bed and vaped until he fell asleep.

A knock on the door woke him. He would have ignored it, but he was thirsty. He still felt good from the grass, but it was fading. He got up and walked to his fridge, grabbed a beer, then looked out the peephole in his front door.

Kendall Collin stood alone in the hallway.

He opened the door, and the spicy smell of her perfume reached out and grabbed him. She was wearing a green fitted top and very short shorts. He forced himself to look up from her legs to her face. What would it feel like to kiss her? To touch her hair? He shook the thought away, angry it had come at all. He blamed the grass. "Hay-o, Kendall."

"I need to talk to you," she said. "Can I come in?"

The words skyrocketed his pulse and imagination. He had to stop this. Figure out what to do about Shay. This was all Belbeline's fault. The things they'd done had opened his mind to obsession. He could barely look at a girl without thinking about pairing up.

And while he had fully intended to pursue Kendall when he'd met her the night of Chord's death, that had changed when he'd learned about Shay. He was going to be a father, whether he — or Jordan or Levi — liked it or not. He had to stop living like a dog.

"Yeah, sure," he said, trying to act like girls came up to his apartment every day. But his place was a disaster again. He never had time for chores. "Uh, can you wait out here for just a minute? I need to check something."

Omar closed the door and tossed his beer can. He picked up all the clothes lying on the floor and threw them on his bed, hoping that would keep him from trying to take Kendall in the bedroom. On his way back to the door, he grabbed six different food containers and three beer cans and crammed them into the trash.

Better.

He opened the door, panting slightly. "Come on in."

Kendall entered. "It smells like paint."

"That's because I, uh, I paint." He gestured toward the kitchen, his makeshift art studio. Kendall walked toward it. He closed the door and followed her, wondering how her legs would look with SimArt patterns up the backs like Belbeline had.

He shook the thought away and focused on the back of her head, but that was no good, either. Omar had always loved painting hair. Kendall's wasn't as wild as Belbeline's or as thick and long as Shay's, but it was real hair, not that straw-like stuff Red had implanted. It looked soft. It probably was.

Walls, why had he vaped so much grass? He tried to keep his thoughts on track. He thought about his Owl plans for tonight, and then pictured the tiny baby pants Shay had made for Naomi's boy. But the smell of Kendall's perfume was like a hook, pulling his eyes back to her again and again.

She had stopped in the kitchen, standing before his easels. One easel had the old Night Owl marquee on it. The other easel held a painting of a little girl's face.

"Who is this?" Kendall asked.

Omar joined her in the kitchen. "Sophie. She was a girl from Glenrock. Her face has, uh, kind of been haunting me." Because it was his fault she was dead.

"She has Shaylinn's eyes," Kendall said.

Omar studied the painting. He *had* given Sophie Shay's eyes. Huh. "I guess Shay has been haunting me too." He removed the canvas and set it, backside out, at the end of a stack of canvasses that were leaning against the wall. He flipped through them. "This one is kind of nice."

He picked it up and set it on the easel where Sophie had been. It was a landscape of Mount Crested Butte with the sun rising behind it.

"It's lovely," Kendall said. "What's this smoke?"

"Jack's Peak. It's a village that used to be up on the mountain. Enforcers destroyed it too."

Kendall walked over to the stack of canvasses. "May I?"

Omar swiped his hand through his hair. "Sure, I guess."

She flipped to the next one, a forest scene painted in dark greens and blacks.

"That's not done yet." It always made him anxious when people saw his art. Part of his soul was bared in each creation. He felt vulnerable. Red must have known how much it would bother him to have a crowd wanting to look, and that's why she'd made that flyer. He didn't understand why she couldn't just move on.

Kendall flipped to a close-up of a pink flower, then to one of a couple kissing in a street.

"That's inspired from an Old photograph I had at home. Papa Eli said they were celebrating the end of a world war."

Kendall turned her wide eyes to his. "The whole world was at war?"

"A long time ago, yes. Before the Great Pandemic."

The next was a painting of Jemma.

"You like to paint people, don't you?"

"I like finding each person's unique beauty, to make others experience something when they look at the painting. It might not be joyful, but it's real. People need to see beauty in each other and have empathy for how we're unique. It's wrong to try to be something we're not."

His words stirred something within him. He'd changed. He used to strive to be just like Levi, but that was a hollow dream. He needed to be himself. Maybe he was finally starting to do that.

"I bet you love mimics, don't you?"

Omar chuckled and looked away. Saying those things had made him feel even more vulnerable. He suddenly wanted Kendall to leave, and she hadn't even said what she'd come to say yet.

She pulled the painting of Jemma forward to reveal an owl, then a deer, then another painting of Sophie, then … "Belbeline Combs?"

Omar flushed, as well he should. He had painted Bel nude, draped in a green sheet. He'd painted two canvases like that. Otley had taken the one he'd given to Bel.

He tugged at the painting, wanting to hide it, but Kendall hung on. "You know Bel?"

Her eyes studied him, wary now, and let go of the painting. "Not as well as you, I suspect."

"I thought I'd taken it out." He set the canvas against the second stack, backside out, relieved to give Bel her privacy from people who didn't understand. "How do you know her?"

"I had dinner with her once shortly after I'd arrived in the Safe Lands. She and General Otley were together, and Lawten Renzor had invited me."

Wow. "You had dinner with the task director general, the enforcer general, and Belbeline? That's mad wild." But that made sense when he recalled how the Safe Lands had bought Kendall from Wyoming. The vulture would have treated her well until his use for her had run out, same as he had Omar.

Kendall flipped to another painting, one of Zane that showed the side where his ear was missing. "Once I became pregnant, Belbeline was assigned as my mentor in the harem."

Omar almost choked. "Bel was pregnant?"

"She lost the child when I was about four months in. So she left, and I was on my own." Kendall flipped to the painting Omar had done of his mom.

Belbeline had been pregnant. Probably every woman in the Safe Lands had been. This place was so strange. And now Shay was pregnant too. But Shay wasn't infected, and that would keep her babies from dying, right? *Please, God, let her babies live.*

Kendall continued to look through Omar's paintings. He'd done City Hall, the park, Lake Joie, a crowd of people wearing different colors of Roller Paint, and one of a very pregnant Naomi, about which he said to Kendall, "Don't tell Jordan. He wouldn't understand."

"Some are more realistic than others. Do you have different methods?"

"Well, some aren't finished. And I do better when someone poses. When I paint from memory, it's hard to get everything just right, especially the lighting."

Kendall flipped all the paintings back against the wall and turned to face him. "I need your help."

Finally. He looked at her, waiting.

"I got a summons from the task director general's office. It didn't say why he summoned me. I've been ignoring it for weeks. Well, my appointment was for this morning, and I didn't go. He wants something from me. It's ... his way."

The task director general was like that with everyone, but Kendall looked terrified.

"What do you mean?"

"Every time I meet with him, he asks me to do something. Usually it's something I don't want to do. And something I can't refuse."

Sounded about right. "You have no idea what he might be asking now?"

She wrung her hands below her chin, like she was praying hard. "I don't know. But I want to disappear, like Jemma and Shaylinn."

Well, she couldn't live in the cabin. The fact that he thought Kendall was pretty would ruin things with Shay. He'd do something dumb. "I can ask Zane to help with that."

"And there's one other thing. I know you're planning to free your children from the nursery. So I wondered ... if you were already going there ... Could you get baby Elyot too?"

"Your son." Walls! Omar had forgotten she had a kid too. "Of course. I mean, once we figure out how. We're still not sure how to get into the nursery."

"I can take you, if you let me come along," Kendall said. "After Lawten changed his mind about letting me hold Elyot — I think he felt he let me visit the nursery. So I know the layout of the rooms, I know where it's located in the MC and everything."

Levi would be relieved to have someone's help with the nursery, but would he accept help from Kendall? She'd dined with Otley *and* Renzor. What if she was working for them? He didn't think she was, but what if? "I'll tell Levi you're willing to help."

"Thank you, Omar."

She hugged him then. He stiffened and held his breath, trying not to smell her perfume, but her hug lasted so long he had to breathe. Her scent filled him with a longing for physical contact, so he pulled back, putting a few inches of space between them. "Kendall, you don't want to be friends with me. I'll just mess it up. I always do."

"I'd rather decide that for myself." She grabbed his face and crushed her lips against his. Whoa. He shouldn't do this, but he gave in to his feelings and walked her backward, slowly, continuing to kiss her, until they reached the sofa. He pushed her down and fell on top. When he kissed her again, she went stiff underneath him.

He moved his weight to his forearms, thinking he'd squished her. "What's wrong?"

She had her hands against his chest, pushing against him. Her eyes were somehow angry and terrified at the same time. "What are you doing? Why did you ... ?"

He flushed and sat up on the edge of the couch, Kendall's feet behind him. "I thought ... You don't want to?"

She shook her head, eyes glazed with tears now. Great. He'd made her cry.

He rubbed his hands over his face. "Sorry, I ... I just assumed." He was an idiot. He wished she'd leave so he wouldn't feel so stupid.

Kendall sat up as well, on the opposite end of the couch, and pulled her feet up until her knees were to her chest. She hugged them to herself, as if putting as much distance between Omar and her as possible without making it obvious. "I'm not rejecting you, Omar. I just don't know."

"No, it's okay." It was good, really. Very good that she'd stopped him. Pairing up was an addiction for him — as strong as his craving for his PV. And Kendall was an outsider. How could he have treated her so poorly? He needed … something. Help, maybe.

"And what about Shaylinn?" Kendall asked. "She told me she loves you."

"She did?" His voice had squeaked the words, and his chest felt like it might explode. Why would any girl love him? Shay especially? He was a mess. And he'd hurt her. He'd been angry and said mean things even when she said she hadn't told Jemma that he was the Owl.

Something occurred to him then. Kendall had been there that night too. "Kendall, do you ever talk to Jemma?"

"On the Wyndo," Kendall said. "We talked about you, actually. She was asking about that girl, Red."

Was *that* why Jemma had attacked him in regards to Red? Kendall must have told her what Red said at the train station. His eyes narrowed. "Did you tell her I was the Owl?"

The way Kendall's eyes shifted to the floor was answer enough. "I'm sorry. I know you told Shaylinn not to say anything, but … It just sort of came out. Are you mad?"

At himself. So disgusted with himself. He'd yelled at Shaylinn, accused her of lying. Insulted her letter writing, the one thing that made her feel good. And then he'd made out with Kendall as if Shay didn't even exist. How could he have forgotten that Kendall had been there when Shay had guessed his secret identity?

God, I'm sorry. Again!

Shaylinn of Zachary wasn't manipulative like other girls. She was different. He never should have doubted her. So, what was he going to do about her? She deserved better than him. He leaned back against the couch and sank into the cushions.

"I really like you, Omar," Kendall said. "I just need to move slow."

"Slow is good." But he was ashamed. He didn't dislike Kendall, but he didn't know anything about her. Getting into a relationship with her would be no different than what he'd had with Red. It would be physical; nothing more. He should never have let Belbeline talk him doing the things they had. If he'd been stronger, he might never ve given in. Then he wouldn't have the thin plague now. And he wouldn't be a depraved animal when women were around.

He smiled at Kendall, tried to make it look sincere. But his hands shook, and he got up in search of his PV. He needed a fix of something, and it wasn't going to be physical.

When Kendall left, Omar went out to fill his PV and to shop for Shay. It was an effort to do penance, he knew, but he couldn't help the way he felt. His credits were blood credits anyway. They may as well be used for someone good. He had a feeling he wouldn't be able to buy her forgiveness, though. Shay was tough, and she wasn't stupid.

When he went to the nest that night he found a pile of messages from Shay that Jordan had brought to Zane. Shay wasn't giving up on her plans, and she was too stubborn to let a bully like Omar stop her. He rummaged through the messages, his stomach twisted in anticipation, hoping. Sure enough, he found one addressed to Omar of Elias in Shay's loopy handwriting. He opened it.

Only those who try to resist temptation know its strength. The spirit is willing, but the flesh is weak. You're stronger than your flesh. Remember, suffering produces perseverance; perseverance, character; and character, hope. Remain steadfast.

It was like she could read his mind. How did she know the very words that would so affect him? He'd have to ask next time he saw her. If he could muster the guts to face her after what he'd done.

CHAPTER
19

Tuesday morning, Mason went to the boarding school, hoping to get a reply from Penelope about the escape plans for Saturday, but the class never came out. What did that mean? He'd gotten there in plenty of time, so he couldn't have missed them. Had a teacher found the note Mason had given her last week? Or was it merely a coincidence?

He walked back to his apartment and text-tapped Levi on his new off-grid Wyndo.

Levi text-tapped back: *What are we supposed to do now?*

Mason replied: *Don't know. I'll get back to you.*

This afternoon Ciddah would take Mason to meet her donors. Perhaps she would help him now. Her confession had broken down a wall between them, but he still wasn't sure how much to tell her. Without Penelope, though, he'd need Ciddah's help to get into the boarding school. He just didn't know how to broach the topic.

"Next stop, Lake Joie Drive, Midlands Central." The train driver's voice came muted and soft over the speakers in the ceiling as the train started to slow.

Mason sat on the train beside Ciddah, who'd taken the window seat. The train looked to be about half full. They were going to meet her donors, to prove to Mason that love and commitment did exist in this place. But Mason had come up with dozens more questions since their dinner the other night, and he hadn't stopped asking them since he'd met Ciddah at her apartment.

The train stopped fully, the doors slid open, and Mason watched as passengers exited the train and new ones stepped on. "Why don't you use a vaporizer?"

"I don't like PVs." Ciddah was practically whispering, her eyes darting from passenger to passenger as if they all might be enforcers in disguise. "There's too big a temptation to supplement your meds, so I take my doses in pill form."

Mason wished Omar would try that approach. "Do you have a medic who gives you a prescription?"

"I used to. But that was before I found out there are stimulants in the ACT treatment."

Stimulants in medication? "What kind? How did you find out?"

The train doors slid shut, and the train rolled forward again. "I overheard something when I testified before the Safe Lands Guild. But I haven't been able to figure out what it meant. Lawten won't give me access to the medical files in the History Center. But since I started compounding my own meds, I've been healthier, though I did experience some withdrawal symptoms. That confirmed that there had been something unnecessary in my meds. So I wanted to make clean meds for Droe and Losira too. I hoped it would help them get stronger after whatever it was Lawten had slipped them. I wanted to compound them myself, but I needed supplies from the pharmacy."

"And you would have had to file a request with Mr. Brock for those."

"Next stop, Verapon Street, Midlands West." The train slowed, softly jerking Mason and Ciddah back in their seats.

"Exactly." She winced, her nose wrinkling. "He would have known if I'd been asking for more than my own personal share. And a lower-level medic is only permitted to compound her own meds, not anyone else's."

The train stopped fully, and passengers came and went. Mason could imagine Mr. Brock's steadfast adherence to pharmacy protocol. "He would have denied your request."

Ciddah's gaze followed a young woman who slipped through the doors at the last second, barely getting inside before they closed. "Not only that, he would have reported me. He's required by law to report anything out of the ordinary."

Which was why she'd framed Mason. The train pulled forward again. "What does ACT stand for?"

"Antiretroviral Combination Treatment. But there's no reason it should contain stimulants."

Mason agreed, but for the sake of argument ... "Perhaps researchers discovered a need. According to Old medical textbooks, physicians used natural plant drugs like coca and cannabis for thousands of years."

"There are safer ways to achieve the same results."

It did seem careless to risk addicting an entire population. "How many doses do people take each day? Of their meds?"

"It varies per patient. There are different stages of the virus, different strains. And meds are prescribed based on diagnosis and age, gender, resistance, and possible side-effects."

"If the meds are not a cure, what good are they?"

"When taken correctly, ACT meds suppress the virus, keep it from mutating, and keep its levels in the blood low enough that they don't cause illness. Basically, they buy us time. But not if they contain stimulants."

Because stimulants weakened the immune system, just as Mason had declared to Ciddah in regard to pregnant women. But she'd already known. She knew so much more than he did about the thin plague. He'd been foolish to think he could discover a cure. He barely understood the virus. The fact that it mutated ... He felt so inadequate. It was impossible to think he could do anything to help Omar and Mia. He'd been arrogant to even consider such a possibility.

The driver's voice interrupted his morose thoughts. "Next stop, Washington Gulch and Meridian Road, Midlands West."

"This is it," Ciddah said, taking Mason's hand and nudging his side. "Come on."

She led him off the train and out onto the street. The trains in the Safe Lands ran above ground on platforms, and Ciddah and Mason had to walk under the track to cross the street. The train rumbled away overhead.

A bustling shopping area filled the corner of Washington Gulch and Meridian. In the dozens of stores surrounding the intersection, Mason recognized only a G.I.N., a Lift, and a Cinnamonster ice cream shop. But as they walked up Meridian Road, the traffic and people thinned out until everything seemed still. The street was now lined with tiny houses on both sides. They were so odd looking, narrow and squashed together, painted colors like bright orange, magenta, or blue-and-green pinstripes. He saw only one lawn of natural green grass, though it had a bright metal sculpture in the middle of the yard that spun in the wind. One house slowly changed colors, morphing from red to orange to yellow to green to blue to purple and back to red.

"Can people use SimArt technology on their houses?" Mason asked.

"Yes," Ciddah said. "It's very expensive, though."

The trill of a motor overhead pulled Mason's gaze to the sky. Another plane headed north to Wyoming, perhaps?

Droe and Losira lived at 423 West Meridian Road in a bright pink box that looked like a giant BabyKakes carton turned on its end. Their lawn was neon-green faux grass with puffs of little plastic flowers in a half dozen shades of pink.

Ciddah rang the bell, which sounded a medley on the other side of the pink walls. Pink. Mason couldn't stop staring at the intense color.

A slender woman opened the door. She was pale and had thin brown hair and violet, electric eyes — definitely contacts. She squealed, as if she knew the very best secret in the entire world. "Hay-o, hay-o, my pearly girl. Come in, come in!" She squealed again and pulled Ciddah inside, giving her a quick kiss on each cheek.

Besides her paleness and a few flaky patches of skin, she did not appear to be ill. Those violet-colored eyes focused on Mason, and she squealed a third time. "Look at you!" She pressed her hand over her heart. "Well, just look at you. What a raven fellow you are. Ohh!" She took both Mason's hands in hers and squeezed, as if they were two little girls about to spin. "Ohh, my. Just precious. Precious! Come in, dear boy." She pulled him inside and kissed both his cheeks as well. "Such a dear boy."

"How are you, Losira?" Ciddah asked.

"Ohh, I'm fine, fine," she said, possibly incapable of not repeating herself. "Well, you took the train? Was it nice?"

When Losira spoke, she hummed the last word of every sentence. *Train* had been pronounced *traaaiiinnnn?* with the lilt of the question at the end. Then *"Was it niiiiiccce?"*

Mason realized his mouth was gaping and he closed it. "Yes, ma'am."

"Ohh!" She pursed her lips, eyes sparkling as if she were holding back a teasing rebuke. "Ma'am. Ohh-kay," she said to Ciddah. "He must think I'm an Ancient."

"I'm sorry." Mason had forgotten the form of address *ma'am* was offensive here.

Losira grabbed his arm and squeezed. "Ohh, I'm just teasing you. Well, I *am* old. Three more years, and I'll be liberated. We might as well be honest about that, right?" She grinned like it was all very exciting.

The woman was bewildering, but Mason couldn't help but like her.

"Ohh-kay, come in and see Droe. He's been talking about you both all day."

"What's he been saying?" Ciddah asked.

"He is delighted to meet the outsider medic and ask him what he knows about teeth."

"Teeth?" Mason asked.

"Droe permatasks as a dentist," Losira said.

"Please explain permatask," Mason said, unfamiliar with the term.

"It's when you have enough training to remain in one field," Ciddah said. "Sometimes it costs the Safe Lands more to train someone else than to keep you in the task, so you get to stay. I permatask as a medic. They could always move me, but no matter where, I'd still task as a medic."

"Do you know much about teeth?" Losira asked.

"I know a little," Mason said, though he doubted it would interest someone tasked as a dentist.

"Ohh, Droe will be so excited. So excited." She rubbed her hands together as if the anticipation was too much to contain.

Droe and Losira's house was tiny and spotless and thankfully not pink inside, but shades of beige and black. Pictures on the walls flashed pictures of Losira and a man in different locations throughout the Safe Lands. They did look happy. They'd entered into a narrow kitchen, and Losira led them past a staircase to a sitting room in the back.

A man stood up from a wingback chair. While he was tall and big boned, his muscles had atrophied to the point where his flaking skin sagged in places. He had a square face and thick black hair and a mustache. No — the mustache was SimArt. Odd. "This the medic?" His voice was hoarse, and he coughed — a barking cough, deep and phlegmy. It sounded like he had a respiratory infection.

"Droe" — which sounded like *Drohhhh* — "This. Is Mason. Ohh, isn't he raven? So raven." Losira all but pinched his cheeks in her introduction. She didn't seem to be afflicted with the same illness Droe had. She walked over to her husband and stood beside him, beaming at Mason.

"I don't know much about what's raven these days," Droe rasped, and the skin under his chin jiggled when he spoke. "What do you know about teeth, young man?"

Mason was about to ask Droe to be more specific, but Losira said, "Well, have a seat. Sit, sit," and motioned Mason to sit on the end of the sofa, which was closest to Droe's armchair.

Mason sat. Droe sat back down as well. Ciddah sat beside Mason, and Losira sat on a footstool beside Droe's chair. Everyone sitting. And looking at Mason. Right; Droe had asked about teeth.

"I know we need teeth to eat," Mason said. "And they also help our speech."

"Quite true, that," Droe said, nodding. "Ciddah said you're an outsider." He paused through a lingering cough. "What kind of dentistry was offered in your community?"

"My mother was the village doctor, which is like a medic. She did everything for the people and animals, including dentistry, though the men handled any problems that arose with calving."

"Calving? What does that have to do with teeth?" Droe asked. "I've never heard that term."

Mason fought back a smile. "Calving is when a cow gives birth."

"Oh, cows. Of course." Droe frowned, likely unable to find any reference for animal husbandry in his sheltered mind.

"Mason was his mother's apprentice," Ciddah said.

This seemed just the thing to bring Droe back into the conversation. "So you were the dentist's assistant?"

"You could say that, yes."

He coughed and hacked for so long that Mason wanted to get him some water. Mason glanced at Losira, who was rubbing Droe's back. When the man finally gathered his breath again, he asked, "What would you do for gingivitis?"

The question was so odd, Mason struggled to keep a straight face. "I'd encourage the patient to brush in painstaking detail twice a day, floss after every meal, rinse his mouth with salt water, drink lots of chamomile tea, and eat plenty of raw apples."

Droe's eyes lit up. "Apples. Delightful. And what about a cavity? What then?"

"We had a few drills that we've scavenged from Old dental offices. Mother would drill out the rot, then melt down Old jewelry — gold or silver only — and once the metal was cool but still soft enough to mold, she'd push it into the hole. She did fairly well. Extractions were rare because — " Droe had begun coughing again during Mason's answer, and the man's face was so red, Mason stood. "Could I get you some water?"

"He'll be fine." Losira winked at Mason and rubbed Droe's back again.

Ciddah took Mason's hand and pulled him back to the couch. She whispered in his ear, "He doesn't like us making a fuss over him. Just keep talking."

Droe's cough was winding down now, so Mason got back to his answer. "Like I said, extractions were rare because, well, once children heard a man getting his tooth pulled, they remembered to brush."

Droe honked a noisy laugh. "Quite so, I'd imagine." A little cough. "No sedatives, then?"

"Droe," Losira said, "you're not going to talk to him all day about dentistry, are you?"

He waved at his lifer, but kept his eyes on Mason. "Just this final question and I'll refrain, I promise." He took a shaky breath, as if fighting off the urge to cough again. "Sedatives, go on."

Mason glanced at Ciddah and they exchanged a quick smile. "We used alcohol. Mother also had a sleep tonic, but it never kept anyone unconscious through an extraction or drilling."

Droe's eyebrows furrowed as he seemed to think this over. "Unpleasant for your patients, I'd suspect."

"Very, I'm afraid. But better than leaving it to get worse."

"True, that. True." Droe leaned back in his chair as if conceding the end of this round of conversation.

"Ohh-kay," Losira said, clasping her hands together and beaming. "Well, tell us all about you, Mason."

He faltered. What should he tell them? That he was a prisoner in this place and wanted to leave? "I'm tasking as a medic in the SC. I live in the Highlands, for now. I'm a vegetarian."

"Outsiders don't eat meat, huh? Probably because of all the worms in it." Droe looked to Losira and added, "Wild animals get worms."

Whaaat ...? Best to let that one go. "I have two brothers," Mason added, in hopes of steering the conversation away from worms in wild game. "An older and a younger. Levi and Omar."

"Ohh, how nice that you all applied for revealing," Losira said. "Droe and I gave three babies to the Safe Lands, but only Ciddah has found us so far. Do they look like you, your brothers?"

It was likely no use to correct Losira's assumption that life in his village was the same as it was here, so Mason merely said, "Somewhat."

"They do all look similar," Ciddah added. "And while I did see the other two probably at their worst, I think Mason is handsomest of the three."

Losira squealed. Mason looked at his shoes.

"Femmes," Droe said to Mason, then to Ciddah, "Can't you see you're embarrassing the man?"

The awkward fun continued until Losira served dinner. She had made vegetarian spaghetti, which Mason appreciated. Throughout the meal, Droe continued to ask questions about "outsider life." Droe and Losira were like an old married couple, though they were not yet forty years old.

"Droe," Ciddah said, "tell Mason your theory about Richark Lonn."

Droe grinned, which stretched his SimArt mustache wide over his top lip. "Yes, well, I can do that." He paused for a heavy cough, which was the first big one he'd had since they'd sat down to eat. "You see now, everyone thinks Lonn went into hiding after Martana's death. Not true, that. Lonn was doing research, got himself caught and fired. He was going to have to retake his task test, despite his being a perma-task medic. They probably would have made him a dentist. Ha!" He slapped the tabletop, which made the skin on his neck and arms jiggle. "Joking, of course. But Lonn's motivations for researching above his level were based on more than his sweet femme's death, of that I'm certain."

Lonn was researching above his level? Like Mason and Ciddah had been trying to do? Mason wondered if there was a way to discover what Lonn had been looking for. "Is there no way to find out what he was researching?"

"Well, now … If I were going to look into it, which I'm not, I'd study his life." He coughed. "I'd bet there's plenty about him in the History Center, if you could get permission to go in."

"We have permission, Droe," Ciddah said. "But our clearance isn't very high."

"Wouldn't need much clearance to read biographies, I shouldn't think."

"I suppose that's true," Ciddah said. "Mason, we should go read biographies."

Mason didn't know how reading a biography would tell them what they wanted to know, but he supposed it was worth a try.

"And," Droe said, "if you have an enforcer friend who could look up the arrest reports on Lonn, I'd bet you'd find something in that too." A slight smile curled Droe's lips, as if he'd offered them some clues and wanted to see if they could solve his challenge.

Mason wished the man would simply come out and say whatever was on his mind. They were days away from their scheduled attempt to free the children. He didn't have time to play scavenger hunt with Ciddah's father unless it was important. But maybe it was. Maybe all this time, Mason had been looking for answers in the wrong place, starting big looking for a cure when he should have started small looking for a clue.

"I'll see if I can find an enforcer to help," Mason said. "Thank you, sir."

"Oh, it was nothing, that." Droe sat back in his chair, looking proud of himself. "Say, did your mother ever extract a tooth from a cow?"

On the train back to the Highlands, Ciddah sat beside Mason — snuggled, was a better word — sitting right up beside him with her head resting on his shoulder. He rather liked how it felt as though she was leaning on him for support.

Outside the train windows, the Midlands flashed by. "I liked your parents," he said, looking down on the top on her head.

"Donors," Ciddah said.

Mason smiled, thinking that even though Droe and Losira hadn't raised Ciddah, they had indeed parented her from the moment they'd met. "I liked them."

She sat up and faced him. "Ever since I met them, I've wanted what they have, but I've never found a man willing to be a lifer. Until I met you."

Mason wanted to clarify that he had no intention of ever being anyone's lifer and again explain his views on marriage, but he held his tongue. "I'm glad you sought them out. I think it gave them a lot of closure from their pain of giving up their children."

"Maybe." Ciddah sighed and looked out the train window. "Love is dangerous, Mason. It exposes you, makes you vulnerable. It's something they can use against you."

Mason still couldn't believe Lawten had altered her parents' meds and threatened premature liberation. Losira seemed to have bounced back from any infections, but Droe's cough concerned Mason. He kissed the top of her head. "I hope we can help them move before Lawten does anything else to them."

She looked up and smiled, so he kissed her lips.

He probably shouldn't kiss her. It only made him want to be with her more. He should ask her about the boarding school. Find out if she could help them. But he didn't want to ruin this moment.

When had his mission for information morphed into a real relationship? Had he given up trying to resist her? If so, what did that mean for his future? Would he ask her to come with him to Glenrock? Leave her parents? Perhaps Droe and Losira would be willing to leave the Safe Lands, and Mason could ask Ciddah to come to Glenrock.

The village would have a female doctor and a dentist, and Mason would have a wife who loved him. Everyone would be happy.

But what about Papa Eli's warning never to marry a Safe Lander? What about the thin plague?

Why were complex relationships so easy to work out in your mind? The imagination was a dangerous thing, tricking you into thinking all was well, that those red flags were really little white ones, to go right ahead and pursue the relationship that was so very wrong for you, that everything would work out fine in the end. And by the time you realized you'd been a fool, that your imagination had tricked you, it would be too late. You would have allowed the girl to imprint herself on your very heart with soul ties so strong that nothing could ever cut them.

Mason and Ciddah's relationship had become symbiotic. It wasn't that they couldn't live without one another. Of course they *could*.

The issue was that neither one wanted to.

CHAPTER
20

W hat is the matter with you?" Levi pulled the covers off Omar, and the chilled air gripped his half-naked body. "You've missed two meetings this week. Get up and get dressed so we can talk." Levi walked to the window in Omar's bedroom, turned his back to Omar, and looked out on the street.

Omar sighed as loudly as he could. His head pounded so hard he wondered if Levi had stabbed a knife into his brain to wake him. He swung his legs off the side of the bed and pulled on the pants he'd worn yesterday. His vaporizer caught his gaze, cradled in a wrinkle of his bed sheets. He grabbed it and vaped a long drag, hoping it would ease his throbbing skull.

Levi glanced back and showed his irritation with a scowl. "I thought the Owl was all you needed for a high, Omar?"

Omar dropped his PV to the bed sheets again. "Leave me alone."

"It's the vapo stick, isn't it? That's the real problem. That's why I can't depend on you."

Omar hated that Levi wouldn't bother to get the terms right in this place. He could quote *The Princess Bride* word for word with Jemma, but he couldn't bother to learn that vaporizers or PVs weren't called vapo sticks.

And it wasn't the *vapers* at all. It was the fact that Omar had become nocturnal in his life as the Owl. He had to sleep sometime. If it was during a rebel meeting or two, so be it. It wasn't like they could make any real plans until Mason heard back from Penny, anyway. They were just talking circles around circles.

Levi walked over to the bed and sat on the end of it. "Get rid of the thing. Or give it to me."

Omar grabbed his PV in case Levi tried to take it. He pulled the covers back up over him and kept his hand with the PV hidden. "I'd just buy another one. I hurt without it." His head was still throbbing.

"Toughen up, brother. Don't be a sissy."

Sissy. The word burned Omar from the inside. Levi had always been a younger version of their father, but the likeness lately was truly horrifying. "You don't understand."

Levi stood and started pacing at the foot of the bed. "I understand that you refuse to tell yourself no. Be a man. Stop juicing up like a flaker. Mason said you almost died once. Is that what you want? You want to die?"

Omar thought hard about it. "Sometimes."

The lines of anger on Levi's face softened. "Why would you say that?"

Omar hadn't meant to say it out loud. There were just too many problems in his life and they'd all piled up on top of him. And now this mess with Shay and Kendall. He didn't know what to do. How to fix it. Kendall had come by twice since the kiss. She liked him. But he didn't want her to like him. He wanted her to go away. Why couldn't he just say so? He wanted to be with Shay, but he couldn't. He wasn't good enough for her.

Was he avoiding giving Kendall an answer so that he'd have her in case Shay gave up on him for good?

"Hey! Answer me." Levi was standing beside him now, at the side of his bed. "Why would you say that?"

236

Walls, he was freaking out. "I'm not going to kill myself, brother. Relax. But I'm tired. I want to be good, but I'm not. I want to be worthy, but I'm not. No matter what I do, it's never good enough for anyone. Never for Father, never for you." And now Shay. "It's my fault we're here, that so many are dead. And I can't fix it. Even when I try to do good, something always stops me."

"Like what?"

"Red. Kendall. Shay. The PV. The Owl. My own fears of never being you."

Levi sighed into a defeated slouch. "You don't have to be like me. Omar, I forgave you for what happened to Glenrock."

Sure. "You said you did, but you still treat me like you don't."

"I do not."

"Whatever." Omar's headache was still strong. He wanted another vape but didn't dare take one until after Levi left. "What do you want, anyway? Why are you here?" And why wouldn't he go away?

"I already said. You missed two meetings, and I wanted to make sure you were okay. I want you to stop being a flaker and help us get out of here."

If it were only that easy. "I *am* a flaker, Levi. And even if I could stop vaping and stop chasing femmes, even if I started dressing like you and talking like you and following you around like some kind of soldier, my skin would still flake because I'm infected."

Levi shrugged off Omar's words. "Mason is looking for a cure."

Not with Levi's agenda. No one had time to do anything when Levi was doling out duties all the time. "He's not going to find one. You think Mason knows more than the medics in this place?" Mason was smart, but not that smart.

"Yeah, well, you and Zane aren't likely going to figure out libera-tion, either."

That was true. So far Omar and Zane had found nothing. Omar lay back down in the bed on his side and pulled the covers up to his neck. "Whatever."

"I talked to Mason about this. He thinks you're addicted to the juices."

Omar huffed a dry laugh. "A sound diagnosis from Medic Mason. But I could've told you that myself, brother."

"Mason also says most people don't stop juicing until they get locked up in rehab, where they can't get it."

"You going to send me to rehab?" Empty threats. Blah blah. Why wouldn't he just leave, already?

"I was thinking of making my own rehab."

"Oh, I see." Omar rolled onto his back where he could get a better look at his brother. "So you're going to lock me in some basement where I won't embarrass you anymore, is that it?"

Months ago, Levi's glare would have made Omar's legs weak. Today, it did nothing. "Stop being difficult, Omar. Look, I think what Mason said about being addicted is a load of dung. Just stop sucking on the vapo stick, and it's done. It's about willpower. You're the one who wanted to be Omar Strong. So prove it. Buck up. But if you keep blowing me off, if you keep missing meetings like you can't be bothered to help us get out of this place, I just might have to stick you in some basement."

Omar sighed, weary of Levi's company. "Is that a promise?"

"You bet."

"Well, gee. Thanks for the talk, brother. It's always nice to know someone cares."

"Good." Oblivious to Omar's sarcasm, Levi nodded like he was finally making progress with his deadbeat little brother. How could anyone be so full of his own self-importance? "I have something else to say."

Omar closed his eyes and dreamed of taking a breath from his PV. "I can't wait."

"You kissed Kendall Collin? She text-tapped Jemma about it."

Great. At least Omar knew for certain which girls couldn't shut their mouth. He really hoped news of his latest blunder didn't get back to Shay. He still owed her a groveling apology for having accused her of lying about the Owl thing. "Kendall started it."

"You're going to be a father, Omar. Act like one."

Omar pushed himself to one elbow and scowled at Levi. "Jemma tell you to say that?"

Levi delivered one last scathing "I think you're a complete failure and waste of space on this planet" glare and walked to the bedroom door.

"Look, I'm infected. Shay's not!" Omar yelled after Levi, who'd left the room. "I can't be with Shay. She's too good for me."

Levi's voice carried back. "You'll hear no argument from me on that, brother."

"Mad good," Omar mumbled. "We finally agree on something. Let's celebrate."

Levi stepped back into the open doorway. "Why don't you come out to the cabin and eat dinner with everyone tonight?"

Omar had been joking about the celebrating part. He fell back to the bed and stared at the ceiling. "I don't know."

"Come on. It will be good for you. Make up with Shaylinn, get Jemma off my back."

So, basically, make all Levi's problems go away. "Yeah, I'll think about it." Thinking ... and ... done. Not going.

"Don't think, just come. I'll see you later." And Levi left.

Omar waited until he heard his front door open and close before he took a long drag from his PV. Then he got up, showered, and ate some stale doughnuts. He pulled a chair from his kitchen table over to his easel. He didn't paint, though. He just sat there, elbows propped on his knees, head in his hands, thinking.

Only one face haunted him at the moment. Shay. Standing outside the cabin. Hurt.

Maybe if he painted her, it would get her out of his head. He set to work, starting with her hair. Black and more black. Then some cinnamon. Add some white to make gray. More white for the glimmers of the tinsel weave. Cobalt to give it midnight highlights. Once he'd gotten the hair right, he painted her eyes. Burnt umber, dark and deep, filled with longing and pain. Eyes that haunted him in so many ways.

His doorbell rang, scaring him out of his obsession. He set down his palette and went and opened the door.

General Otley stood outside with three other enforcers. He handed Omar a sheet of paper and barged past, knocking Omar's shoulder against the doorjamb. "Mind if we come in, little rat?"

Omar should have used the peephole. "Yes, actually." He looked at the paper and saw it was Red's art sale flyer. Nice. That woman continued to get her payback, even when she wasn't trying.

The enforcers followed Otley inside. Omar considered making a run for it, but for some reason he didn't. He kicked the door shut, crumpled the flyer, and tossed it in the trash.

Otley stopped midway between the door and the easel, keeping his back to Omar. "Where have you been, Mr. Strong?"

"Here."

Three heavy pivoting steps and Otley had turned to face Omar. "According to the grid, your SimTag has been here for the past month. It's never once left your apartment. But you have. I've got eyes everywhere, little rat. I think your SimTag is malfunctioning. I don't even see the number on your face." Otley jerked his head, and three enforcers rushed Omar. Two pushed him onto the chair by his easels, the third pulled a SimScanner from its holster and ran it over Omar's body and all around his right hand. His gloves were on the kitchen counter, so he was SimTag free, as Otley had likely been hoping.

"No reading, sir." The enforcer clicked his scanner back on his belt and grabbed Omar's hand. He examined it. "He's cut it out."

Otley stepped in front of Omar's chair, his massive body blocking the ceiling light. "How did you know to cut out your SimTag, little rat?"

"I task at a SimArt shop. I figured it out."

Otley sneered, which lifted one side of his top lip and caused the number eight on his cheek to curl out. "No. I think you've made some dangerous friends. And I think they did this to you."

240

"Careful not to hurt yourself with all that thinking." That earned him a slap from one of the enforcers.

Otley growled low in his throat. "I want to know what you've been doing."

"Maybe I've been pairing up with Belbeline," Omar said, knowing he'd taken his snark too far that time.

Otley punched Omar, knocking him off the chair. His face exploded with hot fire, and he crashed against the legs of his easel. The painting of Shay fell on top of him. He caught it on the palms of his hands and tried to be gentle, but someone pushed down from the other side, smearing the wet paint all over him. When he managed to sit up and slide the painting off him, it was a blob of charcoal gray paint. Ruined.

Omar clambered to his feet and ran at Otley. He was two steps from the overgrown boar when one of the enforcers' stunners hit him. The cartridge bit into his back, overwhelming his nerves. He hit the tile floor hard. More pain. In his right elbow, left hand, and both knees. A second enforcer stepped over him and shot him with a sedation gun.

Omar lay on the floor, smarting and swelling and staring at Otley's shiny black shoes until he passed out.

He awoke to the sound of rattling metal and squeaking hinges. He was in the RC, lying on his face on the cold cement floor. Two enforcers were standing by the open door of his cell.

"Come on out," one of them said. "General Otley wants a word."

"Can't wait," Omar said, his voice a raspy croak. He needed water. And his PV.

It wasn't easy to get up, but he eventually managed and followed the guards out of the RC. He was still wearing his clothes from yesterday. His feet were bare and cold on the cement floor. An itch drew his attention to the 9XX glowing faintly on the back of his hand. They'd given him a new SimTag. And another X. It was about time, really. He felt rather proud of it and walked a little taller.

The enforcers didn't take him to a holding cell, though, but to the lobby. General Otley stood at the reception desk, talking to the femme who tasked there. He caught sight of Omar and walked toward him.

"We Xed you for cutting out your SimTag. Don't do it again. Kept you overnight because I had reason to believe you were that ratty Owl causing all the trouble around here. But the Owl came on the ColorCast last night as always with a whole new list of threats. Thought it might be footage of you, but he was seen on Sopris and Ninth last night attacking an enforcer, so I have no reason to hold you."

The Owl attacked an enforcer? Zane must have donned the costume.

Otley's yellow-eyed stare really freaked Omar out, but he did his best to look indifferent as Otley threw out more warnings. "I'm watching you, little rat. And I can see better than any owl. Now get lost."

It was the first time he recognized that Levi and Otley had a few things in common. But Omar didn't have to be told twice where Otley was concerned. He walked from the RC, even though he wanted to sprint. The sidewalk was wet under his feet. It had been raining. He waved a cab, and before he made his destination request, he asked the driver to check the balance on his SimTag.

"You've got thirteen credits," the driver said, glancing over his shoulder at Omar. "Good thing credit day is coming, huh?"

"Yeah. Look, I'm sorry to have bothered you. Looks like General Otley drained my account. I don't have enough to get me to the Midlands. I'll have to walk."

"Stimming enforcers anyway," the driver said. "Sorry about that, peer. Hey, maybe you'll get lucky. Maybe the Owl will leave you a gift in the night."

"Yeah, maybe," Omar said, getting out and wondering if Zane had taken his place as the Safe Lands' hero.

CHAPTER
21

Mason's two weeks of tasking at Pharmco ended, and the Friday before they were supposed to free the kids, Mason returned to the SC. The moment he arrived, Rimola sent him to Ciddah's office.

"What does she want?" Mason asked, noticing that Rimola's skin was gold today. He must have missed the change in trends.

"She didn't say, valentine, but be nice to her. She's in a good mood today, and I don't want you ruining things with your opinions."

Mason knocked on Ciddah's office door and let himself in. "You wanted to see me?"

Ciddah hopped up from her desk and ran across the room. She wrapped her arms around his neck and greeted him with a lingering kiss that stunned his thoughts and made the Safe Lands seem like a paradise.

"What was that for?" he asked when she finally pulled back.

"For being so perfect. I'm sorry I made you work in the pharmacy. I missed you here."

He stroked her hair. "I missed being here."

Again her lips found his, and the thought crossed his mind that he was getting better at kissing. He no longer felt awkward. Things just sort of ... worked now. And it hadn't even taken very long to learn. He wondered if this were true of all couples or if he and Ciddah simply had more —

The door opened behind them, and they broke apart. Rimola stood in the doorway, one hand on her hip, slouched with enough attitude to host a fight club. "Gee, raven. I told you to be nice to her, but you didn't have to take me so literally. Now, if you sugar sweets are done trading paint, all the exam rooms are full."

Ciddah tossed her hair over her shoulder. "You could have used the intercom."

"And miss breaking this up?" Rimola grinned and left the office.

Ciddah exhaled a long breath. Their gazes met, and she bridged the gap between them and kissed him once more, then mumbled with their lips still touching, "Come tell me when you've set up the patients."

His eyes were still closed when he answered, "Okay," and he felt her lips smile beneath his.

"You're going to go now, right?" Her lips trailed along his jaw and nuzzled his neck.

"Yes." But she was the task director, and if she was going to keep doing that, he may as well wait for her to finish.

The intercom beeped, and Rimola's voice came from the speaker. "Medic Rourke to the reception area. The med supply delivery is here and needs your authorization."

"Oh." Ciddah sighed and her hands fell away. "Got to go." She slipped past him and out the door.

Mason remained in her office for a moment to collect himself, thinking of how good it felt to be loved by Ciddah. Not only did he get to have intellectually stimulating conversations with a brilliant and beautiful woman, but she wanted to kiss him — even seemed to like it. He crossed the hallway to the door of exam room one and lifted the CompuChart from the slot on the wall.

And his joy shattered.

Penelope Colton.

Why?

He knocked on the door. When no one answered, he cracked the door a little and peeked in.

Penelope was sitting on the exam table wearing a white gown and staring at the door. His cousin had always been the leader of Shaylinn and Nell. Personality-wise, she took after Levi more than her own mother or father. She looked older than her thirteen years. Always a tomboy before; perhaps it was the fake eyelashes that were throwing Mason off-kilter. When she recognized him, her face broke into a grin. "Mason!"

He slipped inside and closed the door behind him.

Penelope jumped off the table and hugged him, the paper-like fabric of her white gown rustling in his arms. "You have white stuff on your face, Mason. Powdered sugar?" She reached up and tapped his nose.

He wiped his finger across his nose, and it came away coated in creamy color. He turned to look in the mirror above the sink and saw that his nose and chin were dusted in white, except around his lips, which were pink.

Ciddah's makeup. Roller Paint. Trading paint. Oh.

Understanding the term chilled him into action. He wet a paper towel and cleaned his face. "Why didn't your cla—" No. It would be foolish to ask why her class didn't go out the other day. Lawten was likely listening. "What are you doing here, Penelope? Are you sick?"

She hung her head. "They're making me leave the school. I have to move in a week, and I don't want to say why."

Mason and Levi would never be able to help the kids escape without Penelope's help. "Did someone threaten you?"

"No. But ..."

"Hey, you can trust me. I promise." He lowered his voice to a whisper. "This place hasn't changed me." Though the image of his face covered in Roller Paint popped into his head.

She folded her arms. "Well, you're still a boy, aren't you? And I'm not talking about this to a boy. Papa was right. Boys shouldn't be the doctors of girls. Especially boys you know."

"Oh." He looked at the chart and saw that she was scheduled for a pelvic exam. What? Why would they do that? "Are they moving you to the harem?"

Penelope's face crumpled, and she started to cry. "I don't want to grow up or have a baby or move away from Nelly. I want my daddy and my mom. I'm sick of this place, and I want to go home."

"Hey, hey." Mason put his arm around her in an awkward side hug. She cried a little, and Mason did his best to be patient.

She wiped her eyes. "I wish I were a boy."

"Well, we boys have our share of troubles here too."

She sniffled. "Not as bad as us, though."

"No, you're right about that."

The door opened, and Ciddah swept into the room. "Are you ready, Miss Colton?"

Penelope screamed and hid behind Mason. "Don't let her touch me, Mason. Please don't let her!" Another scream. They weren't the screams of a petrified girl, but one who was trying to manipulate her way out of trouble. Typical Penelope, though Mason couldn't blame her.

"She's terrified," Mason said.

Ciddah twisted her lips. "We'll have to sedate her."

This was his chance to find out whether or not Ciddah would be willing to help him. "Actually, I think there's some mistake here. This patient is scheduled for a pelvic exam, but she claims she's, uh, undergoing menstruation now."

Penelope screeched and pressed her hands over her ears. As if Mason didn't feel awkward enough already.

"Right now?" Ciddah yanked the CompuChart from Mason's hands and tapped around. "The chart says she started last week."

Which explained why Penelope was here today for a pelvic exam. "Perhaps the hormone meds are causing some problems," Mason said, feeling Penelope clench the back of his shirt. "It might be best to reschedule. Maybe give her something for the cramps?"

Ciddah's eyes narrowed as she studied him. She glanced past his arm where Penelope was peeking around his side, then focused her blue-eyed gaze back on him. "I don't see why that would be a problem. Hormone meds can cause irregularity, especially in young girls."

Mason felt Penelope release his shirt.

"I'll tell Rimola to schedule her for next week. Penelope, why don't you lie down, and I'll get you something for the pain."

Penelope scowled at Ciddah. "I don't have to listen to you."

"Explain that to her, Mason, then I'll need you to come and get the meds." Ciddah handed him the CompuChart and left.

He turned around, and Penelope hugged him around the waist. "Thank you, Mason!"

It felt good to get something right after so many weeks of nothing. "Do you take back what you said about men being doctors?"

"No." She gave him a dirty look that only lasted a few seconds before changing into a smile. "But I'm glad you were here."

"Me too." He steered her by the shoulder toward the exam table. "Now lie down. I'll douse the lights. You are a very sick girl." He tried to emphasize his words to hint to her to play along.

"But I don't want to stay here. Will the meds hurt me?"

"Not at all." Mason went to the door. "I'll be back right back with your meds, and we'll figure this out."

But when he stepped into the hallway, Ciddah was waiting. She handed him a CompuChart. "I'll take the meds to the girl. I need you to prep the patient in exam room three." She swept into Penelope's room and closed the door behind her.

What was that about?

Penelope's appearance in the SC wasn't the only surprise waiting for Mason that morning. Exam room three also held a familiar face.

"Mia," Mason said when he entered the room.

She was sitting on the table, giving him one of her haughty smiles. As he set about getting her vitals, it occurred to him that something good had come from the disaster of the raid on Glenrock: he no longer had to marry Mia.

"I heard a rumor that the doctor is in love with you," Mia said.

Mason synced the table scale with the CompuChart.

"Have you slept with her yet?"

He pretended not to hear that. "Please lie back on the bed and put up your feet."

She obeyed him, but continued to pry. "If you do, you'll get the thin plague, just like me."

He activated the scale and accepted her weight in the CompuChart. "It's not the thin plague I fear, Mia, but being used."

She pushed up onto her elbows, scowling. "Rand loves me. We'd be together now if it wasn't for the law that all pregnant women live in the harem. Since everyone else escaped, Ewan won't risk his task to sneak me out to meet Rand. So I can't even see him until I have the baby."

"I'm sorry, Mia." And he truly was. He suspected that Mia was in for much heartache in the coming months.

"Do you think you could ask the doctor to let Rand come to my appointments? I think he'd like to be here, you know, to see me and to see how his baby is growing."

Mason looked at Mia then, and her vulnerability staggered him. He'd never seen her so openly desperate. "It's not allowed." Nor did Mason think Rand would care.

Mia sucked in a breath through her nose, and her nostrils flared. "But *you* could convince her, couldn't you?"

Mason swallowed back his frustration. He had enough to ask of Ciddah right now with getting in and out of the boarding school. "But Mia, what if your Rand doesn't want to come?"

She rolled her eyes at his foolish suggestion. "Of course he'll come."

Mason nodded in an attempt to look positive. "I'll ask Ciddah, but until then, perhaps she'd allow your mother to come in with you. Would you like that?"

Mia lay back on the table and shrugged one shoulder, crinkling the paper beneath her. "Only if she can't get Rand in."

Of course the piano player would rank higher in Mia's mind than her own mother, a woman who'd given up freedom to stay in the harem with her selfish daughter. Mason wished he had the guts to say that out loud, but instead he settled on, "I'll see what I can do."

When Mason stepped out into the hallway, he found Ciddah waiting again. He handed her the CompuChart. "She's ready for you," he said.

Ciddah took the chart and slid it into the slot on the door, then turned and walked down the hall. "Can I speak with you in my office, please?"

What now? Mason followed, bewildered.

Ciddah closed the door behind him, then went to sit at her desk. "Take a seat," she said, motioning to the empty chair before her desk. "I already cleaned it off for you."

The comment made him smile, and he sat down.

"Mason, are we going to have a problem with you tasking here?"

He stared at her, confused. The thought crossed his mind that she'd somehow used him again, but that couldn't be. Could it?

"I cannot continue to argue with you over the decrees of the Safe Lands Guild." She picked up a pen and started writing.

Her words made no sense whatsoever. "What did I do?"

Still writing, she said, "Our people are dying, and we must do everything we can to build a future." She handed him the slip of paper, which said *MiniComms in every room. Be careful.*

Though he'd suspected Lawten might be listening, her words changed everything, erased any last hint of doubt as to her loyalty to Lawten Renzor and the Safe Lands. She had tried to warn him before he said something to Penelope about freeing the children. He had truly won her.

But he needed to play along if Lawten was going to believe this conversation was real. "But the cure. If I could find one ... Will you come with me to the History Center tonight? One last time?"

Ciddah growled as if annoyed by his request, but she grinned and winked as well. "It's a waste of time, Mason. I'll come tonight, but then I think you need to give up this foolish dream of yours and start accepting your new life here."

He sighed as loud as he could. "Maybe you're right." But maybe instead, Ciddah would be the one who started to accept the idea of a new life elsewhere.

Mason and Ciddah left the SC together that afternoon and headed for the Treasury Building, which housed the History Department. Through a series of note writing, Ciddah had allowed Mason and Penelope to have some privacy to plan the boarding school escape. She hadn't even asked for the details. Mason couldn't wait to find Levi later on tonight. But first he wanted to follow up on the lead Ciddah's father had given them about Lonn.

"Shall I wave us a taxi?" Mason asked.

"Let's walk," she said. When they were halfway past the Noble Gardens, she added, "Lawten told me all taxis have recorders. They don't monitor them unless they have reason, but I promise you that they've been monitoring us for a while now. My guess is, at least the last three weeks."

"In the SC? Or everywhere?"

"In our apartments, the SC, my office, the elevators, and taxis. Yes. But not outside. They can't get to us out here."

They walked a moment in silence, and Mason let this sink in. He couldn't remember if he'd said anything incriminating to Mia or Jennifer in their appointments. He wondered how much the enforcers had learned about the people from Glenrock just from listening in.

"I'm sorry I didn't think to tell you before," Ciddah said. "When I saw the girl there, I knew you'd try to make plans with her. I didn't want you to give anything away."

"Thank you," Mason said. "I couldn't let them put Penelope in the harem."

They walked in silence for half a block, then Ciddah looked at him, her eyes wide. "Once the children are safe, are you going to leave?"

"We don't know how to get out," Mason said. "Enforcers have

sealed the storm drains that lead into the canal. But I'll have to go into hiding then. Lawten will know I had something to do with it."

"Will you take me with you?" Ciddah asked. "And my donors? Please? If you leave, I'm afraid of what Lawten might do to them. And to me. Plus … I don't want to be parted from you."

He should reach out to her. Touch her, to show that he cared. He was always forgetting. "Of course, Ciddah." He took her hand and squeezed. Though he didn't know how any of this was going to work. Mason doubted Papa Eli would have supported his desire to be with Ciddah. His great-grandfather would have been concerned about the thin plague. And her religion. With those two issues, they would have never found an elder to act as a witness during their commitment before the elders, let alone consent to mentor them.

How would Levi respond? Would he uphold Glenrock's traditional ways of courting? And was that Mason's goal? He'd only known the real Ciddah for a few days. Perhaps he should slow down a little. Think all this through.

They had dinner at a sandwich shop called Uppercrust, then went to the History Center. Ciddah warned him that it too was monitored with MiniComms.

Mason sat at a GlassTop computer and began by looking up a biography of Richark Lonn. He'd learned some of the information from Lonn's liberation ceremony on the ColorCast. Born in 2037. Richark Lonn had been the fastest medic to reach a rank of twenty. Lifer with Martana Kirst. Together they gave the Safe Lands eight children. Martana died in labor along with the child that would have been her ninth.

"Didn't you tell me Martana Kirst committed suicide?" Mason asked.

"That's a rumor."

"There's nothing here I don't already know," Mason said, then he scrawled on the sheet of paper between them: *I thought your dad was trying to tell me something.*

Ciddah scribbled out "dad" and wrote "donor."

Mason rolled his eyes, then typed "Lawten Renzor" into the search box.

"What are you looking for now?" Ciddah asked.

"Just a hunch." Mason pulled up the task director general's biography and started to read.

Born March 12, 2049 ... "He's thirty-nine?"

"Yes, why?"

"He looks twice that. Ciddah, he's older than your parents?"

"I guess. I never really thought about his age."

Eww. Mason grimaced but a new thought distracted him. "He'll be liberated soon." He continued to read in silence. After graduating from the Safe Lands Boarding School, Lawten Renzor was awarded a medical internship under Richark Lonn.

Mason pointed to the screen. "Did you know that?"

"Of course."

Mason scanned the text and pointed to the next fact he thought was important. Upon Richark Lonn's forced retirement, Lawten Renzor was promoted to chief medic of the Medical Center. Six weeks later he was awarded a chair on the Safe Lands Guild, the youngest man ever to serve on the Guild.

Mason looked at Ciddah. "Six weeks later? Doesn't that seem a little convenient?"

She shrugged and wrote on the paper: *You think Richark's getting fired had something to do with Lawten's promotion?*

"Sure seems that way to me." Then Mason wrote: *We need to look at Richark's arrest file.* That's what Droe had suggested. "I bet there's something in there that will help." Ciddah said Droe had once been a rebel. Mason wondered how many secrets the man knew.

"I guess I don't understand what you're looking for," Ciddah said.

Mason wrote: *It was the way your dad said it.*

Ciddah again scratched out "dad" and wrote "donor."

Mason poked her side, and she giggled. Then he wrote: *Your DONOR wanted me to look this up.* "You have a CompuChart in your bag?" Ciddah often took one home with her.

"Yes." Ciddah opened her bag and pulled out a CompuChart.

"See if you can look up ..." He wrote down: *Martana Kirst's med history.* "Just a hunch." He wrote: *What if Lawten was her medic for the last baby?*

Ciddah took the pen from him: *You think Richark blamed Lawten for her death?*

The dates seemed to fit. "Just look it up." If Mason was right, then perhaps Richark had gone after Lawten because he'd failed to save Martana.

"Found it." Ciddah laid the CompuChart on the surface of the GlassTop, where Mason could read it.

Martana's final delivery had been on September 12, 2068. Lawten *had* been her medic. His notes said the cause of death was likely amniotic fluid embolism, cardiac arrest, and disseminated intravascular coagulation. He read the hospital course.

The patient was admitted to the Medical Center, where she went into labor for her ninth child at 5:58 p.m. During the delivery, the patient became hypoxic and unresponsive. She had three cardiac arrests and developed disseminated intravascular coagulation, which required multiple transfusions. Delivery was accelerated to attempt reduction of the DIC. The infant was stillborn. The patient was temporarily stabilized, but upon transport to the recovery room, became hypotensive. She again went into cardiac arrest. Resuscitative efforts failed.

That a woman could die in childbirth in a place with so many wonderful machines sobered Mason and made him think of Joel. He had always wondered if the Safe Lands medics might have saved his friend, but perhaps there was nothing even they could have done.

"It doesn't seem suspicious," Ciddah said, bringing him back to the subject.

"No." Mason was glad. He hated to think that any medic could allow a patient to die for subversive reasons. He wrote: *But that doesn't mean Richark didn't blame him.*

"I suppose. But, Mason …" She picked up the pen and wrote: *This was 2068. Does Richark's bio say when he started the Black Army?*

Mason wrote: *2068. But he wasn't fired until 2076.* "Eight years after Martana died."

"Then her death and his termination probably aren't related."

Another idea came to Mason. "What if he'd been asking the same questions you were?" He wrote: *Stimulants in the ACT treatment?*

"Then he probably would have come here."

"Maybe." Mason thought back to Otley's visit to his apartment and the enforcer field medic Yarel. *Have you ever tested the blood on a blood meter?*

She grabbed his pen. *Yes. I've tested my blood, the blood of pregnant women, men, children, my donors. Over a dozen people. I was unable to identify or isolate anything that looked like a stimulant. But I know it's there.*

Mason took the pen. *Have you tested just the meds on the blood meter?*

Won't work. Without blood, the control line doesn't show. Makes the test invalid.

Mason dug deep. The meds were designed to be used on infected people. Perhaps the stimulant converted in some way when it reacted with the virus and that's why Ciddah had been unable to isolate it. *Have you tested the meds in uninfected blood?*

There is no uninfected blood.

Mason snatched the pen from her fingers. *I have uninfected blood.* He smiled and wiggled his eyebrows.

Her face shone. "That might work, Mason. That's brilliant!"

They gathered their things and went back to the SC. It was almost eight o'clock, and the place was dark.

"How come you make me task here all night sometimes, but tonight it's empty?" Mason asked.

"I'm on call tonight. Any taps are routed to the MC receptionist, and if there's an emergency, she'll call me. I have you work on nights when the MC is understaffed."

Ciddah turned on the lights in exam room one and pulled on a pair of gloves. "Sit down. I'm going to prick your finger, but if everything looks good, I'm going to draw a few vials. Then we'll have plenty to test."

Mason sat on the chair beside the exam table, eager to see what stimulants might be in the treatment.

Ciddah swabbed his finger clean, then pricked it and ran the blood through the blood meter. "Clean. Amazing, Mason. Your blood is perfect."

He smiled as if that were a compliment.

"I should take your blood pressure too, just to check," she said.

"I'm perfectly healthy. Just do it."

"Okay, fine." Ciddah wrapped a tourniquet around his arm, just above his elbow, then grabbed the pillow off the table and tucked it between his arm and lap, turning his palm up. She swabbed the inside of his elbow with an alcohol wipe, then opened a standard blood test kit and a fresh cannula. "Make a fist."

Mason obeyed, and Ciddah inserted the cannula into his vein. A little pinch. She filled three vials and pressed a cotton ball over the puncture. "Put your finger on that and slowly open your fist."

Mason knew the drill. He held down the cotton ball and opened his fist. Ciddah disposed of the cannula, labeled the vials, and set them on the counter. Then she turned back to him and removed the cotton ball. "Looks good." She put a round bandage over the puncture mark, then released the tourniquet. "Wait here." She stood and walked out of the room.

"Where are you going?" Mason called.

But she was back before he had long to wonder. "I needed some sterile containers so we could test both meds." She put them on the counter. He could hear her ripping open bags and the plastic dishes clicking on the counter.

He stood up to watch her work. She'd set up two little square dishes on the counter, their lids arranged above them. Two med vials sat beside them. She wrote which was which on the sticker of each dish lid. "C. Rourke old meds." "C. Rourke compounded." She released a sample of Mason's blood into each dish, then used an eyedropper to add the meds to each sample, using a different dropper for each one.

"Okay, old meds first." She dropped a sample of the mixed blood and meds onto the blood meter. It whirred. The Wyndo screen turned blue, a sign that the machine was processing.

She sighed and looked up at him, gave a little shrug. "Technology. As fast as it is, sometimes it feels so slow."

"It's pretty amazing," Mason said. "In our village, we weren't able to keep—"

The sound of the elevator's ding and the doors sliding open in the reception area caused them to stare at one another. "That's strange," Ciddah said.

"Safe Lands Enforcers," a man called. "Is anyone here?"

CHAPTER
22

B e right back." Ciddah slipped out of exam room one. Her footsteps clicked over the tile floor as she made her way down the hall and into the reception area. Mason strained to hear her. "Can I help you?"

"Ciddah Rourke?" a man's voice asked. "The task director general has requested to see you immediately."

"Is there some problem? Why didn't he contact me himself?"

"I don't know, Miss Rourke. I'm simply following orders. You'll need to come with us."

"Of course. Let me lock my office."

"Actually, I need you to remain in the lobby while we search this facility."

"Search it for what?"

"SimSearch shows another person at this location. A, um ..." A pause. "Mason Elias. We're to take him into custody."

Mason couldn't breathe. Had Lawten and his enforcers managed to figure out what he and Ciddah had been trying to do?

"Has he done something?" Ciddah asked.

"I'm sorry. That's classified, Miss Rourke."

Multiple footsteps clacked in the lobby, down the hall, approaching exam room one. Mason panicked. He ripped off the bandage that held his SimTag and dropped it in the trash beside the door. Then he opened the narrow clothing closet behind the exam table and squeezed inside. He tried to close the door, but it bounced off the toes of his shoes. He turned his feet sideways, and barely managed to pull the door shut.

At first Mason didn't hear anything. Perhaps they'd gone to a different room? Then a voice on the other side of the closet door spoke.

"I don't see anyone." The enforcer had to be twelve inches from the closet.

"Scan for the tag," another said, this one farther away.

In the confined space, Mason sounded like a panting dog. He held his breath a moment, then let it seep from his lips, praying they wouldn't open the closet.

"It's coming from the trash can," the first man said, his voice more distant.

Another silent, agonizing pause passed. The trash can clunked on the tile.

"Got it. It's stuck to this bandage. He cut it out."

"Stimming rebels, anyway. Call it in, and let's get out of here."

"T33, a 620," the first enforcer said.

A tinny female voice responded. "T33, go ahead."

Footsteps faded from the room as the enforcer answered, "T33, 10 – 26 on Ciddah Rourke. 620 on Mason Elias."

Mason wasn't able to hear any more. The thought crossed his mind that he'd left Ciddah to the enforcers. He should have done something to help her, something that enabled them both to escape. But the enforcer hadn't said he was taking Ciddah into custody. Only Mason. So Ciddah would likely be sent home after talking with Lawten.

He stayed put until long after he heard the elevator ding, hoping they hadn't left behind an enforcer. When he finally climbed out of hiding, his gaze landed on the blood meter. A thrill ran up the back of his neck. He stepped toward it, looked down at the display.

Xiaodrine.

What was Xiaodrine? Mason had never heard of it. To protect Ciddah, he quickly cleaned up their experiment, washed his blood samples down the sink, and cleared the blood meter's memory.

Now to get out of here.

The only yellow security camera that he knew of in the SC was in the lobby. He recalled how Shaylinn had snuck out the emergency exit when she'd first found herself here. But without his SimTag, he didn't have a way to open the door.

In his medic orientation, Ciddah had mentioned emergency overrides in SimPads in case of a blackout. Mason found a scalpel and crept to the back door of the SC. He pried off the pad from the unit, which revealed a green circuit board covered in white and orange components. At the bottom was a black switch. He flipped it, and the door swung open.

Enforcers would likely detect that on the grid, so Mason ran all the way to his apartment in the Westwall. It wasn't until he was standing outside his apartment — using the scalpel to pry the pad off the unit beside his door — that it occurred to him there might not be an override switch on the outsides of doors, as that would enable unauthorized entry.

Sure enough, no switch. He screamed out his frustration and kicked the door, paced back and forth in front of it, then tried to use his shoulder as a battering ram.

When the door swung in, he jumped back, shocked.

Omar stood inside. "Hey, brother. Something wrong?"

Mason ran in and shut the door. "What are you doing here?"

"Otley arrested me. Gave me a new SimTag and a black eye. But he drained all my credits, and I had no way to get back to the Midlands. Do you have any stims, Mase? I could really use a hit of something and my PV's back at my place."

Omar was wearing jeans and a T-shirt and had bare feet. His eye was swollen and rimmed in purple and yellow. A 9XX glowed brightly on his cheek, and thick brown feather SimArt coated one arm.

"So, Otley knows you're here?" If they were looking for Mason, Omar's new SimTag might bring them here first.

"I couldn't very well go to any rebel locations with a legit SimTag, brother. Otley told me not to cut it out, but I want—"

"You have to. Now." Mason ran into his bedroom. His mirror clock read 9:12 p.m. He picked up his backpack and filled it with all his medical supplies: a bottle of alcohol, his scalpels, a box of adhesive bandages, a bag of cotton balls, and a box of rubber gloves. He found his portable Wyndo on his bedside table, then got on the floor to fetch the little metal box holding the ghoulie tag, which he'd taped to a bar under his bed. He grabbed a spare pair of shoes and jogged back into the living room with a full pack.

Omar was running in place, staring at Mason's Wyndo wall screen, which was a blur of colors that made no sense to Mason.

"What are you doing?" Mason asked.

"Playing Metaldrome. I got SimSight contacts a few weeks ago, and they're amazing. It's like stepping inside the wall screen." Omar leaped around the living room, clearly seeing something Mason couldn't.

Mason tossed his backpack onto the couch. "Wyndo wall screen: off."

Omar whipped around. "Hey! Why'd you do that?"

"I need to cut out your tag now. Enforcers are coming. So, sit down and let me get this done. And put on these shoes."

Omar sat on the couch and pushed his feet into the shoes, then twisted his arm so that his fist was bottom side up. "What'd you do?"

Mason crouched beside him and wet a cotton ball with the alcohol. "I don't know. Ciddah said they've been monitoring us. We must have said something they didn't like."

"Then let's do this somewhere else."

Mason swabbed Omar's hand, then the scalpel. "They'll track us. I'd rather your trail end here."

"Do you have any stims?"

"Not a drop, brother. Never tried them."

"Figured. You're smart, Mase, but you already know that."

Mason used the razor to make an incision on Omar's hand. His brother's muscles tensed, but Omar didn't jerk away. Mason pushed out the SimTag with his thumbnail. He left Omar's SimTag on the coffee table and stuck a bandage over the wound. "Let's go."

They slipped out into the hall. It was quiet and Mason headed for the stairwell.

"Where are you going?" Omar asked, running alongside. The number on his face was gone now, as was the SimArt on his arm.

"I don't trust the elevator right now." But they passed under a yellow security camera as they entered the stairwell. They'd have to be far more careful if they were going to make it to Zane's. "We need to hide from the cameras, brother. You're the Owl — how do you do it?"

They rounded the landing for the fourth floor and continued down.

"There aren't as many cameras in the Midlands," Omar said, "and Zane can switch them on and off."

"Then tap Zane," Mason said, as they rounded the third floor landing. "We're going to need his help."

"I can't without a ghoulie tag."

Mason sighed and dug in his pack until he found the little metal box. He opened it and found a thick silver ring. "Put this on and see if it will work." He handed the ring to Omar, who slid it onto the middle finger of his right hand.

"SimTalk: tap: Zane," Omar said.

Mason held his breath, praying it would work.

"Hay-o, yourself," Omar said, continuing down the stairs. "Yeah, we need your eyes."

Good. Mason slowed a little and pulled out his portable Wyndo. He used the Friend-Finder to look up Ciddah's location, moving slowly down to the second floor landing as he read the screen. Her SimTag was at 79 Summit Road, which was on the southeast edge of the Highlands, near the top curve of the bell. He tapped to identify the location as he started down the last flight of stairs. The address came up unregistered.

Was that allowed in the Safe Lands?

Perhaps it was a private residence of some kind, secluded from the rest of the city. Lawten's home, maybe? If so, what did he want with Ciddah?

Next he used the Friend-Finder to locate Ciddah's parents. They were home.

"What are you doing?" Omar asked.

Mason looked up to see his brother waiting at the bottom of the stairwell. "Attempting to locate Ciddah."

"I thought you didn't trust her."

"That was … before." He didn't like not knowing where she was, whether or not she was okay.

Omar turned away and cupped his hand over his ear. "Zane says enforcers are out front, but the back is clear. He says to go to the train station on Snowmass and Washington Gulch."

"That's quite a walk," Mason said.

"Yeah, well, he says enforcers are all over downtown, and this is our best bet."

They pushed out the door and ran through the night. They crossed Gothic Road, which was always the busiest road in the Highlands.

"Slow down," Omar said. "Zane says we'll only call attention to ourselves it we're running."

Happy to. Mason wasn't nearly as physically fit as his little brother. "We have to take the train to Midlands West," Mason said. "Tell Zane. We need to get Ciddah's parents into hiding. Lawten has been using them against her, and she'll keep doing what he asks until she's certain they're safe."

"Are you crazy? Levi will turn purple."

They passed down an alley to Snowmass Road, which had far less traffic, and Mason relaxed a little. "There's nothing he can do once we arrive. We need to get to them before Lawten does."

"Maybe he already has. Have you thought of that?"

Mason wished Omar would stop arguing. "I used the Friend-Finder on my portable Wyndo. Both Droe and Losira are at home."

Omar grabbed Mason's arm and stopped him in front of a Lift shop. "You didn't sleep with her, did you, brother? 'Cause, Mase, that's how I got the thin plague. You might be infected."

The accusation flustered Mason. He pulled free from Omar's grasp. "I have not been intimate with Ciddah." Though he had been careless. One should not be able to contract a blood-borne disease from kissing, but it was certainly possible. "Lawten has been blackmailing her. I simply want to help her." Mason kept walking.

Omar quickly caught up. "That guy is the lowest kind of maggot."

"Yes, well—"

"So you're rebel scum now, brother. Just like me." Omar grinned and punched Mason's arm.

"There's more," Mason said, pausing to look both ways before crossing Rebon Street. "I saw Penelope today. They're moving her into the harem next week, so we made a plan to get them out tomorrow night. But I still have no method of getting into the nursery."

"I got that covered, Mase," Omar said, "but I'm going to need you to help me convince Levi."

"Of what?"

"I promised Kendall Collin I'd get her baby too when we went for our kids. She's been to the nursery and wants to help. She knows the layout."

Excellent. "That's most encouraging. Why would Levi refuse her assistance?"

"Because she's a flaker like me. In case you missed it, Levi doesn't like flakers."

Mason winced at Omar's tone. Clearly Levi had failed to mend his relationship with Omar. The train station came into view in the distance. Almost there. "Levi can't afford to be selective. Why didn't Kendall Collin take her offer to Levi? Or Jemma?"

"I don't know. I guess we kind of became friends."

Mason raised his eyebrows. "Kind of? What about Shaylinn?"

Omar punched Mason's arm again. "Not *that* kind of friend. Walls, you're prude, Mase, you know that?"

"I do. Ciddah and Rimola are always quick to remind me."

"So, you really like that doctor woman?" Omar asked. "What do you think Levi will say?"

"Levi's not going to like having to worry about Kendall's child," Mason said, changing the subject as he headed up the steps to the train platform and locker 127.

Omar kept pace beside him. "Yeah, but if you side with me, he has to agree."

Kendall had always been a nice girl. And Mason felt bad that the Safe Lands had taken her baby. But he didn't want to put himself in the middle of an argument between Levi and Omar. "We'll see."

CHAPTER
23

Levi stood behind the island in the kitchen of Zane's house, observing the people in the living room. Almost everyone had arrived: Beshup and the other four men from Jack's Peak, Jordan, Jemma, Ruston, and Nash. Some were sitting in the circle of chairs, some were standing and talking to each other. Zane, Mason, and Omar should have been there by now. But Ruston had told Levi that Zane was down in the nest, helping Levi's brothers escape enforcers in the Highlands.

Mason and Omar's leaving the grid had not been part of the plan. His brothers were not skilled hunters or fighters, and Levi wasn't convinced Zane would be enough to help them evade enforcers. What could have happened that they needed to flee?

Beshup and Mukwiv approached the island. Levi had been trying to stay away from the Jack's Peak men, distancing himself from another debate. He slipped around the opposite end of the island to where Ruston and his son Nash were standing by the fireplace. Levi stopped beside them.

"What's up?" Nash looked like Zane, with dark hair, pale skin, and deep-set eyes. But Nash had both ears and his skin wasn't flaking. Thin plague free, perhaps? Levi wondered how Nash was dealing with his little brother leaving their underground community and becoming a flaker.

"Trying to avoid another confrontation," Levi mumbled.

But Beshup and Mukwiv were not to be discouraged and followed Levi to the fireplace.

"I've been thinking," Beshup said, edging into the space between Nash and Levi. "We are six men, you are four. Together we have ten. If we split our number between the school, the nursery, *and* the harem —"

"We'll have too few." Levi wasn't going to alter the plans at this late hour. They were sketchy enough as it was.

"Then why not focus on the harem first?" Mukwiv suggested. "With our women free, we'll have more than enough warriors to take back the children."

Levi gave the man the same answer he'd given him before. "If you'd like to take your men to the harem, go right ahead, but without Jack's Peak's help, it'll be difficult to know if we have all your kids. I don't know what they look like."

"I thought we were freeing all the children," Ruston said. "No sense leaving any to be brainwashed further."

Now this again. It seemed everyone had their own "pet agenda," as Zane had called it. "How could we free all the children with so few of us?"

"Our women could help," Beshup said, one eyebrow raised in his calm and silent defiance.

Beshup was really getting on Levi's nerves. "This is not open for discussion."

Mukwiv crossed his arms and grunted the way Chief Kimama was known for. "You are not the chief of Jack's Peak."

"And you're not the rebel leader, either," Ruston said. "You can't pull this off without my help, so I get a say in who gets rescued."

Disagreement from all sides. Levi couldn't take this much longer. Silently, he recited the verse Jemma gave him to help him stay calm. *Refrain from anger, turn from wrath.* "Trying to free all the children makes everything more —" Raised murmurs pulled his gaze to the entrance, where Mason had just come inside with a strange man and woman who looked to be in their late thirties. Safe Landers. Levi could tell from their skin. Omar was the last to enter, and he shut the door behind them. All four were carrying suitcases.

"What's this?" Ruston asked, the tone of his voice incredulous.

Levi couldn't believe his brothers would bring strangers here, and Omar's swollen eye concerned him. "I have no idea. Why would the guards let them pass?"

"The guards trust Omar," Nash said.

Levi and the men crossed the room, and by the time they reached the front door, Zane had exited the top of the basement stairs and greeted Mason and Omar with smiles.

"Wasn't sure you were going to make it there for a bit," Zane said.

"What happened to your eye?" Levi asked Omar.

"Otley."

What? "How did —"

"Levi." Mason beamed like this was some sort of celebration. "This is Droe and Losira. They're Ciddah's parents."

Ciddah? The medic? "Mason, I don't —"

"Their SimTags?" Ruston pushed to the front of the group.

"I removed them and left them in their house," Mason said. "They want to go into hiding. Ciddah wanted to come too, but Lawten took her. I have no idea why."

"I told yoouuuu." Losira smiled like she knew a secret, and her voice was twice as loud as need be. "He loves her. No matter what other femmes he takes into his life, he keeps coming back to my girl."

Mason scratched the back of his neck, forehead creased. "I think it's because she found out something. It's been rumored that Lonn was fired from being a medic and arrested because he discovered something the Guild didn't want anyone to know, right?"

"That's one theory," Ruston said. "What did Ciddah uncover?"

"There's a stimulant in the ACT meds," Mason said.

A grumble rose in the small room. Levi hadn't realized everyone had crowded around Mason and his mystery guests. Was he the only one in the room who didn't understand what his brother had just said?

"Can you prove that?" Ruston asked.

"Yes," Mason said. "We mixed my blood with the meds and tested it on a blood meter. The result was Xiaodrine."

"That's prescribed for obesity, I believe," Droe said.

"Really? I've never heard of it. Before we learned the result, enforcers showed up and took Ciddah. So I wasn't able to talk with her about it. I think they knew what we were doing. She told me they were listening, and we tried to be careful, but ... If we can find out what Lonn was arrested for, I think it might provide a clue as to whether Ciddah and I were on the right track."

"I'll tap my peer in the enforcers now." Zane limped away from the group and down the stairs.

"Lonn never confided anything like this to you?" Mason asked Ruston.

"Lonn didn't trust many people," Ruston said. "In the end, he and Bender were closer than anyone."

This was madness. They couldn't afford to waste time trying to solve some mystery of the past when they had a rescue mission to plan. Levi squeezed Mason's arm. "Can I talk to you for a minute, brother?"

"Talk *to* me or *at* me?" Mason said.

Levi dragged him after Zane, stopping on the landing halfway down the stairs, hoping they wouldn't be overheard. "What *is* this?" he asked, keeping his voice low. "Bringing two flakers to the rebel meeting? I thought you were the smart one."

Mason visibly stiffened at Levi's rebuke. "I had to. Once Ciddah finds out they've gone into hiding, she'll know that Lawten doesn't hold anything over her."

"How? What if he tells her he took them and that he's keeping them somewhere else?" Had Mason even thought this through? And why did he care what the task director general did to the medic?

His brother paled, combed his hands into his hair, and gripped it like he might try to pull some out. "I didn't think of that. Everything happened so fast."

It wasn't like Mason to do something so rash. "I wish you would have asked me first, brother." Now they had no one officially on grid.

"But there was no time." Mason slid his hands down to his face and rubbed it. "If I hadn't left my tag and hid, they would've caught me too. I'd be in the RC right now."

Omar slipped down the stairs to join them. "You should trust Mason. He always does the right thing."

"I do," Mason said. "I try, anyway. But not tonight. I'm going after Ciddah, Levi. And once she's safe, I can think about everyone else. But until then — "

"Whoa! You can't go anywhere," Levi said. "Do you even know where she is?"

"Seventy-nine Summit Road," Mason said.

"That's Champion House," Zane said, coming back up the stairs. "The home of the task director general of the Safe Lands. It's a fortress. No one can get in there."

"Lawten's house," Mason mumbled, then his face hardened. "I'll find a way."

Levi had never seen Mason so agitated. What had come over his bookworm brother? "Let's relax a bit, have our meeting, and once everyone leaves, we'll talk this out, okay?"

"I'm not going to let you talk me out of it, Levi." Mason lowered his voice. "I love her."

That confession hit Levi like a bucket of ice water. "That's just perfect." Levi paced up a few steps, then returned to the landing. "What's wrong with you?" What was wrong with everyone? It was impossible to lead people who did whatever they wanted. How had Papa Eli done this for so many years?

Mason's expression was intense yet apologetic. "I didn't mean to, brother. It just happened. I had planned to ask for your blessing in front of the elders — "

"*Marry* a flaker?" What had come over his dutiful brother? "You can't be serious. Papa Eli said never. And you of all people know what that would mean."

"Irrelevant." Mason's jaw hardened into a determined scowl, but it wavered when his gaze met Levi's. "Ciddah's the one for me." He paused, breathed in and out a shaky breath. "And that's saying a lot."

Ridiculous. The medic had brainwashed the logic right out of Mason. "We'll talk about this later. We need to get this meeting started."

"Hold up," Zane said. "My enforcer friend checked the arrest records for Lonn. Said he was charged with" — he read from his Wyndo — "assault, theft, fraud, conspiracy, criminal impersonation, perjury, making false statements, and obstruction of justice."

Omar whistled. "That's a lot of charges."

"Assault against whom?" Mason asked.

"Three enforcers and one *Lawten Renzor*." Zane waggled his eyebrows.

"What about the conspiracy?" Mason asked.

Zane looked to his Wyndo again. "It says conspiracy against the Safe Lands. That could mean anything."

"He was looking into the meds, just like Ciddah and me," Mason said. "Xiaodrine. I wonder if he knew?"

"I'm more intrigued that he assaulted Lawten Renzor," Omar said. "What do you think *that* was about?"

"Hold on," Zane said. "Still reading."

"We should start the meeting," Levi said. "We only have tonight to plan this — "

"I think I got it," Zane said. "Renzor is the one who turned him in for conspiracy."

"And got a deal for it," Mason said. "Got put on the Safe Lands Guild."

Levi's frustration boiled over. "What is the point of all this? We've got kids to rescue. Who cares about Lonn or Renzor?"

"You're still living under the delusion that your people have a way out of the Safe Lands, aren't you?" Zane said.

Levi didn't like his tone. "We'll find a way out."

"But if we don't," Mason said, "our only hope is to bring down the government by exposing the truth."

"Operation Lynchpin," Omar said.

Levi rolled his eyes. "Fine. Fine! But for this meeting, can we focus on the kids, please?" Levi jogged up the stairs and into the center of the circle of chairs. "We're going to start the meeting now, if everyone can find a seat." Relief rushed into him at the sight of people scrambling to sit down. He didn't know what he would have done if everyone had continued to ignore him. He didn't see Mason's mystery guests anywhere. "Ruston, where are the medic's parents?"

"I took them to one of the bedrooms and got them settled."

Good. At least Levi wouldn't have to worry about them adding their opinions on everything. He'd never have guessed that being a leader was this difficult.

Once the room had quieted, Levi said, "Mason, tell us what you found out from Penny."

"Penelope said if we could get some people on the roof of the Nordic tomorrow night, she'd make sure the board was left up. We'll be able to walk across the board and get inside the school."

"What board?" Nash asked.

"Why tomorrow night?" Beshup asked. "I thought we all agreed to wait an extra week to plan?"

"Because they're going to move Penelope into the harem next week," Mason said. "And she says she can get the kids ready to leave tomorrow."

"Penny in the harem?" Jemma looked like she might start crying, which Levi could *not* handle right now.

"What's Penelope telling the kids?" Zane asked.

"That they're going to run away," Mason said. "Then, if a child accidently reveals something, the teachers will discipline the children rather than tap Enforcer 10."

"I'd like to know *who* she's telling," Ruston said.

"As far as I know, just Glenrock and Jack's Peak children," Mason said.

"That's wise," Ruston said. "We can still offer escape to the others, maybe even kidnap some of the younger ones."

Kidnap? Was Levi really going to be a part of kidnapping children? "Jemma, can you give us the breakdown of what kids are where?" They needed to focus on the kids who belonged to them.

Jemma read from a notepad. "We've got eleven girls in the boarding school: Penny, Nell, Meghan, Ruth, Lucy, Hailey, Kaylee, Rosalie, and the three from Jack's Peak: Heather, Haiwee, and Sarajawea. We've also got eleven boys in the school. Ours are Trevon, Jake, Joe, and Brian, and Jack's Peak has another seven: Etu, Dakav, Sakima, Yas, Chua, Dabooze, and Hakam."

"Penelope said the boys' and girls' dormitories are on opposite sides of the school," Mason said. "We're coming down onto the roof of the girls' dorms, but we'll have to cross the yard to get to the boys'."

"Then there's the nursery," Jemma said. "We don't have any way of knowing how the nursery works. We've got seven there. Three girls: Carrie, Hazel, and Kimi. And four boys: Ben, Mutsiku, Kono, and Kaamp."

"And Elyot," Omar said. "I told Kendall we'd get her kid too since she's going to help us get in."

"What?" Levi said. "How is *she* going to help?"

"She's been there," Omar said. "To see her baby."

Why did Omar always feel the need to surprise him? "Why didn't you say something earlier?"

"So you could say no?" Omar chuckled defensively. "I just need Zane's help with the cameras, and it will be easy."

"I can do that," Zane said. "No problem."

"I'll have to remove her SimTag first," Mason added.

It seemed his brothers were united against him. "I don't want either of you near Kendall's apartment," Levi said. "Zane said they were watching her."

"So we'll have her meet us someplace neutral," Omar said.

"Once you take out her SimTag, take her to the cabin," Zane said. "And she'll have to go into the basements with you afterward."

Jemma would love that. Maybe Kendall and Shaylinn could share a room and fight over Omar. "So tap her, then make a plan to get her SimTag out and get her to the cabin sometime tomorrow," Levi said. "We can go over the nursery plan once she tells us what she knows. How many adults will we need to carry all those infants?"

"I can carry more than one," Omar said. "I'll rig up a harness and strap one to my back. Give me the oldest two. They'll be ... sturdier."

"You don't even know what you're talking about," Jordan said.

"No, he's right," Jemma said. "Eliza used a baby harness for Brian when Ben was born. Don't you remember her walking around with one strapped to her back while she carried the other? And Omar's right about the toddlers being strong enough to handle harnesses. The infants need to be carried more gently." She smiled at Omar. "You're going to be a good dad."

Jordan glared at his sister, then at Omar. Good grief. Jemma just had to turn every opportunity into a chance to manipulate Omar into marrying Shaylinn.

"Kimi is only six months old," Jemma said. "And Kendall's baby is not quite two months. Those are the only two young enough to worry about being extra careful with. And if Kendall carries her baby ..." She shrugged.

"I will carry mine," Tupi said, and Levi guessed he must be Kimi's father.

"Eliza will freak if she finds out Omar is the one rescuing her baby," Jordan said.

Levi couldn't be bothered with unforgiveness over Omar's betrayal of Glenrock right now. "She won't know. None of us are going to be talking to the women about the plans, right, Jemma?"

"Right," she said. "It will only make them nervous. We ladies will be praying for everyone, but please don't give anyone any details."

Levi could only imagine what a nightmare that would be.

"Make sure Kendall knows that too," Omar said to Jemma. "She's got a big mouth."

"I'll talk to her," Jemma said.

Levi pressed on. "So if Omar gets Carrie and Hazel, Kendall carries her own kid and Ben. Tupi takes his child and another, and we need one more volunteer from Jack's Peak to grab the last two."

"I will go with Tupi," Mukwiv said. "Tupi can carry his children, and I will carry Mutsiku and Kaamp."

"Great." Levi didn't know who half these people were. He read from Jemma's notes. "So Omar, Mukwiv, Tupi, and Kendall are the nursery team." Good. One thing done. Levi looked to Beshup. "Do you have a preference?"

"I will go to the boys and Chua," Beshup said.

"And I'll help get the girls out," Nodin said.

"Me too," Yivan said.

Levi thought that over as he watched Jemma write it down. "So we have four going to get the infants. Jordan and I will head up the team that goes after the girls. With Nodin and Yivan, we'll be a team of four. But that leaves only Mason and Beshup to the boys."

"I'll go with Mason," Ruston said. "I'd like to do what I can to bring some Safe Lands children out."

Levi stifled a retort and hoped that Ruston's company tomorrow night wouldn't be a mistake. "Okay, good. Now that we know who's going where, let's talk plans. Zane is our eyes, as always. He'll be monitoring the grid and trying to throw the enforcers off track. The boarding school teams meet here, and Ruston is going to lead us into the Highlands through the storm drains. Ruston?"

"We need to be extra quiet in the drains," Ruston said. "Enforcers have been trying to cut off all exits to the canal. They want to keep you in. So once we get the kids, we bring them back here as quickly and quietly as possible. Then I'll lead you all to one of my basement locations. From there, I'll find you all places to live until you're able to leave for good."

"How will we get to the roof?" Mason asked.

"We'll take the storm drains from here to an alley off Treasury Road, a half block from the Nordic," Ruston said. "We're going to have to take out the doorman at the Nordic. I'll bring two scouts with me. Farran will take the doorman's place. It should be pretty slow at that time of night, so hopefully no one will notice. Nash is going to stay on the roof. He'll tap me if he sees any trouble, but it will be good to have eyes looking down on the school."

Two extra men as lookouts. Levi liked that. "So we go from here, through the tunnels, from the alley off Treasury to the Nordic, take out the doorman, then take the elevator to the roof." Levi met Mason's gaze. "And then Penny is going to leave us a board to cross?"

"That's what she said," Mason said.

"And if she doesn't?" Jordan asked. "The girl does her own thing sometimes."

"If it's close enough for a board, maybe it's close enough to jump," Omar said.

"No one is jumping," Levi said.

"Penelope said she'd take care of the board. If it's not there, something has gone wrong," Mason said.

Levi hoped nothing would go wrong. "Still, our whole plan relies on the existence of this board. Let's take one with us, just in case." Levi would feel pretty stupid if the entire rescue failed because of a lack of a piece of wood that he could have carried himself.

"So we're going to cross some flimsy board, hope not to die, then cross it again, carrying two kids each? That's our plan?" Jordan looked from face to face, like everyone was nuts.

"It's not a flimsy board," Mason said. "Penelope called it the bridge."

"Again … Penny?" Jordan said. "That this whole plan rests on her doesn't make me all warm and fuzzy."

"Just because she doesn't let you boss her around doesn't make her incompetent," Omar said.

Jordan pointed at Omar. "You, shut up."

Could their people look any more mature right now? How was this going to give the Jack's Peak men any confidence in the plan? "Enough," Levi said. "We will bring our own bridge board. But we're going to trust that Penny knows what she's talking about." What choice did they have, really? "Have a little faith, Jordan."

Jordan sat back in his chair. "You're the boss," he said with exaggerated indifference.

Yes, thanks, Jordan. Everything rested on Levi's shoulders. Even if no one listened to him now, they'd blame him if things went wrong. Again he admired Papa Eli for his years of service/suffering. "We cross the board, and Penny should be waiting. She'll lead us to where we need to go from there."

"And she said she'd try to have some children there already," Mason said.

"Everyone be flexible," Levi said. "If we need to shift responsibilities, we'll work it out. But in the end, know we're each getting eleven kids. Make sure to count before we leave."

"Unless I get more," Ruston said.

"Unless you get more." Levi hoped Ruston wouldn't slow them down in his desire to be a savior to kids he didn't even know. "Jemma will make each team a list of names. Call roll before we leave. Good?"

"Mad good," Jordan said.

"What about the SimTags?" Mason asked. "Won't the children all have them?"

"That's on you," Levi said. "You're going to have to remove them."

"All twenty-two?" Mason asked.

"*And* the other seven — eight from the nursery." Zane snickered and shook his head at Mason. "You're going to have to work fast, peer."

"But how can I be in both places at the right time?" Mason asked.

"The school group is going to leave an hour before the nursery group," Zane said. "By the time they walk through the tunnels and go over on the roof and back ... all that takes a while. Dayle will have a moving truck waiting behind the Nordic. It's one of ours, lined with steel and some magnets to hide SimTags. Everyone gets in the truck, and you get to work. The truck will drive you to a location on the west side of Champion Park where everyone but Mason will take a different storm drain into the Midlands. We checked it today, and the enforcers still haven't found it."

"Then Dayle will drive Mason to the Medical Center and pick up Omar's team," Ruston said. "Everyone piles in back, and Mason gets to work on the babies. Dayle will drive back to the drain, and when you get the babies on the other side, we'll have another truck waiting. Omar can drive it up to the cabin for the night. We'll move your women and babies to the basements on Sunday night."

"If we had Ciddah with us, she could do half the SimTags," Mason said.

Again with the medic? "No," Levi said. "We need you with us tonight, brother."

Mason eyed Levi a moment, lips pressed into a thin line. "Then perhaps I should teach someone how to remove SimTags. It's not that difficult. One of Bender's people removed mine."

"You'll be fine," Zane said. "You'll have lots of time. I'm going to broadcast one of the Owl videos we prerecorded at the same time you enter the school. And one of my peers is going to put on the costume and create a disturbance in Champion Park. That should keep the enforcers distracted a bit."

"So it wasn't you in Omar's costume last night?" Levi asked.

"With my limp? Naw, peer. Just someone who owes me a favor."

"He better not mess it up," Omar said. "And do you have any plan for the nursery?"

Hadn't Levi already said? Was Omar not listening?

"Just to the doors," Zane said to Omar. "We're going to have to talk to Kendall tomorrow about what to do once we get in. But here's what I know. The nursery is on the sixth floor of the Medical Center. The nursery team will follow you through the tunnels to an alley off Gothic. Then you're going to walk to the MC. I'll figure out which cameras to tap, so I'll be your eyes. It's going to be tricksy, though. I've never tried to swipe babies from the MC."

"Skottie had a femme who's gatekeeper for the RC," Omar said. "So that's you, Zane. You're our gatekeeper. We couldn't do this without you."

Levi conceded that much. Without Ruston and Zane, they'd be lost. He hated feeling that way, but there was nothing he could do about it. The Safe Lands were like a foreign world. It would be a miracle it they ever got out alive.

CHAPTER
24

It was still dark. But at 5:00 a.m., the moment the clerk opened the Lift on the corner of Anthracite and Winterset, Omar went inside with Mason and sat at a table to wait for Kendall to arrive. Omar used the ghoulie tag ring Mason had given him to purchase a smoothie drink with five lifts of grass, hoping it would stop the itch for his PV. Now that he was off-grid, he didn't have any credits to buy a new one since ghoulie tags never had many credits on them.

"You'd be wise to avoid stimulants, brother," Mason said. "It only complicates your condition."

Ice shot up Omar's spine. "Why does everyone feel the need to tell me what to do? Wait — " He tapped his Wyndo watch to the memo screen. "I forgot that you were an expert on my life. Let me take notes."

"I'm sorry, Omar," Mason said. "I didn't mean to criticize."

Another chill ran over him, one that reminded him that Mason was right. "Look, Mase, five lifts of grass is like vaping a two in a PV. It's not doing much, trust me." But he hoped it would.

Omar took a long drink through the straw. Only two nights had passed since Otley had shown up at his apartment. He'd been itching something fierce since he woke up in the RC. He'd tried going to his apartment last night, but enforcers had been camped outside. Apparently Otley didn't like that Omar had cut out his SimTag the same day he'd been warned not to. Surprise, surprise.

Two nights felt like two hundred. He was still mad at Zane for not helping him get a new PV and some juice. Zane said Omar was better off without them, but Omar needed them — was sick without them. He was so tired, but he couldn't sleep, couldn't even get comfortable. Plus, it was seventy degrees out, and he was freezing. Shivering and shaking like a kitten in a toddler's hands.

Maybe that was the lynchpin: destroy wherever stimulants were created. Without juice to vape, Safe Landers would go insane, government officials included. Then Levi and the rebels could sweep in and take over. It actually wasn't a bad idea. Maybe the Owl could do it. Omar the Owl, though, not Zane's copycat impostor.

"She's here," Mason said. "What in all the lands?"

Kendall trudged into the Lift parking lot holding her birdcage in one hand, a suitcase in the other.

"Could she be any more obvious?" Mason asked. "The whole point of doing this when it's still dark is so no one will see us. But a girl carrying a birdcage is pretty memorable."

It was stupid. If she'd wanted to bring the bird, she could have tapped Omar about it. "I'll wave us a cab."

"Where are we going to put the bird until I'm done?" Mason asked.

"I don't know." Omar hoped this was one of those things they'd laugh about someday. Right now he wanted to wring Kendall's neck. He took another drink, still not feeling the effects of the grass. What if the clerk had forgotten it?

"How about you sit with it while I take her into the bathroom?" Mason suggested.

"Just make it quick," Omar said. "This bird talks."

Mason walked down the hall to the bathrooms seconds before Kendall opened the front door to Lift. Omar got up and took the cage so she could drag her suitcase inside. He carried the bird back to the table and sat down.

Seconds later, Kendall dropped her suitcase beside the birdcage. "What happened to your eye?"

"Meet Mason in the bathroom," Omar mumbled. He repositioned his chair in front of the cage, hiding it as best he could. Now, if the critter would just stay silent. He watched Kendall knock on the bathroom door, then slip inside.

"Give me a kiss. Tch tch tch."

Omar jumped. So much for that plan. Why hadn't she covered the cage? He opened her suitcase to see if she had brought the cover, but clothes blossomed out and spilled onto the floor. Great. No sign of a cover, either. Omar did his best to pack it back nicely.

"Basil's a budgie, budgie."

"What do you have there?" the clerk asked from behind the counter.

See? That bird was guaranteed to cause trouble. "Oh, it's just a dumb bird."

"Juice off, Lawten. You're a shell!"

The clerk eyes widened and he walked over to Omar's table. "You teach it to say that?"

"Naw. My friend's idea of a joke." Omar took a drink of his smoothie. Why couldn't he taste the grass? He wasn't feeling a thing.

"Doesn't sound like much of a friend," the clerk said. "An enforcer hears that, they'll arrest you for slander."

They'd arrest him for more than that. "Yeah, well, that's why I'm trying to get rid of the dumb thing."

The clerk eyes widened. "You selling it?"

"Tch tch tch. Omar's the Owl."

Omar blanched. She'd taught the bird to say *that*? What was Kendall's problem, anyway? "Hey." He kicked the cage. "People are trying to enjoy their drinks." He wished he was enjoying his, but the grass lift must have been defective. Maybe the clerk forgot to add it.

"Did he just say Omar's the Owl?" the clerk asked.

Omar did his best to think fast and make it sound legit. "The bird's name is Omar. He saw all that stuff on the ColorCast about that Owl fellow. Now he thinks he's the Owl."

The clerk laughed. "Walls! That's funny."

"Tell me about it." Omar glanced down the hallway to the bathrooms. *Today*, Mason. His muscles ached — his very bones ached. He sucked down the rest of the smoothie, desperate for the grass to provide some relief.

The clerk squatted beside the cage and looked at Basil. "Well, if you're selling him, I'm interested."

Of course he was. "Yeah? Well, I'm headed over to the Prospector now to meet a potential buyer, but if it doesn't work out ..." Omar pushed up his sleeve and held out his Wyndo watch to the clerk.

"Oh, sure." The clerk tapped his fist against the Wyndo screen, which displayed the clerk's face with his name and ID number underneath.

"Thanks, Keny," Omar said, reading the screen.

"What time is it?" Basil said. "Tch tch tch. Owl. Omar's the Owl."

Omar rolled his eyes at Keny. "I'm warning you. He never shuts up."

"I think he's stimming decked," Keny said. "Well, I should get back. Hope to hear from you."

"Yeah, we'll see."

The clerk returned to the counter, and Mason and Kendall came back to the table.

"I'm going to wave a cab." Omar got up and walked to the door, anxious to get out of there. "Come out as soon as you see I got one." He didn't wait for their answer. *Omar's the Owl?* What had that crazy femme been thinking?

He waved a cab, and they all piled in, but Basil's chatter drew them into another awkward conversation with the driver. Omar had to interrupt Kendall's explanations to give the same story he'd given Keny. Consistency was key in a situation like this. Otley wouldn't have any trouble tracking them if he thought to ask about the bird.

When they were all safely inside Zane's house, Omar let Kendall have it. "What were you thinking, bringing the dumb bird? And why did you teach him to say Omar's the Owl?"

"He copies me sometimes." She frowned and looked at Basil's cage on the living room floor in the middle of the circle of chairs. "I didn't want to leave him behind."

Copies her? "So who did you say 'Omar's the Owl' to?"

Her cheeks flushed and she glanced at Omar, bottom lip pouting like he should feel sorry for her. "No one. Just ... myself."

Kendall had already proved how big her mouth was. She'd told Jemma about the scene Red had made at the train station and that Omar was the Owl. And the bird wouldn't have been there for that conversation. "Are you sure you haven't accidentally told anyone else anything about me or the rebels or the Owl or where you're going?" Omar asked.

"I'm sure. I don't have any friends." And now her eyes were all teary, which made Omar feel like a jerk.

"You do now," Mason said, ever the peacemaker.

Omar picked up Basil's cage and headed for the garage. They needed to get to the cabin unseen, so they were taking the van. Omar carried the "tch tch tch-ing" bird, Mason the suitcase, and Kendall followed them. Nash drove them to the cabin, the bird yakking the whole way. Omar had never been more thrilled to get to a place where everyone thought he was a traitor.

The three of them created quite a stir when they entered the cabin. Jordan came running, gun in hand. Omar wondered if he had any ammo for it yet. Aunt Chipeta ushered Mason up to the attic with Kendall's suitcase. Shay and Jemma came next. Shay looked pale, and he wished he'd thought to get her a pastry from the Lift. Or maybe she was unhappy to see him. Either way, he owed her an apology. He dropped the cage in the hallway and took her hand, pulling her toward the bathroom.

"Is that Basil?" she asked, plodding alongside him.

"I want to talk to you," he said.

"Tch tch tch. Omar's the Owl."

Shaylinn gasped and looked over her shoulder. "Did he just say — ?"

"Yes, and I wish he'd stop." Omar pulled her inside the bathroom.

He shut the door and locked it, then lowered the lid on the toilet seat. "Will you sit down?"

Shay sat.

Omar sat on the side of the tub and took her hand. "I'm sorry, Shay. I was a jerk. Kendall told Jemma that I was the Owl. In case you missed his announcement, she even told the bird. And who knows who else. I should have believed you when you said you kept my secret, but I was too busy being angry. And I said cruel things that I didn't mean. Your messages are so special to people. To me. Will you forgive me?"

She grinned, though her eyes were teary. "Of course I forgive you."

Really? "That's it?"

She tugged on his hands. "Did you want me to yell and make you feel guilty?"

"I guess not." The smile on her face filled him with a rush of joy, and for a few seconds he almost felt better. He wanted to ask to paint her, then wondered how long his paint supplies would be in his apartment before the Registration Department assigned the place to someone else.

"I don't like fighting, Omar."

"I'm sorry." Those words had become his mantra. He really needed to quit screwing up all the time.

"You already said that. No need to say it again." Shay set her hand on the top of his head, and her touch made his heart race. "What happened to your eye?"

"Otley punched me."

"Oh, Omar. Please be more careful." She let her hand fall back to her lap. He wanted to hold it again, but didn't feel like he had any reason to. The tub had started to hurt his backside, so he moved to the floor and leaned against the wall. It was cold and he shivered, his arm hair standing on end. "How do you know what to write in your messages?"

She fidgeted with her hands and her skirt. "I pray and take my best guess."

"'Temptation,' you wrote in mine."

Her cheeks flushed the color of brilliant magenta. Not many people turned so dark when they blushed. Shay and Jordan did, but not Jemma.

"Your PV always seems to be attached to your hand," she said, "though I don't see it right now."

Oh. Her messages had been referencing his temptations to stims, not women. She was spot on with both, though. What was he doing here with someone as good as Shay?

"Do you believe a lie about yourself, Omar?" she asked.

He admired the way her hair curled over each shoulder and into her lap. "If I did, I suppose I wouldn't know it was a lie, since I believed it."

She chuckled, and the sound was light and fun and made him smile. "I never thought of it that way."

But Omar suddenly knew his answer. "I believe I'm worthless."

Shay tilted her head and stared at him, her eyes sad but accepting.

"Nobody ever wanted me around," he said. "But it's not a lie."

"You're wrong." She leaned over and squeezed his shoulder. "I've always wanted you around."

How did she do that? Make him feel so worthy? "Why?"

"Because you're funny and talented and handsome. I loved watching you sit in the square and paint, and you'd always tell us about your dreams, that you were going to do great things. It made me want dreams of my own."

She'd been listening. Always. He wanted to kiss her then, but he stayed put on the floor. Shay was too special to move so fast. He needed to wait for her, to be patient. He needed to make himself good enough for her. Do something to earn her respect. "I'm sorry I was mean to you," he said. "Ever."

She smiled and blushed again, this time putting her hands on her cheeks like she had felt it happen. "Thank you, Omar. But I'll not accept any more apologies from you today."

He winced, overplaying it. "That might not be wise. I mess up a lot."

She leaned over and kissed his cheek. She smelled sweet, like honey, and her hair tickled his neck. "I will always forgive you. Now go away so I can be sick." She set her hand over her stomach and suddenly looked paler than she had before.

Omar slipped out of the bathroom and closed the door. Standing felt good — for three seconds. He stretched, then wanted to lie down and weep at the intensity of the itch.

It struck him as ironic that his father had always threatened to marry him to Shay, a fate Omar had dreaded. How stupid could he have been?

After Kendall had helped them plan out the nursery rescue, the day was filled with agonizing boredom. Everyone sat around, waiting for night to come. Basil was the only entertainment. Some took naps. Omar went down to the basement for a while and lay down on one of the beds, where he tossed and turned, drenched in a cold sweat. But when he couldn't sleep, he decided to go check on Shay. He went upstairs and found Kendall sitting alone on one of the couches in the living room. It was late now — 11:33 p.m. Almost time.

"Will you sit with me awhile?" Kendall asked. "I'm worried about tonight."

Omar sat beside her on the couch. "Worrying won't do you any good."

"Once I get Elyot, where will I go?" Kendall asked.

"Into the basements with us until we can get out of this place," Omar said, wondering how he'd get stims from now on. Perhaps the Owl would need to visit a hit room and help himself. If he didn't get something real soon, he had a feeling he'd die.

"I'll have no way to earn credits," Kendall said. "How will I provide for my son?"

Like he knew how life would be underground. "I don't think they use credits in the basements. I'm sure some of the Natural women can help you figure all that out. Everyone will have the same problems. The Naturals wouldn't bother helping us if they didn't care about how we'd all live."

"Will you help me?"

What did *that* mean? He turned to look at her. "What could I do?"

She bumped her shoulder against his. "Keep me company. Maybe help me raise my son."

His cheeks tingled as the blood drained away. "Kendall ... I don't know anything about raising a kid."

"But you're going to be a father. You'll learn."

Which still terrified him. "Sure, but —"

She kissed him, and he turned his head to stop her. "Kendall, I can't. Shay ..." He should have made himself clear before. "If I'm going to help anyone, it's her."

Kendall rolled her eyes. "She's not like us, Omar. You and me, we have the thin plague. How could you expect to be with her and not infect her? You'd kill her."

Kill Shay? Omar's chest tightened. "I don't know." He hadn't thought about all that — the future. Once they freed the kids, there'd be time to figure everything out. To talk to Shay. See what she wanted. He was only sixteen, for crying out loud. All his life he'd wanted to be treated like an adult, now he just wanted the simplicity of being a kid again.

But his childhood was gone forever.

"I think we could work, Omar," Kendall said, taking hold of his hand. "You and me. Lifers."

Lifers ...?

She kissed him again, and this time he let her, trying to decide if she was right. He didn't want Shay to be infected. But if Mason could find a cure, then —

"Really?"

Shay's voice made him break away from Kendall. She stood in the archway to the kitchen, Jordan's pistol in her hand. Was she going to shoot them?

"You're not a very nice friend," she said to Kendall, and her voice cracked, broken. Then she turned her betrayed expression on Omar. "Either of you."

Omar got up from the couch and walked toward her, slowly, as if trying not to frighten a bird into flight. Her eyes widened and she inched back, shaking her head slightly. "Either of you, Omar."

He reached for Shay's arm, but she backed out of his reach. "Shay, wait." He grabbed her wrist that held the gun and pulled the weapon away, still holding on to her wrist. "It's not what you think."

"Let go." She pulled until her hand squeezed through his grip, then jogged toward her bedroom, so he ran past her and blocked the door. She spun away and slipped into the bathroom. He just managed to get his foot in the opening before she shut the door. It struck his shoe.

"Shay, let me explain."

One of her eyes glared out the opening. "I don't need an explanation." Her voice was a hard whisper. "When in the Safe Lands, do as the nationals do, right? Pair up? Trade paint? Find pleasure in life?"

"Please, it's not like that. I'm different now that — well, I'm trying to be."

Shay rolled her eyes. "Let me know when you grow up." She kicked at his foot, to no avail.

"Shay, please listen. I told her to stop, that I couldn't do it."

"But you did." Shay looked at him through the crack, her eyes teary now. "You made your choice. Just ... Take Jordan's gun. I was bringing it to you. He got ammo for it, but Levi won't let him take it tonight, so he hid it under his bed. I want you to bring back Penny and Nell, okay? I'm going to need someone to help with the babies, and they're my real friends." She opened the door and shoved him. He stumbled back a step, and she slammed the door. The lock clicked.

Gun in one hand, Omar used his other to knock on the door and shake the knob. "Shay? Open the door."

Instead, a door opened behind him. Omar turned to see which one. Jordan stepped into the hall, eyes sleepy. "What's going on?"

Omar hid the gun behind his back, tucked it into the back of his pants. "Nothing."

"Who's in there?" Jordan motioned to the bathroom.

"Shay."

Jordan pushed in front of Omar. "Go downstairs. I'll take care of her."

"Right." Jordan likely thought Shay was sick again. Omar couldn't risk being here when Jordan found out the truth. He turned and strode toward the front door. Kendall said something as he passed the living room. He darted back and found her sitting on the couch. She smiled as if nothing was wrong.

"You and me aren't going to happen, Kendall. Get that straight." He left the cabin and started walking. That girl had ruined everything. Why was he always so stupid?

He checked the gun and found that it was indeed loaded. Panic shot through him. Shay could have hurt herself. But he'd hurt her first. Why did he keep hurting her?

Maybe Kendall was right. Maybe Omar was all wrong for Shay. He was infected and she wasn't. He was dying and she was very much alive.

But she was the only person who made him feel like he could ever be good again. He was pretty sure he'd die a lot faster without her in his life.

He was shivering badly by the time he reached Kokanee Lane. He needed a hit now. Maybe Skottie or Charlz would help him. He hadn't spoken to either in almost a month, but he knew they'd understand the itch. If nothing else, maybe they'd buy him a beer.

CHAPTER 25

"Come on, Shay," Jordan said through the locked door. "Open up."

"I'm fine," she said, yawning over her tears. She was so tired. She should have stayed in bed. Then she'd still be dreaming of her nice moments with Omar before he'd ruined everything. Again.

It wasn't fair. Her parents had been killed. Then the Safe Lands had made her pregnant. And just when it seemed like Omar had noticed her, just when she thought he might actually care about her, Kendall had come along. How could she compete against a beautiful, mature woman like her?

They'd had such a nice talk today. He'd really seemed to care about her. Why was she so blind about boys? And why were boys so dumb?

A wave of queasiness seized her then, and she went to her knees before the toilet. Naomi had promised the morning sickness wouldn't last. But so far, Shaylinn was still sick no matter what time of day. It seemed a terrible joke. If she'd been married and had a husband who loved her, the sickness would be bearable.

But to be so alone…

When she finally exited the bathroom, she found Jordan sitting on the floor against the wall, sleeping. Oh, sweet, stubborn brother. She nudged him. "Jordan, it's almost midnight."

He gasped and coughed. "What's for breakfast?"

"Why don't you go downstairs and make sure the other men are awake?"

He rubbed his eyes. "You okay?"

"Just tired." Though she didn't think she'd be able to sleep until she knew everyone had been rescued.

Jordan pushed up to his feet. "Love you, sis." He hugged her and kissed her hair.

The act brought tears to her eyes. "Be careful tonight, okay?"

He pulled back so he could see her face and gave her that wide, crooked grin of his. "Tomorrow you can see Penny and Nell. My gift to you."

"Thank you. Be safe."

"Always."

Once the men — and Kendall — had set off, Shay found Jemma in the room she and Levi had been using. Her sister lay in bed, staring at the ceiling.

"Chipeta is leading prayers in the living room, but I need a break," Shaylinn said. "Mind if I join you?"

"I'd love it," Jemma said, throwing back the covers.

Shaylinn climbed into bed with her sister, and they nestled close. Jemma began to braid strands of Shay's hair. It almost felt like they were together again in their bedroom in their cabin in Glenrock.

"How are you feeling?" Jemma asked.

"Sick." And brokenhearted.

"I'm sorry, love. Did you and Omar talk? Did you make up?"

Tears flooded her eyes. "He apologized for what he said before."

"That's good, right?"

It had been good. A lovely moment. She was thankful for that, even if it hadn't lasted long. "Later I saw him kissing Kendall."

"What!" Jemma sat up and looked down on Shay's face. "Oh, honey. I'm so sorry."

Her reaction brought Shay's tears to the surface. She hated crying but hadn't been able to control it lately. "Maybe it's just that he's a lot more experienced than me. I don't think he wants to be with a girl so … prude?"

"Ugh. If that's the case, he doesn't deserve you. But I know Omar. I knew him, anyway. I can't believe he'd leave you alone."

"I don't want him out of his guilt, Jem. I want him to love me."

Jemma finger-combed out the braid she'd started in Shaylinn's hair. "Omar should have to earn your love, Shay. If he's not willing, then he's not worth it. Don't risk your heart on a lazy man. He'll take what he wants from you and not give back. And that's not love, honey. That's just not."

Jemma acted like there were a lot of men to choose from in the world. But there weren't. "You never doubted Levi's love for you."

Jemma's expression softened into a smile. "No. My heart is, and always will be, his."

Shaylinn sighed, knowing she'd never have anything like her sister had with Levi. "Why can't I have that certainty? Why do I have so much doubt?"

"Because you are you and I am me. And because Omar hasn't exactly been an unchanging rock of a guy. If we all had the same life, there'd be no surprise. I'm angry that Omar hurt you. He's a stupid boy, and if he were here right now I'd tell him so and whack his head. I hope you did."

"I didn't." As if Shaylinn could ever strike anyone like that. "I told him to bring back Penny and Nell because I'd need help raising the babies."

"Oh, you're a clever girl. Guilting him."

Had she? "I didn't mean to. I'm just tired of feeling so alone." She really did want Penny and Nell back in her life. She missed them desperately.

"You're not alone, dearest. You have me."

Only when Levi and Naomi were busy. "I'm so angry at them both."

"You have a right to be. Sit up and let me finish braiding your hair."

Shaylinn pushed herself up and turned her back to Jemma. "But if I'm angry ... if I judge him, I'm not loving him."

Jemma again combed her fingers through Shaylinn's hair and started a new braid. "How can you love him if he's loving someone else?"

"But I don't think he loves Kendall. He's addicted to doing whatever makes him feel good. And there are too many things that make him feel good in this place."

"But, Shay, that's an excuse. Don't make excuses for him. Men become men by making sacrifices and doing what's hard. He's going to have to decide if he wants to grow up or not. And marriage means something to Omar — I know it does. Despite how he's been acting since we came here, he's *not* a Safe Lander. He's from Glenrock. And his mother raised him to know what's right."

"I don't think he cares about how his mother raised him. Not anymore." Tamera would have cuffed Omar upside the head ten times by now.

"I don't believe that," Jemma said. "The way he paints? As moody as he is? All he's ever wanted was to find the right girl to spoil with all his romantic ideas."

Yeah. "But maybe I'm the wrong girl."

Jemma tugged on Shay's braid. "That's not possible."

But why not? Just because Shay wanted something didn't mean God would give it to her. He might have another plan in mind. "I so believed that God was going to do something big in my life with these babies. And I thought part of it was to finally bring me and Omar together. But I'm just a dreamer, really. Making things up in my head. I wanted what you and Naomi have with Levi and Jordan. I wanted something real. But I don't know how to have a real relationship with anyone." She was only fourteen. But not every person got married. Some stayed single forever.

"There's nothing to know, Shay. You just do your best. You talk. Become friends. See if your life goals are a match."

"See? I don't even know what Omar's life goals are — or mine, for that matter, apart from loving Omar. And I don't think Omar knows his goals, either. So, how could we possibly know if they matched?"

"By talking to each other."

"Every time we talk, someone ruins it. Me, or Omar, or someone else. Now Kendall. I thought she was my friend. I told her I loved Omar. Why would she do this?"

"If she gets Elyot back tonight, she'll be raising him alone. Maybe she wants something real too. But I'm sorry that she felt like her own happiness was more important than her friendship with you."

"I miss Penny and Nell. But even if they were here, they wouldn't know what to say to any of this. These are grown-up problems, and I'm not a grown-up."

"There are no grown-ups, really," Jemma said. "Just old kids who still feel young inside despite the fact that their face no longer looks it."

Shaylinn smiled at Jemma's words. "Is that from a book or a movie?"

"Papa Eli." Jemma tucked the end of the braid into the neckline of Shaylinn's tank top.

"I miss him. He was such a sweet man." Shaylinn fell back on the bed. "Everything was so much easier when I believed I was ugly and Omar would never, ever want me."

Jemma brushed a loose wisp of hair off Shay's forehead and looked down on her face. "Longing is good for a season. And while living in that wanting place might feel safe, it's hiding from real life. Live your life, Shay. And seek out —"

A knock on the door made both girls sit up. Chipeta came in. "Come quick — Naomi's in labor."

CHAPTER
26

The sound of nine pairs of feet sloshing through ankle-deep water set Levi's nerves on edge. He wished they'd all take more care and walk on the sides of the pipe — at least try not to announce their presence to enforcers who might be on patrol.

But despite what Levi wanted, he wasn't fully in charge of this mission. Getting Ruston and Zane's help tonight meant he had to trust them, like it or not.

He and Ruston had done a run-through that morning, so Levi, at least, knew what to expect. They'd already removed the storm drain cover in the alley and covered it with a maintenance sign, so there'd be little delay getting above ground. The bridge board was waiting there too, behind a dumpster. Levi was most concerned with Yivan, who'd tripped three times since they'd started out. He wished they'd left the fifteen-year-old klutz behind.

Soon they were climbing to the surface. Levi waited with Ruston until all nine of the men had climbed up. Jordan retrieved the bridge board and tucked it under one arm. They all had stunners on gun belts Ruston had provided. Even Mason had taken one. But they were SimScanners, not regular stunners. SimScanners read a target's

SimTag, then stunned them, without the shock wires even coming out. And the best part was that the guards' SimScanners wouldn't work on the rebels since they had removed their SimTags. Levi greatly appreciated their odds.

The alley stretched between an auto repair shop and the back of the Nordic apartment building. Treasury Road wasn't much wider than the alley. There were no streetlamps. The west side of the road butted up against a fence that was the back of the ColorCast lot, where they filmed much of what appeared on TV. The east side of the road was the back end of the auto repair shop. From where the road dead-ended at the Midlands wall, it stretched about 100 yards to where it met Eammons, which edged the north side of the Rehabilitation Center.

Levi didn't like being so close to the RC. He removed his SimScanner from his belt and held it by his side.

"Okay," Ruston said, stopping behind the Nordic, where the smell of clean laundry blew strong. "Farran, Nash, Levi, Mason, and Jordan — with me. The rest of you, wait here. We shouldn't be long."

Ruston led Levi and the others down the road, which had no sidewalk until they reached Eammons. They circled the building and stopped outside the front entrance.

"We're at the Nordic," Ruston said. "You ready, Zane?"

Zane's answer came as a soft gurgle from Ruston's SimTalk implant. "Ready. I own the cameras."

Ruston pushed through the front entrance and walked toward the elevators. Levi followed, nerves on high alert, scanning the tiny lobby for the doorman.

No sign.

Ruston reached the elevator and turned. "No doorman, Zane."

"He was there a minute ago," came Zane's muffled reply.

"Should we go?" Mason asked.

Levi was just as anxious to get out of sight. "Not if we don't want to happen upon him on the way back down."

Ruston took a deep breath and panned his gaze across the lobby. "He can't have gone far, and we need to take him out."

"Maybe he went up to one of the residents' apartments to deliver something," Mason said.

Levi started to walk the perimeter of the lobby. It was small, about the size of a living room, with glass windows facing the street. In the far corner opposite the elevator, Levi passed a door to the stairwell. Three more steps, and he came to another door. This one said "Restroom." A stripe of yellow light lit a crack at the bottom of the door.

Levi snapped his fingers three times. The men's gazes locked on his, and he pointed to the bathroom door.

Ruston and Farran came running, clutching their SimScanners. A quick look and Ruston said, "Farran, come with me. Levi, stand watch."

Ruston pulled open the bathroom door and entered, Farran on his heels. Mason joined Levi next, then Jordan, who set down the board and made to follow the men into the bathroom, but Levi stopped him.

"They got it, Jordan."

A loud bang preceded a man's shout. "What are you doing? Get out of here!"

Jordan chuckled, delighted with the situation. "They got the maggot on the pot."

Levi rolled his eyes at his friend's boorish sense of humor.

A minute later, the bathroom door opened, and Farran stuck out his head. "Nash. We need you."

Nash walked past Levi and Jordan and went inside.

"I'm stronger than that weed," Jordan said.

Jordan was simply anxious to be put to good use. "You'll get your chance to be a hero," Levi said. "For now, we trust Ruston." No matter how hard that might be.

Another minute passed, and the three men exited, Nash wearing an extremely tight doorman's shirt.

"Go fetch the others," Ruston told Farran, who headed for the exit.

"What's this?" Jordan asked Nash.

"My dim brother neglected to warn us that the doorman was a child," Nash said.

"Shortest man I've ever seen," Ruston said. "Skinny too. No way Farran could fit into his uniform."

"I couldn't get his pants past my knees," Nash said.

Jordan busted up laughing.

Farran returned with Beshup and the three Jack's Peak teens. Ruston, who was wearing gloves, pressed the Up button on the elevator, and the door slid open immediately.

Inside, Ruston hit the button for five and the elevator sailed up. From the fifth floor, Zane worked his grid magic and unlocked the door to the stairs that led to the roof.

A cool breeze hit Levi when he stepped out onto the roof. It didn't take long to locate Penelope's plank. It was no more than twelve inches wide and stretched four feet across the narrow space between the Nordic and the school. Five stories down there was nothing more than a dead-end alley with a dumpster. Anyone who fell would hit the ground hard.

Jordan walked up beside Levi and stopped, the bridge board under his arm. "I could jump that."

He probably could. "But you won't," Levi said.

"I won't. But I could. And my board is bigger." Jordan hefted it out until it crossed the gap, then he moved it until it was right next to Penny's board. Jordan's was twice as wide.

"Levi," a voice called out from the other roof. "Mason?"

Levi scanned the roof of the school and spotted Penny and Nell standing by a shed that looked like the access to the stairs. Nell squealed and jumped up and down. Levi waved and set his finger against his lips.

"*Girls*," Jordan mumbled. "If we make it out of here with everyone, it will be a miracle."

"Then pray for a miracle," Mason said.

Indeed. Jemma had promised to have the women praying all night, but Levi tossed up a quick prayer of his own.

"So what am I supposed to do?" Farran asked. He'd been planning to act as the doorman downstairs and Nash as the lookout, but the tiny uniform had changed their plans.

"Cross over with us and perch on the edge of the roof overlooking the courtyard," Ruston said. "You see trouble, talk to Zane, who'll talk to me."

While Ruston was coaching Farran, Levi holstered his SimScanner and crossed the board. Penny ran to him and gave him a tight hug.

"I'm so glad to see you," she said.

Nell joined their hug, making it a threesome. Until Jordan and Mason crossed the board, then they each got double hugs as well.

"What's the plan, Pen?" Levi asked.

"Nell and I are the only two girl thirteens. The thirteens and the twelves have their dorm on the fifth floor. The tens and elevens share, then the sevens, eights, and nines share — and both those dorms are on the fourth floor. Then the threes, fours, fives, and sixes are together on the third floor."

Should Levi have memorized that?

"Is that the same for the boys?" Mason asked.

"Yeah," Penny said. "Dakav and Etu, and Trevon, Jake, and Sakima are going to sneak out on their own and meet us in the courtyard, but you'll have to go back for Joey and Brian and the Jack's Peak boys. There's six boys in the littles."

"That's what we call the three-to-six-year-olds," Nell said.

"And the girls?" Levi asked. "You were able to warn them all?"

"Yep," Penny said. "They should be waiting, if they didn't accidentally fall asleep."

"Are the dorm rooms locked?" Mason asked.

"Not the rooms, but the buildings are. That's why I wanted the bigger boys to help, so they could prop open the door to the boys' building."

"And what about guards?" Ruston asked.

"There are two, but they only guard the front entrance to the school."

"They play Wyndo games all night," Nell said.

Good. Levi would take any distraction he could get. "So, my team needs to get Meghan from the fifth floor —"

"No, we got Meghan. She's guarding in the stairwell."

Penny would make a smart elder one day. Levi clarified, "So, my team needs to stop on four and three?"

"Two stops on four and one on three," Pen said.

"And I only need to meet the boys in the courtyard, then go back up to three?" Mason asked.

"Right."

Excellent. "Pen, lead the way," Levi said.

Penny took them into the stairwell, where they met Meghan. After a quick hug, they followed Penny down two flights of stairs to the fourth floor.

"Ruth and Lucy's room is on the left-hand side of the hallway," she said. "And the Hs are on the right: Hailey, Heather, and Haiwee. You guys should wait in the stairwell. Nell will go and get Ruth and Lucy, and Meghan will get the Hs. Once the girls are out in the hall, get them upstairs. Then you guys should spit up. Levi and whoever can come back down with Nell to get the littles, while Jordan and whoever helps the girls cross the board. I'm going to take Mason and his team to the boys."

"Pen, you're so organized you could have gotten out weeks ago," Levi said.

"Maybe. But I didn't know where to go once I got out. Come on, Mason."

Mason grabbed Levi's shoulder. "Good luck, brother."

"And to you," Levi said.

Ruston stopped by Levi as he passed. "If you can free more children, we'll provide for them."

"I'll try," Levi said, though he didn't see how to manage it when there was no time to try to explain who they were. Children would be terrified of strangers in the night trying to steal them from their beds.

Penny continued down the stairs with Mason, Beshup, and Ruston.

Levi took out his SimScanner and followed Nell out into the dark hallway, but Nell waved him back.

"Just wait in the stairs," she said. "If one of the caretakers comes out and sees girls, she'll get mad at us. But if she sees a man, she'll call the guards."

"Okay," Levi said, backing into the stairwell. Bossy things, these girls were.

Jordan had his SimScanner in hand too. "At least there's a window in the door."

"I hate leaving this up to them," Levi said, "but I guess they know this place better than we do."

Levi watched through the window, his heartbeat thudding in his ears. Finally Nell came out. But she had five girls, not two.

"How many was she supposed to bring?" Jordan asked.

"Two," Levi said, cracking the door open.

Ruth came through first. She met Levi's gaze and beamed. Again he set his finger over his lips. Girls were a bundle of squeals, weren't they?

Next came the three strangers, then Lucy and Nell.

"What's this?" Levi asked.

"This is Chetta, Ren, and Leebelle," Lucy said. "They want out."

"I hate it here," one of the girls said. "The others are mean to me, and I love Lucy."

Lucy hugged her and the girl hugged her back.

"Our caretaker makes me do more chores than anyone else," another girl said.

"The boys are always picking on me," said the third. "I hate boys. But not you, because you're our heroes, like the Owl."

"Do you know the Owl?" the second girl asked Levi.

"I do, actually," Levi said. "He's my brother."

Nell squealed and clapped her hands. "I knew it was Omar! He's obsessed with owls and—"

Levi clamped a hand over Nell's mouth. "Enough of this. Yes, you can all come, but only if you stop talking." He turned to Jordan. "Run

300

them upstairs. Start getting them across to the other roof. I'll send Nodin up with the next bunch, then Yivan and I will follow with the third group."

Jordan holstered his SimScanner and saluted him. "You got it, Elder Levi." Then he started up the stairs with the girls.

Nell ran back out into the corridor. Levi watched through the window. After a few minutes, two of the Hs — the girls from Jack's Peak — were coming back with Nell. Levi opened the door and the girls ran into the stairwell.

"Where is Hailey?" he asked Nell.

"She and her friend are trying to talk another girl into coming. The girl wants to come, but she's scared. I'm afraid they're going to wake the others."

Levi looked to Nodin, then Yivan. "Stay here. Girls, we need silence." Then he said to Nell, "Show me."

Nell pattered down the hallway and into the dorm room. Levi followed and peeked in. It was dark, but he could hear the harsh whispers of girls to his left. His eyes adjusted, and he recognized Hailey. A quick scan of the room showed that the other girls were asleep.

He crept into the room and toward Hailey and her friends.

"Levi!" Hailey whispered. "She's scared to come."

Hailey and a second girl were standing beside the bed of a third, who was sitting cross-legged, tears running down her face.

"Hailey, you and your friend stay with Nell and follow me, okay?"

She nodded, eyes wide, and cast one last longing look at the crying girl.

"I'm here to help you, okay?" Levi said to the girl. Then he scooped her up and ran toward the door. The girl squealed, and Levi had to toss her over his shoulder to get the door open. Once he was in the hall, he clamped a hand over her mouth and ran for the stairs. Nodin opened the door, and Levi ran into the stairwell and up a flight of stairs. He didn't dare take his hand off the girl's mouth. He couldn't believe he'd taken her. It was such a stupid risk. Not to mention that he felt like he'd just abducted a little girl against her will. What had become of them all?

Ruston's bleeding heart, anyway.

Levi ran all the way to the roof. Jordan was carrying Lucy across the plank, so he waited for Jordan to return. He looked down to the girl. "I'm not going to hurt you, okay? The scary part is over. We're on the roof, and now we're going to go across and then you'll be safe with your friends. Can I let go of your mouth? Will you be quiet for me?"

She nodded, eyes wide.

Hailey arrived beside him as he set the girl on her feet and released his hand from her mouth. The girl's bottom lip started to tremble.

"What's her name?" Levi asked.

"Kittie," Hailey said.

"Kittie, watch this big guy walk across that plank."

The little heads turned to look. Jordan stepped on the plank only twice as he came back.

"Jordan, this is Kittie," Levi said. "She's a little scared, so why don't you take her first. She's promised to be very quiet. Right, Kittie?"

Kittie only stared at Levi, her eyes as wide as chicken eggs.

Levi grabbed Nell's arm and started back to the stairs. Nodin and Yivan were standing with the stairwell door opened, watching.

Levi waved them ahead. "Down to the third floor."

Nell led the way, clomping down the stairs louder than Levi liked. They reached the third floor and Nell ran out into the hallway. Levi stopped at the door to watch through the window, and Yivan plowed into his back. The door banged.

Levi turned and glared at the boy.

Yivan shrank back. "Sorry."

Levi waited at the window. The first child to appear was Sarajawea, a little girl from Jack's Peak. She wandered aimlessly down the hall, dragging a pillow behind her.

Then Nell stepped out and waved Levi to come. Levi told Nodin to get Sarajawea into the stairwell, then ran to Nell.

"I think we need the other men to help too," she said when he reached her. "They're all sleeping, and I don't know who's who. I think I just woke up the wrong girl."

Levi went back and told Yivan to sit with Sarajawea, then he brought Nodin with him into the girl's dorm. Beds lined both long walls, but some of them were only bare mattresses on wire frames.

"They're on this end," Nell said, leading the way.

Of the five girls left, he was supposed to take two, but Levi could hardly see, and even if he could, he wasn't sure he'd recognize Kaylee and Rosalie if he saw them.

"We'll take them all," he said. "Pick up a girl and carry her to the stairwell. Then come back for the last two. We've got to be quick and quiet, though. Can you do it, Nell?"

"I think so."

"Good. You get this one closest to the door."

Nell started to pick up a sleeping child, Nodin went for another, and Levi walked to the last bed in the row. He scooped up the little girl and held her close, hoping she'd sleep until he was in the stairwell.

They made it there safely, though Nell looked like she might drop her girl. Yivan and Sarajawea were sitting on the steps looking bored. Nodin passed them, taking his girl up to the roof.

"Yivan, help Nell," Levi said, wishing his crew had a little more common sense.

Yivan jumped up and grabbed the little girl, but he got Nell's shirt too and pulled her so hard that she fell onto her knees.

"Let go," Nell cried.

Yivan put down the little girl, who started crying.

"That's Rosalie." Nell crouched down by the crying girl and rubbed her back. "Hey, Rosalie, don't cry. We're going to take you to your momma now."

Levi winced. Rosalie's mother, Susan, had died in the raid. Apparently Nell didn't know that. But her words calmed Rosalie for the moment.

The girl Levi was holding shifted and opened her eyes, staring at him. He was pretty sure she wasn't Kaylee.

"Yivan, take Rosalie upstairs. Sarajawea, can you walk? Go with Yivan and Rosalie?"

Sarajawea stood up, holding her pillow, and stared at Yivan. The boy picked up Rosalie and started up the stairs. Sarajawea followed.

"Okay, that's three. And, Nell, if you take this one, that will be four." Levi handed off the girl in his arms. "I'll go and get the last two, but send someone down to help me, okay?"

"Okay, Levi." Nell started up the stairs.

Levi opened the door and crept back to the dorm. He bent down and examined the first girl, then the second. They both had dark hair. He had no idea which was Kaylee.

He picked up one and set her on the edge of her bed. Her body slumped back over onto her side and she pulled for her blankets. Levi picked up the second girl and sat her on the edge of the first girl's bed. This one stayed upright. He propped the first girl up again so that the girls were sitting side by side. He squatted before them, wrapped an arm around each, and stood. They were light, but the one on the left was slipping. He hefted them up and headed for the door.

He should have propped it open.

He pressed himself against the door, bending his knees until the backs on his fingers felt the knob. He strained to turn and pull at the same time, and only managed to make the door rattle. He thought about putting down the girls, opening the door, and picking them back up, but he kept at the knob until it finally bounced open far enough that he was able to jab his foot into the crack. He had to lean back to keep hold of the girls, but he managed to wedge his other knee into the crack and knock open the door enough to dart out.

He ran to the stairwell door, which was also closed, and set the girls on their feet. One of them started to cry. Levi opened the door and waved them through.

"Go to the stairs," he whispered. *Okay, Mr. Strange Man.* Sure. He couldn't blame the girl for being scared out of her mind.

The second girl stared up at him. "Are you Levi?"

Well, now he knew which one was Kaylee. "Yes. I've come to help you and your friend. Now go through the — "

"You there! What are you doing with those girls?"

A woman stood at the opposite end of the hallway.

Levi shoved Kaylee and the crying girl into the stairwell. "Sit there, Kaylee. I'll be right back."

Levi shut the door and walked toward the woman. "Sorry, I'm a guard, and I heard a noise up here." Yeah, that made a lot of sense. When he was close enough to know he couldn't miss, he drew the SimScanner and fired. The woman screamed, clutched her hand to her chest. Her face distorted into an ugly grimace. She grunted and fell.

Levi holstered his weapon and carried the woman into the girls' dorm. He laid her on one of the plain mattresses, then ran to the nearest made-up bed and ripped off the sheets. He didn't have time to do much, but he whipped the top sheet into a long snake and used it to tie the woman's hands to the wire headboard. He repeated the process with the fitted sheet, tying her feet to the footboard. By then she was coming to, moaning. He found a tiny stuffed cat and shoved its head into her mouth.

It would have to do.

He ran back into the hallway and sprinted to the stairwell. When he opened the door, the crying girl screamed.

"You hurt her! You hurt her!"

Perfect. Levi grabbed the girl and covered her mouth with his hand. "She's not hurt, just sleeping. She'll be fine."

The girl jerked away and bit his finger. Levi growled and reapplied his hand in a way he hoped would keep her from opening her mouth. "Kaylee, come on. We have to run fast up these stairs."

"Okay," Kaylee said.

Levi ran up to the fourth floor, but when he turned back, Kaylee was taking her time, one hand on the rail.

"One step, stop." She stepped up with her right foot, then brought her left foot to join it. "Two steps, stop." Then she stepped with her left foot and brought her right to join it. "Three steps, stop."

Oh, come on, little one. "Faster, Kaylee. Can you go faster?"

"Four steps, stop. Five steps, stop." She increased her speed, but not her rhythm.

Levi would just have to come back for her. He ran up. Around the bend of the fourth floor, he met Nodin coming from above.

"Here," Levi said. "She screams and bites, so be careful." He handed off the girl, and she managed a quick screech before Nodin got a good grip on her mouth.

Levi ran back down until he found Kaylee.

"Seventeen steps, stop. Eighteen — "

Levi tossed her over his shoulder and headed back up the stairs. Just as he passed the door to level five, it swung open.

"Who is out of bed?" a woman said.

Her eyes met Levi's. He fumbled for his SimScanner, but he was holding Kaylee on his right shoulder and couldn't grab it. The woman darted back inside.

"Intruders," she yelled. "In the girls' dorms. Come quickly to the fifth floor."

If she had SimTalk, which she likely did, there was no point in chasing her down and stunning her. So Levi continued on, hoping Mason wasn't far behind.

CHAPTER
27

Mason followed Penelope down the stairs, Ruston behind him, then Beshup. The SimScanner on his hip felt heavy and foreign, despite not being a killing weapon. He hoped he wouldn't have to use it. This whole event had him terrified, not that he'd admit it aloud, especially within Levi's hearing, but all he could think of was that day the enforcers had come to Glenrock and killed so many. Seeing his father and uncle die. Trying to save Papa Eli.

At the bottom of the stairwell, Penelope stopped at the exit door and turned to face them. "When we leave the building, whoever's last, make sure you don't kick out the stick that's keeping the door propped open. Okay?" She looked from face to face, then pushed open the stairwell door and headed into the dark hallway.

They passed by classrooms filled with GlassTop desks and Wyndo wall screens. The wall screens in the hallway flashed images of artwork and assignments. Penelope led them to the front door where a thin aspen branch lay against the doorframe, keeping it open.

Penelope held the door, motioning them to come outside and get behind a hedge of bushes beside the entrance. When the three men were behind the bushes, she carefully closed the door, making sure the branch kept it from shutting fully.

She joined them in the bushes and peeked over the top of one. Mason followed her gaze. A courtyard edged in shrubs separated the girls' dorm building from the boys'. Concrete paths wove through the courtyard, curving and curling to different destinations: a garden of flowers, an area with stone tables, a fountain, a strange sculpture of a horse woman. It reminded Mason of Champion Park and he and Ciddah's picnic. He wondered where she was at the moment and hoped she was safe.

"I don't see them," Penelope said, "but they have to be in there. Let's run!"

She crouched low and jogged into the courtyard, head turning as she scanned the area. Mason stayed on her heels. His adrenaline was so high his hands were shaking.

"Pen," someone said. The voice was low, and if Mason hadn't been straining to hear, he might have missed it.

Penelope took off again, running toward a brightly colored playground.

As they approached, a figure came down the slide, twisting with the spiral until he slid off the edge and stood. Trevon.

Movement in the structure brought several more figures into the dim light of the streetlamp above. Mason recognized Jake and two faces from Jack's Peak, but there were some new children here — children that had to be from the Safe Lands.

"Levi and Jordan are getting the girls out now," Penelope said. "We have to hurry."

"Who are your friends?" Mason asked Trevon.

"Grayn is with me," Trevon said. "And Dakav and Etu brought Holt."

"I didn't dare ask any of the boys in my dorm," Jake said.

"Why not?" Ruston asked.

"Most boys here are filled with the coyote's mischief," Dakav said.

"And Jake's room is the worst," Trevon said. "I wouldn't trust those maggots with my shirt."

Jake grimaced. "They play a lot of pranks on me."

"The rest of you are certain there are no other boys who'd come with us?" Ruston asked.

"None," Dakav said. "Holt and Grayn are different."

"Maybe the littles, though," Trevon said.

"Yeah, they don't cause much trouble," Etu said.

"And that's where we're going now," Mason said. "Though I don't see any reason for us all to go. How many boys are there in the littles?"

"Nine," Dakav said.

They could get all nine. "Okay, then. Penelope, why don't you take Trevon, Jake, Sakima, and ...?" He pointed to Trevon's friend.

"Grayn."

"Grayn," Mason said. "Take them to the roof. The rest of us will go for the little boys. Seven of us should be enough to fetch nine."

"Surely some of the boys will be able to walk on their own," Ruston said.

"That's my hope," Mason said.

"Are you sure you can find your way back to the roof without me?" Penelope asked. "The boys don't know the girls' building."

"You just brought me through it," Mason said. "I didn't forget the way."

"Okay." Though Penelope didn't look happy to be leaving. "Please be careful, Mason."

"We have weapons to use if need be," Ruston said.

Mason tried not to think about the gun on his hip. Hopefully it wouldn't "need be."

"Can I have a weapon?" Dakav asked.

"No," Mason said, "but you can lead the way to the boys' dorm."

Penelope gave Mason one last forlorn look, then grabbed Trevon's hand and dragged him toward the girls' dorm. Grayn, Jake, and Sakima trailed after them.

Mason followed Dakav farther into the courtyard, passing the fountain and the flower garden. Dakav paused at the edge of the courtyard, looked both ways, then jogged to a brown building.

A rock had been used to prop open the entrance to this building, which was identical to the girls' building, only reversed. Again Mason thought of Ciddah. What must it have been like to grow up in this place? They trooped up two flights of stairs and out into the hallway on the third floor.

Dakav pointed to a door on the right side of the hall, then pulled it open and slipped inside. Mason caught the door and peeked into the room. The dim light of a streetlamp outside filtered through the windows, revealing two rows of beds, one on each wall.

"See if you can find yours," Dakav said to Mason. "Explaining things before we leave will make everyone calmer." He sat on the edge of a bed and shook the shoulder of the boy sleeping there. "Yas, time to wake."

Beshup pushed past Mason and walked down the row of beds, examining the face of each boy as he went. Mason followed, but he didn't see Joey or Brian.

"Chua." Beshup knelt beside a bed at the end of the first row and stroked the boy's hair. "Chua, my son, your father has come for you."

Mason hadn't realized Beshup was a father. He knew so little of those who lived in Jack's Peak. Levi and Omar had visited there often, but Mason had been there only once.

The men had roused several boys now, and Mason searched the second row for familiar faces. He found Brian first. The boy was already awake, clutching his blankets to his chin, eyes wide. When he saw Mason, his face lit up in a smile. "We're going to go home?"

"Yes," Mason said, though it wasn't the whole truth. "Can you put on your shoes? We need you to be able to run fast and silent."

"Like Owl Man?"

"Just like the Owl Man, yes," Mason said, amused that so many had heard of Omar's antics. His brother had become a legend in only a few weeks. These people must be hungry for a hero.

Mason found Joey next and told the boy to put on his shoes.

"Where we going?" an unfamiliar boy asked Mason. He had the roundest eyes Mason had ever seen.

"You're not going with us," Brian said. "You gotta stay here."

"That's Weiss," Joey said. "He's not from Glenrock *or* Jack's Peak."

"That's okay," Ruston said. "We're taking all the boys with us. It's not safe for them here."

Weiss's eyes actually seemed to get larger. "The school's in trouble?"

"Yes," Mason said. "And we must get you all out quickly."

"Before Mr. Hemoth comes." Joey looked to Mason. "Mr. Hemoth is mean."

"Is Mr. Hemoth coming with us?" Weiss asked.

"No," Mason said. "He has to stay here."

Weiss raised his hands above his head and jumped. "Hooray!"

"Shh," Mason said. "We must be silent, like the Owl Man, or Mr. Hemoth will catch us."

"He already has," a man said.

Mason spun around. A man stood in the doorway, hands on hips.

"Just who are you people, anyway?" Mr. Hemoth asked.

Before Mason could construct a response, Ruston shot Mr. Hemoth with his SimScanner. Mr. Hemoth went rigid before he fell like a pine tree and hit the floor with a terrible smack. Mason twitched at the sound. The boys stared. Weiss screamed and covered his head.

Mason lifted the boy in his arms and started for the door. "Let's go, boys. Quickly." He stepped over Mr. Hemoth. Weiss wrapped his arms around Mason's neck and nestled his head onto Mason's shoulder. The boy's arms were so short and chubby, Mason felt smothered.

The patter of feet filled the hall behind him as he carried Weiss toward the stairwell. Mason opened the stairwell door and held it. The boy trembled in his arms. Mason gripped him tightly and counted those who passed by. Beshup, carrying his son and holding another boy by the hand. Dakav and Etu, each carrying a boy. Joey and Brian, walking side by side. No Ruston or Holt or their boys. Where were they? Mason peeked down the hall and saw them coming.

Six adults, nine children. They had everyone. Time to get out of this place.

When Ruston passed into the stairwell, he said, "I thought I should tie up Mr. Hemoth."

"Oh." Mason should have thought of that. "Good idea. Thank you."

They quickly caught up to the others. Though Joey and Brian looked to be moving as fast as their little legs could go, they were holding up the back half of the line.

Finally the boys reached the bottom level, where Beshup was holding open the stairwell door. It relieved Mason to have everyone in his sights again. How Levi and Jordan and Omar thrived on such exciting adventures, Mason could not comprehend. Give him an injury to mend over this any day.

They made it out of the building and across the courtyard without incident. As Mason approached the girls' building, the front entrance door came into view. It looked to be closed, but surely that was only the angle. Holt reached it first and turned back. He set his boy on the ground and pulled at the door.

"It won't open," he said.

"Penelope wouldn't have let it close," Mason said. The girl had been extremely cautious.

"I'll be right back," Holt said.

"Wait," Mason said. "Where are you going?" He didn't want to let anyone out of his sight.

"The girls usually leave the bathroom window open so boys can sneak in," he said, walking backward. Then he turned and ran along the side of the building and darted around the end.

"We should get behind those bushes again," Mason said, "where Penelope hid us before. At least until we figure out if Holt can get inside."

"Agreed." Ruston brushed by Mason and stepped behind the bushes on the right of the entrance door. "Come on, boys."

They had barely assembled in the tight space when a horrible siren split the night.

"It's the alarm," Dakav said.

Mason's hopes sank. If they were caught here tonight, all was lost. And what would become of Ciddah? Was Lawten holding her captive? Or was he merely keeping her away until Mason could be apprehended?

"Stay put," Ruston said. "All of you get down."

The little boys squatted into balls. Beshup put down his son and drew his SimScanner. Though the idea of Mason touching his own gun, SimScanner or not, repulsed him, he set Weiss on his feet. "Squat down." He made himself draw his SimScanner and peeked over the bushes.

Lights in the boys' building flicked on, but Mason saw no sign of guards or enforcers.

The front door to the girls' dorm banged open and Holt appeared, a wide grin on his face.

"Go," Ruston said. "Go, go!"

All at once, the boys jumped up and mobbed the entrance.

"Stay with them, Beshup," Ruston said.

Mason squeezed the grip of his gun and kept his finger far from the trigger. He tried to count as each boy went inside, but there was too much confusion.

"Hey, stop!" A guard was running toward them, gun in hand. "G12 to base. Intruders at SLBS. Request backup."

Ruston took off, sprinting toward the guard. He couldn't know whether the guard had a stunner or a real gun. That was true courage: doing what was necessary in spite of the possible consequences.

The guard seemed taken aback by Ruston's actions. "Stop!" He aimed his gun at Ruston. "Put your hands on your head and turn around."

Ruston kept running toward him. The guard fired. Nothing happened, which meant he must be using a SimScanner.

The guard looked down at his weapon and slapped it with his palm, fired it at Ruston again. "G12 to base. We've got ghosts!" Eyes wide, he dropped the SimScanner and drew a second gun. "SimScanners won't work. Copy? Use — "

But it was too late. Ruston fired his SimScanner at the guard first, and the guard went down the same as Mr. Hemoth.

Mason shooed Holt and Weiss inside and held the door open. Ruston picked up the guard's guns and ran toward Mason. He passed by in a gust of wind, and Mason chased after him. The siren was wailing indoors too.

At the end of the hall, Beshup stood, holding the stairwell door as the boys filed through. Panic overwhelmed Mason suddenly. The hallway seemed to stretch out an infinite distance before him. Everything morphed into slow motion. Beshup at the door. The boys going through. Nearly there, Etu and Dakav, each carrying a child. Joey and Brian trotting behind them. Ruston sprinting past Holt, who was waving Weiss to hurry. Weiss, halfway between Holt and Mason, plodding along.

Was Mason in shock? Or was fear taking over his mind?

A ding on his left drew his gaze. An elevator. Its doors slid open and two women stepped out, entering the hallway between Ruston and Holt. Before Mason could think of what to do, Ruston turned back and stunned one. She collapsed.

The second woman screamed and ran three steps toward Holt, but when she saw Ruston, she doubled back to the elevator and pushed the button. The doors slid open, but Ruston shot her with the SimScanner before she could get inside, and she fell in the open doorway. The elevator closed against her legs, then slid open again.

"Hey!" Beshup yelled from the stairwell door, Joey and Brian standing beside him. "I need help carrying these boys up the stairs. They're too slow."

Ruston reached Beshup first and swept Joey into his arms. Holt looked back at Weiss, then turned around and headed for him.

"Stop!" a voice yelled from behind Mason.

Mason turned. A second guard had entered the building and was headed toward them, gun in hand. SimScanner or stunner? That was the question.

He should shoot him, but instead, Mason ran toward Holt and grabbed Weiss on his way, tucking the boy on his hip. "I've got him. Into the elevator!"

But Holt didn't follow. He screamed, clenched his right hand into a fist, and fell to his knees. The guard must have gotten him with the SimScanner.

Mason stepped over the woman and set the boy in the elevator. "Wait right there, Weiss." He holstered his gun and ran back out, grabbed Holt under the arms, and dragged him past the woman, who was now moaning, and into the elevator. The guard pointed his weapon at Mason, but since he had no SimTag, the gun had no effect.

Mason managed to push the woman's body out of the way so that the doors finally slid closed. He pushed the button for five, and only when it started to rise did he breathe. He crouched over Holt and slapped his cheek. He didn't know how long SimScanner stuns lasted. If it was as long as a manual stun, he wouldn't be able to get the boy up to the roof and over the plank.

"Is Mr. Hemoth going to catch us?" Weiss asked.

"Nope. Mr. Hemoth should still be tied up."

The elevator stopped and the doors opened. Mason shooed Weiss into the hall, then dragged Holt out. It wasn't until he'd dragged Holt away from the elevator that he noticed the floor number on the frame of the elevator.

Three.

He lowered Holt to the floor, then leapt over his body to try to catch the elevator. The doors shut and he hit the Up button. Too late. It was already up on five. Should he hit the down button? He watched the elevator numbers count down: four, three, two. There is stopped. Which meant that someone else had called it and it would soon come back to three.

What was he going to do? There was no time. The battle in Glenrock came back to him again, when he'd tried to carry Shaylinn.

He hoisted Holt over his shoulder, but he only made it three steps before his knees buckled. The boy was too heavy. Weightlifting must've been a required course for boys in the boarding school, because Holt's arms were twice as wide as Mason's. He would never make it up two flights of stairs. For the first time ever, Mason wished he'd spent more time trying to build muscle strength.

He glanced at the elevator. It was now on level one. He crouched at Holt's side. "Can you hear me?"

Holt moaned.

Mason had no choice but to hope that was a yes. "We have to leave you, Holt. I'm so sorry. You're a hero for getting that door open, for wanting to leave with us. When they ask you what happened, tell them you heard a noise and went to investigate, and that some strangers were taking the boys and you tried to stop them." Mason took a deep breath. The elevator was on two. "If at some point you can get out into the city, go to the Highlands Department of Public Tasks and ask for Dayle. Tell him Mason sent you. He'll get you to us. Okay?"

The elevator dinged. Mason grabbed Weiss and ran for the stairwell.

"Found some!" a man yelled.

Mason reached the stairwell and yanked open the door. He ran inside and started up the stairs. The door banged shut behind him, then open again. The man was coming, which meant Mason was going to have to shoot him. It was only a SimScanner. And if he did it in the stairwell, he'd have the advantage of being above his pursuer.

He rounded the fourth floor door and ran up the first half toward five. He could hear the man thundering up the steps below him. Mason set Weiss down.

"Keep going up, Weiss." Mason drew his gun. "Up to the top."

The boy scampered up the stairs. Mason looked down the stairs, aiming his gun. He clicked off the safety.

The footsteps grew nearer. A drop of sweat rolled down Mason's temple. The man's head appeared, then his torso. Mason aimed, set his finger on the trigger.

The man saw him and stopped, lifted his arm, gun in hand. "Don't shoot."

Mason winced and fired.

The man grunted, as if fighting the electrical disruption of his nervous system. He toppled backward, fell on his back, and slid down the half flight of stairs until he came to rest on the landing below.

Mason's arms were trembling. He eyed his attacker's motionless body. Falling down concrete stairs could be injurious, to say the least.

He hoped the man hadn't broken any bones or received a concussion in the fall. He should check on him, at least make sure he was still breathing, but the sound of a helicopter pulled him back to his goal.

Ciddah was waiting. And if he failed here, she might be waiting forever.

He holstered his gun and ran up the last level to the roof. The first thing he saw was Ruston carrying Weiss across the board.

Then he saw the bright lights of the helicopter in the dark sky, headed toward them.

Mason ran, hoping the pilot hadn't seen them yet. He crossed the board in two steps and sprinted after Ruston, reaching the door before the helicopter neared the school.

Ruston was taking the stairs, so Mason followed. What if some had taken the elevator? How could he be certain they had everyone? But the elevator would likely beat Ruston and Mason downstairs. It would be okay.

As Mason rounded the landing on the second floor, he drew his gun. He didn't want to use it again, but there might be enforcers in the lobby.

But only Nash was waiting, holding open the front door. Mason stayed right behind Ruston, like a shadow. His breath was heavy, and his side ached from so much running.

"That's all of us," Mason managed to pant out as he passed Nash at the door.

Ruston glanced over his shoulder. "What about Holt?"

Mason shook his head. "He got stunned."

Enforcer sirens wailed in the distance, melding with the drone of the school siren.

Mason thought of Ciddah, wondering if she were at Lawten's home and if Levi would really help him rescue her once they got the children to safety.

He hoped so.

CHAPTER
28

Shaylinn stood behind Jemma, who was crouched at Naomi's bedside. "You were hiding your labor, weren't you?" Jemma asked after another contraction had passed.

"What was I supposed to do?" Naomi lay in bed, sweat matting her hair to her forehead, her cheeks flushed. "If I'd said one word, uttered one groan of pain, Jordan wouldn't have left. And Levi needs him tonight."

"Oh, honey." Jemma took hold of Naomi's hand. "You're so brave."

Naomi rolled her eyes at Shaylinn. "If your sister is going to be like this through my labor, I want her out."

That brought a smile to Shaylinn's lips. "Jemma, stop being dramatic. Naomi needs you, and she can't tolerate such sweetness. Did you forget that she's married to my brother?"

All three girls burst into laughter.

"Jordan is very sweet," Naomi said in an offended tone. Then she winked at Shaylinn. "Just not when any of you are watching."

"Good," Shaylinn said. "I don't think I could stomach seeing him be sweet."

"You can't stomach anything right now," Naomi said.

They all laughed again. It felt good to laugh, but Shaylinn was afraid for Naomi. Her sister-in-law was the toughest woman Shaylinn knew, but she'd suffered two contractions since Shaylinn had entered the room and the pain had been obvious. And Jemma said it would only get worse.

"Mason sent a box of pain meds if you want to try them," Jemma said.

A small shake of the head. "I don't need any of that stuff."

But an hour later, Naomi changed her mind. It took Shaylinn and Jemma a bit to figure out how to load the vaporizer, but once they did, Naomi sucked down the meds like they were water. Soon after she seemed to relax.

"She's very close," Jemma said. "Go get Chipeta and Aunt Mary."

Shaylinn probably didn't need to run, but the whole experience had her terrified. She hurried into the living room, where she found the three women still praying. Eliza was in tears.

"How is she?" Chipeta asked.

"Jemma thinks she's close. She said for you and Aunt Mary to come."

Aunt Mary pushed up from the sofa and trotted out of the room. Chipeta followed.

Shaylinn sat down on the sofa across from Eliza, feeling strange to be sitting with a woman who was crying. She didn't know if she should try to comfort her or not, so she just sat there, feeling useless.

"Did you hear that?" Eliza sniffled. "Listen."

Shaylinn held her breath. A heavy silence descended, then three knocks sounded on the front door. She jumped so high it felt like her heart had stopped. She met Eliza's gaze.

"I thought I heard someone. Maybe they're back already." She got up and ran out of the living room.

"It's too early, Eliza." Shaylinn got up and followed her. "Wait. Don't open the door yet."

But it was too late. Eliza had already cracked opened the door. "Oh, hello."

"Sorry to bother you," a familiar voice said, "but I have an urgent message from Levi."

Eliza gasped and opened the door wider. "What happened? Is it the children? Come in."

Rewl entered and stopped just inside the door. He looked past Eliza to where Shaylinn stood. "Hello, shimmer."

Shaylinn tensed at the sound of his oily voice. Why would Rewl have an urgent message from Levi when Levi didn't trust him? How did he even find the cabin?

"What's the message?" Eliza asked. "Is everything okay?"

"It will be." Rewl reached behind his back and pulled out a gun.

Eliza's eyes flew wide and he shot her.

Shaylinn screamed. Eliza slumped to the floor. A black cartridge clung to Eliza's chest and *click*, *click*, *clicked*, bringing a hint of relief to Shaylinn — it had only been a stunner. But Shaylinn's eyes filled with tears as she stared at Eliza's motionless body and the way her eyes were still open and moving. She stepped toward Eliza.

"None of that now, femme," Rewl said, training his gun on Shaylinn.

"Shaylinn?" Aunt Mary ran out from the back and stopped when she saw Eliza's body. "Oh!"

Chipeta appeared second. "What's this?"

"Back off," Rewl yelled, pointing the weapon at Aunt Mary, then Chipeta. "I've got a job to do, and you femmes are going to let me do it or I'll stun every one of you."

"What do you need to do?" Chipeta asked.

"I'm taking Shaylinn on a little ride."

Shaylinn's heart fluttered. She didn't want to leave the cabin, especially with Rewl.

Aunt Mary started to cry. "Please don't hurt Shaylinn."

"I don't want to hurt anyone, but if you cause me any grief, I will." He waved the gun at Shaylinn. "Let's go, shimmer. We've got somewhere to be."

Shaylinn glanced at the ladies, then moved slowly toward the door.

She didn't know what else to do. She didn't trust Rewl, especially since she was almost certain he'd been the one who had killed Chord.

Rewl slapped his hand against his leg. "Faster — let's go. Open the door."

Shaylinn had to step over Eliza's body to get to the door. She hoped Eliza wouldn't be stunned long.

"You two get back!" He waved the gun at Chipeta and Aunt Mary, and they retreated down the hallway.

Shaylinn opened the door. A black car was parked in front of the cabin.

"Down the steps and into the trunk of that car."

Shaylinn whipped her head around to look back at him. "A trunk!"

"Not your interest, shimmer. You won't be in it long."

Shaylinn walked out into the cool night. A breeze pressed her clothing tightly against her, and she shivered. The trunk was already open. Shaylinn walked to it and looked back again.

Aunt Mary and Chipeta had come to the door and stood watching, looks of horror on their faces. Behind them, Shaylinn could see Jemma kneeling beside Eliza. Rewl backed down the stairs, his steps crunching over the gravel as he neared, still pointing his gun inside the open door of the house. He glanced at Shaylinn. "What are you waiting for? Get in!"

"You're a bad man," Shaylinn said.

"I'm a stimming hero, which you'll see soon enough. Lawten Renzor messed up a lot of stuff. But Bender is going to set it straight. Now, get in!"

Shaylinn climbed into the trunk. It looked like it would be cramped once the top slid shut.

"Lie down on your side."

Shaylinn obeyed. The carpet on the floor of the trunk was scratchy and smelled like metal.

Rewl looked down on her. "You don't have to worry, femme. I'm going to keep you safe. And once you have those babies, you and I can talk paint."

The innuendo made her breath hitch, though she barely understood it. "I will never talk paint with you."

He flashed his striped teeth in a wide grin. "We'll see, neo. We'll see."

The trunk slid closed, engulfing Shaylinn in darkness. She could hear Rewl's footsteps crunch over the gravel, the car door slide open and closed, then the engine purr to life. Then the vehicle rocked back and lurched away.

What could Rewl possibly want with her? How did it involve Bender? Maybe he was turning her over to General Otley as a favor. If so, would Otley take her back to the harem?

She sang songs to comfort herself on the drive, but the journey didn't last long. No more than ten minutes had passed when the car stopped.

Shaylinn tensed, waiting for the trunk to open and Rewl to order her to get out. But he didn't come. After a while she pounded her fists against the lid above. "Hello? Is anyone there?"

"Just me, femme," Rewl's voice came from the front seat.

"Why are you keeping me in here?" Shaylinn asked.

"We're waiting for someone. It won't be long."

Waiting for who? Shaylinn sang to herself some more and prayed. Moments later a vehicle approached and stopped behind Rewl's car. Someone got out and walked over what sounded like concrete.

"You got her?" It was Bender's voice.

"She's in the trunk," Rewl said. "Are you sure we can trust him?"

"No, but I don't see another way."

"He makes me nervous," Rewl said.

"It's our best option," Bender said. "We can't keep doing things the soft way. We need to change if we're ever going to make a difference. This is the best chance we've got right now."

"I hope you're right."

"Come sit in my car with me," Bender said. "She isn't going anywhere."

Shaylinn listened to the shuffling of steps and the sound of power doors rising and falling. Then there was silence.

CHAPTER
29

Omar tapped Charlz. His friend had been about to go out but promised to wait until Omar stopped by. Ten minutes later, Omar knocked on door 322 of the Twister, where Charlz lived.

Charlz opened the door, and Omar was struck by how bad his friend's flaking skin looked. "Long time, peer. Where you been?"

"Keeping busy." Omar followed Charlz into the kitchen. The table was cluttered with stunners. Charlz didn't sit and didn't ask Omar to.

"Why don't you come out with Scottie and me tonight? We're going to Melman's."

Ah, the Safe Lands DarkScene. "I can't. I need your help." And Omar explained about what had happened with Otley, cutting out his SimTag again, and losing his apartment and access to stims. "I've got something important to do tonight, but the itch is so bad, I'm nearly sick. I need something to get me through the night."

"You know I can't get involved in that, peer." Charlz touched his ear as if to say someone was listening. "Otley almost killed me last time I got roped into your plans."

Omar, Charlz, and Skottie used to be enforcers, until Omar had talked them into helping him and they all got reassigned. Was Charlz saying no for real or only because someone might hear? "I just need a hit of something. Anything."

"I can give you a beer," Charlz said, walking to his fridge. "I know how the ache feels, peer, and I'm sorry. But if you vape too much right now, you'll be wasted when you're supposed to be doing whatever tonight." He got a beer from the fridge and handed it to Omar. "And while you can mix stims — vape your downers now then vape some uppers before you head out — I wouldn't risk it when you've got someplace to be. Plus, that's a great way to end up in the MC or premie libbed."

So Omar sipped his beer like it was the most precious substance on earth, then went with Charlz to Melman's, hoping Skottie would have more mercy.

When they found Skottie outside the dance club, he wasn't nearly so prude. "You've been off the vape how long?"

"Two days," Omar said, rubbing the scar on the bridge of his nose. "But I have to be someplace in a couple hours. It's really important that I don't mess it up."

"It's too risky," Charlz said, but Skottie waved him off.

"I think he can take it."

"I can," Omar said. "Thanks, Scottie. Anything you can do, I really appreciate it." He felt pathetic and desperate, but he would keep begging until someone helped him.

They went to the hit room at Melman's and claimed a table in a back corner. But before Skottie would place an order, he taught Omar a few things about the stims he favored. It turned out that Omar liked downers, which helped him relax, took him to a blissful, euphoric oblivion where nothing mattered in the world. Uppers wound him up and made him jittery and anxious but helped him think fast. Grass, brown sugar, and alcohol were downers. Golden ice, white cocoa, and the cocktail mixes were uppers.

"Can I just have some grass and brown sugar? Low doses are fine."

Skottie shot him a dirty look. "Were you even listening to me?"

"He's practically a shell," Charlz said. "I'm telling you, be careful."

Skottie removed two PVs from his pocket and set them on the table. "Charlz?"

Charlz sighed and set his own PV on the table. "I still think this is a mistake."

When the barkeep came again, Skottie gave very specific instructions. "Empty all three of these. Fill one with a four of brown sugar, one with a two of white cocoa, and the third with a five of grass."

Omar got jittery just hearing that order. "Thanks, Skottie. Seriously. I really appreciate this."

"Not a problem, peer." And when the barkeep returned, Skottie handed Omar the brown sugar first. "Now sit here and take your sugar very, very slowly."

Omar did, and all the pain went away. So did his worries. Relief. Sweet relief.

Omar probably would have stayed in the chair at the hit room for a week, but Skottie woke him after an hour and made him vape the white cocoa.

He woke up fast. The euphoria was fast too, came and went in a few minutes. After two days of aching pain, it felt good to feel strong again. Energized. Indestructible.

Then Skottie let him take the PV that had grass in it. "Save this until you need it, you hear me? And come visit me later if you need more of the sweetness."

Omar didn't doubt for a minute that he'd see Skottie the next night.

He left his friends at Melman's and met Kendall and the two Jack's Peak men, Mukwiv and Tupi, at Zane's house. Zane gave Omar a gun belt with a SimScanner. Once they left the house, Omar put Jordan's gun on the other side of the belt. He didn't think Zane would have approved of a real weapon, but Omar knew from his time with the enforcers that many of them carried the dual-action pistols.

They walked through the storm drains and into the Highlands.

Omar felt good. Alive and awake and whole again. The trip passed by in a blur, and soon they were above ground again, approaching the Medical Center from the back parking lot.

"SimTalk: tap: Zane," Omar said.

"You there yet?" Zane asked.

"Yeah. We're in the back parking lot. What do you see?"

"The stairwell is empty. Go for it."

Omar waved the others to follow and walked toward the stairwell as if he had every right to be there. It was a trick he'd learned in his time spent being a rebel. If you looked suspicious, people thought you were. But if you looked like you belonged, people didn't question why you were there.

They climbed the stairs to the sixth floor, and by then Mukwiv was panting pretty heavily. The guy had to be under forty or he would've been liberated like Omar's mother, but Mukwiv had almost as many wrinkles on his face as Papa Eli once had. Tupi was much younger, maybe Jordan's age. They were all wearing black, which had camouflaged them in the tunnels and outside, but would make them really obvious in the MC.

"We're on six, Zane," Omar said. "What do you see?"

"Not a good time. There's a janitor."

"Are you kidding?" Omar wanted to get this done, not hover in the stairwell, waiting to get caught while a janitor mopped the floor. "What do we do?"

"Hang tight. Or you could jump him. I've got the cameras off."

"Zane says there's a janitor out there and that we could jump him," Omar said.

"No," Kendall said. "It's better if fewer people see us."

"He could be cleaning for hours," Omar said.

"I don't think so," Zane said. "He just emptied a trash can and is pushing his cart toward the elevator."

Omar glanced at his team. They were all wearing harnesses to carry the kids. Mary and Shay had made them out of strips of fabric.

Shay.

Hopefully, once they all moved into the basements, Ruston would put Kendall and her kid far away from wherever he put Shay. Maybe Omar could suggest that to Ruston. But no matter where Kendall wound up, he had to apologize to Shay. He wondered if she really would always forgive him. Kissing Kendall had been a pretty major screw-up.

"Janitor just got into the elevator," Zane said. "Go now."

"Janitor's gone," Omar told the others. "Let's go." He pushed open the door and walked down the bright hallway. "Where am I going, Kendall?"

"There's a big entrance on the left, about halfway down," Kendall said. "Wooden doors. A plaque that says Safe Lands Nursery. You should be able to go right in, but stop just inside the front doors. And be quiet."

The doors came into view. Omar opened one and held it for everyone. "Wait right inside," he whispered.

Once they'd all gone in, Omar followed and held the door as it closed behind him, careful not to let it slam. "We're in," he said to Zane.

"All right. Let me find you. The cameras here aren't labeled."

Omar leaned against the wall just inside the door and took a breath from Skottie's PV. It felt good to be back to normal.

They were in a waiting room with rows of chairs and a counter that was dark. A short hall on the other side of the waiting area stretched out for a few yards before turning a corner. Light illuminated the back end of it.

"Got you," Zane said. "You guys were hard to spot. What's your plan?"

"Hold on." Omar waved Mukwiv and Tupi over and stepped close to Kendall. "Zane wants to hear the plan. Talk close to my ear so he can hear you."

When they were all huddled together, Kendall explained. "First we need to stun the femmes at the caretakers' station. It's straight ahead and to the right. Once they're down, we can find the kids. The hallways are a big U, and there are rooms all along it. That's where they keep the babies."

"I see the station," Zane said. "The caretakers are just sitting there talking. Two of them. Have your SimScanners ready."

"I'll take them out," Omar said. "Stay close behind me." He drew his SimScanner and walked forward, trying not to let his shoes make noise on the tile floor. He passed through the waiting area and down the hallway. The light got brighter and he squinted. He reached the corner and could hear voices.

"He didn't even listen to me," a woman said. "So I told him to take me home. And then he got angry, started treating me like I was the one being ridiculous. I mean, I can understand if he has another femme, but to try to pick one up while he's out with me ... I'm sorry, but that's not acceptable."

Omar stepped around the corner. The caretakers' station wasn't as close as he'd expected. He could see both women's heads, just above the top of the high counter that circled them, but they hadn't seen him yet.

He flipped off the safety on the SimScanner, keeping the weapon ready at his side. He strode toward them and reached the counter before either woman looked up.

"You did right," a second woman said. "Did I ever tell you about the time I had dinner with—"

She stopped, and Omar realized the first woman had turned slightly and was now staring right at him. "What do you need, trigger?" she asked. "We're closed."

Omar lifted the SimScanner and shot her, then aimed at the second woman and shot her too before the first had even hit the floor.

"SimTalk: Enforcer 10." A woman's voice, coming from a little office in back of the caretakers' station. "I've got a man with a gun in the nursery. Two caretakers have been stunned."

Maggots! "Someone called Enforcer 10, Zane." Omar heaved himself up against the counter and slid over the top to the other side. He leaped over one of the stunned caretakers and charged into the office. The third woman was cowered behind a desk. "Please don't shoot me!"

"It's just a stunner." Omar fired, wincing at the look of horror on the woman's face as she collapsed. "Zane? Anything you can do about Enforcer 10?"

"I'll try. But you'd better move fast, just in case."

"Spread out," Omar said to the others. "Bring the kids here, and we'll help each other strap them on. Be quick about it. Enforcers are on the way."

Kendall took off for the nearest door. Mukwiv and Tupi ran to the rooms on the left. Omar banged out a swinging half-door and walked to the right. The room on the far right was empty. So were the next three. Then he found a sleeping boy — Eliza's Ben. Omar grabbed him and ran him to the caretakers' station, where Mukwiv was setting down another toddler. Tupi stood cradling a smaller baby in his arms.

"My boy, my boy," Tupi said, nuzzling the kid's neck.

"Love on him later." Omar laid Ben on the floor. The boy's eyes were still closed, and his legs curled up to his chest as he rolled to his side. "We've got five more to find."

"Four more," Kendall said, pushing through the half door and setting little Carrie down on her feet. The toddler's cheeks were red and she was sucking her thumb.

"Find them." Omar ran to the next room. Inside he discovered his cousin Hazel, Aunt Chipeta's youngest. He carried her back to the station and saw that both Mukwiv and Tupi had found another child each. One of them was crying.

Kendall ran out of a room and into another. She came back out. "You guys checked all those?"

"Yes," Tupi said, helping Mukwiv strap a kid to his back.

"And I checked the rooms on this side," Omar said. "Who we missing?"

Kendall's voice came out in a whimper. "Elyot."

Figured. "I'll see if I can wake one of the caretakers." Omar ran behind the counter and slapped the cheek of the first femme he'd stunned. "Where's Elyot?"

She groaned.

Kendall crouched beside Omar. "Baby Promise. Where is he?"

The caretaker's eyes widened, and her voice came out a raspy whisper. "He doesn't live here."

Sure he didn't. "Where else would he live?"

"She's lying. I saw him here before." Kendall grabbed the gun from Omar's waistband and pointed it at the woman. Jordan's gun. "Where is he?"

"Walls, don't, Kendall!" Omar said. "That's not a stunner."

"Good." She prodded the barrel against the woman's chest, then set it against her forehead and held it there. "This is an Old gun. Loaded with bullets that send you to the next life. So, tell me where my baby is, now!"

Omar could only stare at Kendall, horrified. Two of the kids were crying now. He stepped to the side to try to block the view through the doorway.

"I can't," the caretaker said. "If I do, I'll be liberated."

Kendall used her thumb to pull back the hammer. "If you don't tell, you'll die right here."

Omar stared at Kendall in total shock. She could use a gun? "How do you even know how to use that? To pull back the hammer?"

Kendall glowered at the caretaker. "I know all about guns, Omar, and drugs and liars too. My uncle was the biggest liar of all." She jabbed the gun at the woman's forehead again. "Tell me!" she screamed.

The woman shuddered. "He lives at Champion House. The task director general has a live-in caretaker who's responsible for him."

"Why?" Kendall asked.

"An experiment, I was told. His assistant said the task director general wants to see how an infant is raised."

"He took my baby," Kendall said to Omar, her tone wistful yet filled with understanding. "It's all he ever wanted from me."

Omar didn't know what she was talking about, but he didn't like the look in her eyes. The screaming babies probably weren't helping. He reached out his hand. "We'll get him, I promise. Can I have the gun back?"

Her eyes shifted to his, then down at the gun that was still pointed at the woman. She lowered it a little and released the hammer.

Good. He reached for it and —

The caretaker jumped up and knocked into Kendall, stealing the gun. She ran to the corner of the room and pointed it at Kendall, then Omar. She frowned at the gun and used her other hand to pull back the hammer.

Omar froze. He couldn't be certain she'd correctly cocked the gun, but it sure looked that way. "Kendall, get down!" He slowly reached for his SimScanner.

"Don't you touch that!" the caretaker screamed, and Omar lifted his hands where they could be seen.

"What's going on?" Zane asked in Omar's ear. "I can't see in that office."

"The caretaker has my gun."

"I won't let you take our future," the caretaker said. "The children stay here." And she fired the gun at Kendall, the recoil deafening in the tiny space.

Omar quickly pulled his SimScanner and shot the woman. She collapsed. He ran to her and ripped away the gun. Then he looked back to where Kendall had been standing, but she was on the floor. "Kendall? You okay?" He couldn't see any blood, but she was wearing all black.

"Omar?" Zane asked. "Speak to me, peer. That didn't sound like a stunner."

Mukwiv stood in the doorway to the room, staring wide-eyed at Kendall. A kid was strapped to his front.

Omar ran to her side and saw the wetness seeping through her shirt. "Kendall's been shot in the chest. One of the caretakers got my gun." Had the bullet missed her heart? Did it even matter?

"Where did you get a real gun?" Zane asked.

"It was Jordan's," was all Omar could say.

Zane muttered a string of curses. "No one was supposed to bring that."

Omar grabbed hold of Kendall's body, pulled her onto his lap, which left a smear of blood on the white tile floor. *Oh no no.* "We need a medic," he said to Mukwiv. "Zane, we need a medic."

"No, Omar. You need to get out, now. Enforcers are in the building and there are all kinds of medics in the hallways, looking around. Someone will find her."

"You have to go," Kendall whispered.

"We can't leave you like this. We should have brought Mason." Mason would have known what to do.

"The gunfire will have drawn the interest of other people," Mukwiv said.

"Omar, you have to get out of there, now!" Zane yelled. "Enforcers are coming."

"I'm so sorry, Kendall," he said. "I'll get your baby, I will."

"Take care of him?"

"Yes, of course. We all will."

"Wait," she whispered. "I told Otley you were the Owl. Because ... the summons. I went. And Lawten let me see Elyot. My baby was here then. He's so beautiful, my Elyot."

Seriously? Did everyone have a price in this world that they'd betray anyone for? Did Omar have a price too? Shay, perhaps? If someone threatened Shay, what would he to do keep her safe? Could he even —

"There's something else." Kendall fumbled for his shirt and pulled him toward her. For half a second he thought she would kiss him. But she pulled his head past her face, putting her lips by his ear. "When I first got here. Lawten ... He bought me from my uncle, said I was his wife. But when I got pregnant he sent me to the harem. And when I asked why I couldn't be his lifer, he said he already had one. Ciddah, the medic. Tell your brother for me? Mason has always been ..."

Her hand fell away from her shirt, and her eyes were frozen, staring at the ceiling.

"Kendall?" Omar grabbed her shoulder and shook it. "Kendall!"

"We must go," Mukwiv said.

Omar screamed out his frustration and pushed Kendall's body off his lap. But he couldn't look away from her face, the way her eyes stared open at the ceiling. His hands shook as he reached out to close her eyes, something he wished he could have done for his father.

Then he jumped up and ran back out into the caretakers' station. At least half of the kids were crying now. There was so much noise, and they'd just seen adults shooting each other and falling to the floor. And all the blood. Omar wanted to scream for everyone to shut up. Instead he grabbed Hazel and tried to put her leg through the harness.

Mukwiv and Tupi had already harnessed the Jack's Peak children to their fronts and backs.

"Help me," Omar said to Mukwiv.

The older man helped Omar strap Ben to his front, while Tupi strapped Hazel to his back.

All that was left was Carrie, who was crying around the thumb in her mouth. Omar squatted and picked up the girl and settled her on his hip. Three kids weighed a lot more than he'd expected. "Let's go."

Omar pushed out past the half door and walked toward the entrance, shushed Carrie and tried to bounce her. His heart was racing. His limbs shaking. He could feel Skottie's PV pressing against his hip and wanted a vape, but he had no free hands. "Zane? How about those enforcers?"

"Two getting off the elevators now. You're going to have to stun them to get out."

"We've got two enforcers coming." Omar shushed Carrie again. "Can you guys stun them?" He changed the tone of his voice, trying to sound soothing. "It's okay, Carrie." The other babies had quieted, but Carrie's cry was going to give them away.

Tupi drew his gun. Mukwiv already had his in hand. "Should we wait for them to come in?"

"No," Zane said. "Those doors have an alcove that will be good cover. Go, go."

Omar relayed Zane's message. Tupi held the door for Mukwiv, and the two men slipped out. The door started to close, and Omar caught it with his foot. He heard a man yell, shoes squeak on tile. He heaved Carrie up on his hip and crept forward.

"They've got them down," Zane said. "Get out of there. To the stairwell."

Omar pushed all the way out the double doors and into the hallway. Tupi and Mukwiv were waiting. "To the stairs." He tried to run, but the kids bounced so much that Ben's head smacked into his chin, and the boy started to cry. Great, now two were crying. At least Hazel was happy on Omar's back.

"Hold him while you run," Mukwiv said.

Omar pulled his arms tight around Ben and Carrie and jogged toward the stairwell. Awkward, but much better. Ben instantly quieted.

"You've got two more coming up the stairs," Zane said.

Omar warned Mukwiv, who took the lead into the stairwell. "Be careful to keep out of their line of sight," Omar said. "The babies have SimTags and could get stunned."

But Mukwiv and Tupi had the advantage of height as they came down and easily stunned the ascending enforcers. They made it down the stairs. Omar paused at the door to the back parking lot. "Zane? Can we come out?"

"Yeah, yeah. More enforcers are coming in the front, but the back is clear. They still don't know I've hacked the grid and taken over their cameras. Dim shells, anyway."

Omar pushed out the door and walked across the empty, dark parking lot. Carrie had mostly quieted and hopefully would stay that way until they were safely in the truck. In the distance, headlights flashed twice, and Omar changed direction, headed for Dayle's truck.

Just before they reached the vehicle, the back doors opened and Mason looked out. He took Carrie from Omar and set her inside, then pulled Omar up into the back. "You did it, brother."

"Yeah." But not without loss. Another person dead. Omar's fault. Omar's gun. And nothing but bad news about Mason's medic. He dug in his pocket for Skottie's PV, and once he had it in hand, he fell on his knees on a pile of blankets that covered the floor of the truck and took a long drag.

"Where's Kendall?" Mason inched over to help Omar remove Hazel from the back harness and laid her on a pile of blankets.

"May." Hazel crawled over Carrie's body back toward Mason.

"Hey, Hazel." Mason swept her up in a hug and touched her nose. "How are you?"

"Wuv May."

"I love you too," Mason said, setting her back on the blankets. "Though you won't like me very much in a minute." He looked around the interior of the truck. "I thought Kendall went with you. And where'd you get that PV? I thought yours was gone." He moved over and started to unhook the baby from Tupi's back harness.

Omar leaned back against the wall of the truck, keeping one hand on Ben's back. He held the vapor in his chest, shaking, wishing it were brown sugar. Some of the kids were crying and he shut his eyes, wanting this to be over, fighting back tears of his own.

Once everyone was in and the truck was moving, Mukwiv answered Mason's question. "The one called Kendall was killed."

"Killed? How?"

"It's my fault." Omar opened his eyes and met his brother's. "Shay gave me Jordan's gun. We weren't supposed to take anything more than the stunners, but she was worried and ..." Omar squeezed Ben and rocked back and forth, more comfort for him than for the little boy. "One of the caretakers said Kendall's baby is with Renzor."

"Talk about this later," Zane said in Omar's ear. "Get the SimTags out."

Never a moment to rest. "Zane says we have to get out the SimTags."

"Right." Mason shook the shock from his face and picked up a black backpack. "I'm going to need some help holding the kids."

"I'll help." Glad for something to do, Omar scooted across the back of the truck until he was beside Mason.

"It would be best if you held her." Mason picked up Hazel and handed her to Omar, but the little girl clung to Mason's neck.

"May. Wuv May."

Mason had to pry her hands free. "I'm not looking forward to this. It's pretty rough."

"How many you do tonight?" Omar asked, suddenly realizing he hadn't even asked how things had gone at the boarding school. "Did you get the others out?"

"We did." Mason pulled a backpack onto his lap and removed a bottle of rubbing alcohol. "Thirty-four. The kids brought friends, and we only lost one, a Safe Lander. He got stunned, not killed." Mason swabbed Hazel's hand with the alcohol. "Hazel, I have to make an owie on your hand, okay? Omar is going to give you hugs."

Easier said than done.

Mason used his scalpel to slice the side of Hazel's hand. She shrieked, a high-pitched sound louder than any siren. And her tears were contagious. Carrie and one of the Jack's Peak kids started to cry too.

The next fifteen minutes were horrible. Babies screaming, tongues curled, faces red, blood and more blood. But Mason worked quickly and kept calm and soon had a collection of seven SimTags in a little plastic container.

"Knock on the wall, will you?" Mason asked Mukwiv, who was closest to the inner cab wall.

He did and the truck slowed to a stop.

"I'm just going to toss this," Mason said, "then we'll be good to go."

Mason slipped outside and returned in seconds. He closed the door, motioned to Mukwiv to pound on the wall again, and the truck sped away.

"What did you do with it?" Omar asked.

"Threw it in a dumpster."

Omar did his best to hold Carrie and Ben on his lap as Dayle drove toward the storm drain. The kids were still whimpering. At least they didn't have much farther to travel. It was dark enough in the back that Omar let himself cry for Kendall.

Once Dayle stopped, Mason helped Omar get the kids back in the harnesses. Then they carefully descended into a storm drain that would take them to the Midlands.

They had to go very slowly so they wouldn't slip and hurt the kids, whose cries were so loud Omar was certain they'd be caught any minute. He almost didn't care. What was the point, really? Death would win in the end. It would take them all.

Zane had left a truck for them in the Midlands, and once everyone was loaded up, Omar drove it to the cabin. He came upon the building slowly, making sure there were no other vehicles out front. The place looked deserted. He checked his SimTag detector just to be sure, then turned the truck around and backed up to the porch. Then he shut off the truck and got out to open the back doors. By the time he reached them, Mason was already out and knocking on the front door of the cabin, Hazel and Ben in his arms.

Aunt Chipeta opened the door. "They're here! Oh, Hazel, my sweet baby!" She took her child and started bawling.

Mary pushed out onto the porch, her girth filling the doorway. "Any word from Levi?" Mary's kids were older, and she was the only mother here without a child to hold.

"When we were in the tunnels, Zane told me they were back," Omar said. "Hailey and Meghan are fine."

Mary hugged Aunt Chipeta and squealed. Eliza came running next and claimed Ben. Mukwiv and Tupi carried the Jack's Peak children into the cabin, and Mason went back to the truck to pick up Carrie, whose mother had been liberated with the other women over forty a few months ago. He handed her to Mary. Omar shut the truck doors.

"Mason." Aunt Chipeta waved him inside while still holding Hazel. "Come and check on Naomi. She had her baby. It's a boy!"

Another baby. Mason hurried inside, and the women followed, leaving Omar alone outside. He could hear the tearful reunion from where he stood outside by the truck. He imagined the mothers embracing their children, crying but happy. Such a scene would make a nice painting. He should go and watch. After all, he had helped bring about this great reunion. See? Not everything he did turned into a disaster.

But Kendall was dead. So he stayed outside, vaping and wishing he hadn't taken Jordan's gun. He should go inside, find Shay, apologize. And he needed to tell Mason what Kendall had said about the medic woman, but he was tired of doing hard things. For now, he just wanted to stand here in peace and grieve and —

The door flung open and Jemma ran out. "Omar!" She ran down the porch steps. At first he thought she must be glad to see him, but then he noticed her bloodshot eyes. "Rewl took Shaylinn."

Icy fear dripped through Omar. "Took her where?" How did he even know about the cabin? And what did that mean for the rest of them? Were they safe here?

"He stunned Eliza, then threatened to shoot Aunt Mary and Chipeta if Shaylinn didn't go with him."

This was very bad. What did Rewl want with Shay? Or had he done this for Bender? "Did he say where they were going?"

"No. He made her get into the trunk of his car. It was a big black car."

The ice in Omar's chest melted into heat. "When was this?"

"About an hour ago."

Omar needed help and fast. "SimTalk: Zane."

"Hay-o, peer," Zane said. "Make it to the cabin yet?"

Omar relayed what Jemma had said about Rewl kidnapping Shay. "Can you track his car?"

"Give me a minute," Zane said, then he mumbled to someone. "First let me do this for —" A sigh. "Fine. Omar, Levi wants you to drive the women and kids to my place. He's very ... concerned about everyone's safety in the cabin. Now let me check on the car. I'll tap you back." And the implant went silent.

Move everyone right now? Omar took a deep breath and glanced at Jemma, who had tears in her eyes. "Zane's trying to track Rewl's car."

Jemma blurred before him, and Omar realized tears had filled his eyes as well. Would the madness never end?

Jemma's lips pursed into a scowl, and she slapped the side of his head.

"Ow! What was that for?" Did mothers teach that to their daughters? Because that was exactly how his mother always struck him, right down to the stinging ear.

"For kissing Kendall. What's the matter with you?"

Oh. "I ..." What was the point of trying to explain? "Kendall's dead."

Jemma's anger melded into shock. "What do you ... why would you say that?"

"Because it's true. Because she got shot with Jordan's gun that Shaylinn took from under his bed to give me so I'd be safe in case enforcers showed up with real guns." He screamed into his hands then. "It's my fault. So stupid."

Tears rolled down Jemma's cheeks. "I didn't even realize she hadn't come back with you. Where's her baby?"

"He wasn't there. I have to find him, though. I promised."

The door opened and Aunt Chipeta stood there wearing Hazel on her back. She must have taken one of the harnesses from Mukwiv or Tupi. "Omar, Jem, would you like something to eat? I'm warming up a casserole."

And so they went inside, silent, both of them dazed. Omar nearly stepped on Carrie, who was toddling around the kitchen with her thumb in her mouth. Eliza and Mary and several of the babies were missing, likely in one of the rooms. No sign of Mason either, so he must still be talking with Naomi. The Jack's Peak men were sitting in the living room, Mukwiv on Jordan's chair, Tupi on the couch, still holding his son. Omar sat beside him. This was where he and Shay had talked together. Where Shay had kissed his cheek when he'd given her the painting.

Where Kendall had kissed him.

Mason walked into the kitchen then, and Jemma greeted him.

Omar should tell him about the medic and Renzor, but his SimTalk implant spoke first. "You. Have a. SimTalk tap. From … Zane."

"Answer."

"Omar," Zane said. "I found Rewl's car. But, peer, he's parked at Renzor's place. Champion House."

Why had he taken her there? Omar cursed. How could they possibly—

"Omar, language!" Aunt Chipeta crouched to cover Carrie's ears. They were all staring at him: Mason, Jemma, Mukwiv, Tupi…

"Rewl took Shay to Champion House," Omar said.

"What's that?" Jemma asked.

"Then let's go," Mason said, hands on his hips like this was nothing more difficult than sweeping the carpet. "He's got Kendall's baby, and Ciddah's there too."

"Wait. What's that mean?" Jemma asked.

Ciddah the medic. His brother might not be so eager to rescue the woman if he knew she didn't want to be rescued. "It's not that easy, Mase. Zane said that place is a fortress."

"There must be a way," Mason said.

"Yeah, you're going to have to give me some time on that," Zane said in Omar's ear. "You'd have to be invisible to break into there."

Omar thought on that word: *invisible*. "I could create a SimArt design," he said. "I'd have to get body implants for it to work, but I could make my skin all black or something. Sneak inside. Hide in the shadows?"

"Walls, that's clever, peer," Zane said. "I don't think we have time for you to get that made. But let me check a few things. I'll also see if I can pick up any enforcer chatter for that location. Maybe I can find out if something is going on there."

"Get back to me as soon as you can." And the connection died. Omar let his head fall back against the couch.

Jemma walked over to where he sat and looked down on him. "What is Champion House? Where's my sister?"

"It's where Lawten Renzor lives," Omar said. "It has very high security."

This set off Jemma's tears again, and she walked over and hugged Mason.

"Could we not save this rescue until after we free our women from the harem?" Mukwiv said. "That would give you all more time to make a plan."

"The harem women are safe for now," Mason said. "We don't know what Rewl wants with Shaylinn or what Renzor wants with Ciddah or Kendall's baby."

"Why would he have Kendall's baby there?" Jemma asked, then turned to Omar. "And why would he take Shaylinn?"

"I don't know." Omar didn't know anything. He just wanted to make sure Shay was okay. Then he wanted to visit Skottie and vape the sweet stuff. But there was no point holding back what he did know. "Okay, listen. Levi wants you guys to get in the truck and drive to Zane's. He doesn't like that Rewl, and therefore Bender, knows where we are. So you may as well pack up and go while it's still dark."

Aunt Chipeta stepped into the archway and handed Mason a bowl of something steamy. "Move tonight?"

"Do you want to lose Hazel again? Yes, move tonight." Omar felt like a jerk, but there was no point trying to be nice if everyone wanted to argue. "Mason, before she died, Kendall said Ciddah and Renzor were lifers. I'm sorry. I'd still like your help going after Shaylinn, but if you'd rather drive the truck to Zane's, that would be fine."

Mason eyes widened and he frowned slightly. "I – I don't ..."

"But Naomi just gave birth," Aunt Chipeta said.

"She'll be okay as long as she doesn't have to walk," Jemma said. "Did you tell Levi about the baby, Omar? Now that they're back, Jordan should know."

"Would anyone else like something to eat?" Aunt Chipeta asked. "Omar? You other men? Forgive me, I don't know your names."

"Sorry," Omar said. "This is Mukwiv and Tupi from Jack's Peak."

"Nice to meet you," Aunt Chipeta said. "Would you like something to eat?"

"Yes, thank you," Mukwiv said. Tupi nodded.

"Omar?" Aunt Chipeta said.

"No, thanks." Omar didn't think he could keep anything down.

Aunt Chipeta passed out bowls of noodles and beef. Jemma told them about Naomi's labor and more about Shaylinn's kidnapping, then she asked Mason to tell which kids he saw at the boarding school.

The question seemed to surprise Mason, like he hadn't been listening. Omar felt bad for upsetting him with what Kendall had said.

"Um ... I saw all the boys. And quite a few mentioned the Owl," Mason said with a glance at Omar. "You're a legend with the kids, brother."

"Really?" The fact that the kids liked the Owl made him smile despite his pain.

"You. Have a. SimTalk tap. From ... Zane."

Omar stood and walked out of the room toward the front door so he could hear Zane better. "Answer."

"Okay, peer. We've got the makings of a plan here. Why don't you put me on speaker, if you still have your Wyndo watch, that is."

"Oh, yeah, hold on." Omar walked back into the living room and tapped "speaker" on the watch. "Listen up, everyone. Zane wants to talk." When the room quieted, Omar said, "You're on speaker, Zane."

"First, I'm supposed to say that everyone not going after Shaylinn needs to pack up and move down here. Also, Levi says Jemma is not to go after Shaylinn."

Jemma scoffed and folded her arms. "Tell Levi that I said —"

"That Naomi had the baby," Omar said, hoping to prevent a fight. "It's a boy, and they're both fine." Right? He looked to Jemma, who nodded, though she was still scowling.

"I'll do that," Zane said. "Now, here's what I learned. There's a big enforcer bust scheduled for six this morning at Champion House. Several teams have already been deployed. They're armed with dual-action pistols."

Omar looked at Mason. They both knew what that meant: guns that could both stun and kill.

"You think they're going to bust Lawten for something?" Omar asked. "Can they do that? Isn't that like the sheriff arresting the president?"

"The enforcer general runs the enforcers but also heads investigations to protect the Safe Lands. If he found the right dirt on Renzor, he could arrest him," Zane said. "It's pretty intriguing. As I see it, you have two options: Go in now, or wait until it's over and see where they take Shaylinn, then plan to get her from there. My guess is they'll take her back to the harem, and that's our next target anyway."

"Yes," Mukwiv said. "Do not risk exposure and capture when we could take more time and make a safe rescue of all the women."

"But they're going in with real guns," Mason said. "Anyone can get killed in the cross fire. I saw it happen in Glenrock. And I don't trust Otley not to shoot Shaylinn just to make us mad."

"Otley's a psychotic maggot," Omar said. "I'm not leaving her there, knowing he's involved."

"I agree," Jemma said.

"Do you have any way of helping us, Zane?" Omar asked.

"I had nothing until you suggested the SimArt and my dad reminded me of TRO."

"What's that?" Omar asked.

"Hold on," Zane said. "Ruston is tapping in."

"Omar, you hear me?" Ruston asked.

"Yeah, we hear you. Go ahead."

"The Technology Research Organization was originally called Technology Research Teams. It was founded just after the Great Pandemic. Its job was to go out into the world and rescue technology. If the Safe Lands were to keep moving forward, they needed to learn how to create things. Teams were sent out on assignment to bring back the knowledge of creating everything from industrial machines to pharmaceuticals."

"That's how the Safe Lands were able to keep so much technology from the Old world?" Mason asked.

"Yes. And to keep creating new technologies. Over time, there was no more need to rescue Old technology, and the Safe Lands changed TRT to TRO. Now they work on new inventions."

"And this will help us rescue Shay?" Omar asked.

"I know a guy," Ruston said.

Omar smiled at Mason. Zane and his father were a lot alike.

"He owes me," Ruston went on, "and a while back he showed me what he was working on. You've seen WyndoFlex screen, yeah?"

"Like my watch?" Omar said.

"Exactly. Well, my contact, he's got a couple full suits of it."

"Why would anyone want their body to look like a TV?" Jemma asked.

"That's not the goal," Ruston said. "If you have a screen on fabric, it can reflect whatever you want it to reflect."

"It can reflect its surroundings," Mason said, eyes wide.

"Exactly," Ruston said. "These suits use cameras to record what's behind them and project that onto their fronts."

"You think he'll let us borrow them?" Omar asked.

"No. But like I said, he owes me a favor. How many in your rescue team?"

Omar took a deep breath and met Mason's gaze.

"Two," Mason said.

"Two. Fine. Nash will pick you up in twenty minutes."

"We'll be ready." Omar disconnected from Zane, eager to do something more than sit around feeling useless and guilty and sad. "Finish eating, brother. We're going to visit Champion House."

CHAPTER
30

I need to be there," Jordan said. "Hogs teeth, I should have been there already!"

Levi and Jordan were in the nest with Ruston and Zane. "Just wait, Jordan. Until I figure out what I'm doing. Please." Levi looked back to Ruston, who'd forbidden anyone to leave until the enforcer chatter on the boarding school escape had died down. "I'm elder of Glenrock. I'm their brother. And I know more about this sort of thing than they do. I should be going with them."

Ruston stood and stepped into the tunnel. "Come with me."

Levi sighed and followed the man out into Zane's basement.

Ruston gestured at the ratty old couch. "Have a seat."

Levi didn't like feeling as though he was about to be manipulated. He sat down.

"A good leader has sense enough to pick good men to do what needs done and enough self-restraint not to meddle," Ruston said. "Trust your men."

"And if Mason and Omar were skilled at breaking into fortresses — if I'd assigned them to such a chore — I might trust them with it. But Mason's a doctor, and Omar is ... Omar."

"Omar has shown himself to be clever and persistent. With Zane's eyes and my connections, I don't see why they can't succeed."

Maybe. "At least let me and Jordan go help move the women and babies over here."

"Again, there are two men to help, and the women are also quite capable. There is no reason for you to leave."

Levi rubbed his eyes. He didn't like how Ruston was treating him like a prisoner, even if he made sense. "I can't just sit here and wait."

"Then don't. You and I need to make plans on how to divide the children. I can't do this without you. Only you know your people."

"I gave you Jemma's list." What else did the man want?

"A list of children's names. I need to know the families so I can place them together. Haven't they been separated long enough?"

"More than," Levi said.

"Make a new list while I'm gone."

Levi stood up. "Wait, where are *you* going?"

"I can't get your brothers the help they need without going out. I'll be back long before they start their mission. Then I'll want to see your list."

"Take Jordan, then. Drop him at the cabin when you pick up Mason and Omar. He's going to drive us all crazy if you don't."

"Agreed. I will have him go with Nash."

"And what will I do while my brothers risk their lives?"

"You could sleep. It *is* the middle of the night. Or you can sit with Zane and watch your brothers. We'll be able to see most everything on the cameras."

That was some consolation. "Then that's where I want to be."

Ruston nodded once, as if Levi had passed some sort of test. "When I return, we'll figure out where to place the families. And after that, I want to talk to you about something ... special."

Levi narrowed his eyes. "Are you going to start asking favors of me like Bender did?" Because Levi didn't think he could take much more of that. He was elder of Glenrock. That might be only two dozen people, but they were his responsibility. No one else's. And he didn't want them made into slaves, himself included.

"No, nothing like that," Ruston said. "See, I have a theory, though my son thinks I'm dimmer than a dead Wyndo screen. But I think that you and I are kin."

CHAPTER
31

Ciddah couldn't possibly be Lawten Renzor's lifer. Mason told himself this for what must have been the one hundredth time since Omar had passed on Kendall's message. The mere idea made him sick. Kendall had had the tendency to exaggerate. She must have misunderstood. She must have.

Aunt Chipeta and Jemma were well into directing the packing up of the cabin when Nash arrived with Jordan, then drove Omar and Mason to the TRO, which was a warehouse ten blocks away that said "Safe Lands Industries" on a sign out front. It was still dark out. According to the display on the windshield, it was 4:07 a.m.

"What's Safe Lands Industries?" Mason asked Nash as they made their way to the building's entrance.

"Nothing," Nash said. "The TRO has always kept a secret location for their research facility. Trying to keep the technology away from thieves and rebels and Luella Flynn."

Omar snorted a derisive laugh. "I understand the need. That woman's persistent."

His little brother was still wearing one of the baby harnesses. It looked funny on him, but Omar had left it on, saying he might need it if they found Kendall's baby. Mason had wrapped a scalpel, three alcohol swabs, and three bandages in a strip of denim and shoved them into his pocket. If they were going to rescue Ciddah and the baby, he'd need to remove their SimTags. And he didn't want to risk not having supplies in case Shaylinn had been re-tagged.

Nash opened the door at the front corner of the warehouse, and they stepped inside a small reception area. Two hallways stretched out on each exterior wall, white walls and thin gray carpeting. The place was dark and appeared to be deserted. Nash paused, looking both ways as if he wasn't certain where to go.

"Ever been here before?" Mason asked.

"Nope. SimTalk: tap: Zane." Nash peeked down the hallway on the left. "Hay-o, bro. We're at the TRO. Where am I going?... Gotcha, thanks. SimTalk: end tap." He walked down the right hallway. "We go this way."

They followed Nash down the hall until they came to an open area. A two-story wall ran perpendicular, enclosing the office portion of the building on the front end of the warehouse. The rest of the warehouse spread out before them. Only a quarter of the ceiling lights were lit up. On the right perimeter wall, shelves stuck out like the teeth of a comb, holding small objects Mason couldn't identify. The rest of the space held strange vehicles and machinery, each in its own squared-off section of floor.

"I'd love to walk around here sometime," Mason said.

"Dream it," Nash said. "If they find out we were here, they'll probably move the place."

Nash led them along the office wall toward a long gash of light that spilled across the dark cement floor. An open doorway. As they approached, Mason heard voices.

"B – But ... but why the suits?" a man asked. "Anything else, I ... I wouldn't flinch to let you b – borrow."

"We need to be invisible." Ruston's voice. "This is the fastest way."

"Do you have a ... a slower way of b – being invisible?"

"Maybe," Ruston said. "I'll tell you that when we return the suits."

They reached the doorway and entered a laboratory. Not a medical one, though. This one was filled with GlassTop computers and Wyndo screens, tables covered in stacks of fabric, and racks of white jumpsuits. Ruston stood beside a man sitting at a GlassTop computer console that had six screens.

The man turned his attention to where they walked through the doorway. He was in his mid-thirties, with flaking white skin, a cropped brown beard, and a thatch of messy hair. His eyes were wild, like a cornered animal.

"This is Mason and Omar, and you know Nash. Boys, this is Lhogan Rayscott," Ruston said. "He's a TRO engineer."

"I'm not comfortable with … with this, Ruston," Lhogan said. "If anything hap – happens to these suits, you'll see me p – premie lib – libbed."

Mason and Omar stopped just inside the door, but Nash walked over to the computer where Ruston stood. "We could set it up as a break-in," Nash suggested.

"No one is sup – posed to know where TRO research takes p – place," Lhogan said. "If it b – became known that the facility had b – been compromised, they'd likely liberate us and train new … new researchers."

Mason saw no logic in such fears. "Surely they wouldn't kill the people who know the technology."

"No one is above lib – liberation in the Safe Lands. Do you know … know what TRO founders went through to rescue technology from the Old world? P – People of Old were selfish, hiding technology from each other to make a p – profit. They didn't share. And they didn't take p – precautions. And when the world ended and no one was left who knew how to do anything, it wasn't easy to figure it out. And TRO made sure it won't hap – happen again. If the Guild needs to get rid of us, they b – bring in new p – people. The tutorials train them."

The idea of tutorials intrigued Mason, as did the man's stutter. "Are these tutorials only for the TRO or for other tasks as well, like medical procedures?"

"There are tutorials for every … everything. B – But they're only shown to p – people in task training. Ruston, the suits are going to be too b – big."

Ruston walked over to one of the racks and fingered a white sleeve. "Better too big than too small."

"I sup – suppose." Lhogan got up and produced a plastic bin from a shelf on the corner, from which he removed three tiny plastic boxes. "B – Before you ask, Mr. Mason, without getting overly tech – technical, these are simp – ply contact lenses that have MicroTag resisters emb – bedded into the p – polymer. P – Put them into your eyes, and once I activate the SimSuits, you'll b – be able to … to see one another."

The idea of trying contact lenses thrilled Mason. "Are they sanitary?"

"I always clean them b – before put – putting them away," Lhogan said. "B – But you should all wash your hands at the sink." He gestured to an industrial sink in the corner.

"What about my SimSight lenses?" Omar asked.

"Take them out," Lhogan said. "You can't wear b – both."

"Do you have something I can put them in? They were really expensive and I don't have any more credits."

Seriously? Was Omar really worried about something so trivial at a time like this?

"I sup – suppose I can find something." Lhogan went back to the shelf.

Mason washed his hands and returned to Lhogan's desk. "How do you get them in?"

"Ah, yes. Well, p – put one on the tip of your finger, cup … cup side up. Make sure there's no dust. If there is, I've got some solution here somewhere." He wandered over to the shelf again. "Ah, here we are." He carried a little white bottle back to his desk. "Use your other hand to p – pull your skin away from your eye and p – put in the contact. Go … go slowly. And try not to b – blink or move your head. Oh, and b – before you let go of the contact, make sure to center it on your … your eye. Move it around if necessary."

"It's easy, Mase," Omar said, removing one of his SimSight lenses to the tip of his finger.

"When you think ... think it's in and you let go of your eye, b–blink slowly. It might hurt as you b–blink out any air bub–bubbles."

"It doesn't hurt," Omar said. "But I don't see anything yet."

Omar had them in already? Mason was still holding his first on his finger.

"That's b–because I haven't turned you on," Lhogan said. "And you're not wearing the ... the suits."

Mason managed to get in both his contacts. They made his eyes feel wet, as if he were going to cry. He blinked, and a tear rolled down his cheek.

"Now the suits." Lhogan walked to the rack of suits and looked through them. He lifted one off the rack. "This is the smaller of the two pro–prototypes." He handed it to Omar, then gave Mason a second suit. "Not to offend you, b–but these suits were designed to ... to fit some of our undercover enforcers."

Mason wasn't offended. "Strength alone does not make a man."

Lhogan flashed Mason a rare smile. "I like that. Very ... very good."

The suit weighed as much as chest waders and were just as stiff, though the fabric was thinner and bright white on the outside. The inside was black.

"P–Put them on over your clothes. You'll need the extra p–padding."

Mason moved his surgical kit from his pocket to a front pocket on the suit and made sure it didn't show, then slipped off his shoes and stepped into the suit. But then he realized the suit had built-in feet with rubber tread on the bottoms. "Wait, should I have kept my shoes on?" Mason asked.

"Yes, sorry. And there are snaps inside the ... the feet to fasten over your shoes and keep them tight."

Mason stepped out of the suit and carried it and his shoes to the nearest chair. He sat down and put his shoes back on, then put his feet into the legs. He found the snaps, which were attached to a lining pouch that covered his shoes. He fastened them, then pulled the legs up and threaded his arms through the sleeves and into the gloves. The suit zipped up from waist to chin and sagged around his middle, clearly designed for someone built like Jordan. At least Mason was a few inches taller than Omar.

"How do these work, anyway?" Mason asked.

"It's SimTech illusion technology ap – plied to a different surface," Lhogan said.

Fine, but that didn't explain anything. "But what's SimTech illusion technology?"

"It's the technology of creating illusions on different surfaces. In a p – person's b – body, that's done b – by imp – planting a SimTag for ID numbers and SimArt. For Wyndos that's done with ... with MicroTags."

"So the suit is filled with MicroTags?" Mason asked.

"Sort of. Think p – polymer light-emitting diodes. We emb – bed them into 140 Denier p – polyurethane p – polyester, ap – apply a film of p – poly methylmethacrylate, followed by a layer of p – poly muslin. That makes the ... the fabric."

It sounded fascinating, but Mason didn't understand most of what Lhogan had said. "There must be a lead tag, right? Like the hand tag that speaks to additional SimTags in the body?" Mason thought of Omar's SimArt tattoos that came and went when he wore his gloves.

"P – Precisely. We cut out the suits from the ... the fa – bric and sew them up. A CamTag is sewn into each suit in the ... the front right shoulder. After that we pro – program the micros to the lead and test them. The MicroTags in the fa – bric simp – ply rep – plicate the ... the feed. Just like the lead SimTag controls the others in the b – body, the CamTag controls the other MicroTags in a suit. They've never b – been used for any real tactical situation b – before. I'm not p – positive they'll work in all environments and ... and temp – peratures."

"Why wouldn't they?" Omar asked.

"I ... I don't know. That's just it: we would never send an enforcer into danger wearing a ... a suit that we haven't fully tested. And we're several months away from completing the testing on … on the SimSuits."

"They're the only chance we've got." Mason appreciated Lhogan's risk when he clearly would rather not let them use the suits. "Thank you for letting us use them."

Lhogan blinked, eyes still wide and paranoid. "Yes, well, let me get you the … the hoods, and I'll make sure you're all showing up on my … my GlassTop."

The hoods were white with no eye holes or openings for the mouth and seemed to be made of the same fabric as the suits. But when Mason put his on, he could see through it and breathe. "How does this work?"

Lhogan's rare smile returned. "You ask that a lot, Mr. Mason. The hoods are made invisible by adhering a … a light-emitting p – polymer skin to the b – back of the fabric."

"This is amazing," Mason said. Omar looked like a human-shaped snowman. "When will it make us invisible?"

"Once I turn you on." Lhogan sat at a GlassTop computer and started working. Mason walked behind him and watched over his shoulder. Lhogan opened a program that brought up an animated version of a man wearing a suit. "This is for suit one, which is the … the small suit." Lhogan's fingers made dull thuds against the GlassTop as he typed. Mason looked to Omar, who was standing by a rack of belts.

Omar disappeared.

Fascinating. "Omar! You've vanished," Mason said.

"Whoa." Nash walked out into the middle of the room. "I can't see you at all!"

Mason strained to see his brother and caught the faint outline of his bulky suited form moving around, like a ripple in the surface of a lake. The cameras didn't quite work perfectly. The line was off a bit, but he really had to be looking to see it. "That's amazing."

"Thank you." On the screen, as Lhogan tapped away, the image of the man in the suit changed to another. "This one is yours," he said.

Mason stepped back and waited for it, his nerves tingling. He held his hand in front of his face and glanced at Lhogan's GlassTop, and when he looked back to his hand, it was gone. A puzzling thrill of panic shot through him. His brain knew his hand was still there, yet part of him still reacted to the fact that it could not be seen.

Mason waved his hand and caught a slight vibration in the air. These were incredible inventions. Who would ever know to look for them? With these, the rebels could do almost anything in the Safe Lands. And if the enforcers began using them...

He tried to locate Omar in the room and found he couldn't. "How will we not run into each other?" Mason asked. "Or see each other if we need to? I thought the contacts —"

"I need to activate the ... the contacts, and then you'll see," Lhogan said, tapping away.

"I see Mason!" Omar shouted. "You're a blue blob."

Mason's lenses suddenly activated as well, illuminating a blue form across the room.

"There is a ... a number on the chest and b – back of each suit. Number one is the small suit, um ... Omar. Mr. Mason is number two."

Mason could barely see the white outline of the number two on his chest. The number one on the back of Omar's suit was much larger.

"What about weapons?" Omar asked. "Won't they see them if we're carrying?"

"The suits have a ... a flap at the waist that covers where a b – belt can be worn. I don't have any weapons for you, though."

"I've got weapons in my truck," Ruston said. "Lhogan, do you have the link for Zane to run these?"

"Ah, no. I'm running them."

"Are you sure you want to be involved?" Ruston asked.

"I have to b – be. What are you using them for, anyway?"

"We need to pay a little visit to the Champion House," Omar said, punching his palm.

Lhogan's eyelids fluttered. "Did I ... I mention if anything happens to ... to these suits ...? Or if you're caught ...?"

"Yeah, you did," Ruston said.

"Just let Zane run them and you won't have to worry," Nash said.

"The – the suits are my responsibility. If I give the … the eyes to Zane, I've got nothing b – but your word that you'll return them. I … I trust you, Ruston. But I … I don't know these b – boys, I don't know where Zane's GlassTop is, and I certainly don't trust whatever crazy ad – adventure you're planning at Champion House. My eyes only. F – Final offer."

Mason walked around the room, playing with the suit. He didn't quite understand what Ruston and Lhogan were talking about, but he felt badly that Lhogan was feeling pressured to help them.

"Can Zane at least watch the feed?" Ruston asked. "If he can't see …"

"Yes, I … I can do that. But if he tries to … to hack me, I'll move the feed and … and he's out."

"He won't hack you," Nash said. "He's a good boy."

"What's his – his message ID?" Lhogan asked.

"Techwiz dot sl," Ruston said.

Lhogan tapped it in. "I … I still don't like this. I'm risking every – everything. The p – price is much higher than what I owe you."

"Then I owe you now," Ruston said. "Can you record the lens feeds?"

"I can."

"Do it. My guess is that these two will see something tonight that will be useful for blackmail. If anyone comes after you, show it to them and promise that the Owl will show it to everyone in the Safe Lands if anything happens to you."

"The Owl?" Lhogan asked. "You think Task Director Renzor is involved in … in something sinister?"

As far as Mason was concerned, Lawten Renzor was always involved in something sinister.

"If not him, someone who wants to frame him," Ruston said. "Either way, we should know soon enough."

Lhogan sighed. "I'll re – record it. B – But if they don't see anything that can b – be used as b – blackmail, I won't have anything to use to pro – protect myself from any accusations."

"If nothing happens, you won't need to protect yourself," Ruston said. "And, like I said, I'll owe you."

"Well, everything is ready," Lhogan said, pushing back from the GlassTop. "Take good care of – of them."

The suits, of course, not Mason and Omar's lives.

"They won't get a scratch," Omar said.

Mason hoped it was true.

CHAPTER
32

Omar was glad to have the loaded gun on his hip, even if it had betrayed him once tonight. He wouldn't have felt safe going up against Otley and those dual-action pistols with only a stunner. He needed the same heat Otley would be packing, that overgrown boar.

Nash drove the DPT truck down a winding road filled with massive homes, headed for Champion House. The three of them sat side by side in the cab — a tight squeeze, with Omar in the middle.

The suits gave them an advantage. Tonight he was the Invisible Owl, embarking on his most daring mission yet. The suits were hot, though, and Omar was glad he'd removed the hood for the drive, but every time he looked down and his body came into view, glowing blue, he jumped. He completely forgot the contacts in his eyes three times in the space of five minutes. He needed sleep — and Skottie's PV, which he couldn't get to with the suit on.

He burned at the idea of Shaylinn in a car trunk; sweet Shaylinn who never said a mean word to anyone, who prayed for people and wrote kind messages, who'd been forced to produce *two* babies, who loved him in spite of the wretched person he was...

Who'd seen him kiss Kendall.

He was sick. Sick with it all. The Owl was supposed to make a difference. But he needed more time to plot Operation Lynchpin. And this ... complication with Shaylinn and now Kendall's death ... None of it was helping him keep his focus.

Why was he so stupid? He could have stopped Kendall's kiss. Stood up. Moved away. Then Shaylinn wouldn't have gotten upset, and Omar would have had more time to think about the gun. Might have decided to leave it behind. Then Kendall would be —

"SimTalk: tap: Zane." Nash pulled into a driveway in front of a massive green house and killed the headlights. "Yeah, what's going on just above, uh ..." He squinted to see the house number above the door ... "Fifty-three Summit Road?"

Omar glanced out Nash's driver's side window. In the distance, where the road curved around a bend and up the hill, a dozen taillights glowed.

Shay was up there. He wanted her out, and he wanted Rewl and Otley and Renzor to pay. Maybe it would all end tonight with three bullets from Omar's gun. Bang, bang, bang. And they lived happily ever after.

The crack of the gun flashed in his memory. Kendall falling. Nothing happy about that.

"Let me put you on speaker," Nash said, tapping his Wyndo watch, which looked identical to Omar's. The time was 5:06 a.m. "Go ahead, Zane."

"Enforcer troops have been deployed to Champion House." Zane's voice came out tinny through the watch speaker. "You've got a collection of eight enforcer vehicles up there. Chatter tells me they're not going in until six."

"Why wait?" Omar asked.

"No idea," Zane said. "The way I see it, you can either wait until they move in, then follow. Or you can sneak past them now."

"Can we do that?" Mason asked.

"With those suits you should be able to walk right up the middle of the road, but if there are enforcers on foot, I wouldn't risk it. Walk in the ditch or something. And you might avoid walking in front of headlights. Might make shadows. The real problem is the gate. It's shut. And it has to open for you guys to get through."

"You can't hack it?" Omar asked.

"Nooo. Their security is too good. I can get in and watch, but if I so much as turn a camera a millimeter, they'll see me and lock everything down. You're going to have to walk up there and wait for it to open, then walk in along with the vehicles. There's no other way."

"Can't we climb over?" Omar asked. "Are the fences electrified?"

"Not that I know of," Zane said, "but they're ten feet high and topped with some nasty barbed wire. I don't think you have time for that. And if you mess up those suits, my dad will kill us all."

Not to mention they'd be visible again.

"Is there a back gate?" Mason asked. "One that's easier to get through?"

"It's identical," Zane said, "and you'd have to hike around the perimeter or drive back out Summit and go all the way around to Forest Lane to get to it."

"That's too far," Nash said.

"No storm drains here?" Omar asked.

"They're closed off. Have been for years. And none of us have ever had a premie lib wish to risk exploring them. Stop arguing with me. I've checked this. Trust me. Walking in with the cars is your only option. And there will be guards at the guardhouse, so keep an eye out for them too."

"We've got the advantage of being invisible," Mason said. "That greatly decreases our odds of encountering danger."

Yes, and Zane would be looking through the cameras. And didn't that engineer say Zane would be able to see through the contacts too? "Can you see what we see, Zane?" Omar asked.

"Only one at a time. I'm looking through your eyes right now, peer," Zane said. "Your eyelids keep drooping. Need a nap?"

Desperately. And another breath of brown sugar wouldn't hurt. "I'm fine."

Zane chuckled. "I've got no control over what I see, though. Lhogan's running the vids. If I need to switch to Mason's eyes, all I can do is message Lhogan and ask nicely."

"What about Rewl's car?" Omar asked. "Where is it?"

"Let me look." Omar could barely hear the tap of fingers on glass. "His is the first car outside the gate. Go ahead and get closer. You might be able to see if he still has Shaylinn."

Omar sure hoped so. "All right. We're going."

Omar and Mason got out and said good-bye to Nash, who promised to wait with the truck. They walked down the center of the street, headed for the hill. Their suits swished like snow pants. The rubber soles under his feet scuffed on the concrete.

"Think we should get off the road?" Mason asked.

"Not 'til the corner," Omar said. "The houses and sidewalk should end there, then we can walk in the ditch."

They came to the last driveway before the corner, about a stone's throw from the nearest enforcer car. Omar had been such a fool to believe that being an enforcer would make him happy. To think he'd given up a peaceful life in Glenrock with Shay to lick Otley's and Renzor's boots.

And now he'd lost everything.

He wished he could get at his PV right now. He could really use a vape.

He caught himself being negative again and shook it off. What would the Owl do? Something good, not mope about everything. He was going to rescue Shay and get her to Ruston's basements. She was going to have a peaceful life, even if he couldn't.

Omar led Mason down into the ditch, trying to walk carefully in the fake green grass. He couldn't hear as well with the hood on. He kept his gaze bouncing from his feet to the road, inspecting the parked cars they walked past. So far, the enforcers were just sitting inside the vehicles, two to a car, from what he could see, talking with each other as if this was merely another routine bust.

They had to be wondering, didn't they? What kind of bust goes down at Champion House? Whatever Otley had planned, it was going to be big news. He was surprised Luella Flynn wasn't here with her cameraman.

Four cars in, Omar could clearly see the front gate and the guardhouse behind it, the windows lit up in bright yellow light. And Rewl's black sedan was parked right up against the gate with its driver's door rolled up, open to the night air. He walked through the ditch until he stood across from the door. No one was inside. He stared at the trunk, tempted to walk over and look inside. "No Rewl in the car," Omar whispered to Mason.

"He's in the one behind," Mason said.

Sure enough, when Omar looked through the windshield of the second car in the line of vehicles, he saw Bender in the driver's seat and Rewl sitting beside him.

"It's so weird to see them like this. When I first met them, I thought they were heroes," Omar said. "Yet here they are with Otley. Maggots, anyway."

"Do you think Shay's still in the trunk?" Mason asked.

The lights on Bender's car were off. "I'm going to find out."

"They'll hear you," Mason hissed.

But Omar was already halfway up the shoulder of the road. His boots backslid a few steps on the incline, but he moved faster and reached the top.

At the edge of the road, he stayed put a moment, making sure no one had heard him. When nothing happened, he started across the road. Bender's headlights were off, so he walked between the two cars. There was about ten feet between them. He stared through the windshield of Bender's car to where Bender and Rewl were talking, laughing, like this was all part of some game. But their windows had to be closed, because Omar couldn't hear their voices at all. Good.

He squatted by the trunk, made a fist, and knocked on the back. The gloves muted the sound. "Shay?" He kept his eyes on Bender and Rewl and tried to measure his voice. Loud enough for her to hear, but soft enough so that no one else could. They hadn't seemed to hear him, so he tried again. "If you're in there, answer quietly. It's me, Omar."

"Omar! Help me!" Shay's voice bordered on hysteria. "Get me out of here."

Bender and Rewl's heads both twitched in the direction of Rewl's trunk. Omar held his breath until he saw them relax and start talking again. "Quietly, Shay. Calm down. Listen, I can't get you out just yet. People are watching."

"Please, Omar. Please get me out." She had quieted her voice, at least, but her tone sounded petrified.

He was no good at saying the right thing. What would she have said to him? He struggled to remember one of the hundreds of Bible verses his mother had made him learn as a child. "The Lord's your shepherd, Shay. Don't be afraid. What can these maggots do to you?" Close enough. He wished he could just jump in the front of this car and drive it away, which he couldn't do without taking off the suit to reach the ghoulie tag. Plus there were two dozen enforcer vehicles blocking him in. But at least he'd found her. When she didn't answer, he asked, "Shay, did Rewl say anything about what his plans are?"

"He said Lawten Renzor did bad things and that Bender was going to make everything right."

Cryptic. "Did he say why he needed you? What he planned to do with you?"

"No. Well, he did say that he was going to keep me safe until I had the babies, then we could, um, 'talk about painting.'"

Painting? Omar pictured his easel and the picture of Shay Otley had ruined. Rewl didn't paint. Not that Omar knew what Rewl did in his spare — "Wait. Shay, you mean trade paint? Does Rewl like you?"

"He wanted to take me dancing once. And he said Bender is his father. And he told me that he wasn't infected. That he's a Natural."

Both had grown up in the basements, yet both had turned their back on that life. Rewl might be a Natural, but the only reason he wasn't infected was because he was a creepy shell who probably scared the femmes away. No, that was unfair. He didn't really know Rewl at all, except that the maggot had put Shay in a trunk. And for that, he would pay.

"Shay, listen. I have to go."

"No! Don't leave me."

"I won't be far away. But I can't get into the trunk, so I have to wait until they take you out, okay? I'll be close by."

"Please don't go." Her voice was laced with tears again. "Omar? Omar, are you there?"

The electric hum of a vehicle door opening split the silence. "I'll grab it." Rewl's voice. Outside the car.

Still crouched on his toes, Omar spun around. Rewl was on top of him, headed back to his car, going to cross between the two vehicles from the passenger's side of Bender's car to the driver's side of his. Omar shrank as close to the bumper as possible, but Rewl slammed into him and tripped.

Omar didn't wait to see what happened. He scrambled around the back of the car and up the passenger's side.

Another door slid open. "What happened?" Bender's voice.

"I tripped over something. Someone was there."

"Where? You saw someone?"

"No, but I—"

"Then get in the car," Bender said. "Otley's coming."

Otley. Rewl's headlights were off too, so Omar crossed in front of the car and looked down the road. Headlights were approaching on the wrong side of the road, headed his way. Omar crouched in front of Rewl's car, waiting.

An enforcer's Jeep stopped beside Rewl, who was still standing at the back of his car. The passenger window on the Jeep slid up onto the roof. "What are you doing out of your vehicle, little rat?" Otley said.

"Talking to Bender."

"Get in and follow me." Otley's Jeep sped by Omar's hiding place and pulled up to the front gate.

Omar ran after it, then to the left side of the road to stay out of the way of Rewl's car. He turned back and located the blue figure that was

Mason in the ditch beside the guardhouse and waved his brother to follow.

When Mason caught up, he asked, "What's our plan?"

"We follow them in. Shay's still in Rewl's trunk, so I'm going to stay with his car and try to get her out. You stick with Otley and look for your medic and Kendall's baby. If we don't see each other inside, once you get the medic and the kid, get out of the house. We'll meet behind the guardhouse, inside the fence. We'll probably have to wait for the gate to open before we can get out, but I guess we can figure that out later."

"Sounds good," Mason said.

Mad good. They passed through the gate just as Otley spoke to the guards at the guardhouse.

"Safe Lands Enforcers. We have a warrant to search these premises."

CHAPTER
33

The iron gate rattled as it slid open on wheels. Mason walked behind Omar, who was shadowing Rewl's car. He didn't know what to think of his little brother becoming a father, but Omar had certainly grown protective of Shaylinn. Mason was glad of it. Maybe it would give him some focus in life.

The mansion was made of gray stone and was so massive that its roof looked like three mountain peaks. Bright yellow light shone out narrow windows. A grassy lawn — real grass — surrounded the building. The drive split ahead. To the left it went straight around the back of the house. To the right it circled the yard and ran back to the front gate. A fountain and a rose garden decorated the center of the circle. The smell of roses made the early morning air sweet. The sky was growing pink. Almost dawn.

General Otley drove to the right. Rewl continued on toward the back of the house. Mason waved to Omar and ran to keep up with Otley.

The man stopped his Jeep in front of the house and got out. Mason looked back and saw that the other vehicles had followed Otley. Bender got out of the second vehicle in line, while enforcers climbed out of the others. They all wore gun belts laden with weapons. From what Mason could figure, they each had a SimScanner, a stunner, a dual-action pistol, and some kind of stick.

Four men in black suits met Otley at the bottom of the steps.

"I'll see that warrant now," one of the men said.

Otley pulled a piece of paper out of his inner jacket pocket and handed it over. "Signed by the Guild. It's good."

The man glanced over the paper and sighed. "There is no pregnant girl here. But search if you must." He led the way up the wide steps and rang the bell. Otley followed, Bender at his side. Mason stayed with them, keeping on the far edge of the steps so as not to touch anyone. The enforcers followed.

The front door opened, revealing a young man dressed in a black suit. "Yes?"

"General Otley has a warrant, Mr. Berg. His men will be conducting a search. And my men will be accompanying them."

"Of course. Well, come right in, General Otley. I'm the butler. The task director general was not yet awake at this early hour as he *is* on vacation. But he'll be with us shortly. He's asked me to see you to the small parlor."

Otley grunted. "Bender, Nicol, Leech, Robb — with me. The rest of you, wait here."

Mason slipped into the house after Otley. The foyer was wide and square, floored and trimmed in dark wood. It had walls painted cream. Long red, navy blue, and cream-patterned rugs covered much of the floor. A dark wood staircase wrapped up the left-hand side of the foyer, carpeted in the same colorful rug. The ceilings were higher than what Mason knew to be normal. Fancy iron furniture and tables lined each wall amid vases and statues. Directly in front of Mason stood a life-size bronze-and-iron statue of a woman and three large dogs, each on its own leash. Where the railing curved at the foot of the stairs, a vase filled with fresh, long-stemmed roses stretched as tall as Mason.

Once all the enforcers had entered the house, Mr. Berg closed the front door and crossed the foyer to an open walkway at the bottom of the stairs. "Right this way."

Otley stomped after the butler, his boots clumping over the shiny wood floor and thin rugs. Mason followed closely and carefully, making sure to keep his distance from everyone else. Would Ciddah be with Lawten? Or would she be somewhere else? At this hour she'd likely be sleeping. Where might the bedrooms be in such a house?

The "small parlor" was as big as Mason's old house had been. The walls were also cream, which made the room look bright. There were eight sofas — four cream and four red — and at least a dozen wing chairs, all arranged to face the middle of the room. Tables and lamps and mirrors and vases and pillows ... the place was cluttered yet looked immaculate. A brown piano as big as a car sat in one corner of the room. A fire in a marble hearth crackled on the opposite wall. Two archways led out the back of the room, one on either side of the fireplace. To the bedrooms, perhaps?

Otley walked up to a mirror hanging above the fireplace. He bared his teeth and picked them with his thumbnail. The men in black suits filed inside the room, followed by Bender and the three enforcers. They stood in a line behind one of the red sofas.

Lawten's assistant, Kruse, entered then, still pink-skinned and bald, and still wearing the same black SimArt hand on the side of his head. He led the way for his boss, who was frail and hobbling like an old man. Mason had never seen the task director general walking, and now he saw why. No one should move so slowly at thirty-nine years old. Why was his condition so accelerated? Ciddah had said she'd loved him once. Did love go away like a stomachache? Mason didn't think so. It must hurt to see someone you love waste away from illness. She couldn't really be his lifer, right? He'd betrayed her.

The head of Lawten's security carried the warrant to Kruse, who started to read it.

"General Otley," Lawten said, "what right have you to barge into my home at this hour?"

Otley turned away from the mirror and stood with his hands

behind his back. "I have a warrant for your arrest and to search your house."

Lawten lowered himself onto one of the red chairs. "And what am I being arrested for?"

Kruse stepped up behind the couch, just to Lawten's right. "Kidnapping and conspiracy against the Safe Lands, according to this." He handed it to Lawten, who waved it away.

Lawten crossed one leg over the other. "Preposterous. Who have I supposedly kidnapped?"

"Baby Promise," Otley said.

Mason edged toward the far wall and peeked out the doors there. A formal dining room. Perhaps the bedrooms were upstairs.

"Baby Promise is here as part of an experiment, General Otley," Kruse said. "I can produce the paperwork if necessary."

"And now that we've cleared that up, what conspiracy do you accuse me of?" Lawten asked.

Mason started back toward the door he'd come in, intent on reaching the stairs.

"We have reason to believe you helped several outsider women escape the harem," Otley said. "That you bring them here to receive medical check-ups from Ciddah Rourke."

"Miss Rourke is my lifer," Lawten said. "And I've never brought any harem women to my home."

Even though he'd been prepared for it, the statement shook Mason. And Otley's accusation of medical check-ups compounded the doubt in his mind. He reminded himself that Otley was trying to frame Lawten. The Glenrock women had never come here for check-ups. So Ciddah was here for a different reason, but what?

"We'll see, Mr. Task Director," Otley said. "My enforcers are going to search your home."

Lawten narrowed his eyes at Otley. "And who will your men find, General Otley?"

"How could I know?" Otley said, innocently.

"Oh, I think you know. This isn't the first time you've tried to set me up. All of the dead in Glenrock. I know you ordered your men to kill."

"The outsiders were armed. I warned you it might be necessary."

"But you fired first. And it made me look bad. That's what you wanted, wasn't it? To make me look incompetent?"

"You've served the Safe Lands well for many years, Mr. Task Director. Because of that, I'm willing to negotiate."

"I'm listening," Lawten said in a low voice.

"Resign as task director general, and I'll dismiss the charges. No X. No record."

"No task?" Kruse said.

"Oh, he'll task," Otley said, "just not as the TDG. And not in the Highlands. Or the Midlands."

Mason had heard enough. It wouldn't be long before the remaining enforcers were let inside to do their search. He slipped out of the parlor and went up the stairs.

CHAPTER
34

When Ruston returned from helping Mason and Omar, he and Levi and Beshup went over the list of Glenrock and Jack's Peak families until Ruston had found a basement location for each to move into. Then Levi sat beside Zane and watched on the video screens as Mason and Omar walked through the gates surrounding Champion House, invisible to the enforcers they were walking beside. So strange.

"I can't believe I'm seeing this," Zane said. "I mean, I knew Bender and Rewl were doing their own thing, but seeing them walk beside Otley..."

Ruston, who was standing behind Zane, squeezed Zane's shoulder. "I know, son."

"But what are we going to do? Bender and Rewl, they know the basements as well as anyone."

"We keep doing what we do and trust God will continue to protect us. He has from the beginning, you know."

But Zane sighed heavily, like he didn't like that plan. Levi wanted to ask Ruston what he meant by "God," but his brothers were approaching the gate. Levi was thankful that Jemma and the others were already on their way here. But if Ruston's basements weren't any safer than the cabin, what was the point?

"I wish we could hear what they're saying," Zane said. "I don't know the cameras so well inside, so bear with me." He switched the view on one of his six screens to a camera on the front porch, looking out at the approaching vehicles. No sign of his brothers, though on another one of Zane's screens, Levi could see through Omar's eyes as the second car branched off and Omar followed it.

Seeing his brothers walk into danger and having no ability to help them was strange. Levi didn't like feeling so helpless. There was nothing to do but watch and pray.

He glanced at Ruston, who stood beside him, arms folded as he watched the screens. Could the two of them possibly be related? It seemed insane, but Levi hadn't been able to stop thinking about it the entire time Ruston had been gone. "That was quite a statement you left me with," Levi said.

Ruston grinned without removing his gaze from the monitors. "Got you thinking, did I?

Thinking you're mad. "I'd like to hear why you think we're related."

"Good," Ruston said, "because I'm happy to explain."

Zane groaned and turned on his chair. "He's always telling it. The *Tale of the Outsiders* has been a legend to basement kids since before I was born."

"Because my father told me stories of *the* Elias McShane," Ruston said, "the smart young man who got away from the Safe Lands and took his family into the woods to live off berries and rabbits."

Zane spun back to the monitors. "As if people would eat a rabbit."

But the back of Levi's neck prickled at what Ruston had said. "Elias McShane was my great-grandfather."

Zane's twisted his chair around again, eyes narrowed. "Hold the flavor."

"Didn't I say so, Dathan? Didn't I?" Ruston broke out a wide smile and grabbed Zane's shoulder. "The stories are true!"

"Dathan?" Levi asked.

"My real name," Zane said. "We all have fake ones to use above ground. I was born Dathan McShane."

"And I'm Seth McShane," Ruston said, "named after my — "

"Papa Eli's father?" This was too weird. McShanes in the Safe Lands? How?

"You called Elias McShane 'Papa Eli'?" Ruston asked, as if the mere idea was ridiculous.

But Levi wasn't jumping ahead to that until he got more answers. "How can you be related to Papa Eli's father?" No one from Glenrock had ever moved into the Safe Lands. Papa Eli would have said, wouldn't he?

"First, let me show you this." Ruston went to the ammo shelves and pulled a rifle down from the very top.

Levi's heart fluttered at the familiar weapon. "That's my gun! How did you get it?"

"Dathan told me about it after he went with you to shoot out those transformers. He said it looked a lot like mine and that you claimed it came from Arizona."

"For the record, I thought it was merely interesting," Zane said. "I did not believe my dad's crazy stories were true."

Ruston pulled down a second rifle from the top shelf. "This is my gun. It belonged to *my* great-grandfather, Seth McShane." He handed the rifle to Levi.

It didn't have the engraving Levi's had, but they were almost identical.

"I've got a guy loyal to me in the enforcer's evidence warehouse," Ruston said. "And after you got thrown in the RC, I had my guy steal the gun. When I saw the engraving, I knew."

Levi turned his rifle over, baring the engraving on the bottom of the stock. But he knew what it said: *Elias McShane — March 22, 1996.* "It's Papa Eli's birth date."

"That's right. And when Dathan told me so many of you were nines, I pieced things together. See, our family are all nines too."

Levi looked at Zane, but he wasn't wearing his gloves right now. "But Zane, er, Dathan … He's a five." Levi hadn't forgotten that.

"It's fake," Zane said. "I can program SimTags to bear any number. Nines get too much attention from Safe Lands medics, so we always use lower numbers. I've got Mason's eyes on the screen now, by the way. Lhogan switched suit two to the main feed. I wish he'd give me access to his GlassTop so I could see all his screens."

Levi looked at the second screen. Mason was standing in a fancy room with General Otley, Bender, Lawten Renzor, and Renzor's weird assistant. "No sound?"

"Nope. All we can do is watch," Zane said. "Unless Omar taps us."

"What do you know about Seth McShane?" Ruston asked.

"Uh …" Jemma would know the story better. "Papa Eli's father sacrificed himself so that Papa Eli and his friends could get out of the Safe Lands. He distracted the guards and got arrested and put in jail. Papa Eli said they'd never have gotten out otherwise. As far as we know, no one else ever got out."

"So Seth McShane is a legend to your people, and Elias McShane is a legend to mine." Ruston smiled. "Isn't that something?"

Bewildering was a better word. Levi didn't think it had ever occurred to Papa Eli that his father might start a new family in the Safe Lands. "Papa Eli always made his father look like a, uh …" What was the name of those men of Old who didn't marry? "A missionary priest?"

That seemed to tickle Ruston, and he hooted in laughter. "Once those gates closed him in, Seth McShane had seven more children."

"Seven!" Levi couldn't believe it. "Papa Eli only had four, and he was a lot younger."

"I still can't believe Elias McShane was a real person," Zane said. "All this time I thought it was just a story."

Levi had greatly respected and admired his great-grandfather, but it was weird to hear people talk about Papa Eli like he was some kind of legend. "Otley shot him," Levi said. "In the raid. But he died later when I found him." Died right in front of him.

Ruston's eyes bulged. "He was still alive? After all this time?" He walked across the nest and sat on the chair in front of the green wall. "How?"

"He was ninety-two," Levi said, smiling, "and he could still keep up with me on hunting trips."

"Ninety-two? That's stimming ancient," Zane said.

Ruston just stared at Levi, his expression awestruck. "I can't believe you knew him."

"Lived in the same house as him," Levi said. "You must have old people in the basements, right?"

"Old people, yeah," Zane said, "but none that old."

"We don't have great access to medical care," Ruston said. "If our elderly get sick, we can't take them to the MC."

"Because they'd be liberated," Levi said. This place was nuts. "Do you have the thin plague?" Levi asked Ruston.

"Not me. Some Naturals do, most don't."

"I'm a flaker, Levi," Zane said. "Go ahead and hate me."

"I don't hate you." But Levi doubted that was enough to convince Zane, whose words brought a rush of shame over Levi. No one had helped him more than Zane. "Liberation," he said, thinking of his mother. "What is it?"

"Ah, that I can't tell you," Ruston said. "We've tried to figure it out for years. And we have some men in very high positions within the Safe Lands government too. But the Guild is very careful with the truth about liberation."

"Could it be death?" Because that's the only thing that made sense to Levi.

"Could be," Ruston said. "Killing Xed people would be one thing, but I can't imagine it would help the Guild's cause to kill the innocent."

"We have to find out what it is," Levi said. "There's got to be a way."

"Then we need to take down the government," Ruston said.

"Operation Lynchpin," Zane said.

"What's that?" Levi asked.

"Omar's idea for taking down the government," Zane said. "He thinks we need to do something that will cut off the food or water supply to the people, which would force everyone to leave the Safe Lands. And it *could* work, but enforcers have a lot of supplies stocked up. And they can always take flights to Wyoming to get more."

"So find a way to cut off access to flights?" Levi suggested.

Ruston shook his head. "Only a few helicopters are kept inside the walls. The rest are out at the Old Crested Butte airport."

"Are any of your people pilots?" Levi asked.

"I wish," Ruston said. "Flight is a heavily guarded task in the Safe Lands. They have the test programmed to select only two new pilot candidates each year. And even though we have a man in registration, the pilot positions are always assigned by the task director general."

"And the tutorials for pilots are kept in some vault. Not really, but it sure seems that way when I've tried to — Mason's leaving the room," Zane said, drawing Levi's attention back to screen two, which showed that Mason was walking up a fancy staircase.

Be careful, brother, Levi thought, wishing he could see Omar too, wishing he was there to keep them both from getting killed.

CHAPTER
35

Shaylinn forced herself to calm down as the car rolled forward. Omar would come back. He had to avoid being caught or he couldn't help her. He'd be back. He'd promised.

But she didn't know what to make of Omar's promises. Loving him was easy, but trusting him was hard. At least he'd come for her. *Omar* had come. Not Levi or Mason or even Jordan. That had to mean something, didn't it? She repeated the verse Omar shared — or at least tried to: I trust in God and won't be scared. What can man do to me?

Man could kill her. But then she'd be in heaven with her mother and father and grandparents and her brother Joel, and she'd be happy. That wouldn't be so bad, right? She recalled a quote Jemma loved. "If we find ourselves with a desire that nothing in this world can satisfy, the most probable explanation is that we were made for another world."

The car left the smooth road and rocked over jagged terrain before coming to a stop on an incline. Shaylinn slid forward and pressed her hands against the back of the trunk to hold herself steady and protect her head.

She struggled to turn until she had her back to the wall, which was a bit more comfortable. If she thought too much about where she was, that she was trapped and couldn't extend her legs, panic fluttered in her chest. So she forced her thoughts elsewhere. But Shaylinn was torn. She wanted to get out, yet staying in the trunk might be safer. At least the trunk was a barrier between her and Rewl and his icky teeth.

But then the trunk slid open. Shaylinn covered her face with her hands, hoping that whoever it was would think she was sleeping.

"Get out," Rewl said. "Don't make me drag you."

Shaylinn blew out an angry breath and pushed herself to a sitting position. "You don't have to be mean."

Rewl stepped back from the car, his gun trained on Shaylinn. She looked beyond where he stood and gasped. Rewl had parked on a grassy hill beside a castle made of smooth gray rocks. Lights lit up the doorways and balconies like yellow stars glowing in the dim light of dawn. The sky was pink with purple-gray clouds, and the pine trees that loomed beside the house were black silhouettes against it.

"It's beautiful." Who might live in such a place? She wished Jemma could see it.

"Hurry up." Rewl lunged forward and grabbed her arm. He pulled so hard that she scrambled to get her feet underneath herself so she wouldn't fall onto the ground.

They walked up to the house, and once she was level with the back patio, she saw the pool. "Oh!" Like a mirror of glass, it stretched out from the back of the house, surrounded by the patio made from slabs of gray rock that matched the castle. Fat stone bowls edged the pool and were filled to overflowing with dark pink and purple flowers. Shaylinn breathed deeply, enjoying the mixed scent of the spicy sweet flowers and pine.

Rewl grabbed her arm again and pulled her along the patio onto a porch of wood slats. Just ahead, an enforcer was holding a door open for them, and they entered an oval-shaped room. The walls were paneled in light pine, and the floor was stone. Ugly blue-and-peach-flowered chairs sat around the perimeter except where three long closets broke the space. The closets had no doors and were filled with outdoor clothing and skis and helmets.

"Where am I taking her?" Rewl asked the enforcer.

"I'll show you."

The enforcer led them down a hallway that was covered in paintings of landscapes. She wondered if Omar would like them. They took a narrow, wooden stairway up to the second floor and walked down another hallway. This one was twice as wide as the one downstairs and covered in soft beige carpet that reminded her of the harem.

The enforcer opened a door and held it. Rewl nudged Shaylinn inside and remained right behind her.

"Wow." Shaylinn stopped inside a bedroom. Almost everything was white. The bed was fat with white pillows and a fluffy blanket. Curtains ran floor to ceiling over the balcony windows. The carpet was a background of green covered in white flowers and leaves. Here and there accents of jade and gold complemented the room.

A baby's gurgling pulled her gaze to one of two green wingback chairs sitting before a golden hearth. A blonde woman was sitting in one of them, holding an infant. Ciddah, the medic Mason loved.

"Oh," Shaylinn said, wondering if Ciddah was helping Rewl or not.

"Talkative one, isn't she?" the enforcer said.

"Wait here to be discovered," Rewl said. "And don't try to escape." He walked out of the room and the enforcer closed the door, leaving Shaylinn alone with Ciddah and the baby. What did that mean, *Wait here to be discovered*?

"You *can't* escape," Ciddah said. "I've tried and failed three times since I got here."

So Ciddah was a prisoner too? Shaylinn was glad, for Mason's sake. "Is that your baby?"

Ciddah rocked the baby in her arms. "It's Kendall Collin's baby."

Oh, dear. Kendall must have been very upset when she didn't find her child in the nursery. Omar probably had consoled her. Shaylinn scowled at the idea.

Stop it, she told herself. Jealous thoughts could change nothing. They would only make her angry.

"Why did he bring you here?" Ciddah asked.

"Something to do with getting the task director general in trouble." Shaylinn sat on the second wingback chair. It was soft. "Omar is here. He's going to rescue me. Us, if you want to come."

"Omar?" Ciddah raised her eyebrows. "Isn't he the one who got your people into trouble in the first place? The one who OD'd?"

"Yes, but he's changing. Or starting to, anyway." He just needed people to believe in him, like Shaylinn did — or tried to.

"Have you seen Mason lately?" Ciddah asked, and, for some reason, the worry in the medic's eyes made Shaylinn blush.

"I saw him tonight — last night, before they left."

"Who's they?"

Should she tell Ciddah about freeing the children? It might not be wise. Mason had said once that he didn't trust this woman. Shaylinn suddenly realized just how he felt — to love someone you couldn't trust. It was an awful feeling.

"Just some people from my village," Shaylinn said. "Why are *you* here?"

"Because Lawten Renzor is insane. He thinks I am his lifer. And whether or not I like it, whether or not it's true, he has claimed me as such."

CHAPTER
36

Omar didn't dare attack Rewl when he had the stunner pointed at Shay, so he waited and followed them into the house. And what a place! Omar's senses were on overload as he took in the ornate decor. He tried not to look, and instead focus on Shay and Rewl and where they were going. But a painting on the wall in the hallway stopped him cold.

He'd seen this painting in one of his Old art books. It was called *Starry Night*, and it had been painted by Vincent van Gogh in 1889, one hundred and ninety-nine years ago.

How could it be here? How could it even exist still? The frame looked new, so it must be a copy, perhaps a giclee. Omar leaned close to study the strokes, but footsteps on the wooden stairs pulled him away. Shay.

He found the staircase and walked up as softly as he could, coming out into a plush hallway, marveling at yet another painting on the wall.

Just ahead, the enforcer opened the door. Shay and Rewl went inside. Omar could hear low voices but couldn't make out what they were saying.

Should he go in or wait? He didn't know. The enforcer was standing in the doorway, so until the man moved, Omar had no way around him.

Then Rewl came out and closed the door behind him. "Stand guard here until I come back."

Rewl walked back toward Omar, so Omar turned and darted into the stairwell to wait for Rewl to pass by. But when he turned back, Rewl was coming down this staircase. Idiot! Why hadn't he stayed up in the hallway?

He turned and crept down ahead of Rewl, as quickly and as quietly as he could manage. He crouched under the van Gogh, fighting the urge to look at it. He drew his stunner, and when Rewl appeared, he fired. Rewl collapsed in the hallway. Omar ran to his side and dragged him to the nearest open door. A small bathroom. Perfect.

He pulled Rewl inside and shut the door. Rewl's eyes were squeezed shut, so Omar slapped his face and used one finger to push up his left eyelid.

"Hey," Omar said. "You stole the wrong girl, you know that?"

Rewl frowned. His eyes flickered around the room, unable to find Omar's face.

"That's right. I'm haunting you, you traitorous maggot. So, Bender is your dad, huh? Did he kill Chord or did you do it for him?"

Rewl moaned, as if trying to speak but unable.

"You're both pathetic. Trusting Otley for anything is insanity. He *will* betray you. It's what he does."

Omar looked for something to tie Rewl up with, but he couldn't find a thing. So he stunned him again and darted back out into the hall.

At the van Gogh, he leaned close and could see the individual brushstrokes and the thickness and texture of the paint. The swirling strokes directed his gaze around the peaceful scene. The church steeple and the tree both pointed to the heavens. Man and creation worshiping their Creator, perhaps?

Or maybe pointing upstairs to Shay.

Omar crept up the stairs, knowing that the painting had been no copy. Someone must have sought out the treasure to hang it here, in a random hallway off a kitchen. That such paintings still existed had never occurred to Omar. To think he might scavenge the world in search of masterpieces of Old.

A thrill grew in his chest at the very idea.

Four steps before he reached the top of the stairs, a blur of blue light walked by on the hallway above.

Mason.

Omar lunged up the last few steps to join his brother.

CHAPTER
37

Mason stopped in the hallway, staring at the enforcer who was leaning against the wall outside a door, looking bored. Could that be where Ciddah was? Or Kendall's baby? So far, every other bedroom door had been open and no one had been in any of them.

Mason reached for his stunner, yet hesitated. What if that was a bathroom, and the enforcer was merely waiting for his partner? Mason might be making more trouble for himself. He would wait. Though he didn't have much time to spare. He wished that Omar was—

Something shot past his left arm. A crackle. The enforcer seized up and slid down the wall into a heap on the floor, a stunner cartridge stuck to his chest. Mason spun around and saw the glowing blue form of his brother.

"Got him," Omar said. "Why don't you go say hello to your medic?"

"She might not be in there."

"Well, that's where Rewl took Shay," Omar said.

Mason ran to the door and went inside. It was a bedroom, white and bright and totally empty.

Behind him, a voice whispered. "I don't see anyone."

Mason turned around. Ciddah stood, pressed against an

indentation in the wall beside the closet, holding a jade vase as if to slam it over the head of whoever might enter.

Behind him, Omar pulled the guard inside the room, which to Ciddah likely looked like a man sliding across the floor by himself on his back with his feet in the air. She screamed.

Mason darted forward and pressed his hand over her mouth. "Ciddah, it's me, Mason."

She dropped the vase and her eyes bulged, rolling in their sockets as she looked for him.

"We're wearing suits that make us invisible," he said.

Her eyebrows sank and her fingers felt for Mason's hand on her mouth, then up his arm. He released her mouth. "Mason?" she whispered.

"When Omar closes the door, I'll take off my hood."

"Guess I'll close the door, then, brother." Omar dropped the guard's feet and stepped over him. The door clicked shut. "Where is Shay? I saw her come in here."

"Here." Shaylinn's voice came from the closet.

Omar darted past Mason toward the closet. Mason removed his hood.

A breath tremored past Ciddah's lips as her eyes grew wide again and looked him up and down.

"What? You don't like my outfit?" Mason said.

A smile chased the fear from Ciddah's face. "I thought I'd never see you again."

"Not see me? Were you afraid you'd go blind?"

She laughed, a breathy laugh, then grabbed his ears and kissed him.

Mason let the moment take him, lost in the feelings she stirred within him. If this was not real love, then Mason would never understand it.

Omar cleared his throat and Mason pulled away, though Ciddah's fingers slid down his arm and took hold of his gloved hand. Shaylinn was holding a baby, standing beside Omar, who looked to be nothing more than a severed head, floating slightly higher than Shaylinn's.

They were both staring at them.

"Kendall Collin said you were Lawten Renzor's lifer." Omar raised one eyebrow as if daring Ciddah to deny it.

Omar ... Now was not the time.

"He's obsessed with this idea of creating an Old family. And he mentioned moving away." Ciddah looked up into Mason's eyes and squeezed his hand. "You don't believe I still care for him, do you? I don't want to go with him." Her eyes flicked back and forth from one of Mason's eyes to the other. "You do. Mason, no. I love *you*. I want to stay with *you*. I want my donors to come too and —"

"Explain later." Omar flashed Ciddah a fake smile. "Right now we need to get out of here."

Mason wanted to shake Omar for his "help" in regard to Ciddah. He only felt more flustered and confused now.

"Do you invisible men have a plan of escape?" Shaylinn asked.

"I think we should put the girls in the SimSuits," Omar said, already zipping down the front of his. "That way we'll be sure they get out safely."

"Excellent suggestion." Mason unzipped his suit as well.

"I'm going to wear that?" Shaylinn shifted the baby to her other arm and reached for Omar's invisible middle, patting it with her fingertips.

"What about Baby Promise?" Ciddah said.

"I'm wearing a harness," Omar said, shrugging off the sleeves of his suit. "The same one I used to carry Ben. One of you will have to put it on."

"I will," Ciddah said.

"You saved Ben?" Shaylinn said, beaming.

Omar stepped out of one leg of his suit. "We saved all the children, except ..."

"Except what?" Shaylinn asked. "Is it Jemma?"

Omar struggled to get his other foot out of the suit. "Nothing. Never mind."

"Jemma is fine." Mason didn't think now was the time to bring up Kendall's death. He could imagine the effect the news of Kendall's death would have on two frightened women. It would not expedite their escape. Mason left his SimSuit on the floor and removed his surgical kit from the pocket. He unrolled it on the bed.

Omar took off the harness he was wearing. "We can give you our suits, but not the contact lenses. So you'll have no way of seeing each other. Hold hands or something, so you don't get separated."

Mason took the harness from Omar and helped Ciddah put it on. "I need to remove your SimTag next, Ciddah, or they'll be able to track you. Did they give you a new one, Shaylinn?"

"No," Shaylinn said. "I just got here."

"Mason, what about my donors?" Ciddah asked.

He met her eyes. "Your *parents* are in hiding. Omar and I got them to safety on Friday."

"Oh, Mason!" She threw her arms around him and hugged him so tightly he could feel her heart beat.

He wanted to linger in her arms, but he made her sit on the bed. "Hold still so I can do this."

Omar took the baby so Shaylinn could get into his SimSuit. While Mason removed Ciddah's SimTag, he shared what he'd overheard from General Otley. "It seems like it won't be long until he's the task director general. Though I don't know why he wouldn't just wait a few more months until Lawten is liberated."

"Because then the Guild takes a vote," Ciddah said. "And if Otley can make himself look like a hero before then, he stands a better chance of getting the job."

"That's madness," Omar said. "It will be worse for everyone then. Do you think he'd really let Bender be enforcer general?"

"Bender has no enforcer experience," Mason said. "I believe Otley is manipulating him." He taped a bandage over the incision on Ciddah's hand. "Sorry I can't do better than that right now."

"It's fine," she said. "You were right about our land: It's anything but safe. In fact, the only place I've ever felt protected has been in your presence."

Mason took hold of her hand. "Then I will never leave you."

"Wow," Omar said. "Keep that up and you two are going to make me sick." Omar pulled Shaylinn to the bed. She was now the one with a floating head. "Sit and hold the baby for Mason. And you" — he nodded to Ciddah — "put on Mason's suit, will you?"

Ciddah got up from the bed and Shaylinn took her place. She hugged the child to her chest, which looked so strange with her body being invisible. "You're going to cut him?"

"I have to. They'll track his SimTag otherwise."

Omar stood guard at the door, stunner in hand, while Ciddah got dressed in Mason's SimSuit and Baby Promise screamed. Mason worked fast, though, and once Kendall's child was bandaged up, he quickly fastened the boy into the harness Ciddah wore, then zipped her up until she was only a floating head too.

"How will we get out?" Shaylinn asked. "I don't know where to go."

"You'll stay with us unless something happens," Omar said. "And if it does, get out of the house and walk to the black truck that's parked at a green house around the corner. Nash will drive you to Zane's place."

"Can't we just go to the cabin?" Shaylinn asked.

"Not now that Rewl knows where it is," Mason said. "Everyone will be at Zane's now."

"Just get out of the gates," Omar said. "Zane says they can find you wherever you are as long as you keep the suits on. So get out and look for Nash. If you can't find him, sit somewhere and wait. He'll come find you."

Ciddah took hold of Mason's hand, and the thick suit glove felt strange against his skin. "I don't want to be apart from you ever again," she said.

He looked down into her eyes. He wanted to say that his love didn't change when they were apart, but Omar would mock him, and he still didn't know with absolute certainty that she was being honest. "Stay alive, please. That's your only task now."

"I will, if only to see you again." She kissed him, and Mason couldn't believe how happy a person was capable of feeling.

"I think it's time for the hoods," Omar said, a little louder than necessary. Then he mumbled, "Walls, you two are worse than Jemma and Levi." He laughed, then added, "And Levi agrees."

Mason and Ciddah broke apart, and Mason's cheeks burned. He'd forgotten that people were watching through his eyes. He lowered the hood over Ciddah's head and she vanished from sight. It was difficult to find the snaps with the suit already activated. He found the first two, but the third must have been twisted under the hem somehow because—

The door burst open. "Don't move!"

Rewl walked into the room, gun trained on Mason, then Omar, then Mason again.

"You can't shoot us both at the same time," Omar said.

Mason was glad to see that his brother had gotten Shay's hood on in time. Perhaps if he were able to stall Rewl, Omar could get the girls out. He looked for his stunner, then realized it was still strapped to his belt, which was coiled on the floor at his feet.

"Where are they?" Rewl asked. "Where's the baby? I can hear it."

The baby cooed from somewhere near the closet. He hoped Ciddah hadn't gone inside, but then he saw her blue form inching along the wall toward the door.

Rewl stepped forward and motioned Mason to walk to the foot of the bed, where Omar was standing. Mason backed up slowly as Rewl moved toward the closet. Rewl turned quickly, so that his back was to the closet and his gun aimed at Mason. He pulled the closet door aside.

Empty.

Rewl frowned and looked at Mason. "I don't understand."

His aim drooped enough that Mason took his chance. He tackled Rewl, knocking him into the open closet. Mason's hand and temple scraped the wall as they fell. His elbow struck the metal runner for the closet doors, and pain coursed up his arm.

"Go, Omar! Go!" Mason yelled, both hands on Rewl's gun hand, pushing it away from him. No matter what, he had to hold on long enough for them to get out of the room.

Somehow Rewl got on top and jammed his knee against Mason's abdomen. Mason froze, as if paralyzed. His diaphragm was stuck in the inhale position. Too much air with no place to go. His spine instinctively curled. Rewl untangled himself and stood, then he shot Mason with the stunner.

The electricity from the stun cartridge was stronger than Mason would have imagined. His muscles seized and felt like they were being stretched beyond their limits. The pain surprised him as did the fact that he had no voice, no motor control at all. Yet he was completely cognizant of his surroundings. Rewl was searching the room. Mason saw him look under the bed and behind the chairs and curtains, out on the balcony.

Yet Mason couldn't move. It was the strangest sensation he'd ever experienced.

And then the cartridge ran out of current. Mason's body relaxed, though every nerve still felt like it was vibrating.

"He's there," Rewl said to someone. "Pick him up and follow me."

Two enforcers appeared over Mason. Hands descended upon him, and he was dragged out of the closet and from the room. The enforcers carried him through the house, down the stairs, following Rewl, and while Mason's body no longer hurt, his muscles had yet to resume taking instructions from his brain.

It truly was a fascinating experience.

Suddenly the enforcers stopped. They were in the small parlor again. Lawten was there, sitting on the same red chair. Kruse sat beside him now. Two enforcers stood behind Lawten and Kruse, guns in hand. Two of the bodyguards in black suits lay on the floor. Stunned. Dead. Mason couldn't tell. The others weren't present. Bender sat on one of the beige sofas across from them. General Otley was standing before the fireplace.

"Well, surprise me," Kruse said. "It's the handsome medic. I did not expect *that*."

Otley turned and looked at Mason, then at Rewl, who walked farther into the room.

"What's this?" Otley asked.

"The girls are gone, sir," Rewl said. "All I found in the room was him and his brother."

"Gone?" Otley roared. "How? Where? And what about the baby?"

"I don't know," Rewl said, his voice so low it was barely audible.

Otley narrowed his eyes. "*Which* brother did you see? He has two."

"Omar," Rewl said.

Otley walked up to Rewl. "And where is Omar now?"

"He got away, probably with the girls and the baby."

Otley drew his gun and shot Rewl. The gun let off an airy pop.

Mason's arms flinched then, fear bringing his muscles back into action. He knew that sound. It was the same sound he'd heard when they killed his father.

Rewl collapsed, and Bender jumped up from the sofa and stared at his son. "You — What did you do?"

"What was necessary," Otley said. "Clearly Mr. Renzor is working with those outsider rats. But without the girl and the child, we have no proof of kidnapping charges. So find Omar Strong, find the girl, and find the child. Now!"

The two enforcers holding Mason dropped him on a chair and ran out of the parlor. Mason sat there, legs still shaky, staring at Rewl's body, wondering if there was anything he could do. He tried to move his hands and only one finger curled.

Bender crossed the room and knelt at Rewl's side. He pulled his son onto his knees, leaving a circle of red stained onto the rug. A breath released from Mason. Too much blood loss. Too late.

He could only stare and pray that Omar and the girls had gotten out.

CHAPTER
38

Shaylinn clutched tightly to Ciddah's arm as they followed Omar down the hallway. He turned a sharp corner, and when the girls caught up, Shaylinn saw him standing three steps down a half-flight of narrow, wooden steps, looking back up, waving them to come.

Omar turned, but before he took another step, footsteps clattered up the steps from below. Shadows jostled on the wall of the landing. He spun back to them. Shaylinn reached out and took his hand, and he ran up the steps and darted ahead, pulling Shay along. She had to run to keep up, and she squeezed Ciddah's arm even tighter.

Omar ran past the room the girls had been kept in and followed the hall until it turned a corner. Here the passage stretched out the length of one room before it turned yet again and ended in a grand staircase. Shaylinn thought she saw the front door at the bottom of the stairs. They were almost free.

Omar went down the steps quickly and silently. Shaylinn tried to be silent as well. She could hear little Elyot fussing and hoped no one else would.

Just as Omar stepped off the stairs, General Otley swept out from a doorway on the right.

"You!" Otley grabbed the front of Omar's shirt and swung him around, jerking Omar's hand from Shaylinn's and knocking over a vase of roses with Omar's feet. The vase fell with a crash, spilling water and porcelain and flowers across the floor.

Shaylinn bit back a scream. Footsteps on the stairs behind them signaled the approach of two enforcers.

"Did you find the girls?" Otley asked the enforcers, still holding Omar's shirt as Omar struggled to get away. His words were heavy and mean, like punches.

"No sign of them in the rooms, sir."

Shaylinn clutched Ciddah's arm and watched Omar reach for a shard of the broken vase.

"Look again."

"Yes, sir." The enforcers turned and scurried back down the hallway.

Omar stabbed the shard into General Otley's leg, which made the beastly man growl. With a flick of his arm, he threw Omar through the archway and stomped after him, disappearing from sight.

A tug from Ciddah, and Shaylinn followed her down the stairs. When they reached the bottom, Shaylinn could see into the room where General Otley had gone. Omar lay on the floor on his back, General Otley's foot on his chest. *Don't hurt him!*

"Where's the girl, little rat?" General Otley leaned on Omar, pressing down with his foot. "Where's the infant?"

Omar grabbed the general's boot and twisted out from under it. He rolled up into a sitting position and pushed back on the floor, panting slightly. "I don't know anything about a girl or an infant." Omar took a breath. "Or a rat, for that matter. Me and my brother were looking for a new house, and we liked the looks of this one."

Otley kicked Omar's stomach, making Omar slide over the wooden floor. He rolled onto his chest and moaned.

"Leave him alone." Mason's voice. Somewhere deeper in the room. Shaylinn saw the back of his head above a fancy red chair. Why was he just sitting there?

Someone hitched in a muffled sob, which drew Shaylinn's gaze to Bender, kneeling on the floor, cradling Rewl's head in his lap, blood staining the floor beneath them.

Shaylinn lost her breath.

They should do something to help. But what? If only Shaylinn had a stunner. She would shoot Otley and end all this.

The baby let out a long, gurgling coo. Ciddah pulled on Shaylinn's arm, and, reluctantly, Shaylinn followed Ciddah, but her eyes stayed on Omar until she could no longer see him.

She heard him moan again and gasp for breath, so she increased her grip on Ciddah's sleeve until her fingers ached.

Ciddah turned the knob on the front door, and it swung it open. An enforcer on the porch turned to look, a gun in his hand. Ciddah pulled Shaylinn back as the enforcer walked through the open doorway. He looked up the stairs, then into the room where that horrible man was hurting Omar.

Ciddah towed Shaylinn behind the enforcer, out the door, and down the steps. Shaylinn looked back to see the enforcer step outside again and close the door, shaking his head. She stumbled over a rock and almost fell.

"Sorry," Ciddah said. "I just really want to get out of here before they catch us."

But the tears lacing Ciddah's voice were obvious, and Shaylinn started to cry too. She didn't want to leave Omar and Mason behind, but there was nothing they could do, not without help and not with a baby in their care.

She prayed that General Otley would let Mason and Omar live.

CHAPTER
39

Omar had been watching from where he lay on the floor. He could barely see the foyer. But he'd seen the blue suits walk to the door, open it, saw the enforcer come inside and look around, and then the blue suits had gone out and the front door had closed again. The girls had gotten out. They were safe. And Omar was done being a kicking bag.

He scrambled to his feet and picked up a lamp from a table by one of the sofas. He ripped off the shade and threw it at Otley. The enforcer general batted it away, but Omar took the lamp by the fixture and bashed the base over Otley's head.

Otley growled. It started low and rose to a scream that turned his face a mottled shade of magenta. Omar grabbed a vase and threw that next, but it only bounced off Otley's chest and landed near the chair Mason was sitting on. Omar didn't know what had happened to his brother, but he didn't look so good.

Otley went for his gun, so Omar dove behind a sofa. Great plan, *Owl*. Now what? He'd only needed to stall long enough for the girls to get away. Now that they had, he needed to get Mason and get out.

Footsteps over the floor had him momentarily paralyzed.

"He's come 'round the piano side," Mason said, his voice slurred.

Omar crawled along the back of the couch and around the corner just as a bullet pierced the floorboards. He bit back a curse and crawled faster. Real bullets from an enforcer-issue dual-action pistol. Omar reached for his own gun, but it was gone. It had likely fallen out of his waistband when Otley had been using him as a kickball.

"Gunfire is our cue to leave, Mr. Task Director," Kruse said.

"You're not going anywhere," Otley said.

Omar looked around for a place to hide or for anything he could use as a weapon. He was almost to the fireplace, which had a rack of tools beside it. The poker hanging by the little broom and shovel might work. He started crawling toward it.

"You're going to shoot me, General Otley?" Lawten asked. "The bullets would match your gun, and you would be caught."

"Maybe you got hit by a stray. I was shooting at one of your rebels when he attacked me. Unfortunate accident."

"You'd still be liberated for my death," the task director general said. "And you know what that means."

"I will *never* be liberated."

"It's that or the Ancients," Lawten said. "I didn't think you liked them. And I doubt they'd accept you, treasonous as you are."

"Enough of this. Hay-o, rat! How do you like this?" The gun fired again, a pop of exploding air. Mason screamed, and it tapered into a whimpering groan.

Oh no. Mason! Fire shot through Omar. He grabbed the poker and crawled to the end of the couch.

"You want me to shoot him again, rat? I kind of like making holes in him."

Unbelievable maggot of a human being. Omar peeked at the scene. Mason was doubled over in the chair, pressing his hands to his thigh. Omar couldn't see his face. Otley stood only a few paces ahead of Mason, gun still pointed at him, his back to Omar's side of the room. To Otley's right, Bender sat on the floor cradling Rewl's body. And

Renzor and Kruse were standing across the room, near the exit to the foyer.

What now? Even if he managed to strike Otley, with Mason's leg injured, they wouldn't be able to move fast enough to get out of —

"Tell me something, Mr. Elias," Lawten said. "Who shot first when the enforcers came to your village?"

"General Otley shot first," Mason said in a tight voice. "I'll never forget. He said, 'One kill each. Sleep the rest of the village.'"

"Witnesses, general," Lawten said. "And I bet he's not the only one."

Again anger coursed through Omar. That overgrown boar had killed his father on purpose? Why hadn't Mason ever said so? Omar had to try to take him out.

He ran out from behind the couch and bashed the poker against the back of Otley's head.

Otley roared and wheeled around, his gun still in his hand. Omar hammered the poker down over Otley's forearm. Once. Twice. The gun clattered to the floor and Omar kicked it away.

Otley punched Omar, who dropped the poker and fell against a wing chair so hard he knocked it over. Omar hit the floor but flipped himself onto his stomach and scanned the rug for the gun. He saw it on the floor by Mason's foot. Mason must have seen it too because he moved his foot and carefully pushed the gun under his chair.

Otley stalked over the carpet, looking for his gun while growling low under his breath. When he didn't find it, he walked back toward Mason. As he passed, Omar grabbed his boot and yanked with all his strength.

Otley tripped and fell on his knees. Omar tried to slip past him to get to Mason, but Otley snagged the back of Omar's shirt. Omar snapped back and landed on his rear in front of Otley, who wrapped his arm around Omar's neck.

Omar's breathing ended right there. He struggled against Otley's hold, but there was simply no way he could get free. His head started to tingle. He rolled his eyes up to focus on Otley's face and reached for the tusk in the man's nose.

"Don't you dare," Otley said.

But he did. Omar took hold of the metal, winced, and yanked hard. A scream burst out of Otley that sounded like a boar stuck in barbed wire. Blood fell hot and wet on Omar's neck, but Otley's grip lessened enough that Omar slipped away and crawled to his brother's chair. He reached between Mason's legs for the gun, but his fingers knocked the weapon farther away. It slid to the other side of the chair.

Omar got up to go around for it, but an enforcer picked it up. Two other enforcers stood behind the first, guns in hand. *Maggots.* Omar put his hands up.

"I'm going to break your neck, rat," Otley said, stepping toward him. Blood had painted a glossy red, three-inch stripe down his lips and beard and onto his uniform, and it looked like he had only one nostril. "And once your brother sees you die, then I'll break his."

A gunshot rang out. Loud and Old.

Omar jumped. Mason yelled. But neither brother fell.

Otley's body tipped like a felled tree and smashed onto the floor, rattling the nearest lampshade. Behind him, Bender was pointing Jordan's gun in the direction of where the enforcer general had been standing.

Omar stayed put, waiting to see what Bender would do next. But he dropped the gun and looked down at Rewl's face.

"Thanks," Omar said to Bender. He grabbed Mason's sleeve and pulled it. "Let's go, brother. Can you walk?"

Mason looked almost green and his eyes were closed. "Ciddah?"

Good grief. "Come on, Mason. I need you to stand up, brother."

"Oh, no. You're not going anywhere," Renzor said.

Omar had almost forgotten the creep was there, now standing over by the walkway to the front door. "We saved you," Omar said. "You'd be dead if it wasn't for us."

Renzor waved a few enforcers into the room. "He wouldn't have killed me."

"Yes, he would have!" Omar said. Renzor was a fool to think otherwise. "Wait. Is this because my brother stole your medic woman?"

"I'll find her," Renzor said, narrowing his eyes. "Ciddah belongs to me."

Omar snorted a sarcastic laugh. "Really? Because I don't know if you've seen them together but, uh … I just don't think she likes you anymore."

"Arrest them," Renzor said.

"Down on the floor," one of the enforcers said. "Hands on the back of your head."

And there was nothing to do but comply.

CHAPTER
40

After two days in the Medical Center, Mason joined Omar in the RC. Two more nights there and Mason and Omar were transported to Champion Hall to appear before the Safe Lands Guild. That seemed a bit rushed to Mason.

Their arms were bound behind their backs from the moment they left their cell, and they remained bound as they were led down the wide hallway toward the auditorium.

Luella Flynn stood beside the auditorium doors, armed with her signature microphone and accompanied by her cameraman. "Mr. Elias," she said, "do you know the whereabouts of Ciddah Rourke and Baby Promise?"

Mason smiled at her. "That's one story you'll never get." He hoped. He prayed again that Shaylinn and Ciddah had made it to safety. They must have if Luella Flynn was looking for the story. And since Otley had killed Rewl, perhaps Bender wouldn't be so eager to betray the location of Ruston's basements. Bender had been in the RC too, but he'd been taken out yesterday and hadn't come back.

The guards pushed Mason through the front doors. Every step hurt. His leg was still sore from being shot, though he knew he was doing remarkably well, considering. If he had doctored his own gunshot wound, he would still be in bed.

The auditorium was icy cold, and the sweat on his body made him shiver. The place seemed small compared to how large it looked on the ColorCast. The paint job was hideous: purple floor, orange theater seats, and lime-green walls. Omar probably thought it was artistic, but Mason didn't dare ask his brother anything with the guards and their stunners so close.

Mason did *not* want to be stunned again. Or shot, for that matter.

Omar didn't look so good. The RC had given him a mercy vape, but he was suffering from a pretty bad withdrawal.

The auditorium seats were filled with people. Tables edged the front and side walls and sat up on platforms, like a dais. People in black robes with pointed hoods that hid their faces sat behind the tables. There were six people on the left, six on the right, four in front, and Lawten Renzor, right in the middle of the front table, the only person on the platform not wearing a robe.

"What's with the creepy death hoods?" Omar whispered to Mason.

"Silence!" the guard on Omar's right yelled.

The guards led Mason and Omar down the center aisle and up into a raised box with half walls. It reminded Mason of the witness boxes people sat in during trials of Old, though rather than facing the audience, this box faced the front—faced Lawten.

The guards instructed Mason and Omar to stand at the front of the box, then they stood behind them. On the dais, Lawten was talking with a hooded person, their heads cocked toward one another as if Lawten were having a conversation with Death.

Mason was glad they'd freed everyone, truly, but the only thing that really mattered to him right now was that Ciddah had chosen Mason over Lawten. She loved Mason and no one else. Knowing that gave him the strength to stand before Lawten.

An enforcer dressed in a formal black uniform walked to the front of the room and faced the audience. He stood directly under the place where Lawten sat. "All rise."

The audience stood, but Lawten and the hooded people remained seated.

"The distinguished court of the Safe Lands Guild is now in session. Task Director General Lawten Renzor presiding. Please be seated."

Rustles and murmurs filled the auditorium as the audience sat.

Lawten spoke next, his voice amplified through speakers. "Good morning, Ancients of the Safe Lands and ladies and gentlemen of the audience. Calling the case of the Safe Lands versus Mason Elias and Omar Strong. Be advised that national status has been revoked from these two men. The safety of this land and its people make it necessary for this Guild to invoke Ancient authority over such outsiders. We allowed them into our fair city on Fortune's faith, and they have not measured up. Therefore, they will not be permitted legal counsel or a right to testify on their own behalf."

Mason glanced at Omar, who raised his eyebrows. This shouldn't be surprising, but it made Mason's gut churn. They were going to be liberated, he was certain.

"Colonel Stimel," Lawten said. "Are you ready with the facts?"

A man seated in the front row stood and approached the enforcer, who was still standing at the front of the room. Colonel Stimel was the enforcer Mason had seen the day he'd barged into Lawten's office.

"Ready for the Safe Lands, Mr. Task Director General," Colonel Stimel said.

"You may proceed," Lawten said.

"Mr. Task Director General, Ancients of the Safe Lands, ladies and gentlemen of the audience, the defendants have been charged, and their charges read thusly: removal of SimTag identifiers from their bodies, theft of government property, trespassing, kidnapping of Safe Lands nationals, possession of illegal firearms, assault on Safe Lands officers, and war crimes against the Safe Lands. You, the Ancients, have read the evidence against them. I encourage you to see that they are guilty as charged."

"Thank you, Colonel Stimel. Does the Guild have any questions at this time?" Lawten asked.

"Are the accused infected with the thin plague?" a scratchy voice asked from the right-hand side of the room. One of the hooded people.

"Yes." Lawten looked down his nose at Mason, and his beady eyes seemed to rake Mason's courage into shreds. "Both outsiders ignored my warnings and contracted the virus from Safe Lands nationals."

"He's lying!" Mason yelled. "I don't have it!"

The enforcer behind him pulled his stunner and pressed it against Mason's back. "None of that, now."

"Another outburst and you are to stun him, officer," Lawten told the enforcer.

"Yes, sir," the enforcer said.

Mason shot a quick look at Omar. He had supposed these hooded people wouldn't liberate someone clean, that they'd rather lock him in the donation room until he turned forty. But Lawten wanted payback for Mason's rescuing Ciddah. That was what this whole trial must be about, that and it was Omar's third X.

So Mason smiled at Lawten, imagining Ciddah and her parents sitting with Levi and Jemma over a nice meal, caring for Baby Promise, Lawten's son.

Lawten looked away from Mason around the room at the hooded people. "Any other questions?"

No one spoke.

"Very well. The evidence has been presented," Lawten said. "This Guild will vote. All in favor of liberation?"

A chorus of "Aye" made Mason jump.

"All opposed?"

Silence.

"The Safe Lands Guild finds the defendants guilty of all charges. It is the judgment of this Guild that both men be liberated without delay."

"Well, this should be fun," Omar said.

Fun wasn't the word Mason would have chosen, but at least, for them, the mystery of liberation would finally be solved.

Discussion Questions

1. Levi thinks Safe Lands "flakers" are the enemy and that the outsiders should stay out of the Safe Lands business, focusing instead on rescuing their children and getting out of the Safe Lands. What do you think of his perspective? Is he right or wrong?

2. The owl is a symbol of freedom for Omar, who desperately wants to be free. What are some ways Omar has sabotaged his desire for freedom?

3. In chapter 7, Zane tells Omar, "What you do doesn't matter as much as who you are. But you have to decide who you are. Who you *want* to be. And no one can decide that for you." What do you think of this statement? Do you agree? Disagree? Either way, have you thought about who you are? Is that who you want to be?

4. Guilt is a recurring theme in this story. Which characters suffer from guilt? Why?

5. Compare the lives of Mason and Ciddah. How are they alike? How are they different? Is their love real or is it merely infatuation?

6. Omar and Shaylinn both want to do something to help the people of the Safe Lands. What does each of them choose? What are the strengths and weaknesses of their plans? What do their plans have in common?

7. While marriage and families don't exist in the Safe Lands, there are exceptions. What are lifers and what are Naturals? How are

they similar and different from one another?

8. Omar believes the lie that he is worthless. Do you believe a lie about yourself? If so, what is it?

9. In chapter 25, Shaylinn comforts herself with a quote from C. S. Lewis: "If we find ourselves with a desire that nothing in this world can satisfy, the most probable explanation is that we were made for another world." What do you think this means?

10. Mimics are rampant in the Safe Lands. And as Zane told Omar, people mimic more than fashions. Where do you see mimics in our world today? What are the advantages and disadvantages of such behavior?

ACKNOWLEDGMENTS

Huge thanks go to Larry and Crystal Nielsen and Michael and Lindsay Vernor for helping me with the science in this book, and to Jason Joyner for helping me with the doctor scenes. Thanks also to Shannon Dittemore and Chris Kolmorgen for reading this book at the last-minute speed of light. And as always, big hugs and thank yous to my team: agent Amanda Luedeke, editors Jacque Alberta and Jeff Gerke, marketers Sara Merritt and Marcus Drenth, the whole team at Zondervan, author support Kara Christensen, Andy and Angie Lusco, Stephanie Morrill, Melanie Dickerson, Nicole O'Dell, and Go Teen Writers. And to Brad, Luke and Kaitlyn Williamson for all your love and support.

Captives

Jill Williamson

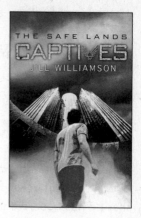

One choice could destroy them all.

When eighteen-year-old Levi returned from Denver City with his latest scavenged finds, he never imagined he'd find his village decimated, loved ones killed, and many—including his fiancée, Jem—taken captive. Levi is determined to rescue what remains of his people, even if it means entering the Safe Lands, a walled city that seems anything but safe.

Omar knows he betrayed his brother, but helping the enforcers was necessary. Living off the land holds his village back. The Safe Lands has protected people since the plague decimated the world generations ago ... and its rulers have promised power and wealth beyond Omar's dreams.

Meanwhile, their brother Mason has a position inside the Safe Lands, and may be able to use his captivity to save not only the people of his village, but also possibly find a cure for the virus that threatens everyone within the Safe Lands' walls.

Will Mason uncover the truth hidden behind the Safe Lands' façade before it's too late?

Available in stores and online!

Replication

The Jason Experiment

Jill Williamson

What if everything you knew was a lie?

Martyr—otherwise known as Jason 3:3—is one of hundreds of clones kept in a remote facility called Jason Farms. Told that he has been created to save humanity, Martyr has just one wish before he is scheduled to "expire" in less than a month. To see the sky.

Abby Goyer may have just moved to Alaska, but she has a feeling something strange is going on at the farm where her father works. But even this smart, confident girl could never have imagined what lies beneath a simple barn. Or what would happen when a mysterious boy shows up at her door, asking about the stars.

As the reality of the Jason Experiment comes to light, Martyr is caught between two futures—the one for which he was produced and the one Abby believes he was created to have. Time is running out, and Martyr must decide if a life with Abby is worth leaving everything he's ever known.